Kat Black lives with her husband and daughters in the
South of England where she spends a great deal of her
time avoiding reality, and amazingly gets to call it a job.
Kat loves to hear from readers and can be contacted via
www.katblack-author.com

D1136492

KAT BLACK
Melting Ms Frost

AVON

AVON

A division of HarperCollins*Publishers*
77–85 Fulham Palace Road,
London W6 8JB

www.harpercollins.co.uk

A Paperback Original 2014
1

Copyright © Kat Black 2014

Kat Black asserts the moral right to
be identified as the author of this work

A catalogue record for this book is
available from the British Library

ISBN 978-0-00-754076-1

Set in Sabon LT Std by Palimpsest Book Production Limited,
Falkirk, Stirlingshire

Printed and bound in Great Britain by
Clays Ltd, St Ives plc

MIX
Paper from
responsible sources
FSC™ C007454

Find out more about HarperCollins and the environment at
www.harpercollins.co.uk/green

Writing this book has been quite a journey, one that would never have started without my editor at Mischief Books, the talented and tireless Adam Nevill, who not only approached me with an amazing opportunity, but who also had faith that I could rise to the challenge. I'm hugely appreciative for his encouragement and support. Without him *Melting Ms Frost* would not exist. I'd like to also express my gratitude to the team at Avon for making that 'amazing opportunity' available, and for getting me through the experience (relatively) unscathed.

There are various kind and patient people from the Vienna Tourist Office to thank for their advice on their beautiful city. Likewise, the generous help provided on the Irish Gaelic language by Oideas Gael in County Donegal. Any mistakes/ bending of facts/stretching of truths are my own.

As writing is such a solitary business, it's all too easy to get lost in your own words and end up where you don't want to be. I'm therefore indebted to three fabulous and well respected book bloggers who agreed to take time out of their busy reading and reviewing schedules to cast their critical eyes over my first draft scribblings. Mandi Schreiner at Smexy Books, Nix at Scorching Book Reviews, and Jennifer Porter at Romance Novel News – thank you all for your constructive views which helped get these characters knocked into shape. They're much better for it.

Lastly, to my neglected family and friends – who've been at risk of forgetting what I look like during my absence of the past year. You'll probably never know just how much your patience and unflagging belief has meant to me during this process. Heartfelt thanks and love to you all. I look forward to spending some time together before I disappear back down into the word mines to begin chiselling out the sequel!

For Rob, Ellie and Lottie with all my love.
Anything is possible.

ONE

'Let's get to work then,' the redhead in the razor-cut skirt suit snapped, pivoting on her heel to bring an end to the pre-dinner staff meeting. Without so much as a glance to the left or right, she marched off towards the kitchens and the office space beyond, leaving the click of her strides to cut through the silence blanketing the restaurant dining room in her wake.

From where he leant back against the glossy expanse of the lacquered cherry wood bar, arms folded over his chest and one ankle crossed in front of the other, Aidan Flynn kept his features schooled and gave her retreating form an appraising once-over. Starting at the tightly rolled twist of her hair, he ran his gaze past the rigid set of her shoulders to the purposeful swing of her hips – then followed the long line of her legs all the way down to the soles of her spiked black stilettos before releasing a slow whistle under his breath.

So. That was the woman he'd been hearing so much about. Café Cluny's general manager, Ms Annabel Frost. His immediate boss.

Beginning the visual ascent back up over her tailored

curves, he had to admit that as far as first impressions went, she made a hell of an impact. Not least because she actually seemed to live up to every word of warning he'd received from his colleagues during the week he'd been on the job. There'd been so many horror stories, so gleefully imparted, that he'd taken a lot of what he'd heard with a good-humoured pinch of salt, suspecting the truth had been embellished as part of some joke to wind up the new boy.

But having just seen the alleged villain of those tales in action for himself, he had to assume that most of the gossip was, in fact, true. Despite having never met him before, she'd treated him with the same cool indifference she had the rest of the staff, singling him out only when he'd spoken up to make a point of introducing himself – and only for the shortest and sharpest of exchanges. Even fresh back from a week's leave, the only chilled vibe Ms Frost was giving off was an eyebrow-icing arctic blast.

She was stunning too, no question. That striking ruby-red dye job and matching lipstick lent her a vibrant air severely at odds with the glacial personality that characterised her name to a T. It had been a good thing she'd demanded the room's undivided attention when she'd swept in a short time earlier, as he doubted he'd have been able to drag his fascinated gaze away from her even if he'd wanted to. From what he'd been admiring of her alabaster complexion and green eyes, he'd bet his boots there was a natural redhead lurking beneath all that cosmetically manufactured armour – because armour was exactly what that polished and prickly exterior represented, he had no doubt. There was more to Annabel Frost than met the casual eye, and just what it was she was trying to hide behind that tough outer shell had him intrigued.

It wasn't until the kitchen door swung closed behind her, the sight prompting a collective sigh of relief to hiss around him like so many punctured tyres, that his attention was pulled from its internal reverie and back into the midst of the loosely gathered group of his colleagues.

'The Bitch is back,' one of the commis chefs muttered as the starched white huddle of kitchen staff broke away and started towards their shiny steel domain without any of the irreverent banter Aidan had grown accustomed to hearing from them over the past week.

The rest of the staff began dispersing to complete their interrupted preparations for a busy service. Amid the subdued, grumbling shuffle, Tim, the fair-haired head waiter who'd taken a far more amiable approach to the role of acting manager in Annabel Frost's absence, stopped by the bar and clapped a palm on Aidan's shoulder. 'Sorry to have to say I told you so, mate,' he commiserated privately in his chummy, Australian twang.

Before Aidan had a chance to answer, sweet-natured Donna was there as well, using the guise of friendly concern to lay a hand on his forearm just below the turn-up of his white shirt sleeves, the touch to his bare flesh as suggestive as it was shy. 'She had no right to treat you that way, Aidan.' She gazed up at him prettily, eyes shining with empathy and open infatuation. 'You mustn't let her get you down.'

'Not a problem,' he assured her with a flash of a smile, straightening and using the excuse of heading back behind the bar to break the contact without hurting her feelings. The little waitress had been signalling her interest from the outset but, as keen and lovely as she seemed to be, her gentle femininity did nothing for him.

Taking up his station beside Jon, Cluny's junior barman, he wondered what Donna's delicate sensibilities would make of the fact that, far from getting him down, the arbitrary tongue lashing he'd just received from his new boss left him not only up, but very nearly hard, too, within the confines of his uniform black trousers?

3

In all honesty, he had to wonder at the visceral response himself. Self-restraint and control had always been his trademarks where the opposite sex was concerned – even towards its most eager members. Why he'd react so instantly to a woman who appeared to be so unaccommodating, so thoroughly unpleasant, was a mystery. After what he'd been through over the past few years, he would have thought he'd have had enough of impossible challenges, but apparently not. All his addled brain could seem to think about was what a pleasure it would be to drag the haughty Ms Frost off her high horse and teach her to enjoy kneeling, naked and obedient, at his feet.

Turning his attention to the task of slicing lemons for the night ahead, he ducked his head and let the fall of his unruly hair curtain a slower, altogether darker, kind of smile.

And if she insisted on kicking and screaming against him every inch of the way as he was certain she would?

Even better.

From her front-of-house position behind the lectern-style reception desk, Annabel took one of her regular moments to sweep a gaze over the packed restaurant, checking that everything in her world was running as it should – staff busy but attentive, service efficient, customers content.

With its reputation for being classy but never stuffy, Cluny's was popular all year round, and tonight, against the backdrop of opulent festive finery, the ambience was even more sparkling than usual. In addition to the artfully dimmed lighting, the twinkle of hundreds of tiny white fairy lights helped cast a magical glow over polished wood and snowy linen, while the spice-scented tealights flickering at the centre of each table bounced reflections off gleaming glassware and lent an attractive golden hue to the animated faces of the diners. The atmospheric background strains of easy jazz were overlaid by the lively buzz of chatter, and punctuated by the chink of

4

cutlery against china. Mixed with the succulent aromas of rich seasonal dishes, the crisp scent of winter woods was conjured by the seven-foot gold and red decorated Christmas tree standing prominently in the window, and the garlands of berry-studded greenery hanging in deep swags from the cornicing. The look and mood were perfect: a blend of effortless sophistication and relaxed elegance that gave no hint of the exacting standards and obsessive attention to detail that were needed to achieve them.

Satisfied, Annabel ran her eye over the bar area opposite, only to find the new tousle-haired senior barman, the one who'd dared speak out of turn during the earlier staff meeting – Andy or Adam or something – looking back at her. It wasn't the first time that evening she'd caught him staring, and it certainly wasn't the first time she'd felt a spike of irritation in reaction to the cocky challenge in his look as he smiled, holding her gaze for a fraction too long.

Not another one.

Rather than encourage him by returning the smile, she let her lips purse. Handsome, vain and tripping on testosterone – she recognised the type only too well. It was hardly worth being surprised any more by the number of men who seemed to have no clue how to take female authority seriously; who thought it was okay to play up their manly attributes to bluff, bully or charm their way into blurring the line between the professional and the personal.

Well, she'd come across enough 'charmers' in her life not to be impressed by this one. As tall, dark and handsome as his particular attributes undeniably were, his allure wouldn't work here. Not with her. Already beyond annoyed to have come back from a stressful week off to find that an emergency replacement for the previous head barman had been drafted in without her approval, she was in no mood to put up with any disrespectful crap.

Noting that the handful of stools at the front end of the bar were empty now that the last of the night's bookings had been seated at their tables, she clipped the top back on her fountain pen and laid it down along the open spine of the reservations book. Smoothing the already flawless line of her pencil skirt, she stepped from behind the desk. Time to teach the pretty new boy his place.

The smile she directed at customers as she crossed the room dropped the second she entered the narrow area between the polished bar and the mirror-backed wall of shelves displaying an impressive array of bottles. By contrast, the smile from the man standing a few feet in front of her broadened in welcome, lighting up his handsome face and stopping her in her tracks.

Wow. There was no denying the killer impact of it – shame he'd mistaken her for a willing victim. Lifting her brows and tilting her nose just enough to be able to look down it, she went straight for the knock-down.

'Is there a problem over here?' she demanded. 'Only you seem to be spending an awful lot of time standing around staring into space instead of working.'

Rather than jumping to attention and spewing excuses or false apologies as she expected, the target of her disapproval simply let the smile slide, sending her a sideways look instead – a stunning flash of silver through a tangle of black locks – and took his time rinsing the dregs from a cocktail shaker down the sink. She caught the soft, southern Irish brogue she remembered from earlier as he turned to send a suddenly stricken-looking Jon off to the kitchens in search of fresh mint.

The show of unhurried confidence and the relaxed stance of his rangy frame only served to nettle her further, as did the too-casual turn-up of his sleeves – which exposed a most distracting display of muscle flexing along lean forearms as he reached for a towel and wiped his hands.

'Annabel, isn't it?'

The sound of her name snapped her attention back up to his face as he turned from the sink at last. 'It's Ms Frost, actually,' she informed him in her coldest tone. 'And I asked you a question.'

His gaze met hers head on for the first time, leaving her to feel the shock of impact of the most arresting pair of pale eyes she'd ever seen.

'I think you know very well that I've been working,' he said, sweeping that gaze over what she had to admit appeared to be a spotless and organised area. Slinging the towel over one shoulder, he began sauntering her way, offering a crooked smile that belied the intense focus of his scrutiny. 'Just like you know that "space" isn't what I've been staring at.'

Unused to being answered back by a subordinate, Annabel felt her own eyes widen at his audacity, but she didn't miss a beat. 'I have to say I don't like your attitude.'

His brows flickered upwards, but otherwise unfazed, he kept walking towards her, moving with an effortless grace that only reinforced his air of confidence. He didn't stop until he got right up close. Too close for her down-the-nose glare to compete with his height. So close her gaze was forced up to meet his unwavering one.

And for the second time in under a minute, Annabel found herself distracted. This near, the guy was not just handsome – he was breathtaking, with strong-angled features and the bold slash of black brows accentuating the almost iridescent quality of those irises that she now saw were ringed by a dark border of charcoal.

With bare inches to spare between them, he lowered his face to hers a fraction more, the pull of that near-transparent gaze strong enough to hold her captive. He pitched his voice so that only they could hear. 'Well, now. So far that makes us equal. Because I don't think much of yours, either.'

She almost spluttered then. None of her staff had ever had the nerve to speak to her in such a way. 'I beg your pardon?' She drew back a step, thrown but determined to maintain her appearance of aloof superiority. 'You can't talk to me like that, I'm your manager.'

'Oh, I know who you are, *a mhuirnín*,' he said, and before she had a chance to question the unfamiliar sounding word, he followed her retreat, re-closing the space between them. 'You're all I've been thinking about for the past few hours.' He visually traced the contours of her face. 'I confess, I can't help wondering what you look like with that glorious hair let loose.'

'What?' Annabel floundered, caught off guard by his forward manner. Not only was he more handsome than she'd thought, he had the arrogance to match. 'Are you always so rude?'

He looked bemused. 'Was I being rude? That wasn't my intention. I was simply following your lead and being direct. Are *you* always so hard on new members of staff?'

He was questioning *her*? 'That depends entirely on the impression they make. Most know how to behave better.'

The jibe was met with nothing more than an easy laugh. 'I'm sure they do, once they've come face to face with you. Do you insist on the same criteria for friends and lovers – does everyone have to be on their best behaviour to meet with your approval?'

Annabel couldn't believe her ears. Was the guy for real? 'That is absolutely none of your business.'

'True.' He gave a small shrug. 'But it doesn't stop me from wondering, Annabel.'

'Stop calling me that. With the exception of the head chef and owner, I expect every employee to refer to me as Ms Frost.'

'That's very traditional,' he said with a teasing glint in his eye. 'And surprisingly strict. How about when you're out for drinks after a long shift? Surely you relax the formality then – let that hair down a little bit?'

And encourage precisely this sort of over-familiarity? No. 'I don't fraternise with my staff.'

'I'm sorry to hear that,' he said with a very good show of sincerity. 'Why not?'

'Again, that has nothing to do with you. I don't think you've quite grasped the meaning of "none of your business".'

Her rebuff only made him smile. 'Oh, I've grasped it. But let's just say that I'm curious by nature.'

He was *unbelievable*. 'Well, you know what curiosity did to the cat?'

As though searching for the answer, he looked off into the distance for a moment. 'Correct me if I'm wrong,' he said, turning that unsettlingly direct gaze back on her with a slow spread of a smile – one that looked very different from the open, friendly expression he'd used a minute ago, 'but wasn't it the cat that got the cream in the end?'

She might have imagined it, but that last seemed to be delivered with some sort of subtle suggestion that packed a surprisingly potent punch, causing her breath to hitch.

'You're getting your metaphors mixed,' she snapped to cover her reaction. 'Let's hope you find it as easy to mix drinks because I'll be keeping a close eye on you.'

'I'll have to make sure I give my best performance then,' he said, accepting the challenge with a slight bow of his head as they both noticed Tim coming up to the bar with an order. 'I'm sorry to have to cut short our informative introduction, Ms Frost, but as you can see I've work to do.' He flashed her a dazzling smile. 'And I've just discovered I have a very tough boss to please.'

She glared in response. 'Just so long as you remember that. You really don't want to test me.'

Yet as she spun away, she got the distinct sense from his expression that testing her was exactly what he wanted to do.

TWO

Finishing up for the night, Aidan switched off the gleaming chrome coffee machine as Tim came through from the kitchens, whistling a jolly yet totally unidentifiable tune into the stillness of the now empty restaurant.

Swinging close by the bar, the waiter flung Aidan's overcoat across the polished surface. 'C'mon, time to get out of here,' he announced. 'Fancy a quick beer? I'm parched.'

'Sure,' Aidan agreed, rolling down his shirt sleeves as he made for the open end of the bar. After his earlier one-to-one with Annabel Frost it had to be said he was feeling more than a little dry-mouthed himself.

With Cluny's sitting smack bang in the middle of Soho, they wouldn't have far to look to find refreshment. Ringed by the world-famous shopping precincts of Oxford and Regent Streets – which at this time of year teemed with locust-style swarms of Christmas shoppers – and the theatres of Shaftesbury Avenue, the square mile parcel of the bustling West End was steeped in a colourful history of hedonistic iniquity and represented the beating social heart of London.

Having shrugged off the seedier side of its gangland and sex industry past, the multicultural urban village of modern

Soho continued to celebrate its identity as a free-spirited party playground. With its labyrinthine streets and laneways crowded with a multitude of cafés, bars, restaurants and clubs, it was the perfect location for establishments such as Cluny's to thrive on a clientele ranging from colourful local residents and creatives, to tourists, shoppers and theatre-goers.

As Aidan and Tim made their way through the late-night streets – still lively under the twinkle and glow of the city's Christmas light displays now that the festive party season was well underway – they passed several such pubs, bars and clubs without stopping. Noticing that Tim was striding out like a man with a predetermined destination in mind, Aidan was happy to be led along, enjoying the constant stream of the ex-Sydneysider's amusing and irreverent banter.

Coming to Old Compton Street – the loud and proud main GLBT artery of Soho – Tim's chatter abruptly cut off to be replaced by a sudden obsession with tweaking strategic strands of his short blond hair. When he slowed to turn into the doorway of a bar called the Louche Lounge, Aidan saw he even gave his collar a snappy tug before stepping inside.

A moment later he had to wonder why his colleague had bothered with the primping. The interior of the bar was so dark that it was doubtful anyone would be able to appreciate his efforts. With only a dim pink glow providing the bare minimum of illumination, Aidan had to squint to avoid falling over anyone as he made for the nearest free space at the bar.

'What are you having?' he asked Tim, thankful that the music was set to a mellow midweek sound level that allowed for communication via a semi-raised voice rather than a full-blown performance of unintelligible shouts and charades.

Without answering, Tim pulled at his sleeve and kept moving, not stopping until they'd reached a section of the bar already two-deep with customers.

'I'm buying,' he informed Aidan with all his attention focused on the bar. Or more specifically on the hard-bodied twenty-something guy in the black vest top serving behind it. With his cropped hair, smudged black eyeliner and leather dog collar buckled around his neck studded with crystals depicting the word 'BITCH', he seemed to be very popular with the punters.

Feeling a sharp jostle against his shoulder, Aidan turned and looked up into the garishly made-up face of . . . well, of what he could only describe as something resembling a pantomime dame straight off the stage. Swaying next to him, the vision of sequin-bound brawn topped his own six-one height by roughly half a foot, with most of that elevation coming courtesy of a voluminous platinum blonde wig. As there seemed to be little correlation between the dame's swaying and the rhythm of slow, soulful funk being pumped through the place, Aidan guessed the movement was alcohol induced.

When roughly two hundred and fifty pounds of hairy Amazonian teetered into him again, he stopped guessing and decided it definitely was alcohol.

'Sorry, guv,' a gravelly voice escaped from between the crooked slash of bright orange lips. 'It's these bleedin' 'eels.'

'Eels?' Aidan asked, somewhat alarmed.

'Yeah. 'Eels.' A big hand gestured downwards. 'Don't know how the birds manage to walk in 'em.'

Looking down to see the vision's meat-slab feet crammed into an oversized pair of court shoes, Aidan grinned in understanding. 'Ah, heels. No problem.'

'Don't usually go round dressed like this, see? I'm a cabbie for chrissakes,' his new companion declared with a disgruntled belch. 'S'those bastards over there made me do it.' He gestured over his shoulder with his thumb. 'Friends they call 'emselves. S'me birthday. Forty today so they dressed me up

13

and lugged me out like this. The missus'll have a bleedin' fit when she sees me. 'Ere.' He nudged Aidan with a beefy arm as a space opened up at the bar in front of them. 'You gettin' in there for a drink or what?'

'Ladies first.' Aidan gestured, careful to keep his toes out of the way as the huge cabbie lurched forward in search of more drink he really didn't need.

On Aidan's other side, Tim had also managed to edge to the front of the crowd.

'Tim, my lovely!' the 'bitch' behind the bar cried when he spotted the blond. 'You back *again*?'

'Stu.' Aidan heard Tim answer with a reserved coyness he wouldn't have expected from the garrulous Aussie. After the order had been placed and Stu had turned away to the fridge, Aidan leant in a little and raised a questioning eyebrow.

'I'm working on it,' Tim said, correctly interpreting his expression as Stu turned back, planted two bottles of lager on the bar and popped the tops. With a wink he took the proffered money from Tim's hand before moving off to serve the next calf-eyed customer.

'Good luck with it,' Aidan said, taking the bottle Tim passed him as they began to push their way back out of the waiting bar crowd.

'Thanks.' Tim sighed wistfully when they'd found a less cramped area, clinking the neck of his bottle against Aidan's. 'And congratulations,' he added after they'd both taken a few thirst-quenching swallows of the cold Spanish beer.

'We're celebrating?' Aidan asked.

'Too right. You survived your first shift with Little Ms Frosty. How was it?' Tim peered at him intently through the dark. 'I don't see any blood.'

Aidan laughed. 'No blood,' he confirmed, and held up his fingers. 'Not even any frostbite.'

'Lucky. I saw her come gunning for you at one point. What was that all about?'

Aidan shrugged. 'Not much. Just establishing a few ground rules, getting better acquainted.'

'Crikey, Aid. Might as well get chummy with a shark, mate.'

'Yes, I got a good flash of her teeth.' Aidan smothered a smile at the memory of his snappy manager and took another swig from his bottle. 'Apart from work, what do you know about her?'

'Hardly anything.' Tim shrugged, his gaze slipping over Aidan's shoulder towards the bar. 'I don't reckon there is anything except work where she's concerned. I've been at Cluny's for over a year and haven't ever heard her talk about her personal life, haven't seen any evidence of family or friends even existing. She doesn't seem interested in taking much time off for holidays either. I think she only disappeared last week because of some sort of crisis.'

'So you don't know whether she's in a relationship?'

That got Tim's full attention back. He nearly choked on a mouthful of beer. Despite the dark, the horrified look he gave Aidan was obvious. 'Mate, you're shitting me. Don't tell me you're interested?'

'I like to know who I'm dealing with, that's all,' Aidan hedged with an easy smile. He'd been telling himself all night that it would be wise to ignore the crackle of anticipation Annabel Frost had sparked across his entire nervous system. Even though he'd seen no evidence of a wedding band or engagement rock glinting on her ring finger, it would be better to leave the lure of this particular provocation well enough alone. No sensible man would risk stirring up the kind of trouble he was contemplating – not on the job, not with a superior.

But there was the rub. Even though he liked to think he

15

wasn't totally lacking in wisdom, if there was one thing he'd always thrived on, it was risk. And maybe having been forced to play things safe for the past few years meant it was that very element that made this such an impossible prospect to resist. He'd certainly enjoyed sparring with her. And as an introductory round it had proved quite informative. He'd learnt that not only was she sharp-tongued, she was dismissive and emotionally closed, and he'd been left even more fascinated by her than before. Judging by the way she'd reacted to the various baits he'd set, he suspected that the only way he was likely to get past her cold exterior was by turning the heat up. High.

'Better the devil you know, et cetera.'

'Yeah,' Tim puffed out a breath. 'Well just remember you *are* dealing with the devil.'

Aidan looked at him. 'If she's really that bad why are you still working for her after a year?' And Tim wasn't the only one, Aidan had noticed. For all the badmouthing he'd been hearing, it seemed most of the staff at Cluny's had been there long term.

Tim shrugged, his gaze wandering in the direction of the bar again. 'The pay's great, as you know. And it's the best-run restaurant I've worked in.' He raised his beer to his lips but paused as he seemed to think. 'Even though she's a nightmare, I guess the Ice Queen is bloody good at her job. She's got that place operating like nowhere else I've ever seen.'

Aidan's own take was that maybe Annabel Frost was bloody good at her job precisely because of her nightmarish reputation, not in spite of it – but he kept the thought to himself and wondered how much more information he could manage to get out of Tim without raising suspicions.

Tipping his bottle to his mouth, he drained the last of his beer. 'That barely touched the sides. Got time for one more?'

He cast a glance over his own shoulder at the bar before flashing a smile at Tim. 'My round, but you can order.'

'Oh, Tony, you are wicked. You shouldn't say such things . . . I know. Yes, I miss you too.'

Bag and keys still in hand, Annabel stood in the hallway of her flat, frozen with astonishment and anger as she listened to her mother's voice coming from the other side of the closed bedroom door.

'No, we can't. Bel says I'm not to meet with you . . . Of course I can make my own decisions. But as I'm staying with her, I suppose it's—'

'Mother, that's enough!' Annabel grasped the handle to fling open the door, only to discover it was locked. 'Hang up the phone now,' she shouted, hammering on the white-glossed wood for good measure. Had her mother lost her mind?

There was a moment's silence, a rush of hushed words, then her mother called out in an overly sweet voice, 'Bel, is that you?'

'You know it is. Now open the door.' Annabel waited as she heard rustling sounds of movement approach and the click of the latch being released.

Shorter than her daughter but with the same green eyes and fiery colouring handed down from some distant Celtic ancestor, Ellen Frost opened the door in her nightie. 'How was your day, darling?' she asked with a bad attempt at a look of innocence and her eyes swimming with a bright film of gin.

The smell of the spirit hit Annabel straight away. 'I can't believe you're in contact with Tony,' she said, voice tight with disapproval.

'I'm no—'

'Don't, Mum. Don't lie to me. I heard you.' She felt the

17

weight of disappointment pull at her expression. 'What were you thinking? You told him where you are for God's sake.'

Her mother at least had the decency to look shamefaced at going back on their agreement. 'Oh, Bel, I didn't mean to. I only said I was with you, I remembered not to tell him where you live.'

Annabel sighed in frustration. That wasn't the point.

'So you see. No real harm done.' Her mother smiled, and as easy as that relieved herself of any blame. 'Poor thing, you do look tired, shall I make you a cup of tea?' She patted Annabel on the cheek as she slipped past and wove her way down the hall to the tiny galley kitchen.

'Don't try and change the subject,' Annabel said as she followed. 'This is serious. I want to know why you were talking to that . . . that scumbag.'

'Do you have to call him that? He's not the monster you think.' Tea obviously forgotten, her mother took a glass from the draining board and reached for the bottle of gin on the worktop, looking surprised to find it empty. Annabel was surprised too. She'd bought it only the previous day. A bottle gone in just over twenty-four hours wasn't good. Especially when only one person was drinking.

'He's sorry for what happened,' her mother continued, clutching the glass and looking around as though she'd discover something else to put in it. 'That's what he phoned to say, that he's sorry. Deep down he's a good man who just had a run of bad luck.'

Oh, that was too much. Tony Maplin was no such thing. He was a thieving, lying gambling addict who'd taken her mother for everything she owned.

'He used you, Mum. He tricked you, stole from you and then deserted you – leaving you to deal with the bailiffs on your own! Have you forgotten that?' She glared at her mother. 'Because I haven't. It will take me longer than a few

18

gin-soaked days to forget the state you were in watching your whole life being pulled from under you, losing everything you owned.' Everything except the damn mobile phone Annabel had given her for emergencies and hadn't thought to change to a new number. Not that she'd thought for a moment that Tony would have the nerve to try to get in contact with her mother after the way he'd run out and left her. 'That's what Tony is, that's what he does for you. And after all that I can't believe you're stupid enough to even speak to him!'

For her own part, Annabel doubted she'd ever forget the events of the previous week – from her mother's hysterical phone call for help, to the subsequent dash Annabel had made to Norfolk, where she'd arrived too late to stop or postpone the process of eviction as the bank repossessed the house Ellen had shared with Tony.

Her mother stood rigid for a minute, fighting to hold back tears. 'If you think I'm so stupid then perhaps I should go,' she said stiffly.

Seeing the welling up doused the flare of Annabel's temper with guilt. The poor woman had been through enough without her adding to the heartache. 'No of course you're not going anywhere.' She put her arm around her mother's shoulders. 'You need to be here until we can get you sorted out. I know I seem harsh, but I just want you to be careful. I don't want to see you get into another mess like this again.'

Releasing her hold, she took the glass from her mother's hand and filled it with water from the tap. 'Come on, it's late. I think we're both too tired for this right now. Let's get you into bed.'

Annabel made short work of getting her mother settled for the night. Turning off the bedroom light, she was about to pull the bedroom door closed behind her when she heard her mother mutter bitterly into the darkness, 'You think it's so easy to judge but you don't understand. You've never been in love.'

It was the gin talking, she knew, so she tried to let the hurt pass right through her. But she couldn't deny the ring of truth to the words. If she'd never been in love it was because of what this woman's choices had shown her it could be. 'From what I've seen of so-called love, Mum, I'm happy to do without, thanks. Sleep well.'

It took her another half hour to go through her nightly ablutions and make up the sofa in the sitting room into her temporary bed. Climbing under the covers, she lay down and let out a huge sigh. What a night. One sticky situation averted, one still unresolved. Snagging her smartphone from the coffee table, she reopened the email she'd received the previous evening from Cluny's owner and re-read it.

Annabel,
   Thanks for letting me know of your intended return tomorrow. I trust that means your family emergency has been resolved.
   During your absence, and in response to the staffing situation caused by Keith Dally's unexpected departure, I took the liberty of installing one Aidan Flynn behind the bar as a suitable replacement. Comes personally recommended.
   Am due in for dinner on Saturday so will see you then.
   In haste.
   Richard.

A *suitable* replacement? Richard Landon couldn't have any idea just how *unsuitable* Mr Aidan Flynn was. Where on earth had he found the arrogant jerk? Before leaving work, she'd tried to find out a bit more about him – where he'd come from, how he'd been hired so quickly. But with the apparent speed with which he'd been 'installed' there was as yet no record of him on the computer, no employee file containing relevant details, and no signed contract. It seemed that Aidan Flynn had just appeared like a bolt out of the blue.

Switching off the phone, which itself yielded no useful information to help answer her questions, she put it back on the table. Twisting to turn off the side lamp, her eye snagged on the photo frame sitting atop her bookcase. Even in the semi darkness she could picture clearly the age-faded image it held. Taken on a summer's day in front of an old limestone built inn that bore a sign reading 'The White Harte', it showed a giggling five-year-old girl with a blaze of coppery hair held aloft in the arms of a laughing man dressed in chef's whites. She felt a familiar ache in her chest as she stared at the photo, and realised that her earlier thoughts towards her mother had been unfair. She had known real love once, and had it tragically ripped from her. Who was Annabel to judge her for trying to find it again, even if she did seem to look in all the wrong places?

Switching off the light, she settled down and closed her eyes, but instead of her exhausted mind letting her slide into sleep it kept returning to the confrontation she'd had with the Irishman. Rather than feeling confident that she'd set him straight on expected behaviour at Cluny's, she had a feeling there was more trouble brewing.

THREE

A glowering Annabel was the first thing staff encountered as they arrived for the lunch shift the following day. Positioned behind the reception desk, she made no secret of the fact that she was clocking everyone in.

Having fronted up in good time himself as it was Jon's day off, Aidan was polishing glasses out of the washer when, at precisely eleven fifteen, she called a meeting of the front-of-house staff. There was a brittle edge to her ice-cold demeanour as she berated them collectively on the state of the near-perfect dining room. He noticed that no one argued with her as she set two waiters to work cleaning the inside of the already almost spotless plate glass windows, and two more on the equally immaculate mirrored panelling that ran the entire length of one wall above the banquette seating.

One of the kitchen hands was unfortunate enough to arrive at that point, eyes widening as he stepped through the door and saw the meeting underway.

'Uh . . .' he started, before freezing under the stare Annabel cast his way.

'Don't bother with an excuse. You're late. You're off this shift. Turn up on time to the next or you'll lose that one too.' He didn't utter a word as he slunk straight back out of the door.

Before it had clicked shut, Annabel had moved onto the fingerprint smudges on the back of the wooden dining chairs setting the remaining serving staff to work polishing every chair in the place. For Aidan she picked the job of dusting the shelves behind the bar.

'Already done,' he said, feeling the air around him thin as every one of his colleagues sucked in a breath, presumably shocked by his audacity at having answered back. Annabel herself raised an eyebrow at him and walked slowly around to the back of the bar. As she inspected the shelves – which he and Jon had indeed started dusting last night, and that he had finished this morning – he fancied he caught a quickly concealed flash of annoyance when she failed to find anything amiss.

Plucking a glass from the half emptied washer, she held it up to the light. 'The glasses need polishing.'

And as she'd been sitting right across the room from him there was no way she didn't know that was what he'd been in the middle of doing when she called her staff meeting. 'I'm just about thro—'

'Mr Flynn,' she interrupted him with a sigh of impatience. 'That's not a request nor is it up for discussion. It's a direct order. I say the glasses need polishing. All of them.' With a triumphant glint in her eye, she set the glass down on the bar with enough force to act as a punctuation mark before turning to stride off towards the kitchens.

The evening service was well underway by the time she decided he was due another dose of her authority.

'Annabel,' he acknowledged as she swept into his space.

She cast him a withering look before ignoring him in favour of carrying out a thorough inspection of the bar area, paying particular attention to the glasses.

23

'I can assure you they're all immaculately polished,' he said, running his gaze just as thoroughly over her from head to toe. 'Like you.'

That made her pause momentarily but she still didn't engage with him.

He closed the distance between them so he could lower his voice. 'What does it take to get that perfection all ruffled, I wonder? What makes you let that hair down?'

She narrowed her eyes on him. 'That's enough.'

He smiled, pleased to have her on the hook. He'd been right, it seemed that touching on the personal was the easiest way to bait her. 'Are you always so defensive?'

'The more relevant question here is are *you* always so offensive?'

Clever. She had a quick wit to go with the sharp tongue – he liked that. 'Tell me what offends you the most about me, *a mhuirnín*?' he asked with a grin.

'What is that you're saying?' she demanded suspiciously. 'You've used it before.'

'*A mhuirnín*? It's a Gaelic term.'

'Do I even want to know what it means?' she muttered. 'Something unsuitable, I'm sure.'

He regarded her. 'I get the impression you have a habit of thinking the worst of everyone and everything. Why is that?'

She gave a put-upon sigh. 'Because that way I'm seldom surprised or disappointed.'

He leaned towards her slightly. 'It means "sweetheart",' he said softly and could tell by her reaction that this was one of those seldom occasions. He'd managed to surprise Ms Frost.

It didn't take her more than a moment to recover. 'I'm not your sweetheart.'

'But are you anyone's?' He gave her an enquiring look. 'Who gets to whisper terms of endearment into your ear at the end of the day, Annabel? That's what I'd like to know.'

Annabel stared at her barman, wondering how he'd managed to wrest control of the exchange. Again. She needed to assert her authority and set some boundaries. Fast.

'Listen to me, *Mr Flynn*. I don't know what sort of working environment you're used to, but here your behaviour is inappropriate.'

'I'm afraid I can't agree with you, *Ms Frost*. I've done nothing inappropriate.' He smiled in a way that added a silent 'yet' to the end of his statement and pinned her with a piercing look. A look of such open hunger it was impossible to misread the passionate intent in the shimmering depths.

It was also impossible to ignore her body's immediate response – a pulse of heat low down in her pelvis, a reaction that, given the situation, was as unexpected as it was misplaced. Shaken, she stumbled back a step, instantly annoyed at herself for giving ground, for letting a few unruly hormones get the better of her. Since when had overly familiar insolence become sexy?

Drawing on her indignation, she straightened to her full height and came right back in his face. 'If that's what you think then keep it up,' she challenged him through her teeth, savouring the rush of satisfaction it gave her to know she held the power to pull rank on him. 'And I'll have no option but to instigate disciplinary procedures.'

She watched his straight brows rise to form elegant arches. That infuriating smile grew wider to showcase a set of strong, white teeth. 'You'll punish me?' he asked without the faintest hint of concern just as something caught his attention. Gaze flicking to the side, he backed off to spear a couple of straws into a pair of mojitos sweating on a nearby tray and pushed the lot towards a drive-by waiter. They were barely alone again when he returned his attention to her, the smile gone, that keen scrutiny intent on her as he said, 'Tell me. Is that the sort of thing that would turn you on, Annabel?'

With that, the ability to breathe momentarily deserted her. She felt her mouth moving, but stolen by shock, there were simply no words to come out. The man was outrageous . . . and the flip-flopping sensation deep in her belly was nothing but pure astonishment, surely?

'No.' Tilting his head to the side, Aidan answered his own question before Annabel had the chance to find her missing voice. 'Despite the dominatrix image you like to portray, I don't think that's really your style.' His focus became laser sharp as he studied her. 'Now, maybe if we were to reverse the roles . . . ?'

Again, that unmistakably suggestive tone, that carnal gleam that prompted a set of images in her mind, disturbing snapshots of this stranger bending her to his will with piercing eyes, strict words, firm hands – visions that should have left her feeling offended and angry but which swamped her with something that felt more like warm, tingling pulses of excitement instead.

Confusion over her own reaction left Annabel unable to work out her next best move. She turned to face the shelves rather than let her adversary see her uncertainty, or worse, any trace of that warped sense of excitement.

'That's way out of line,' she said, pretending to straighten a row of already perfectly aligned highball tumblers to buy herself time to gather her flustered wits.

But in the next instant he was there behind her, giving her no time at all. 'You started it,' he said softly. Keeping her attention trained on the glasses, she felt him crowd close without touching, his proximity making her skin prickle with awareness, the heat of his body radiating against her spine.

'Ms Frost, is that a blush I see staining those cheeks?' he

murmured in her ear, his tone rich with satisfaction, his breath whispering over the side of her neck, stirring the tiniest of hairs. 'Lovely. I bet you blush when you come, too – bet that pure white skin flushes rosy all the way down to your chest. Am I right?'

She couldn't help it. Her stunned gaze flew up to meet his in the mirror. The reflection showed him looming behind her, taller by half a head, the width of his shoulders blocking her view of the busy room beyond.

'I've been trying to picture it, you know, how you'll look when I drive you to that moment of surrender.'

Speechless, she shook her head in rejection of his words even as she was engulfed by the arousing, visceral effect they wrought on her body.

She was appalled – by his actions, by her own reaction, by this situation that had got way out of hand, way too fast. A part of her was aware that she should move away, reclaim her personal space, put a stop to this blatant sexual harassment. But the sheer intensity of him seemed to scramble her brain. For the first time in a long while she felt at a total loss for what to do.

At least she had the sense to grab onto the counter top as, gazes still locked, she watched the man behind her lean even closer to trickle the words, 'I'm going to find out, Annabel,' into her ear without a trace of doubt in his soft tone, just absolute conviction. 'Soon.'

Scandalised, electrified, Annabel felt the hairs on her arms rise. But it was the glimpse of something so resolute, so *steely* in the depths of that grey gaze that triggered an injection of adrenaline into her racing bloodstream.

She closed her own eyes, feeling herself sway. She couldn't look at him any more, couldn't listen. She needed a moment to breathe, to remind herself that she was in charge. She needed to think, to wrench back control and slap a verbal warning in this guy's face. Hard. But how could she hope to force the words out through a throat squeezed too tight even to draw a wisp of air?

'Um, excuse me? Ms Frost, Aidan?' A tentative female query intruded from behind, making Annabel's eyelids pop back open and bringing the reality of the crowded, noisy room crashing back into her clouded consciousness.

Keeping a one-handed grip on the counter top, she spun as her captor stepped back to reveal Donna standing on the other side of the bar.

'Sorry, I, ah – need another bottle of Rioja for table nine,' the diminutive waitress said, her gaze jumping between them and a little crease denting her brow. 'And three sparkling waters.'

'Coming right up.' Aidan's voice was pitched once more in cordial Irish tones, as though nothing dark or dirty had recently passed his lips. The friendly smile he gave the waitress stayed on his face as he turned back to Annabel.

Annabel held herself rigid as he came in close and reached around her to retrieve the glasses from the shelf behind. 'Why don't you wear your hair down for me tomorrow?' he murmured in her ear before moving away to fill the order.

Aware of Donna's inquisitive look still on her, but too stunned to trust herself to speak, Annabel snatched at the flapping ends of her control and pulled them tight as she turned and stalked back to the reception desk, relief at her escape warring with anger. Walking away, when the very act of doing so made her feel like she was the loser in the exchange, left her far from happy despite being the only sensible course of action to take. Even in her floundering, stuttering state she'd been aware that things had not been going her way, nor were they likely to improve while her usually quick-firing synapses were shorted out by shock.

Feeling the sting to her pride, she was adamant this was

only a temporary retreat, not an outright defeat. Now that she knew what she was dealing with, all she needed was a bit of time to arm herself appropriately before she went back in on the attack and showed the foul-mouthed Irishman who was boss.

It was hardly her fault that every time she told herself she was ready, she'd suddenly start noticing a million and one other things that demanded her urgent attention, denying her the opportunity to do just that.

Of course the delightful Ms Frost didn't disappoint him, turning up for her next shift with her hair pulled into the tightest bun Aidan had ever seen, and which left her barely able to blink. Even the fuck-off-and-die scowl she sent him in return for his amused grin of acknowledgement was hampered, but not enough for him to mistake it for anything other than what it was.

After she'd made a point of avoiding him following Donna's interruption last night, he hadn't known quite what to expect of today. But certainly fronting up for work to find he wasn't neck-deep in shit had been a promising start. As sure as he'd been about his instincts regarding his uptight manager, he'd taken a hell of a risk plunging into the deep end to test the icy waters the way he had. Having decided that hard and fast was the only way likely to break through Annabel Frost's frozen surface was one thing, but making those types of moves on any woman – let alone one who held the power to sack him from his job – could prove dangerous. The fact that he hadn't been read his employment rights on the spot or later found skewered on a stiletto heel in a dark alley was all shades of interesting. Especially given the murderous looks he'd been treated to.

Making it obvious that, despite his continued healthy existence, Annabel considered him *persona non grata*, she was careful to avoid him, sticking to the dining area and doing her best to work the edge off a seriously black mood by harrying the wait staff. Given the amount of time she spent sliding livid little glances his way and chewing at that ruby-red bottom lip while she no doubt perfected her plans for bloody revenge, Aidan knew that keeping her distance wouldn't do her the slightest bit of good. He had her right where he wanted her – so wound up she'd have no choice but to address the situation between them at some point.

That point didn't come until the busy dinner crowd had thinned down to the last two tables of espresso and brandy stragglers. All but done setting his work area to rights, he glanced up to see a tightly wrought bundle of female indignation striding towards the bar with an all-business jut to her chin and her shoulders thrown back. Her jacket had been shed earlier in the evening, letting him appreciate her fine posture so beautifully accentuated by her close-fitting white shirt.

Watching as she approached, he felt a warm wash of anticipation spread through his gut. Last night the element of surprise had awarded him the upper hand, but now that she'd had time to recover and regroup, he couldn't wait to see how his faux-dominatrix planned to play this out.

'Aidan,' she began, sticking her nose up at him as she had previously but this time tellingly keeping the solid barrier of cherry wood between their bodies.

He hid his pleasure at hearing her say his name for the first time and pondered how thrilling it would be to have her naked and within reach the next time she dared to use that uppity tone, leaving him no option but to correct her for it.

Fuck. He nearly staggered with the speed his body responded to the thought of how *that* scene would go down.

Too much, too fast, Flynn, he cautioned himself. *Rein it in or you'll lose the game before it's even started.* Placing the last dirty glass in the washer he straightened to look at her, feeling a delicious telltale tug in his groin as he did so.

'Annabel?' he replied, noting the slight flinch she tried to contain at the familiar form of address. A reckless part of him hoped she'd dare to demand that he call her 'Ms Frost' so he had an excuse to get his hands on her before the night was through. Game strategy be damned. Those barbed looks of hers had been pricking his nerves all service, leaving him unusually impatient to exercise his more dominant side.

Something of his thoughts must have shown, because she swallowed and refrained from calling him on it. Pity.

'I'm sure that on reflection you'll agree your behaviour towards me last night was unprofessional and unacceptable,' she said instead, lifting an expectant eyebrow and plainly looking for his agreement. Like the rest of her, her brows were immaculately groomed, leaving him wanting to trace the winged arches with the pads of his thumbs as he held her head cradled between his hands. While he was about it, he'd skim across the top of her cheekbones, as well, learning the delicate lines of her bones just before he speared his fingers deeper into her bound hair and forced her face up to accept his kiss . . .

As his gaze dropped to her mouth, he noted that his distracted silence had caused those red lips to tighten into a thin, hard line. They loosened only so that she could launch into him.

'On that basis, and under current employment laws, consider this your first formal warning. In case you're not familiar with the standard terms of our contract, I can tell you that any continuation of harassment will result in a maximum of two further warnings, which, if ignored, will end in eventual dismissal.' Every inch of her expression showed the fierce satisfaction that prospect obviously gave her.

Prepared speech over, Annabel Frost faced him down, presenting an outward demeanour that could freeze the balls off a brass monkey – green eyes so cold they fairly glinted with little chips of ice, features tight with disapproval, shoulders set with determination. Oh, she was that good. If he hadn't been standing directly opposite her and didn't know what to look for, he'd have missed the rapid flicker of the pulse point at the base of her throat telling him she wasn't quite as composed as she looked. Inwardly, she was either mad as hell that she couldn't boot him right out the door, scared to her marrow that he'd found a chink in her armour, or reluctantly aroused by the things he'd said. Aidan was willing to put his money on a dizzying mix of all three.

'And if I don't ignore them?'

She looked at him for a moment. 'If you're prepared to apologise and ensure that you'll never behave in such a personally offensive manner again –' she paused as though the next words were sticking to her tongue and leaving a bitter taste there '– then, officially, matters need go no further.'

It wasn't hard to tell which outcome she was hoping for. She wanted him gone.

'Ah, I see. Well, I refuse to apologise for something I found so enjoyable. And I won't be made a liar by promising not to do it again when I have every intention of doing so – at every given opportunity. It's too much fun watching you get your tight white panties in a knot.'

And that put the first real crack in Annabel Frost's tightly held control. A flash of temper warmed those irises before she gritted her teeth. 'I've just told you not to talk to me that way,' she ground out. 'Leave my underwear out of it!'

'Now there's a fine idea.' He beamed, unable to resist jumping into the mile-wide opening she'd unwittingly given him. 'Why don't you come in tomorrow without any?'

Her eyes snapped wide and her cheeks reddened. 'You're perverted!'

Oh, if only she knew.

'Why, thank you, Ms Frost.' He wondered how warm that gorgeous, flushing skin of hers would feel to his touch. Wondered whether she'd ever accept his *perversions* and let him draw the same pretty glow from elsewhere on her body.

'And disgusting,' she spat, almost as if she'd read his thoughts, although the sudden rapid rise and fall of her chest suggested she was at least as excited as repulsed by his words.

'Careful now,' he warned her in a dead gentle voice. 'Insults will only lead to punishment.' He noted her flinch as he stressed the final word, the reaction to the mention of discipline almost as interesting as the one she'd showed last night.

'You wouldn't dare lay a finger on me.'

'Oh, I'd dare to use more than a finger,' he parried, enjoying the clash of wills. 'Much more. There's a whole world of erotic torment I'd like to introduce you to, Annabel.'

'You might find that difficult,' she sneered, but he detected an underlying tremble in her tone. 'Seeing as I'll never let you touch me.'

He flashed her a knowing smile. 'Now here's the funny thing.' Resting his elbows on the bar, he leant towards her, catching the faintest tease of her scent intensified by the rising heat of her skin. 'I don't need to touch you to make you mine. Soon, all I'll have to do is look at you across the room to make you gasp and shiver and know you belong to me.'

'Don't be so ridiculous.' Despite her continuing bravado, she retreated a step. 'Even if I didn't find you obnoxious I have a rule not to get involved with staff.'

'Rules were meant to be broken.'

'Not this one, I can assure you. I'm not *yours*' – she emphasised the word with contempt – 'and never will be.'

Aidan pulled back, straightening and changing his smile to one of 'if you say so', which infuriated his sparring partner to the point that he could almost hear her mentally stamping her foot.

'Why are you doing this?' she demanded, unable to hide the snap of petulance in her tone. The sound of it shot straight to the centre of him. Honestly, he hadn't felt so susceptible to a woman's temper in ages. If he wasn't careful, he'd find his control in tatters. No doubt about it, Annabel Frost knew how to push his buttons.

Just like he was getting to know how to push hers.

'Apart from wanting to get to possess every inch of you? Because I recognise a need in you that I understand and know how to fulfil.'

To her credit, she was quick to rally and stand her ground. 'How presumptuous.'

He gave an easy half-shrug. 'I'm a good judge of character, Annabel.'

'Really? Well, do share your expertise and tell me what you think this supposed *need* is, then.'

He paused for a moment, letting her sarcasm wash over him, watching her bristle as her discomfort grew. 'All this attitude.' He swept a hand up and down, the gesture encompassing her from head to toe. 'And the hard-nosed face you present to the world, it's part of a cover to hide your true nature, to bury the desires you're too afraid to admit to.' He could see a spark of wariness flare in her eyes, sense her bracing herself, ready for denial and defence. 'That yearning you have to surrender control, the need you feel to let someone else take charge, care for you, see to your pleasure.'

For a split second her eyes grew huge, telling him she knew exactly what he was talking about. God, that flash of sweet vulnerability shot a bolt of fire all the way down his spine and into his groin, and made him want to bend her over the bar right then and fuck her until she was soft and pliant and delirious with pleasure.

'A doormat?' she spat, currently about as soft and pliant as a steel spike, and every bit as sharp. 'That's what you think I am?' The laugh she gave him was hollow, dismissive. 'You must be blind.'

'I can see perfectly, thanks. Right through the bratty façade to the strong, capable woman beneath. Doormats don't do it for me.'

'And arsehole misogynist control freaks don't do it for me. Sounds like we've got a terminal case of incompatibility.' The triumphant note in her voice said she thought she'd got him – thought she'd won. That false sense of security left him hiding a fierce grin. God, she was fun to play with.

'Now that's where you're wrong,' he said, taking her high colour and glittering eyes as proof of how much she was also thriving on the exchange – even if she didn't realise it. He wondered how long it had been since a man had done her the courtesy of standing up to her, of trying to engage with the real Annabel Frost. 'If you think I don't know that your body is every bit as fired up as your brain at what we're doing here, think again.'

She looked about ready to explode – with anger, and frustration, and a heat he reckoned she'd rather die than admit to. And he knew once again he'd called it right.

Instead of letting rip at him as she so obviously wanted to do, Annabel glanced across the room at the remaining customers and contented herself with muttering, 'Insufferable bastard,' under her breath, providing him with the perfect excuse to turn things up a notch.

'I've given you fair warning, Annabel. You speak to me like that again and I'll come at you.' It was the first time he'd let his tone drop all the way to its deepest register and

35

he noted that the stern words hit their target. The shift in her demeanour was subtle but instant as some long buried instinct pricked up its ears to the underlying sense of power. 'And regardless of where or when or who's watching, I *will* put my hands on you then and leave you in no doubt as to who belongs to whom.'

Just as well she didn't know the trouble he was having not putting his hands on her right there as she stood gaping, those luscious lips doing the same cute fish impression they'd done the previous evening as she tried and failed to find her voice. Now he wanted nothing more than to push her to her knees and watch his hardening erection inch into her mouth, stretching that perfect 'o' wide until her wet heat encased him and her lipstick left a brand like a scarlet cock ring.

Annabel, it seemed, had different ideas. Apparently considering that retreat would be the better part of valour, she turned her stiff back on him and strode away. But not before Aidan had noted the darkening of those green eyes as her pupils dilated with desire.

Jesus. He was sure his own pupils were in much the same state as he watched her go, tamping down hard on the urge to vault right over the bar and give chase. The force of his need thrummed through his bloodstream, making his fingertips, toes and every damned thing in between ache with each thud of his heart.

At least now, after another intriguing exchange, he was certain he'd been right. Under that solid cold layer of ice, the real Annabel Frost was a firebrand. And even though he'd only begun chipping away at the outer edges of the frigid surface, Aidan could already feel himself scorched by flames of lust – flames that would need the hell beaten out of them once he made it home.

There he'd stretch out on his bed and heighten the

self-service experience by fantasising that she was there with him, red hair tangling around her porcelain nakedness as she begged and writhed against the bonds holding her spread-eagled and helpless across his sheets.

FOUR

Annabel was beyond relieved to find the bar area devoid of antagonistic Irish libertines when she arrived at Cluny's the next day, much later than usual and failing to convince herself that her tardiness had anything to do with avoidance tactics.

Aidan Flynn was a problem. A big one that needed sorting ASAP.

Having generously given him the benefit of the doubt the previous evening, she'd ended up getting her efforts flung back in her face without a hint of remorse. The man was intolerable. An immoral maverick who should never have been employed – certainly *wouldn't* have been employed if she'd been given her usual say in matters. If only Richard Landon hadn't chosen to act without consulting her, she wouldn't now be the one left to pay the price for somebody else's rushed mistake.

To add insult to injury, she wasn't even allowed the satisfaction of kicking Mr Flynn's degenerate arse straight back into whatever gutter he'd crawled from. Instead she was legally obligated to follow a strict set of steps aimed at protecting his rights even though it was obvious he wasn't interested in listening or conforming to the accepted rules.

Well to hell with waiting until he had exhausted each and every one of his statutory rights as he seemed to be intent on doing. She wanted him gone. Sooner, rather than later. Fortunately, tonight was the night that Richard Landon was due to host a pre-Christmas dinner for a table full of friends as he did every year, and although he'd made it clear that these occasions were for pleasure, never business, Annabel wasn't about to pass up the opportunity to lodge a quiet complaint in his ear. He was a shrewd businessman who understood that his restaurant had a public reputation to uphold. She was sure he'd be horrified to learn that he'd hired such an objectionable individual, a man who didn't seem to respect authority or care less about the consequences of his questionable actions. If she was lucky, she'd be able to get him to agree to Aidan Flynn's instant suspension while the attendant formalities were dealt with.

Pushing through the door into the kitchens, she barely registered the sudden exaggerated burst of activity from the full complement of staff already present – a sight that would normally have filled her with satisfaction but today just highlighted the extent of her distraction as she passed through with barely a glance to either side.

Shit. She couldn't afford such lack of focus. Tonight of all nights. Familiar with her boss' exacting expectations, she really should be busy cracking her whip to ensure that every last detail of the evening's food and service was beyond reproach.

Shoving through the fire door leading to the staff facilities and office, she strode down the short corridor pulling off her overcoat and determining to get her head back in the game. All she needed to do was play it cool, get through the next few hours and then this whole nasty episode would be behind—

Annabel froze in the act of swinging open the office door, her grip tightening on the handle as she noticed that the internal door leading to the cellar was ajar. Her gaze flicked instantly to the filing cabinet beside her desk, where the drawer containing the spare set of keys sat open. Obvious sounds of movement and a stream of appreciative, softly-accented mutterings floated up the stairs from the room below.

Bloody, bloody man! What did he think he was up to now? Her simmering resentment flashed to a hot, fast boil. Leaving the door to swing closed behind her, she marched across the small room, pausing at the top of the stairs.

'What the hell are you doing down there?'

'Annabel?' came a cheery reply. 'Hello. I was thinking maybe you weren't coming in today.'

Whether it was the nonchalant tone or the snide reference to her timekeeping that had her curling her hands into fists she didn't know. Who did he think he was? And how was she supposed to keep a cool head when it felt like the top of it was about to blow off? Tossing her bag and coat onto the desk, she stomped down the stairs.

'I said, what do you think you're doing? The cellar is off limits to unauthorised staff. Who gave you the key?'

'Well now, the boss phoned about this dinner he's got on tonight for a few of his cronies he's wanting to impress.'

That stopped her just as she stepped down onto the dusty concrete floor. By the light of the single bare bulb hanging from the cobwebbed rafters, Annabel spotted the bane of her life over by the far wall. 'Mr Landon phoned?'

'He did.' Fiddling about on the wooden bench top built into the bottle racking system that spanned the entire wall, Aidan Flynn didn't even have the decency to turn and face her. 'And as you weren't available, we discussed what he wanted from his fine, private collection here and he told me where to find the key.'

Oh, that grated. She glared at that broad back, at the

glossy tangle of black hair curling down to his collar, her teeth grinding and her hands itching to reach out and – what exactly? Clamp around that thick neck . . . thump between those wide shoulders?

'Well I'm here now,' she snapped, probably nowhere near as disturbed by her violent thoughts as she ought to be. 'So you can leave it with me and get back upstairs to the bar.'

'Not to worry.' He turned then and strode towards her holding a tray laden with bottles. 'I'm all done.'

Annabel fumed to see his sleeves rolled up to the elbows again. For fuck's sake, between that and the unruly bed-hair, did the guy have no idea how to even present himself properly for work?

Instead of heading straight up the stairs, he stopped in front of her. 'I just need you to take this for a minute,' he said, pushing the tray at her so quickly that Annabel had no option but to grasp it or let the lot fall to the floor.

'There now, be very careful with that,' he advised, tapping a light fingertip on top of one of the bottles. 'This Louis XIII cognac alone is worth about £1,300. Add the rest and we're looking at in excess of three grands' worth of the boss' rare booze. Have you done as I asked?'

It took her a moment to realise he'd fired a question at her.

'What?' She frowned up at him before noticing that silvery gaze locked on her, bright and sharp as a predator's, and every bit as merciless. Her scalp tightened as she suddenly became hyper-aware of the situation she'd let herself blunder into: alone with a man she knew was nothing but trouble.

'Don't play with me, Annabel.' The voice he used did nothing to reassure her. The soft edges of his accent were gone, leaving his words clipped. His tone was the same deep one that had made the bottom fall out of her stomach last night – stern, unyielding, commanding. 'Are you wearing nothing under that skirt, like I asked?'

The bottles on the tray tinkled as she gasped with a mix of alarm and outrage. 'Of course I'm not!'

'Of course you're not,' he confirmed with a particular relish that set off warning bells in her head. 'First you refuse to wear your hair down and now this.' He slipped a hand into his hip pocket and drew out a black-handled waiter's friend. 'You might like to take the opportunity to note that defiance only increases my determination.'

Seeing him flip out the serrated foil cutter from its slot at one end of the multi-function bottle opener made Annabel's pulse trip. 'Wha-what do you think you're doing?' She stumbled back half a step on unsteady heels, freezing on the spot as the bottles rattled and threatened to topple over.

'What would you like me to do?' Aidan Flynn asked, the little blade and those pale eyes glinting under the harsh overhead light as he began strolling in an arc around her. 'Would you like me to cut through the chains of respectability that are holding you back? Free your wild side?'

Annabel's heart leapt into her throat. She tried to keep an eye on him at the same time as keeping the tray steady.

'This is outrageous. You can't treat me this way. I'm your manager, not some sex toy for you to play your sleazy games with.'

The shivers running over her skin had little to do with the subterranean chill. The air itself down in the cellar seemed to be getting thinner, making it difficult for her to draw a decent breath. When her adversary stepped out of sight behind her, alarm turned to panic, causing the bottles to clink and clank. 'If you dare touch me I'll scream!' she threatened in a rush.

'I agree,' his voice sounded softly over her shoulder, so close it made her jump and fight to rebalance the tray. 'When I do get around to touching you, you will scream. Loudly and repeatedly with pleasure. I'll make it my mission not to let you stop until you're hoarse.' The warmth of his presence started to seep through the fine wool of her fitted jacket, blanketing her spine just like it had when he'd used his big body to corner her behind the bar the other night. She'd never known anyone to give off such heat – it chased away the chills yet doubled her shivers as he continued to murmur in her ear. 'But I promise you that won't be tonight. It won't be tomorrow either, maybe not even next week. No matter how much you end up begging for it, Annabel, I won't touch you until you're properly ready for me.'

Even though she had no reason to believe him, the rush of relief that his words brought left her shaky. Of course he wasn't going to do anything to her. Not even someone as unscrupulous as Aidan Flynn would go that far in a business premises full of people.

'Lucky me then,' she managed to push out in a voice that sounded far steadier than she felt. 'Because that will be the far side of never.'

He chuckled, the warm rush of his breath brushing against her neck, the caress making her skin tingle and grow warm. Why did her traitorous body react to him that way when her mind had the good sense not to?

On the move again, Aidan Flynn appeared from behind her other shoulder and completed his full circle appraisal with a few deliberate steps. Coming to a halt in front of her, he tilted his head down and smiled right into her eyes. 'And lucky for me I'm a patient man. It'll be worth the wait.'

Annabel stared, unable to look away from that Machiavellian smile which triggered another bout of physical treachery – this time a chain reaction of flutterings that ran right down to her core. Even when he was acting the prize arsehole in a dirty, dank cellar there was no denying the potent attractiveness of the man. Not that that was any reason to let him get away with such behaviour. Unlike her mother, Annabel

43

didn't believe that good looks were ever an excuse for bad manners. She couldn't wait to see how quickly she could wipe that smug expression off his handsome face. 'Will it be worth losing your job over? Because you can consider this your second verbal warning.'

'Noted,' he said without a moment's hesitation. 'And yes, you're worth that and more, Annabel.'

She blinked as she felt her confidence deflate. If he was bluffing, he was damned good – she couldn't detect anything but absolute certainty in his tone or expression. She realised she'd have to pull out the big guns if she stood a hope of winning this particular round. 'A charge of sexual harassment?'

His expression didn't change. Not by so much as a nervous twitch of an eyelid.

'Now here's where we have a difference of opinion,' he said, resuming his slow paced circling. 'What you're calling harassment, I simply consider a statement of intent.' He disappeared from sight again. 'I want you, Annabel,' he breathed. 'And from the way I read your reactions to me, I know you want me too.'

'You don't know the first thing about me,' she told him, fighting the tremors that skated across her spine as she sensed him moving behind her.

'Oh, I know enough. I know that rude words whispered in your ear make you catch your breath,' he murmured over her shoulder, making her nearly prove him right, if only she'd had any breath to catch. 'I know that dirty talk about the things I'm going to do to you makes your skin flush with heat.' He paused and brought his head down closer to her neck, taking an audible draw of air as he breathed in her scent. When he spoke again, his words came slower, his voice a low, throaty scrape over her nerves. 'I know that a stern tone, softly delivered, makes your pupils dilate and your pulse flutter.' God help her if she couldn't feel that flutter now. 'And I know that all those reactions mean you like what you hear, Annabel.'

'I do not,' she insisted, senses reeling as body and mind pulled in different directions. She yelped as she felt a tug on the hem of her skirt. 'What the hell are you doing? You said you wouldn't touch me.'

'I'm not touching you,' he simply said. 'I'm touching your clothes.'

'Well stop it!' she squealed, the thin veneer of her composure cracking as she felt the hem line rise up her thighs. 'You're wrong. I don't want this.'

And just like that the pull on the fabric was gone. The warmth radiating against her spine withdrew, leaving her back suddenly cold.

'Don't you?' His ever-calm voice sounded from a step or two behind her. 'Then why are you still standing there?'

The question clanged like a bell, the shock of the words reverberating around the quiet cellar. 'No one's keeping you here against your will. You're free to go any time you want.'

The moment he'd said it, she knew he was right. Why was she standing there taking this like she didn't have a choice? Mind spinning with confusion, pulse pounding in her ears, breath sawing in and out, she couldn't begin to fathom the reason. Or perhaps was too frightened to.

The bottles set up an almost constant chiming and her arms trembled with the effort of holding the tray aloft. After a moment she heard the soft crunch of a footstep behind her and realised she still hadn't moved – couldn't seem to make herself move.

She felt her tormentor step up close again, registered the rich male scent of him that chased away the dank smell of cellar.

'I mean it,' he said into her ear, his soft Irish lilt barely

45

audible over the rush of her blood that was increasing to a roar. 'All you have to do is take the tray and walk up those stairs now and you'll be rid of me.'

Yes. Of course that's what she must do.

Take the tray.

Walk away.

Before her brain could connect the messages to her feet, Aidan Flynn returned to stand in front of her and Annabel made the mistake of letting her gaze meet his. Once caught, there seemed to be no resisting the magnetic pull of those extraordinary eyes, no way of stopping the flow as they somehow drained the will to look away right out of her.

Was this how a rabbit felt, trapped in the headlights – breathlessly aware of the imminent danger yet rendered powerless to act against it?

'Go, and I swear I'll never bother you this way again.' The hurtling vehicle of her destruction came a step nearer, came as close as the tray between them would allow. 'But is that what you really want? I understand why you're fighting me, because that's your default setting – to fight when you sense something threatening your tightly controlled world,' he said in a deceptively quiet, compelling voice while those liquid mercury depths held her enthralled. 'But despite your denials there's no getting away from the fact that at least a part of you likes the idea of staying, of surrendering to the temptation to just let go for a change. A part that yearns to hand over the control and simply enjoy the pleasure I want to give you.'

Annabel felt her stomach bottom out. She'd known desire before. She'd been in the clutches of excitement and the grip of fear as well, but never anything like this. Never this para-lysing collision of all three. As soon as Aidan Flynn broke that hypnotic eye contact to begin prowling around her again, she gave her head a little shake in the hope of clearing it.

Then the words, 'And I do want to give you pleasure,

Annabel – so much pleasure,' were whispered into her ear on a hot breath that seeped down through every atom of her being like a drug. No one had ever said such a thing to her in such a way, never made such a promise with such longing. She knew that even if she somehow managed to get her feet to move, her knees wouldn't have the strength left to carry her up the stairs. She closed her eyes as a hopeless little sob of defeat bubbled up in her throat.

She expected him to gloat over the sound – hoped he would, so the tone of his self-satisfied triumph would ignite her anger and burn away this strange stupor. But instead, all she heard was a deep exhalation, as though Aidan Flynn had been holding his breath for a very long time.

'Trusting is the hardest part.' His voice, though still soft in her ear, had acquired a rasp that scoured over her skin. 'But it's also the best. I won't do anything to betray it. Just let go and give all the control over to me.'

As she felt the pull on her skirt resume, Annabel doubted she had the ability to do anything but. She stood there, half thrilled, half appalled, and fully dazed by the fact she actually appeared to be submitting to a virtual stranger's whim. It had to be a dream, she decided, letting the darkness behind her eyelids convince her that was the case. This would never happen in real life.

True to his earlier word, Aidan Flynn didn't let his fingers so much as brush her skin as he raised the figure-hugging fabric up over her hips. Perversely Annabel found a shameless part of her willing him to touch her now that he'd said he wouldn't – perhaps because it had been so long since any man had? Imagining the feel of his hands on her flesh – wondering whether that first contact would be gentle or rough, his fingers smooth or callused – had a warm sensation blossoming between her trembling thighs as she felt him slide the skirt up around her waist.

Then she heard his footsteps circle back around in front of her. 'Open your eyes for me, *a mhuirnín*,' his voice instructed after a moment.

It was too much. She'd rather die of her shame than have to see it reflected back at her from those deep silver pools. She gave a sharp shake of her head.

'Open your eyes, Annabel,' he repeated, his voice dropped into that low tone that suggested she disobey at her peril. 'Now.'

When she forced her eyelids apart, she saw him standing a little way back, arms crossed over his chest and head tilted at a slight angle. He made sure she was looking at him before he dropped his gaze to run it down over her from head to foot. Then he took his time raking it back up over every inch.

He re-met her eyes with a slight shake of his own head and a look that gave her the impression she'd be sorry. 'Tights, Ms Frost?' One dark eyebrow raised. 'Really?'

With that, he unfolded his arms and moved towards her, dropping smoothly to crouch at her feet. Instinctively, she shifted the tray to keep an eye on what he was doing, but froze when the movement set some of the bottles into a precarious wobble.

'Careful now, you need to keep nice and still,' he warned as, out of sight, she felt her tights being stretched away from her skin.

Annabel gasped in disbelief. *Was she really letting this happen?* Her blood rushed so fast she felt faint. *She couldn't . . . He wouldn't . . .*

He did.

With a tugging shred and tear, he took to the gusset with the blade of the foil cutter, exposing her thighs to the chill air. 'Oh, Annabel. So pretty. That underwear is way too lovely for me to destroy.'

And instead of reacting like any sane person and getting out of there or telling him were to go, she seemed preoccupied with trying to remember which set she was wearing.

The silence stretched, so heavy she could almost feel the weight of the tension closing in on her. When Aidan spoke at last, his voice was roughened to the point of gruffness. 'Christ, you're beautiful. I can just see the colour of your curls through the lace. A natural redhead, I knew it.' He pushed back to his feet and her belly clenched when his gaze pinned her again, the clear silver clouded to a darker shade of grey. 'I look forward to seeing more of you.'

Annabel watched dumbly as he reached out to level the drooping front edge of the tray with a finger, stopping the suddenly forgotten bottles from sliding to the floor.

'Like the sound of that, do you? Good. I want you to think about how it's going to feel to have me spread your legs so I can see all your secrets. How it will be to have me hold them wide so you can't hide.'

'Please.' Her voice was breathy and desperate as the bottles shook along with her entire body. The twitch and burn of her locked muscles and the dizzying pound of her blood were so acute she feared she wouldn't be able to hold on much longer. 'I'm going to drop the tray.'

Mouth dry, heart hammering, Annabel watched as Aidan smiled and reached towards her. But rather than help with the tray, or touch the throbbing ache of need his words had started between her legs as she realised she was silently willing him to do, he pulled her skirt back down into place and checked the elegant, leather-strapped watch on his wrist.

'But right now,' he said with regret, 'it's time for another busy night, Ms Frost.'

Bewildered by the sudden change in pace, she watched him tuck the waiter's friend back into his hip pocket and take the tray.

'I have to say I'm going to enjoy watching you work knowing you're secretly exposed for me.' He turned for the stairs and, in the rapidly cooling heat of the moment, she realised he was actually walking away – walking away and leaving her there. 'Remember that, every time you catch me looking.' His retreating voice floated down the stairwell. 'I'll be wanting you to tell me how it made you feel.'

FIVE

Sweet Jesus. He was in trouble.

Stepping out onto the pavement, Aidan paused to do up his jacket and suck in a fortifying breath, letting the brisk night air ease some of the heat of his ardour. Thank God that shift was finally over. And thank God he'd managed to get through it without doing something stupid – or downright illegal – like laying Annabel Frost out over one of the tables, sliding up her skirt and taking a taste of her through that diaphanous pale pink satin and lace right under the scandalised noses of the customers.

Just the thought had him fighting the urge to spin around, push back through the doors and turn the explicit fantasy into the ultimate X-rated reality. Forcing himself to move in the opposite direction, he started off down the street towards the Tube with long, purposeful strides, determined to put as much distance between himself and Cluny's as quickly as possible.

Since the moment he'd cut away his lovely manager's tights and uncovered those pretty panties and fiery curls, the knowledge of what was there under that figure-hugging skirt had been torturing him. The erotic vision of that delicate lace

51

and feminine terrain so rudely framed by the shredded wreck of her tights had been all but seared onto his retinas, tormenting him every time he so much as blinked.

'Hey, watch it!' He was slammed back to his surroundings as he jolted hard against another body. It was a clear, cold Saturday night but despite the near-freezing temperature, Soho was in full party mode, the streets clogged with an overspill of weekend revellers amid a dazzle of coloured lights and a cacophony of sounds.

In the swirling mass it was impossible to tell who he'd run into. Raising his hands in a general gesture of apology, he started off again at a slower pace, trying to keep at least half his attention on where he was going.

He hadn't spoken to Annabel again since he'd left her standing, shaking and enticingly submissive, in the cellar – hadn't trusted himself to be able to keep his cool if he got too close. The woman was damned near irresistible. How he'd ever found the strength to walk away from the temptation of her and make it up those cellar stairs without tripping over his iron rod of a hard on, he didn't know.

He'd come *that* close to breaking his own promise – to touching her. And that would've been a great shame. It was way too soon.

Brought to a stop at a busy intersection, he joined a clutch of people waiting to cross the road and puffed out a frustrated breath, watching it cloud in the cold air. He had no one to blame for his agitated state but himself. Having felt he'd had no choice but to come on dangerously fast and strong or risk having his advances batted away like an annoying gnat, the stunt he'd pulled down in the cellar had been designed to throw Ms Frost off her guard, make her flustered and breathless. He never for a moment expected her to let things go so far. If she really was as averse to his advances as she liked to insist, that would have been the moment she'd have put a stop to things. But she hadn't, and the encounter had ended up being so intense, her first act of surrender so captivating in its reluctance, that he'd wound up well and truly caught by his own game. He'd only just found the strength to stop before he took things too far, only just resisted the temptation to cut through that flimsy barrier of lace and pull it from between her trembling thighs.

He'd hardly been able to take his eyes off her since, as much out of a surge of possessiveness as voyeuristic fascination to see how she'd cope with her secret state of *déshabille* while fulfilling her frontline public role. For her part, she'd been staunch in her refusal to so much as glance his way, spending a good portion of the evening tucked behind the reception desk, making only the occasional necessary foray to the boss' table and tactically retreating every time Aidan approached to take care of anything drink-related. On the surface, she'd seemed to go about her business with her usual display of cool professionalism, but even in the artful gloom of the restaurant Aidan had been able to pick out the delightful blush shadowing her cheeks, the vaguest hint of self-consciousness any time anyone got a bit too close.

The traffic lights changed and he let himself get pushed forward with the crowd while his mind continued to pull back in the direction of Annabel Frost. Although he had more sense than to ever admit it out loud, those glimpses of uncharacteristic vulnerability appealed to his dominant side in some primal predator-and-prey way that didn't give a flying fuck for the enlightened advances of social evolution, sexual equality or political correctness. The sight of that strong, independent woman trembling because of him was more potent than a double dose of Viagra.

Coming to the Tube station entrance, he jogged down the stairs, resigned to the fact that for the time being he was in for another long night with his fist and his fantasies. At least he could console himself with the knowledge that Annabel Frost was likely to be in a similar situation – able to think of nothing but him, and in for just as restless and rocky a night.

Annabel lay glaring at the numbers glowing red across the face of her digital alarm clock, counting down the minutes until the radio would spring into life and signal that it was time to get up. Though to be honest, she'd never felt more like keeping to her bed . . . or sofa in this instance.

Far too much of the night had been spent watching time crawl past instead of sunk in the re-energising sleep she needed to help her deal with the nightmare her waking life had become. Over and over again into the small hours, that scene in the cellar had replayed in her head, until every sordid, shameful second of what had happened was indelibly imprinted on her memory.

She'd been in a state of shock at the time, she'd come to realise. She must have been, otherwise how else could she explain what had happened? That she'd let a man she hardly knew and certainly didn't like do the disgraceful things he'd done? Allowed him to control and degrade her in a way she'd sworn never to let any man do?

Worst of all – how had Aidan Flynn made her feel like she'd enjoyed it?

It seemed absurd now to think he'd been able to steal her will so effectively using nothing but the mesmerising power of those eyes and the hypnotic tone of his voice. It was even more disturbing that her body had reacted so readily to the cool authority of his words. It frightened her to consider that maybe she was more her mother's daughter than she'd realised – that despite her determination not to make the same mistakes, she was destined to let the wrong type of men walk all over her, control and ruin her life.

Groaning, she rolled onto her back and flung an arm across her face trying to blot out the cold clarity of morning that illuminated more than she cared to see. Because, as much as it pained her to admit it, there was just no denying the rush of desire she'd felt as Aidan Flynn had calmly taken command and uncovered her – no ignoring the needy ache that persisted between her legs even still.

As if that wasn't humiliating enough, *he*, by contrast, had seemed totally unaffected by what he'd done to her, simply walking away and leaving her exposed and wanting and mortified. The second he'd disappeared up the cellar stairs, taking the force of his will and whatever strange, spellbinding charm he wielded with him, she'd come back to her senses with a jolt, nearly collapsing on the spot as her knees had threatened to give out.

She'd had no option but to remove what remained of her tights, of course. Then it had taken all her nerve to appear on the restaurant floor shortly afterwards and brave it out as though nothing was amiss while every step, every swish of movement, reminded her of her state of undress. With the knowing weight of Aidan Flynn's stare bearing down on her, she'd barely found the presence of mind to exchange pleas-antries with Richard Landon, let alone take him aside as she'd planned.

After what she'd let happen, how could she have even contemplated making serious allegations? She'd have had to recount the story of what had gone on in that cellar and that would have cast as much doubt on her character as on Aidan Flynn's. Maybe even more so considering the fact that while he had avoided laying so much as a finger on her, she hadn't done a thing to put a stop to the proceedings . . . hadn't run, hadn't screamed, hadn't fought. If she thought her case sounded flimsy to her own ears, she could only imagine how it would have sounded to her boss. Having watched the way Richard

Landon and his all male guests had so casually included the Irishman in their conversation, their rounds of laughter – automatically accepting him into their boys' club – she'd decided the only thing to do was keep her mouth shut.

Jumping as the radio blared into life and filled her sitting room with the chirpy jingle of a Christmas pop song, Annabel lashed out at the off button and sprang up from the sofa. As hiding under her covers was unfortunately not an option, she had no time to waste on feeling sorry for herself. There were things to do. Important things like trying to salvage what was left of her pride and working out how best to deal with Aidan Flynn now that the situation had become much worse than she could have imagined.

By the time she arrived at Cluny's, Annabel was done beating herself up. Shit had happened. There'd been a moment of insanity. It was over. The roil of self-loathing that had been clouding her mind had settled into cold, hard clarity, letting her focus her thoughts and feel like her old self again. She was a twenty-seven-year-old professional, not some gutless girl. Calm, controlled, and cutting; she could take on anything when she had a cool head. Anything up to, and including, the manipulative sexual deviant who was behind the bar amid cleared shelves and a forest of bottles as he checked stock levels.

The irony wasn't lost on her that someone so fucked up on the personal front could be pretty near faultless from a professional standpoint. Hard-working, self-motivated, dedicated – her nemesis was the type of employee she'd normally fall over herself to hire.

A quick visual sweep of the restaurant showed the only other member of staff in sight to be Donna, who was out of earshot on the far side of the dining room polishing cutlery. The waitress gave a guilty little jump when she spotted

Annabel stepping through the door, quickly dropping the dreamy smile she'd been directing towards the bar.

Annabel wasn't surprised. The meek little mouse seemed just the type to fall for the autocratic lord and master act. And thinking about it, surely someone like that was the perfect woman for Aidan Flynn? Agreeable, dependent, compliant. Yet for some reason Annabel couldn't pick up the smallest vibe of the waitress' interest being returned.

Lucky Donna.

Having decided on the quick rip plaster method as the best way of dealing with this painfully sticky situation, she marched straight from the doorway towards the bar, the sound of her heels striking the floorboards drawing Aidan Flynn's attention from the clipboard he was marking.

The frown of concentration creasing his brow cleared as that silvery gaze locked on her. Annabel fought the pull for a breathless second as the space between them seemed to tunnel and contract. Those translucent depths that had seen far too much of her last night sharpened with an intensity that left little doubt they were remembering every intimate inch. Under that penetrating look she felt exposed, stripped all over again, vulnerable . . . then everything snapped back into place as she saw one of his infuriating smiles start to curl his lips.

'Ann—'

'Don't!' she interrupted, flinging her palm up to stop him. 'You've got nothing to say that I want to hear. So just keep quiet and listen to me.'

Black brows jumped almost to his hairline, grey eyes flashed as they sparked with interest and – seriously – was that a glint of *amusement* she saw?

Well, let him see how funny he found this. She narrowed her own eyes. 'I don't like you,' she told him. 'I don't like the things you say or the way you think you can behave towards me. This is not your personal playground, this is a place of business. And I don't like that you're in it,' she enunciated tightly. 'Take a word of advice and don't go getting yourself comfortable because I'm going to have you out of here so fast it'll blow that smirk right off your face. Until that happens, I don't want you anywhere near me at any time. Understood?'

Aidan Flynn's only reaction was to sweep what looked suspiciously like an appreciative gaze over her. 'Yes, ma'am.'

More mockery? Annabel felt her icy resolve begin to melt under a renewed blast of anger. Why was she surprised? Rather than give him the satisfaction of seeing that he riled her, she spun away and strode towards the kitchens, unable to help snarling over her shoulder, 'And roll your fucking sleeves down!'

SIX

Aidan gave three quick raps on the office door then pushed it open without waiting for a response.

Across the room, Annabel stiffened where she sat at her desk, talking into the phone.

'. . . calling to confirm that Chef and I will have everything ready for the Christmas Day menu tasting tomorrow afternoon at three.' That green glare flashed at him as she emphasised her next words. 'I very much look forward to seeing you again then, Mr Landon, and having the opportunity to discuss a number of matters with you.'

Disconnecting the call, she dropped the handset back into its cradle. 'I told you I didn't want you coming near me,' she said to Aidan by way of welcome. 'Are you deaf or just stupid?'

He paused and used the excuse of narrowing a disapproving gaze on her to check her over. Oh, yeah – as he'd predicted, her night had been every bit as rough as his. Annabel Frost was tired and grouchy and just the tiniest bit dishevelled, with wisps of hair escaping from a slightly skew-whiff bun and curling down to her collar. She'd removed her jacket and he wondered what would happen if he were to peel her white shirt aside and blow those soft red tendrils against the sensitive curve between neck and shoulder. Could he transform her barely contained tremors of tension into trembles of pleasure? Make her shiver and moan for him right there in her chair? From the way she'd reacted to him every time he'd got near – so responsive to even the slightest verbal stimulation – he'd not only put money on the shivers, he'd double the odds for a scattering of goose bumps as well.

Aidan didn't know whether it was his look or the lowered tone of his voice as he said, 'I'm neither, Annabel, as you well know,' that had her shifting uncomfortably.

'Then why are you here?' she snapped. 'If you think I'm going to put up with—'

'Reorder form for the bar,' he interrupted, holding up the piece of paper in his hand.

That stopped her dead. She obviously hadn't expected anything quite so mundane, because for a moment she stared at it in surprise. When he started across the room, she blinked and seemed to pull herself together.

'Fine, just leave it there.' She nodded towards the furthest corner of the desk from where she sat and ignored his outstretched hand.

Rather than put the form down he kept hold of it and settled one buttock cheek on the corner of the wooden surface closest to her instead.

'No!' Annabel gaped at him, eyes popping with horror. 'What are you doing? Don't you dare sit there.'

Surely she was beginning to understand that he'd dare a lot in his efforts to get close to her, to force her to engage with him rather than retreat. Resting his forearm across his thigh, he clasped his wrist with his free hand, bent towards her and fired his opening shot. 'Tell me now, Ms Frost, what's got you in such a snit?'

'Snit?' She glared at him. '*Snit?*' she repeated and he saw her swallow in an obvious effort to get control of her voice which was rapidly escalating to an out-and-out shout. 'I'll tell you what's got me in a fucking snit, you arrogant arse-hole. You!'

He felt a tug at the corner of his lips as he fought to deny a smile. Ms Frost was about to blow her ice-cool top. Good. He'd take her hot and bothered over frigid and aloof any day – a thought which ignited a spark of excitement in the pit of his belly. 'I gathered that much. But why?'

'*Why?* Are you kidding me! Where should I start? Oh, I know, how about with you *assaulting* me!'

'Assault is it now?' He nodded slowly as he absorbed that, all too aware of the knife edge he was on with his behaviour, of the risk of taking things too far. But he'd decided that if shock tactics were the only way to put a crack in Ms Frost's defences – the only way to draw her out – then it was a chance he had to take. 'Then why is it that I'm here and not being fingerprinted down at the nearest police station?' He watched her carefully as he waited for her reply – watched her struggle and fail to come up with a satisfactory answer. He had one, but he didn't think she'd care to hear it just yet. 'As far as I understand, it's only assault if either party doesn't consent.'

'I *don't* consent!' A heated blast of temper blazed through the thin cold shell of Annabel's control. She slapped her palms against the desk top hard enough that he felt the angry blow reverberate through his backside to his spine. 'I've never consented. I've done nothing but tell you that I don't want your attentions, that I'm not interested.'

And if every one of her physical reactions to him didn't contradict those words, he'd have left her alone from the start. He leant in closer, just to drink in those reactions, liking the way her eyes flashed at him, the way the paleness of her skin had warmed to a rosy flush, the way her chest rose and fell with rapid breaths. She looked vibrant, volatile . . . beautiful. 'But I don't recall you saying no when it mattered, Annabel.' He broke the news to her in a calm tone, knowing she wasn't going to like the truth behind his next words. 'I gave you the opportunity to put a stop to this last night and you didn't take it. If you're uncomfortable with your decisions or the discoveries you're making about yourself, don't think you can make yourself feel better by throwing accusations of assault and non-consent at me. If you want to pick a fight, fine, but you'll have to come up with a genuine argument.'

He'd been right, she didn't like it. She looked as though she wanted to kill him. Right there and then with her bare hands. Slowly. God, the woman excited him.

'Fine,' she spat. 'There are plenty to choose from. Where should I start? With you undermining my authority? Or sexually harassing and humiliating me? What about ruining my clothing and . . . and exposing my underwear?' She glared at him.

'OK,' he said after a moment. 'First off, undermining your authority? If you're talking about your position here, can you tell me of a single instance where I've done anything in front of any other members of staff or customers that would call your authority into question?'

He knew full well he hadn't, but he let her have the time to think about it for herself. No matter how disrespectful and depraved she might consider his behaviour in private to be, she'd never find him doing anything to publicly demean her.

'I didn't think so,' he eventually said into the telling silence. 'And for the record, that's not just coincidence. I've been careful, Annabel, and I always will be. You have my assurance on that. What's going on between us has nothing to do with your professional standing. This is strictly personal and private and I intend keeping it that way.'

'There is *nothing* going on between us,' she insisted through gritted teeth, but he didn't feel the need to correct her. Not when the chemistry between them was off the charts enough to prove otherwise. 'Secondly, we've already covered the sexual harassment thing and nothing has changed.' She looked as though she had plenty she wanted to say about that but he carried on without giving her the chance. 'As for ruining your clothing . . .' He gave a shrug of acceptance. 'You're right, I'm going to have to cop that one fair and square. But come on, we're talking *tights* here – those things were beyond hideous and deserved to be destroyed. I'll take you shopping and replace them with a pair of silk stockings.'

Annabel curled her lip at him. 'Don't bother. I'm not some doll for you to dress up.'

It wasn't dressing her *up* he was interested in. 'And as for exposing your pretty underwear.' Leaning forward, he lowered his voice. 'Oh, Ms Frost. That little pair of panties. I haven't been able to stop thinking about them. Do you want to hear about the torment they've been putting me through?'

'*No!*' Looking like she'd touched a live electric cable, Annabel shot away from him with such force she sent her chair rolling backwards from the desk. 'I don't want to hear another word. She snapped with more than a hint of desperation before she ordered, 'Get out.'

The curt dismissal she'd issued to Aidan rung in Annabel's ears, but like that sense of morbid fascination which made it impossible for people to look away from the scene of a crash, she found that part of her *did* want to hear about it. Not that she'd be foolish enough to ever admit such a thing.

It appeared, though, that regardless of her clear statement to the contrary, Aidan Flynn was determined to share the details anyway.

'You don't want to hear how I've been unable to forget that teasing glimpse they offered of you through that delicate barrier of lace?'

Annabel gasped, as in front of her, Aidan unfurled his spine and rose from his spot on the edge of her desk, placing the piece of paper there in his stead. 'Don't want me to tell you how tantalising a picture you made?'

'No.' Gripping the arms of her chair, Annabel pushed her soles against the carpet, backing the chair further away from him until she hit the wall.

'You don't want to know how hard for you I was down in that cellar?' In three slow, sauntering strides he was in front of her, so close that the fabric of his trousers brushed against the outside of her knees as he placed his feet to either side of hers. Further up nearer her eye level, the crotch area of those same trousers strained across a large bulge she couldn't help but notice.

Oh, for the love of . . . was that *all* him?

'How hard I've grown every time I've thought of that scene since?'

'No!' Annabel dragged her own eyes away from the bountiful sight and dug her heels into the ground to put more space between them. But there was nowhere left to go. Mindlessly, she grabbed at the hem of her skirt instead and held it tight to her knees with both hands.

Her racing heart skipped a beat as Aidan Flynn leant over her, hands reaching out . . . But rather than put them on her, he gripped the arms of the chair, boxing her in with those forearms he hadn't bothered to cover, the long, lean muscles cording to hold his weight. A wave of his body heat crashed over her and what little space there was between them fairly crackled with static.

'You don't want to hear how I've wished I'd gone that extra step and cut that little scrap of lace from you as I'd wanted?' he rasped, his desire-clouded gaze locked on her. 'Taken them for my own?'

Trapped, Annabel shook her head, trying to ignore the

dizzying rush of her pulse, fighting to override the unwanted, yet unmistakable, response of her body as every nerve ending quivered. He was toying with her, she knew – toying with her like a cat did a mouse. She could see it in the mischievous glint in his eye.

'No,' she said, her voice sounding smaller and less steady than she'd like. 'I don't want to hear it.'

He was close, looming over her, studying her intently, ready to pounce. 'Why not?'

'Because it's crude and disgusting.'

'Is it?' he asked. 'Or is it just natural and honest?'

'I . . .' she began and had to stop to clear her dry throat. 'It doesn't matter. Either way I don't like it.'

'And I don't think that's true. I'm picking up all sorts of signals that tell me you *do* want to hear it, that you *do* like it. Why pretend otherwise?'

Because she didn't want to have to contemplate the truth. 'The only thing you're picking up from me is revulsion. That, and the determination to see you gone from here as soon as possible. Now get away from me.'

The chair creaked under his weight as he tightened his grip on the arms and leaned even closer. 'Tell me. Did you enjoy the feeling of being exposed last night? It was obvious you were thinking of nothing else all service.'

Oh, she'd been thinking of other things, but nothing she was prepared to own up to. 'I felt violated. You tricked me into holding that tray, took unfair advantage.'

'Is that so? From what I know of your character so far, Ms Frost, there's no way you'd have let me do what I did if some part of you didn't want it. You'd have hurled that tray right back in my face then used the broken bottles to gut me on the spot.'

She gaped at him. 'And smashed thousands of pounds' worth of alcohol?'

65

He looked at her for a long moment, that clear gaze probing deep. 'Do you think the cost of the booze would have really been a factor if you'd felt genuinely threatened or violated?' he asked, his gentle reasoning pricking right through her protective outer layer of resentment. 'The tray was just a prop, Annabel. Think about it and you'll see it was nothing more than an excuse to make it easier for you to give up control.' He blinked and a spark of something mischievous lightened his eyes. 'And I have to say I was surprised by how quickly you gave it up. For someone so determined to come out on top, you caved with barely a fight. What do you think that says about you?'

She really couldn't bear to think. Couldn't bear to bring herself to listen to the inescapable ring of truth his words carried. Attack was her best form of defence. Always. 'Perhaps you should be more concerned with what you think it says about you, that you consider it acceptable to use cheap tricks to try and get women?'

He smiled, undeterred. 'I'm not trying to get women. Just you. And I think it says I'm a man determined to get what I want, by any means necessary. That makes me dedicated and resourceful at the very least.'

'It's nothing to gloat over!' she shouted at him, exasperated. 'What you did was unscrupulous and sordid.'

'Extremely. And so enjoyable I'd do it again in a flash.'

'Not to me you won't,' she assured him.

'Be honest now, Ms Frost. You liked it, didn't you? Were you driven to distraction, kept awake half the night, like I was?'

Her distraction was none of his business. She shot him a withering look. 'I know you think you're being sexy right now, Mr Flynn, but again, I have to say that what I mostly feel is disgust. I'll never think about you that way.'

'Soon, every time the merest thought of pleasure crosses

your mind, you'll think of me, Annabel, I promise you. In fact, I'll wager it's started already. Have you learnt your lesson? Did you come into work ready for me today? Is that why you've got that death grip on your skirt – because you're bare for me under there?' he asked before dropping his voice to a whisper that had her clenching every muscle in her body to keep from squirming in the chair. 'Why don't you open your legs and show me? I can't stop remembering how pretty you looked through that lace; I've been driving myself mad wondering when I'll get to see all your secrets.'

God, he was shameless, and with the speed he kept turning and twisting the argument it was a miracle she didn't have whiplash. 'I have nothing to show you apart from your third and final warning. This one you'll need in writing. Now get away from me so I can type it up.'

'Nothing nicer than that?' He leant over her a little more, his gaze flicking down the neckline of her shirt.

Annabel jerked one hand from her skirt to her top, clutching the fabric close to her chest, trying to ignore the fact that her every nerve ending had lit up in response to his words.

Aidan's eyes flicked back up to hers. 'I hate to tell you this, but despite all your protestations, your body is telling a different story. Are you always so responsive?'

She refused to answer him, refused to acknowledge the tingling in her breasts, the sensation telling her that her treacherous nipples were hardening. She didn't dare breathe in case the movement made the evidence visible against her shirt.

'It's all right, you don't have to tell me. I'm going to enjoy finding out for myself. I'm going to take all the time I need to discover all sorts of intimate details about you.'

Annabel blocked the picture that popped into her head, but not before the image of herself trapped beneath his weight and moaning under his mouth had shot a white-hot bolt from chest to pelvis. 'I said get *away* from me,' she ground out.

He held her narrow-eyed glare for a second then flashed a dazzling smile and straightened. 'Oh, Ms Frost. There are going to be fireworks when we eventually get it together.' He turned and headed for the door.

Watching him go, Annabel sucked in air to keep from passing out with relief. 'Why don't you do me a favour and hold your breath until the day you think that's going to happen?' she sniped at his retreating back, determined to have the last word.

She barely refrained from hurling the stapler against the closing door in response to the low chuckle that came drifting back over his shoulder.

SEVEN

'Why don't you open your legs and show me?' Aidan coaxed the reluctant goddess seated in front of him.

Wearing nothing but a white bra, black hold-ups and glossy killer heels, her thighs pressed firmly together and wrists bound to the arms of the office chair, she raised her eyes to meet his.

Aidan felt the impact of that green gaze punch right into his chest and groin, where it simultaneously took hold of his heart and his manhood and squeezed. He'd never seen anything as beautiful as the vision Ms Frost presented. Never wanted anything so much that certain parts of him literally ached with longing.

'I have nothing to show you,' she insisted, her red lips clipping short each word.

His gaze slid down the pale loveliness of her torso to where he could see the very top of her triangle of russet curls peeping like licks of flame from between her upper thighs.

'Now I know that's not true. I've already seen a glimpse for myself, Annabel, remember? I've seen – and now I want to touch.' In fact, his fingers tingled with the urge to plunge into that intimate fire and burn. Returning his gaze to her face, he fixed her with a look and dropped his tone. 'Open for me.'

He saw her reaction to the voice, saw her clench her fists even as she moved to obey, the battle within allowing her knees to fall only an inch apart. It was all the sign he needed to tell him that she wanted this as much as he did. She wanted to let go, to trust him, but couldn't.

'Wider,' he persisted, sterner still – assuming control, easing the burden of choice. Providing her with the excuse she needed to surrender herself up to him.

Another inch, nothing more. But she hadn't yet given him an outright 'no'. God help him if she made him stop now – his heart would give out under the strain.

Deciding to risk testing the tough road, he took a step closer, letting the tips of his shoes touch the tips of hers. 'Open your legs,' he warned. 'Or shall I do it for you?'

A spark of temper flashed in her eyes at that, and as he'd anticipated, she took up the challenge. Giving him a defiant glare she opened her legs half way.

It wasn't nearly enough. He needed her to give him everything. So he could give her everything in return. 'Wider still, Annabel. Don't play with me.'

All she gave him was one of her contemptuous little laughs. 'I'm not the one looking for a sex toy,' she sneered. 'If anyone's playing, it's you.'

He couldn't resist the attitude, the hint of provocation she threw straight back at him. 'Very well,' he said, positioning his feet between hers. 'My game. My rules.' Using the outer edges of his shoes he pushed hers wider and wider in turn until she was completely open to him. Open and vulnerable and so heart-stoppingly desirable that he dropped to his knees, worshipping the heavenly sight of her as his right. 'Winner takes all,' he rasped, reaching his tingling fingertips towards their fiery prize.

Rather than scorch him on contact, she was warm to his touch – soft and slick and silky smooth. The breathy moan wrenched from her throat resonated through him, ricocheting between every deep pleasure spot and leaving his body humming like a tuning fork.

Under his caresses, Annabel's eyelids drifted closed and her features softened. If she was a goddess, then witnessing the power he had to transform her thus made him feel like a fucking god.

'We've both waited too long for this, Ms Frost.' Reaching his free hand over her shoulder, he found and released the clip holding her hair and let the red locks tumble free. Threading his fingers through the luxurious mass, he fisted a handful at her nape and pulled, tilting her head back, holding her fast. 'I'm going to make you come for me now. I'm going to watch the pleasure of it on your face. I'm going to drink the sound of it straight from your mouth.'

Behind him the computer on her desk beeped.

Annabel's eyes sprang back open; her thighs snapped shut, trapping his hand. 'You'll need that in writing,' she said, attempting to manoeuvre the chair towards the desk.

'What?' Aidan tried to release his hand from between her legs but found it stuck fast. Annabel ground herself against it, her breathing changing to short, sharp pants, her body tensing with urgency.

'Now. I need to type up my orgasm *now*,' she gasped, and as the computer beeped again she flung her head back against the hand he still had in her hair, her mouth stretching wide . . .

Eyes flying open and with a mighty gasp of his own, Aidan shot upright and stared around him, disorientated. The remnants of the dream rapidly faded to bring him back to the reality of his bedroom. His bed. Light seeped in around the window blinds, illuminating the room and telling him it was already morning.

71

'*Jesus.*' His pulse pounded, his entire body was set rigid – very rigid, he noted with a wild glance to where the rumpled sheet tented over his lap.

The beeping sounded again. Not from Annabel Frost's computer but from his phone on the bedside table next to him, announcing that he'd received a message. Whoever wanted him, they'd have to wait. Because even more unsettling than the physical overload currently bombarding him was the astonishing psychological activity that had brought it on.

He hadn't dreamt – or at least been able to recollect having done so, according to the science – in three years.

Pushing the covers aside, he swung his legs off the mattress and set his feet to the floor, needing to feel the solidity of the ground beneath him while he let the significance of what had just happened sink in. For more than a thousand nights his sleep state had been a blank void of nothingness, an endless black hole – and while he'd told himself that oblivion was preferable to the prolonged period of nightmares and sleeplessness he'd suffered prior to it, the loss had left him feeling strangely bereft. To have that void suddenly filled was more than a little overwhelming.

He scrubbed his hands over his face to remove the last traces of sleep and then splayed them through his hair, feeling the shape of his skull, the long thin line of scar tissue running behind his ear – reassured to find everything still in its right place. After the coats had finished running every post-operative test they'd been able to think of on him, and tried to hide their continuing bafflement over his dreamlessness, they'd said that *if* the anomaly ever righted itself, it would likely be by degrees. A gradual process with not much more to offer than the odd flicker or fragment here and there to start with. And yet the dream he'd just had of Annabel Frost – the first one he was aware of in so long – had exploded across the screen of his slumbering mind with the clarity of a high-definition, Technicolor feature film.

Apparently science wasn't as exact as it purported to be after all.

His phone beeped again and, releasing his head, he reached across to pick it up. The display showed him he had a missed call and voicemail. Recognising the number, he pressed to play the message.

'Ah, shit.' Disconnecting a minute later, he checked the time and texted a quick reply before tossing the phone onto the bed. Just when he thought things couldn't get any more complicated with Annabel Frost.

Pushing to his feet, he headed naked to the en suite wetroom, acknowledging that what had started out as an exciting challenge was fast becoming something much more. And he didn't think his increasing preoccupation with his manager was merely a result of his self-imposed no touch rule – the rule he was coming to regret making with every sexually frustrated fibre of his being.

As convenient an excuse as it made, he suspected physical denial was only partly responsible. What he was starting to feel for Ms Frost went deeper than simply wanting to satisfy the flesh.

Hitting the brushed steel control panel for the shower, he waited for the water to run hot. God knew the last thing he was looking for at this point in time was to get himself tangled in anything serious. But already Annabel was too far under his skin for him to believe this could be a casual affair, the fun distraction he'd first envisaged. Looked for or not, she was turning out to be something special. The fact that he'd been able to find her in his dreams was confirmation of that.

Watching white clouds of steam billow against the back-drop of the black slate walls he tried to work out how he felt about it. Certainly not as trapped or claustrophobic as a freewheeling bachelor-about-town who lived by the motto 'Life's too short' might expect to be, he realised – which in itself should be enough to scare him off.

But far from instilling a feeling of fear, the thought filled him with a sense of fierce anticipation. The question was, did he want to pursue it . . . see where it led? Did he even have a choice any more?

Stepping under the high-pressure jets, he let the cascade of water drench him from his hair down, washing away the dream daze still muddying his mind. The one thing he knew for sure was that the nature of the game was changing – quicker than he'd like, thanks to that phone message – and he was going to need to get his head clear to keep up with the play.

Annabel was half way through unpacking and putting away the weekly groceries when her mother shuffled into view in the kitchen doorway.

'Gosh. You've been busy early, darling.' Ellen yawned. 'Why didn't you let me know you were going shopping? I could have come and helped.'

Annabel took in the dressing gown and slippers. 'Not to worry. I had to be up early anyway, so I thought I might as well get it out of the way.'

'But it's Monday, isn't it?' Her mother frowned. 'I thought the restaurant was closed on Mondays? You work so hard I'd have thought you'd appreciate the opportunity of a lie-in.'

A lie-in would be blissful, but it was all Annabel could do to try to eke out a decent night's sleep on the too small, too hard sofa as it was. Why would she willingly spend more time tossing and turning on it than was strictly necessary? Still, the current sleeping arrangements had been her choice so there was no point in mentioning her discomfort and making her mother feel bad.

'Apart from the next fortnight when we're open seven days a week for the festive rush, Cluny's is usually closed on Mondays. But I have to go in for the Christmas menu tasting with Mr Landon today, remember?' And for Annabel the hours couldn't pass fast enough until she'd be face to face with her boss and able to stick the shit big time to Aidan Flynn. 'Plus, we agreed to make a start on that box of paperwork of yours this morning. Why don't you get dressed while I finish putting this stuff away and make us some coffee.'

Unsurprisingly, her mother didn't look very keen at the mention of paperwork – the damning, black-and-white proof of her financially ruined life. She came further into the kitchen.

'I could help,' she said, stalling for time and starting to poke about in the top of the still full bags while Annabel reached and stretched around her. 'Did you remember to get more gin, darling? We're clean out.'

Ready for just such a question, Annabel performed an exaggerated *how-stupid-am-I?* eye roll. 'I knew I forgot something,' she lied, having no intention of continuing to support her mother's unhealthy habit. That was the main reason she'd left her sleeping instead of taking her along to the supermarket. 'I'll get some next time.'

'Oh, no problem,' her mother said, still checking out the contents of the bags on the counter without actually unpacking anything. 'I can easily nip out and get some while you're at your tasting.'

Annabel had to bite her lip against the *no* that wanted to come out. Although her mother sometimes seemed as naïve as a child, she was a grown woman. A woman who'd just been through hell. While Annabel might not want to play a part in aiding something she didn't agree with, what right did she have to try to stop her mother acting for herself?

'Could you just . . . ?' Hands full of items for the fridge, she herded her mother backwards towards the doorway. Her kitchen, while modern and well equipped, was far too small for them both to work around each other. Like the rest of the flat, it epitomised the trend for compact urban living, which meant there wasn't space enough to swing the proverbial cat. But Annabel didn't mind. With property prices the way they were in London, she counted herself fortunate to be able to call even this tiny slice of the capital her own.

'If you could just leave me some money before you go,' her mother tagged on lightly.

Springing upright from where she bent at the open fridge, Annabel blinked at her. 'But I gave you some on Saturday. Don't you remember?'

'Of course I remember, darling. I'm not quite senile yet.' Ellen gave a tinkling laugh. 'But that was days ago.'

'Two days ago.' Annabel didn't join in the humour. 'And it was a hundred pounds, Mum.'

'I know. London is so expensive, Bel. I don't know how you manage. Your money's gone before you know it!'

Frowning, Annabel closed the fridge door. 'Gone where?' she couldn't resist asking, although she tried to keep her tone casual. Her mother seemed to play down how she spent the long hours that Annabel was at work. What if she was buying even more drink, hiding a worse problem than Annabel knew about, doing serious damage to her health? 'I didn't think you were getting up to much.'

'Oh, I'm not. But I needed a few things. Women's necessities, you know. It soon adds up.' When Annabel still looked questioning, her mother's expression began to crumple. 'I'm sorry, Bel. I'm so grateful for everything you're doing for me but I didn't realise I had to keep receipts for what I spend. I'll make sure I do so in future.'

Seeing her mother's green eyes start to well up, Annabel decided to drop the subject. She wasn't entirely happy doing so – a hundred pounds was a lot of money to fritter away, even in London – but with the mountain of admin they had to get through this morning, she needed her mother in a relatively switched-on mood.

'Of course you don't have to keep receipts. The money was yours, Mum, a gift. Don't worry about it now. Go and get dressed while I put the kettle on.'

Once the rest of the shopping had been put away and the coffee prepared, Annabel grabbed a plate and arranged the selection of fresh pastries she'd picked up as a treat to help sweeten the unappetising task awaiting them. She carried the lot through to the small dining table set against one wall of her sitting room and retrieved the storage box containing the documentation of her mother's financial straits – or the bits of it she'd been able to scrape together at least. Ellen's record-keeping had always been haphazard at best.

Taking a seat and pouring herself a cup of coffee, she removed the lid of the box and pulled out a handful of papers. Scanning each one, she began sorting them into piles on the table in front of her.

After ten minutes she'd finished her second cup and worked her way through the entire box with still no sign of her mother. She called out.

'Yes, darling,' came the reply. 'Just coming.'

After close to another ten minutes, Ellen finally appeared. Settling into the chair opposite Annabel she said 'Oh, lovely,' and helped herself to a pastry and coffee. Annabel resisted the urge to mention that the pot was now only lukewarm. These delays were costing them time and, with one eye on the clock, she didn't want to waste even more of it on making one fresh.

'Right, I've split everything into more manageable piles,' she started instead, sliding a writing pad and pen across the table top towards her mother. 'Let's start by making a list of what's to do in order of priority.'

Ellen's nose scrunched up in dislike. 'You can't just work your way down from the top?'

'Me?' Annabel levelled a look across the table. 'I'm not doing this, Mum. I'll help, but this is your business. You have to do it.'

Her mother let out a forlorn sigh. 'But it's so tedious. You know I don't usually bother with all the boring paper bits myself.'

Annabel's own sigh was more impatient. 'And look where that's got you. It *is* tedious, I know, but it's necessary. And you need to learn how to do it for yourself so you don't get into this sort of mess again. I've already dealt with the most urgent matters for you, but there's still a load to be sorted out – accounts to be closed, change of circumstance notifications to be sent out, creditors' demands to be answered. Not the sort of things that can be put aside and ignored.'

'Yes, I know you're right, darling. It's just that I'm so hopeless with numbers. I wish I was more like you.' Ellen picked up the plate of pastries and offered it to Annabel, who took an almond croissant. 'Such a clever girl. Much cleverer than I'll ever be. And so beautiful too.' Her mother peered at her across the table as she bit into the sugary, flaky croissant. 'In fact, you seem to be positively glowing at the moment, Bel. Have you met a man recently?'

Annabel nearly choked on her mouthful as she snorted. Had she met a man recently? No, she'd met the devil incarnate. And any 'glow' was probably the still smouldering embers of the hellfire he'd been raining down on her.

'You have!' Ellen crowed with glee. 'I can see it in your eyes!'

Really? Would they be the same eyes that were watering madly as a result of the crumbs she'd just breathed down her throat? Pouring some coffee into her cup, she gulped it down, grateful it had had time to cool.

'Come on, darling, do tell.' Now that her mother had the bit between her teeth, there'd be no stopping her. No matter that she was galloping off in completely the wrong direction in her usual blinkered fashion. Annabel knew only too well that as far as Ellen was concerned a man was the answer to everything.

'There's nothing to tell,' she said, clearing her throat and wiping the tears from the outer corners of her lashes. 'I'm not seeing anyone if that's what you mean.'

'But you've *met* someone,' her mother persisted. 'It's obvious in the way you look, the way you're carrying yourself.'

Oh, this was ridiculous. 'Mother, I promise you, the only person I've met recently is . . . is some complete bastard who's making my life a nightmare at work. Now can we start on the list, please?'

'See. I knew I was right! What's his name?'

'What? What does that matter? Didn't you hear me say he's a nightmare?'

'You like him,' Ellen pronounced with a glint in her eye.

'What?' Annabel hated to repeat herself, but, really, what else was there to say? 'How did you leap to that conclusion from "complete bastard"?'

Her mother brushed that aside with a little 'Phssht' sound. 'You've always been prickly about boys, Bel. But I'm your mother, darling. I see right through you.'

What was with everyone at the moment, thinking they could see her innermost workings? Was she suddenly made of glass? And if she had always been prickly about the opposite sex, her mother had always been too damned blind to their faults. Having lived with the consequences of that blindness, Annabel wasn't about to change her ways for anything. Reaching for the closest stack of papers, she pulled them towards her.

79

'Is he handsome?'

She pretended not to hear the question, not to see in her mind's eye the stunning flash of silver irises contrasted with black hair, a lopsided smile . . . 'First off, you need to call these—'

'Oh, he must be.' Ellen clapped her hands together in delight. 'You're blushing!'

'I am not blushing,' Annabel insisted despite being able to feel the heat radiate from her cheeks. She pushed up the sleeves of her suddenly-too-warm wool sweater, cursing her fair colouring which made even the mildest flush stand out vividly. 'I'm getting frustrated because we need to get this sorted. Now, see this—'

'Is he tall?'

Annabel closed her eyes and took a deep breath. 'He's nothing important, Mother. Just an overbearing, ill-mannered barman. This, on the other hand –' she waved a county court notice between them '– is something very important indeed.'

But her mother didn't seem to think so, already losing her focus on the present. Her attention wandered over Annabel's shoulder, gaze going to the photo sitting on top of the bookshelf. 'Your father was lovely and tall,' she mused, getting a faraway haze in her eye as she looked back into the distant past. 'And you were always such a daddy's girl; I think that's something you'd definitely look for in a man.'

At the mention of her father, the usual ache set up in Annabel's chest, a muted echo of the fingers of fear that had squeezed tight around her heart on the day she'd had the solid foundation of warmth and strength and safety torn from her young life.

How different would things be now if only . . . *No.* She cut the thought off. Pushed aside the past as she tugged her sleeves back down. What ifs were pointless. They didn't help solve the problems of the here and now.

Looking at the trance-like expression on her mother's face, she decided that the immediate here and now was going nowhere fast. As disappointing as it was not to have even made a start on the paperwork, at least the day wouldn't be a complete waste – she still had the prospect of engineering Aidan Flynn's imminent downfall to look forward to. And with her stress levels running at an all-time high due to the pressures she was under at both work and home, she really needed something to give soon.

She checked the time and pushed to her feet. 'Listen, Mum. I have to get ready now. How about we try tackling this again tonight?'

'Hmm?' Her mother's attention meandered back to the present. 'Oh,' she said, blinking. 'I'm out tonight. Sorry, darling, did I forget to mention it?'

'Yes.' Annabel was surprised. 'Where are you off to?'

'To some book club thingy. I got in touch with an old friend and she invited me along. I thought it might be a good idea to start getting out and meeting some new people.'

'That sounds great. Who's the friend?'

'Oh, no one you'd remember.' Ellen inspected her nails.

'Where's the book club?' Annabel cringed inside to hear herself. This must be what it was like being a parent – trying to satisfy those protective instincts without sounding interrogative and suspicious. And failing.

'Not far, I don't think. I've got her address written down somewhere. I'll have to get a taxi as I don't really know my way around yet.' Ellen gave her a needy look. 'If you could leave me that money we discussed?'

'I can let you have twenty pounds. That's all I've got on me.' Trying to stretch her budget to cover the extra expense of supporting the two of them meant that cash was getting tight. Luckily, her own day-to-day expenses were minimised by her season travel pass.

'Twenty's fine, Bel,' her mother said, although she didn't quite manage to hide her look of disappointment. Annabel took comfort from the fact that after paying for taxi fares there wouldn't be much left over to spend on booze.

EIGHT

'No way in hell.' Dressed immaculately in her usual crease-free perfection, it appeared that Annabel Frost's only concession to 'day off' casualness was the substitution of her sharp black skirts for a pair of low-rise grey trousers draped with a hip-hugging chainlink belt, and the semi-letting down of her hair. Aidan noted that it was almost as long as it had been in his dream. Worn in a sleek ponytail instead of its usual tight bun, he could see the end flicking from one shoulder of her crisp white shirt to the other like the tail of an angry cat as she shook her head in denial. 'Mr Landon *always* gives final approval on the Christmas Day menu dishes. Why would he send you? He barely even knows you.'

Quickly closing the door on the damp, blustery afternoon weather before a gust of wind had a chance to drive the sleet in to splatter against the polished floorboards, he made his way through the quiet of the closed restaurant to where Annabel stood by the only table laid up for dining, looking like she'd just swallowed an entire place setting. As well she might, considering it was only a matter of hours since she'd slapped the envelope containing his final written warning on the bar as she'd strutted past without a word or glance.

'He didn't get hold of you?' Aidan's stomach muscles tightened as her glittering green eyes now tracked his approach. He felt the force of that glare like a physical touch scoring across his skin. She was beyond gorgeous when she was furious, but knowing he still had worse news to break than the fact he was the boss' 'taster' replacement, he bit back on the type of smile likely to incite violence. 'He had something urgent come up.'

Annabel snatched her phone from where it lay on the white cloth to check the screen. 'But that still doesn't explain why *you're* here. Why would he even think to contact you?'

Coming up on the opposite side of the table, Aidan shed his coat and draped it over the back of a spare chair before picking up the printed sheet of paper from the place setting in front of him and cast an eye over the list of tasting dishes to be served. 'Let me find us something suitable to drink and then we'll sit down and talk about it.'

'I don't want a drink,' Annabel said as he turned and headed for the bar. 'I want to know what the hell is going on.'

He knew she did. He also knew she wasn't going to be happy once she found out the truth. It would change the dynamic between them and, although he'd known she'd have to find out some time, the more he thought about it, the less he liked his hand being forced so soon.

'Did you hear me?' she demanded, the stomp of her footsteps following after him.

'I heard you,' he replied, not stopping and not turning around as he felt the nerve endings in his fingertips react to the petulant bite of her tone.

'Well? I want answers.'

And she deserved to have them. But bastard that he was,

half of him was hoping that if he let her frustration simmer for a little longer she'd lash out at him. Because if she lashed out, he'd have no choice but to break his promise and touch her before things changed irrevocably between them. In the name of self-defence he'd have the excuse to grab her, hold her. Wrap his arms around her tight as the length of that lithe body struggled and thrashed against the length of his and she fought to scorch him with her temper, cut him with her curses, maybe even scratch him with those lethally manicured fingernails. And he was so ready for the contact that every fibre of his being was strung taut with wanting.

'I think we'll go with prosecco,' he said, swinging around the end of the bar before he did something stupid like turn around and reach for her. Just because he was ready didn't mean she was. 'It's the perfect aperitif – the bubbles wake up the taste buds, the acidity cleanses the palate. It'll be dry and light enough to complement Chef's starters, too.' Not to mention it would loosen Annabel Frost up a bit. If she attempted to eat anything in her current state of choler, she'd end up with a world class bout of indigestion.

'It doesn't matter whether it can sing and dance and do the sodding dishes, let alone go with the food.' She glared at him over the bar as he retrieved a bottle from the chiller and placed it between them. 'Seeing as I can't imagine being able to swallow down even a single mouthful.'

That must have been the first time they'd been in agreement on anything. And it would probably kill her to know it. Pulling two champagne flutes from the uniform ranks lining the shelves, he placed them alongside the bottle. 'All the more reason for you to have one, then. In case you choke.'

It looked for a moment as though she might reach across the bar and choke *him*. Maybe it was the fierce gleam of anticipation in his eyes as he silently willed her to do it that warned her off.

'Fine!' she said with a sharp exhalation. 'If it'll get us off the riveting subject of drinks, and onto why the hell you're here, I'll have water.'

'That doesn't sound very exciting.' Aidan ripped away the foil, took a hold of the cork and started twisting the bottle.

Those ruby-red lips pursed and her delicate nostrils flared as she breathed in. 'Not that it's any of your business but I have a rule never to drink at work.'

'Ah. Another rule.' He paused as the cork eased out with a soft pop and a fizzle of air. 'But not one you'll have to break because, technically speaking, Ms Frost,' he lowered his voice as though confiding a secret, 'it's your day off.'

He could almost hear her counting slowly in her head for patience as he began to pour.

'Water,' she repeated through gritted teeth. 'And tell me why you are here.'

Relenting, he filled only the one flute and grabbed a bottle of mineral water and a tumbler. 'The reason Richard Landon sent me in his place,' he said, unscrewing the cap and filling the glass while keeping half an eye on her for her reaction, 'is because he was calling on the bonds of family ties to help out in an emergency. I'm his nephew.'

Honestly, the poor woman couldn't have looked more winded if she'd taken a medicine ball to the solar plexus. Her mouth dropped open slightly. God help her if she started with the fish thing again. With the way the morning's dream had left him wired, he didn't think he'd be able to stop himself from pushing something between those lips – his fingers, his tongue, his stirring erection.

It would have to be his tongue, he decided. He hadn't been able to stop wondering how that red-painted mouth would taste – if Annabel Frost would be as sharp and tart as she seemed.

'But . . .' she managed to say, ignoring the tumbler he pushed towards her, brow creased in confusion. 'You're Irish.'

He couldn't quite smother his smile in reaction to that nonsensical observation. 'I am. So is my aunt, Bronagh – Richard's wife.'

It didn't take long for all the pieces of the puzzle to fit together. A look of appalled comprehension flashed across Annabel's face and without a word she reached out, picked up the full flute of prosecco and drained it in several gulps.

'Are you fucking kidding me?' she snarled, banging the empty glass back down. Behind the furious glare she gave him he could see flickers of worry as she no doubt considered the worst-case implications that came attached to that bit of news. But in typical Annabel Frost fashion, she tried to hide whatever fear or vulnerability she might be feeling by staying on the attack. 'There's no way I can get rid of you now, is there?'

Wanting to reassure her that he was no threat to her professionally, Aidan picked up the bottle and tipped it over the empty glass. 'Annabel—'

'Oh, don't bother with a refill,' she interrupted. 'There's no way I'm sticking around for this farce. I refuse to stay in the same room as you, let alone sit at the same table and eat.'

She spun to leave, her ponytail snapping against her shoulder blades with each step. Her behind swayed, each rounded arse cheek perfectly accentuated in turn by the form-fitting cut of her trousers. *Christ.* He was only human, helpless to stop his mind instantly stripping away her clothing and torturing him with a picture of how she'd look naked on all fours in front of him, that silky red tail of hair wrapped tight around his fist to hold her leashed for his driving thrusts as he took her from behind, hips slapping against the delicious curves of that derriere.

Before he could clean up his thoughts enough to take action to stop her leaving, the kitchen door swung open and the bristly face of Cluny's head chef, Anton Dubois, popped into view. When the chef's gaze jumped from Annabel to Aidan, his bushy eyebrows flew up to the band of his towering white toque.

'*Mon ami!*' he cried. 'What a surprise, you are here to serve the wine for my festive feast?'

'No, Chef. Lucky me, I'm here to eat your excellent cooking. The boss isn't able to make it. I'm here in his stead.'

At that, the chef slid his gaze back to Annabel then puffed out his cheeks and gave a Gallic shrug. '*Bon.* So we are ready to commence?'

'Actually, no—' Annabel started, reaching to collect her belongings heaped on the other spare chair at the table.

'Yes,' Aidan said firmly, cutting her off. 'We're all ready, Chef. Bring it on.'

The Frenchman's head disappeared, his string of quick-fire instructions silenced as the door swung closed.

Annabel rounded on Aidan. 'How dare you speak for me?' she said in a voice tight with barely contained fury. 'How dare you think you can use your relationship to my boss to set something like this up, to manipulate me? This is my livelihood you're fucking with!'

'I didn't have anything to do with "setting this up",' Aidan told her calmly as he filled the two flutes. 'I understand that this is a shock but Richard really did have an emergency and, rather than cancel, he asked me to stand in.' Placing the bottle on the bar, he made a point of looking directly at her. 'I also understand that this is work, Annabel, and I respect that it's important to you. You have my word that I'll be on my best behaviour today. No games.'

'Best behaviour.' She gave a derisory snort. 'Do you even know what that is?'

With a full glass in each hand, Aidan made his way back across the room. 'I guess you're about to find out.' Setting the glasses down on the table, he pulled out one of the chairs but, rather than taking a seat, he raised an eyebrow at Annabel and waited to see if she'd accept the challenge or run.

With a huff and something that looked suspiciously like a flounce, she ended up in the chair opposite him. 'I'm only staying because of my commitment to Cluny's and out of respect for the effort Anton has put in.'

'That's fair enough,' Aidan said, seating himself.

Annabel wasn't to be placated. 'I can't believe how despicable you are, using your connections to think you can get away with abusing me.'

Shaking his napkin out, he dropped it onto his lap. 'How could I have used my connections to do anything to you when you knew nothing about them?' He eyed the range of cutlery gleaming like deadly weapons on the table but refrained from removing a single piece from Annabel's reach. He could congratulate himself on his bravery if he managed to survive the next couple of hours.

Not to be derailed by something as simple as a flaw in her argument, Annabel changed her line of attack. 'And how underhand, keeping secrets. Were you sent to spy on me?'

'No. I suppose the most sinister accusation you could level at this would be mild nepotism. I was in the market for a job. My uncle – knowing you needed a barman – was in a position to offer me one. That's it, Annabel. I didn't come here to spy, nor to undermine your authority, nor to take your job from you.'

'And I'm just expected to believe the word of a *liar*?'

Aidan sighed. 'I didn't lie. I just never admitted to it.'

'That's as good as the same thing. There couldn't have been any decent reason not to own up to who you are straight away.'

'Couldn't there? I didn't own up because I had no interest in being granted any special treatment. And once I'd met you, decided to pursue you, I needed to be able to gauge your honest reactions without any other influences coming into play. You can't deny that knowledge of my "connections" would have changed the way you dealt with me from the start.'

'I still wouldn't have liked y—' Annabel stopped short at the reappearance of Anton Dubois from the kitchen, leading one of his commis chefs who bore two plates.

'So,' the chef announced. 'First we 'ave the wild salmon tartar with organic cornichon foam and the toasted seaweed crispbread.' He gestured for his nervous-looking assistant to place the plates on the table. The young man did as he was bid, depositing Annabel's with such speed he practically hurled it into her lap as though afraid he'd lose an arm.

With a tut, Anton sent him scurrying back to the kitchen before turning to beam at Aidan and Annabel. '*Bon appétit!*' he declared, and instead of leaving, crossed his arms over his barrel chest as he settled his feet shoulder-width apart and waited for them to start.

Aidan, in turn, waited for Annabel to grudgingly lift her fork before he took a mouthful of his own and made the big Frenchman smile with his noises of appreciation. As he set about demolishing the artfully presented plate of food he noticed that Annabel matched almost every one of her mouthfuls with a slug of prosecco – more in the hopes of blurring her unhappy reality, he guessed, than out of any real appreciation for how the lightly sparkling wine complemented the briny freshness of the salmon cleverly balanced with the sharper tastes of lime, coriander and red onion.

The tasting went on, and Anton continued to hover and fuss, extolling the virtues of the ingredients and preparation techniques of each dish like a proud mother hen clucking over newly hatched chicks. And he had every right to preen his feathers as dish after dish of sheer decadent delight was produced. Wafer thin slices of juniper smoked goose breast served on a salad of cranberry and orange and winter leaves. Venison infused with the flavours of clove and ginger. Roast partridge accompanied with an earthy chestnut and truffle stuffing. Unctuous sauces rich with port and brandy. Between the chef taking the role of unwitting chaperone, the abundance of delicious food, Aidan's strict adherence to his promise to behave, as well as the small glasses of wine he served up, it didn't take as long as he anticipated for Annabel to start relaxing.

He wouldn't go so far as to say she was actually enjoying herself – until it came time for the desserts. Then her reaction to the selection of sweet and sticky treats was nothing short of a revelation, transforming the starchy Ms Frost into such a sensuously abandoned creature that he was concerned he'd gone and got her drunk in spite of his careful efforts to avoid just that. He reckoned a pissed and pissed-off Annabel Frost would be a handful of hell he could happily do without.

But whether she was drunk or not, it became obvious it was her sweet tooth rather than the wine that had her ahh-ing and mmm-ing and flicking her pink tongue out to lick traces of spiced pear syrup and rich cinnamon cream and cognac butter from those signature red-coated lips, making Aidan want to lean across the table and kiss the sugary lipstick right off her mouth.

With an effort, he managed to stay in his chair and make do with the delights of Anton's sticky plum pudding, all the while transfixed by her blissed-out smile and shifting to ease the increasing pressure behind his flies as he thought of all the things he'd be prepared to do to get her to smile like that for him.

NINE

From the way Aidan Flynn kept staring at her mouth, Annabel was convinced she had food stuck between her teeth. Resisting the temptation to lick her cutlery clean of every last smear of heavenly salted caramel goo, she set her spoon and fork down on the final empty plate of the day and excused herself to pay a visit to the ladies' room.

While a check of her reflection revealed nothing amiss in her mouth, it did show a set of very rosy cheeks. She'd only ever been an occasional drinker and although she didn't think she'd consumed all that much over the past couple of hours, she supposed the warm flush must be from the wine – likewise the light-headedness and warm fizzing feeling in her stomach. Though with Aidan Flynn's strange power to unsettle her it was hard to tell.

And if she *had* accidentally indulged in a few too many drinks, who could blame her? The afternoon had started badly enough when her nemesis had shown up in place of Richard Landon, effectively scuppering yet again her plans to get rid of him. But that had been nothing compared to the bombshell he'd then dropped concerning the family connection. That vital piece of information had changed everything and made her realise how close she'd come to disaster with her intention of taking her complaints to her boss. What if Richard Landon already knew what his nephew was like? If she didn't want to jeopardise her own job, she realised she'd have to think very carefully how to handle this situation from now on.

In the face of all that, numbing the shock had seemed the most attractive option. But even in her slightly inebriated state, Annabel knew that being tipsy around Aidan Flynn couldn't be a good idea at all. Despite him living up to his promise to behave and his show of surprisingly agreeable manners so far, it would be foolish to forget that his default settings sat firmly in the region of devious. She had no doubt that the truce he'd called was a temporary one, and if she wanted to avoid any unnecessary strife it would be smart to put a safe distance between them before he reverted to type.

By the time she made her way back to the dining room, the table had been cleared and Aidan was carrying the dirty glasses to the bar.

'Can I interest you in a coffee?' he asked as she started collecting up her belongings.

She shook her head. 'I have to have a word with Chef and then I need to get home,' she lied. What she really needed was at least a double espresso to help clear her head enough that she could remember how to get home. But that matter was between herself and her favourite little café; it had nothing to do with him.

'Sure?' His quizzical expression made it plain he thought she should have one.

She looked across the room at him, touched by his display of concern . . . *Hang on. What?* That wasn't right, was it? How come she was suddenly reading him as caring rather than condescending?

'I'm sure.' She gave herself a mental shake, cross that she'd been foolish enough to drink too much and compromise her judgement around such a man. 'I, ah, have an appointment at the hairdresser's in half an hour,' she improvised.

'But you just said you needed to get home,' Aidan challenged, adding the touch of a smile to the quizzical look.

Crap. This was why she didn't drink. Alcohol scrambled the brain. 'Yes. My hairdresser comes to me. At home.' *Shit*. She needed to get away from him and shut up. 'So I should, er, get going,' she said, heading for the kitchen at a brisk pace. 'See you tomorrow.'

Not waiting for a reply she pushed through the doors and bore down on Anton Dubois to discuss the new menu dishes. Ten minutes later she checked to make sure the dining room was empty before leaving.

Two streets across, Chino – the best coffee shop in Soho in Annabel's opinion – was doing its typical roaring afternoon trade with minor scuffles breaking out in the doorway as a steady stream of customers tried to manoeuvre their way in and out around each other while putting up or taking down umbrellas.

With the worst of the weather shaken off her own compact umbrella, Annabel joined the end of the queue. Counting six people in front of her, she gave an impatient sigh and rummaged in her bag until she found her purse. Opening it up she rifled through the sections hunting for her customer loyalty card.

'You're a little liar, Annabel Frost.' The Irish accent whispered in her ear had her fingers freezing and the hairs on her neck rising.

Spinning around in shock, she stumbled on her heels. 'What are you doing here?' she squeaked, swaying slightly as she looked up into the handsome, grinning face of Aidan Flynn. 'Are you following me?'

'Well now, as I've been sitting in the corner over there for the past quarter of an hour,' he replied, indicating a spot at the end of the window bar with a couple of vacant stools – one draped with a dark coat and an open newspaper spread over the counter top, 'I think I should be asking that question of you.'

'Of course I'm not following you!' Annabel had never heard anything so ridiculous. 'I just wanted to pick up a coffee on my way to the hairdresser's.'

'Home, *a mhuirnín*,' Aidan said, making her frown up at him in confusion. 'The story was that you were going home.' He elaborated with a shake of his head and a chuckle. 'Not only are you a liar, you're an appallingly bad one.'

She opened her mouth to tell him that was rich coming from him but he held up a hand to forestall her argument. 'No. I'm not going to fight with you while you're obviously the worse for wear. Just tell me what you're drinking and go guard my newspaper for me before someone claims it.'

'I don't . . .' she started. 'I can't . . .' she tried again. Aidan Flynn waited silently, watching as she struggled to find a valid excuse to refuse, a testing spark in his eye. She could try telling him to get lost, but recalling how bloody-minded he'd been on the subject of beverages earlier at Cluny's, she realised it would be easier just to agree and get it over with. 'Oh, all right.' She gave in gracelessly, fearing she was making a serious mistake but desperate for a shot of caffeine. 'I'll have an espresso.' She spun away and headed off for the spot he'd indicated, rudely leaving him to pay for it himself.

Settling herself side-on on one of the free stools at the window bar, Annabel took a peek at the open paper as she loosened her scarf. She half expected to have caught him poring over the personal ads, hunting for innocent victims like the pervy stalker type he was. But apparently he was more in the mood for global politics today. That wasn't such a surprise either. Given his alpha tendencies, he was probably checking on how his plans for world domination were progressing. Slowly, if he was going about conquering it one restaurant manager at a time, she mused, covering her amused snort with a cough when a few odd looks from nearby tables were cast her way.

Hoping at least that Aidan wasn't watching her make a spectacle of herself, she swept her gaze over the interior of the café. Finding his attention focused on the activity in front of him, she allowed herself the opportunity to surreptitiously check him out. It wouldn't do to give him the satisfaction of catching her staring at him, providing him with any extra ammunition to use against her and inflating that already rudely healthy ego of his.

Not that his self-confidence wasn't justified, she had to admit. Tall and leanly muscular, with his dark good looks, untamed mop of hair and quick smile, there was no denying that he represented a very sexy, slightly roguish, package. Was he handsome, her mother had wanted to know? Oh, yes.

His casual look today of a dark, long-sleeved jersey, well-fitting faded jeans and chunky biker boots accentuated the width of his shoulders, the curve of a tight set of glutes and a pair of long, strong legs. He carried the look with same masculine elegance as he did his smarter, tailored work clothes. There was no doubt that he was a beautifully put together man. And as he'd demonstrated over the past few hours, he was more than capable of being good company when he wanted to be, entertaining, attentive, well mannered. Almost gentlemanly.

In fact, even now his easy charm had the baristas laughing and almost falling over themselves to serve him, and more than a couple of the female customers were unashamedly ogling him. She'd noticed it happening at Cluny's, too – the way he drew lingering looks as though he were magnetic.

If he was aware of all the attention when he turned and made his way across the café, he didn't give any sign, not sparing a glance for anyone but her. When he sent her one of his crooked smiles, she felt the full force of all that dangerous male appeal impact against her chest, pushing the air from her lungs. She tried to quash the warm thrill that ran through her. No matter how attractive, or civilised his current behaviour, being the sole focus of Aidan Flynn's attention was a bad thing, she scolded herself. Capital B.A.D.

'Apparently you're a regular here,' he said, coming up, setting the cups down and dropping with easy grace onto the stool beside hers. 'And you drink doubles, with sugar.' Facing her, he hooked one boot on the foot rail under him and left the other planted on the floor so that his long leg stretched out beside her, cordoning her off from the room and enclosing her into his space. It was a blatantly possessive manoeuvre, one that could be read as a protective gesture, although it reminded her more of a hunting technique she'd once seen on a wildlife programme, used by a wily predator to separate the prey from the herd. The phrase 'moving in for the kill' suddenly took on a whole new level of meaning, sending another thrill of awareness through her.

Instead of running for her life like she should, she offered a 'Thank you', proving what she already knew: that too much alcohol could turn even the most sensible person into an idiot. She felt her heartbeat pick up as she braced herself for the inevitable attack of gratuitous dirty talk.

'You're welcome.' He picked up his cup. 'I'm so full this will probably come running out of my ears. Anton excelled himself today.'

Having been expecting the worst, the innocuous question

98

threw her. 'He did,' she replied with caution, reaching for the packet of sugar on her saucer. 'He's a talented chef.'

'Very. He also did an admirable job of keeping the staff suitably terrified and in line while you were away. Did you have a nice holiday?'

Annabel froze in the act of ripping open the packet. 'Why do you want to know?' she asked, suspicious of entering into personal territory.

'Why?' He raised his brows at her. 'Because that's generally what people do when they're sharing a coffee, Annabel – they chat to each other. Exchange pleasantries. Socialise.'

Well, the smile he gave her was certainly open and convincing enough to make her want to believe him. She stared at it, at the way it reached all the way up to his eyes and made them crinkle in the corners. They were stunning eyes, as she'd had reason to note before – framed by thick black lashes and with those light irises that reflected his moods, like the surface of a lake mirroring a changeable winter sky.

'Annabel?'

She blinked at the sound of his voice, noticing that his smile had widened into a full-out grin. She felt herself flush. Had she seriously just been sitting there mooning over Aidan Flynn's eyes? *Likening them to lakes?* Good God, she must be drunk. It was way past time to try to sober herself up and get out of there.

In her eagerness to cover up her embarrassing lapse, she found herself blurting out precisely the sort of personal information she'd rather keep to herself. 'It wasn't a holiday. It was just a break. Personal issues.'

What? Why had she told him that? Upending the sugar into her cup, she gave it a quick stir and took a swig, hoping the scalding liquid might sear her tongue to the roof of her mouth and render her incapable of speech. At least the negativity of her reply should be enough to put him off. People expected pleasant platitudes in response to such standard polite questions, not uncomfortable truths.

But she should have known that Aidan Flynn was not 'people'.

'I'm sorry to hear that. I hope you got things sorted?'

She made sure he caught her little sigh of annoyance. 'I'm working on it.'

Instead of taking the hint and letting the subject drop when she didn't elaborate further, he prompted, 'Sounds complicated.'

'Relationships are.' *Jesus Christ, blabbermouth. Put a sock in it!* 'It's private.'

'Ah.' He gave a sympathetic nod. 'A lovers' tiff?'

'No.' Then actually quite impressed by how close to the truth his guess was, she gave a short laugh. 'Well, not mine anyway.'

'I see,' he said with a little smile and, as though he had no further interest in the subject, he picked up his coffee cup and turned his head to look out of the condensation-clouded window at the darkening afternoon street scene, sinking into an apparently satisfied silence.

Was that it? She peeked warily at him. Was Mr Stubborn really letting go that easily? His handsome profile gave nothing away, half hidden as it was by that mass of black hair. Such beautiful hair – if worn a touch too long. Thick, wavy and so glossy she wondered whether he used products to achieve such a shine. It looked soft, so silky that her fingers would just slide through . . .

Aware that her hand had risen and was hovering with intent between them, Annabel snatched it back and looked away. But not before she'd seen Aidan Flynn's eyes trained on her again and his lips pressed just a little too tightly together.

And that was all it took for her to start spouting off at the mouth in an attempt to cover her embarrassment – telling him how she'd had to make a mercy dash to her mother's side when her lover of the past five years had run out leaving her broken-hearted, penniless and facing an aggressive pair of bailiffs sent to seize all of their property. How she'd had to help pack up what precious little there'd been left of a lifetime's worth of physical possessions, move her now homeless mother into her own tiny flat and begin the frantic task of damage limitation on her finances, freezing any surviving joint lines of credit, negotiating repayment deals with debtors.

And once she'd started spewing personal details, it seemed the flow of words would not stop. With her tongue well oiled and her frustration fuelled by alcohol she found herself telling him more – about how her mother's appalling taste in bad men went way back. 'She was terrified of being alone after my father died, so desperate to fill the emptiness in her heart that she started throwing herself at any man who looked her way.' About how unfortunately, the kind of men her mother attracted were chancers and users who'd taken advantage of her vulnerability, her soft, giving nature, to milk her dry of affection and money and leave her broken.

When her brain caught up with her mouth and she realised how much of her personal life she'd given away, she stopped abruptly. 'God. I don't know why I'm telling you all this.' She pressed her hands to her blushing cheeks, hating that the unexpected emotional outpouring left her sounding melo-dramatic and needy but also aware of a strangely relieved feeling, as though some pressure valve had been flicked open inside her.

'I'm glad you are,' Aidan said as though it was no big deal. Apart from the odd gentle prod, he had been sitting in thoughtful silence throughout. 'I get the impression you haven't shared even half of it with anyone before, despite how hard it must have been for you – seeing your mother repeatedly hurt like that, being the one to have to pick up the pieces.'

He was right, she hadn't told anyone because there hadn't really been anyone to tell. From the moment she'd been old enough, she'd been too busy working to have time to socialise, to keep up her friendships from school. Because it had been hard. Hard enough that she'd sworn never to let the same happen to her, promised herself to be strong and independent and never have to rely on anyone else for her happiness. But she hadn't expected someone like Aidan Flynn to empathise with that.

'Er, thank you.'

He gave her a quizzical look. 'For what?'

Annabel shrugged, feeling so uncomfortable she wanted to squirm. 'For being so, I don't know – *nice*.'

He laughed then, and she actually felt the deep, earthy sound reverberate in her chest as though her heart was jumping around behind her ribs.

'No need to sound so surprised. I am nice.'

With his handsome face lit up with relaxed humour it would be easy to be fooled. 'No you're not. You're a liar.'

'We've already established that I'm not,' he countered easily and gave her a look. 'But you are.'

Damn him for always having an answer. 'You're arrogant and controlling and predatory.'

Instead of parrying in his usual fashion, he let the smile fade as his look sharpened. 'Like the men your mother chooses?'

'Yes. Just like them.' She made a point of meeting the look, steeling herself against the penetrating grey. 'Domineering arseholes. Trouble.'

'Not all dominant men are arseholes by default, Annabel.

Just like not all strong, independent women are stereotypical bitches.'

Wait. Annabel felt her brows draw together. Was he calling her a bitch, or saying she wasn't one? For God's sake, how long until the effects of this wine started to wear off? She was having trouble keeping up.

Falling silent, she watched as he picked up his cup to drain the last of the coffee. His forearms were covered for once which should have pleased her but left her feeling strangely disappointed instead. At least he had equally nice hands, she noticed – strong, long-fingered and dextrous. She'd seen him work with those hands, seen him handle delicate crystal with the lightest of touches and wrestle heavy crates with sure strength. Would they be as deft, as confident when caressing a woman's body? Her body? How would it feel to have them on her, touching her? Looking at the size of his hands dwarfing the tiny espresso cup, the thought made her heat up and shudder.

'*Jesus*, Annabel.'

The rasped words had her gaze flying up to his face. He was staring at her with a new intensity, his previously relaxed demeanour tightened with tension.

'Whatever the hell it is you're thinking now,' he said through a tight jaw, 'I suggest you stop.'

Oh God. He knew she'd been thinking intimate thoughts about him and he looked ready to pounce. She made a grab for her bag and umbrella. It was officially time to go.

In her haste to slide off the stool, she stumbled on her heels and reached out to steady herself. In the next instant she was lodged in the space between Aidan's legs, the palm of her free hand clasped to his upper thigh. She stared dumbly at her fingers splayed across the worn denim, aware that beneath the soft layer of fabric he felt warm and hard and strong.

103

And warm, so very warm. Had she already noticed that?

She ordered herself to let go, but as usual her body seemed deaf to reason when it got too near Aidan Flynn. Instead, almost of their own accord, her fingers squeezed tighter, testing the firm muscle. When it didn't give at all under the pressure, something low inside her rolled over.

At the sound of Aidan's sharp breath, she raised her eyes to meet his, found the silvery lustre already darkening, pulling her in. And for the life of her, all she wanted to do in that moment was let go – dive in and sink down to the depths where the promise of pleasure glinted like lost treasure. Was that glimmer even the real thing, or the shiny lure of fool's gold?

There was only one way to find out.

This close, the heat rose off him, washing his rich, male scent over her. Her breath came short as she leaned in, closing the distance between them, drawn to that heat, that scent. Aidan didn't move, his own breath escaping from his slightly parted lips to mingle with hers. She dropped her gaze to them, wondering if they'd feel as soft as they looked when they pressed against hers – what they'd taste like beneath the lingering traces of coffee. Annabel licked her own lips as though they could already reveal the flavour of him. The whisper of a curse fell from Aidan's mouth into the last inch of space between them, so close she felt the brush of it tingle against her damp flesh.

'Well, are you leaving or not?' a testy-sounding voice demanded, jerking Annabel's attention to her side. A middle-aged woman with a coffee-and-mince-pie laden tray and an arm full of bulging shopping bags gave her an impatient glare as she edged proprietorially towards the vacated stool.

With the spell broken, Annabel blinked, aware of her thudding pulse. What the hell had just happened? She'd been about to kiss Aidan Flynn, for fuck's sake.

Worse, she still felt the urge to do it. But looking back at him, she realised he hadn't moved so much as a muscle. Just like that episode in the cellar, he appeared completely unmoved. How humiliating. Hadn't she just been talking about not making the same mistakes as her mother? And here she was proving herself equally as weak and gullible and making a fool of herself.

Mortified, she snatched her hand from his thigh. 'It's all yours,' she told the woman as she barged past Aidan's leg and rushed for the door.

TEN

He knew it the moment he stepped into Cluny's the following day and saw her. The darting, shifty-as-all-hell look Annabel Frost flicked his way from across the room told him loud and clear that she'd done more than just think about him after she'd bolted so abruptly from Chino.

'I wouldn't bother looking so happy,' Tim warned him as he bustled up with an armful of linens. 'She's on the warpath today. Poor old Donna's been copping an earful for the past ten minutes.'

'Why? What's happened?' Aidan asked, looking over to where the little waitress stood wide-eyed and hunch-shouldered in the face of Annabel's wrath.

'Who knows? She spotted a mark on one of the tablecloths that came back from the laundry and just went ballistic. She's insisting that every table in the place be stripped, changed and re-laid. Every. Table.'

Interesting. While Tim mightn't have any idea what the problem was, Aidan's guess was that not only had the lovely Annabel got down and dirty with herself to relieve the arousal that had taken hold of her over coffee, she obviously wasn't happy about having done so. He hoped that meant she'd

106

been thinking of him while she'd been doing . . . Jesus, whatever the hell it was she'd been doing to herself. A slide-show of stunning X-rated images ran through his mind, leaving him to acknowledge that, despite what he'd told her yesterday, Annabel had been right to sound disbelieving about him being nice. Smart woman. If she knew even half the things that went on inside his skull she'd never think of him and nice in the same sentence again.

'Mate, I'm telling you, you're asking for trouble. Keep your head down or she'll have that grin off your face in no time,' the Aussie said as he started off in the direction of the kitchens.

It seemed like sound advice, but convinced as he was that he'd been instrumental in creating the situation, Aidan was unable to heed it. Instead, he made for the two women with a view to drawing some of the heat off Donna. Noticing his approach from the corner of her eye, Annabel stopped mid-tirade and turned towards him.

'Mr Flynn. I need a word in my office,' she said stiffly before stalking away without so much as another glance towards the waitress, who sagged with instant relief.

Following Annabel through the fully staffed but silent kitchens, Aidan ran the gauntlet of exaggerated looks and theatrical slit-throat and hanged-man gestures the chefs mimed at him as he passed.

Once in the office, Annabel made straight for the opposite side of the desk, putting the solid object between them. For a moment she looked as awkward as he'd ever seen her, green gaze jumping around the room as though searching for an escape route before she took a slow breath and trained her eyes roughly in his direction.

'About yesterday. The personal issues I mentioned. I wanted to ask you to keep the details to yourself.' She spoke in a stilted manner, suggesting that now that she knew his full identity, she was weighing every word she said to him with caution. 'I'd prefer to keep my private life separate from my professional one.'

No wonder she looked so uncomfortable. With the way she perceived him as her mortal enemy, he imagined how having to ask him for a favour must stick in her throat. He'd known that discovering his family ties would change the way she felt she could act towards him, and this effort at forced politeness was the result. He'd also known that once the liberating effects of the wine had worn off, she'd regret the fact that she'd let herself open up to him. And he supposed he should feel guilty that he'd intentionally taken advantage of her booze-loosened state to slip through her defences and gently prise open the high security vault labelled 'private'. But in all honesty, he couldn't muster any remorse for his actions. Not when he'd learnt so much about what made up the foundations of Annabel Frost's hard outer surface.

'And you'd trust me not to say anything if I gave you my word I wouldn't?' He started moving closer to the desk, noticing for the first time the bloodshot tinge to her eyes and the brow furrowed with tension.

'I don't see that I have much choice but to trust you,' she snapped. 'It's too late now to do anything but try and appeal to your honourable side.'

'So you think I have an honourable side?' He grinned, because from her tone it was obvious she didn't think any such thing.

She gave him a baleful look through her red eyes. Under the glare of the unforgiving lighting in the office, her pale skin had a pasty look and a fine sheen of perspiration. Her hands trembled slightly.

'Have you taken anything for that hangover?' he asked her.

Annabel shook her head, and instantly looked like she

regretted the movement as she turned a bit green. 'I tried earlier but I brought it straight up again.'

He frowned at her. There was no way she should be feeling so rotten after the relatively small amount they'd consumed at the tasting. True, she'd been quick to succumb to the effects, but still . . . 'Do you always react badly to alcohol?'

'I don't know. I don't really drink.'

'Ah, Annabel. I'm sorry.' He felt a twinge of guilt in his chest. 'I should have been more careful serving you the wine yesterday.'

She gave him a surprised look, which soon turned sheepish. 'I think it might actually have more to do with the bottle I bought on the way home.'

His brows shot up at that.

'I know,' she said crossly, rubbing at her temples. 'It seemed like a good idea at the time.'

'It always does,' he sympathised. 'Why don't you sit down for a minute? Let me get you something to help.'

'I don't need any help,' she insisted, automatically slipping back into defence mode, trying to keep him at arm's length. 'The only thing I need is to know that my private business will stay private.'

Aidan had to admit he was getting a little bored with arm's length, not to mention frustrated with her skewed idea that somehow being independent meant she had to be isolated. Melting Ms Frost was turning out to be more of a challenge than he could have anticipated. But the greater the prize, the tougher the game – and he already suspected that winning this one would bring him more satisfaction than he could have ever imagined.

'I'll make you a deal. If you let me administer a medicinal hair of the dog, I'll promise never to divulge a word you've told me.' Not that he ever would anyway, but he was enough of a gambler to recognise a bargaining chip when he was

109

handed one. And he was enough of a player to know how to use it to his advantage.

Annabel seemed to wilt as her energy waned, draining all the remaining fight out of her. She suddenly looked so young and fragile that he wanted to lend her his strength, wrap her in his arms. He doubted she'd be able to muster much resistance if he tried it, which is why she'd never forgive him if he did.

'Fine,' she muttered, dropping into the chair and bracing her head in her hands as she leaned her elbows on the desk.

'I'll be right back.' Leaving her like that, he stopped off in the staff room to remove and hang his coat before making his way to the bar. Ignoring the questioning looks from his colleagues he mixed a drink and delivered it back to her in a matter of minutes.

When he placed the highball tumbler in front of her, she eyed it as though it was a glass of cyanide. 'What is it?'

'Essentially, a Bloody Mary. But with an added Flynn twist.'

'Which is?' she asked suspiciously.

'I'm not at liberty to divulge, I'm afraid. Family secret. You'll just have to trust me.' He paused to let the significance of his words sink in. Whether or not she picked up on the deeper message they conveyed, she still looked distrustful.

'There's nothing sinister in there, I promise,' he assured her. 'I'll warn you that there is a dash of alcohol but I've been as light-handed as possible without compromising its efficacy. Start with small sips until your stomach feels more settled, but make sure you drink the whole lot. Give it about half an hour and you should start feeling better.'

He left her again and joined Jon behind the bar, helping ready everything for the upcoming service. When Annabel next made a front-of-house appearance, he was pleased to see it was with a slight glow to her cheeks. The gentle pink bloom suited her much better than her previous bilious hue.

Catching him smiling at her, she sent him a look of grudging gratitude before settling into her usual routine of treating him with cool disdain.

It wasn't much in the way of progress, but it had been worth it. Every hard-earned inch of ground he won got him closer to his goal. All he had to do was make sure he kept up the momentum so she didn't have the chance to retreat.

By the end of the evening, Annabel could feel the effects of Aidan's amazing restorative hair of the dog starting to wear off. She hadn't been able to identify the secret ingredient, but figured maybe that was a good thing. Given its near magical abilities that had her flying through a busy service, she had to question the likelihood of it even being legal.

Packed up and ready to leave, she received a call from Richard Landon, who apologised for missing yesterday's tasting.

'I admit to being surprised to find out the family connection between you and Aidan Flynn,' she made a point of telling him. He needed to know that she wasn't happy with being misled.

'Yes, sorry about that. He asked for discretion and I respected it.' There was a pause before he continued. 'Annabel, Aidan's not had an easy time of things recently.'

She shouldn't think so, if he went around behaving the way he did. Was that Richard's way of admitting that he knew what he was like?

'I believe Cluny's is a good place for him to be. Bronagh and I are very fond of him.'

Well, if he did know, that made it very obvious that she couldn't take her complaints to him, could forget about getting rid of Aidan Flynn. It looked like she was stuck.

When the conversation was finished, she made her weary way through the spotless empty kitchens to the dining room, flicking switches and plunging Cluny's into darkness as she went. With the security shutters down over the front windows and all but a few lights left on, the restaurant lay in peaceful semi-darkness that was heaven on her gritty eyes and sore head.

Detouring towards the bar to return her empty glass, she froze as she heard a grunt and a scraping sound from the other side of the cherry wood counter. Her heart jumped into her throat. A moment later the messy, black-haired head of Aidan Flynn appeared as he straightened with two cases of wine in his arms. Spotting her standing there as he hefted them onto the work surface in front of him, he flashed her one of his ever ready smiles.

Annabel noticed that the sight of a familiar face did nothing to slow her pounding heartbeat. As well acquainted as she was becoming with the darkly attractive features, looking at them now did little to calm her. More and more she found herself falling under the spell of the roguish beauty of those smiles. In fact, it was how she'd pictured him last night in her bed when she'd—

'I thought everyone had gone,' she said, cutting off the perilous direction her mind had been taking before she could give herself away. This man was proving to be too observant for words. She needed to stay on her guard around him.

'Everyone has. I'm just finishing up.' He inclined his head to the glass she held in her hand. 'Did the Flynn Special do the trick?'

'Yes. Thank you. I was just going to return this.' She lifted the glass as she forced herself to approach the bar, feeling that silvery gaze studying her.

'To be honest, you look as though you could do with another one.'

Placing the glass on the counter top, she took an immediate step back and shook her head. She felt too tired to stay and

112

play his games, too deflated that no matter how hard she fought against him, Aidan Flynn always seemed to gain the upper hand, managed to ensnare her in his trap a little bit further. But most of all – after the way she'd practically thrown herself at him yesterday – she feared her own resolve to keep clear of him. 'No. I need to go.'

'Another hairdresser's appointment?' he asked with a grin.

Annabel cringed inside at the tease, felt herself flush. 'No.'

'Then surely you can let me mix you another for the road? What's the point in suffering if you don't need to?'

For God's sake. Could he not for once just give her a break and take no for an answer?

'There is no point. That's why I want to leave, so I don't have to suffer *you* needlessly,' she said with all the annoyance she could gather, which even to her own ears didn't sound like much. 'You can finish whatever you're doing tomorrow. I want to lock up.' She turned and headed for the door, eager to get out into the fresh night air. She'd only made it a few steps before he spoke again.

'You know, for all your tough-as-nails reputation and fighting talk, Ms Frost, you tend to do an awful lot of running away. Why is that, I wonder?'

She stopped on the spot, uncomfortably aware of the ring of truth to his words. She was running. As fast and hard as she could from the ever-increasing lure of him. She'd sooner stick hot needles in her eyes than admit it out loud, though.

She gave him a look over her shoulder. 'Perhaps you'd find that people would be more inclined to stick around, Mr Flynn, if you weren't so disagreeable.'

'Perhaps. But I don't think that's the real issue here.'

Oh, no way was she touching that particularly fishy piece of bait. Turning away, she started for the door again.

Not that ignoring him stopped Aidan Flynn for one moment. 'I think it's because you're afraid.'

'Afraid?' Keeping her eyes fixed on the door, she gave a dismissive little laugh that she hoped covered her growing discomfort at how accurate his observations were. 'I'm not afraid of you.'

'Not of me,' came his calm reply. 'I'd say you're more afraid of yourself.'

Keep walking, she ordered herself as the discomfort spiked to panic. How did he manage to keep hitting the bull's eye on targets she barely knew existed?

'That's ridiculous.'

'Is it? Then prove it.'

Her hand faltered as she reached out for the door latch, her stomach muscles clenching at the hint of demand in his tone.

Don't bite. Don't bite. Ignore him.

'Stop running, Annabel.'

A part of her thrilled to hear those words, wanted nothing more than to listen, obey, give in to the temptation of him. She knew if she turned around now she'd see a matching glint of demand in those dangerously captivating eyes.

So don't do it. Don't look at him.

'Stay and have a drink.'

Don't fall for it. Just do not—

'I dare you.'

ELEVEN

'You dare me?' Voice laced with incredulity, she spun and gave a snort of derision. 'How old are you, ten?

'Soon to be thirty-one, as it happens,' Aidan Flynn informed her from across the room. 'And don't pretend you're too mature to take up a dare. You're every bit as competitive as I am.'

There was little point in attempting to disagree with his declaration when they were standing there staring each other down like a couple of gunslingers at high noon.

As far as stubbornness went, Annabel would say they were pretty evenly matched – but not absolutely on equal footing. Whereas she knew she wore her bloody-mindedness on the surface like a suit of armour, his seemed to come from a deep reserve of self-possessed patience, a centre of calm resolve that she knew she lacked. That disparity made it tough enough to compete with him on a good day, but on a day like today when she was nowhere near her best, she was already proving that she had no chance of keeping up with him.

As things stood, he'd already backed her into a corner where, whatever decision she made, she lost. Leave, and she proved him right – stay, and she gave him exactly what he wanted. No matter how she looked at it, she couldn't see a way out that didn't leave Aidan Flynn the winner. After a minute, the effort involved in trying to find a loophole became too much and the painful pounding in her head forced her to make a choice.

She had to go with the one that would at least show them both that she wasn't a coward.

'Fine.' She started away from the door, giving a casual shrug as though the thought of being alone with him didn't unsettle her at all. 'One drink.'

Too weary to keep standing once she'd retraced her steps back to the bar, she climbed onto one of the stools – keeping her coat buttoned up and her bag on her shoulder – and watched to see what the magic ingredient was that went into a Flynn Special. She soon found her concentration wandering, distracted by the sight of Aidan working with his typical speed and efficiency, twisting and turning his body with agile grace as he reached for bottles left, right and centre.

By the time he slid a full tumbler in front of her, she felt a little dizzy just from watching. As he began to quietly tidy everything away again, she reached for the glass, keen to feel the benefits from another dose of the magic cure.

When the area was once again clear and clean, Aidan leant his forearms on the bar opposite her and clasped his hands together. She'd noticed that his shirt sleeves were rolled up as usual, but after yesterday's embarrassing little episode involving her fantasising about his hands, Annabel made sure she kept her gaze well away, busying herself with stirring the contents of her glass with the straw.

'Annabel,' he said after a moment. 'I'd like to ask you a question.'

She stiffened but didn't reply, just gave him a wary look, which naturally he took as an invitation to continue.

'I'm interested to know why you think it's so important that no one knows about your private life?'

Oh no, just because she'd accidentally opened up to him yesterday didn't give him the right to get all touchy-feely, to dig deeper and psychoanalyse her. She'd given too much of herself away already.

'Listen, while I appreciate that you've agreed to keep things to yourself, it's really none of your business. I should never have said anything about it. I don't want, or need, your pity.'

He looked taken aback. 'Pity? I don't pity you. I admire you – your drive, your independence. You've worked hard to gain your success. You should be proud of what you've achieved.'

'I am proud. But I don't need you to patronise me about it.'

His brows flew up and he gave a disbelieving laugh. 'Now you think I'm patronising you?'

'Of course you are. Don't pretend to respect me when all you really want to do is degrade and abuse me.'

His expression darkened. 'I don't want to do any such thing.'

'Really? I must have misheard you when you said you wanted to take control of me, use me like some sort of puppet.'

'Let's be clear,' he said, pinning her with an intense look. 'I want you to submit to me, Annabel, but only in the sexual sense, and only for the profound pleasure it will bring you, as well as me. For that arrangement to work, I can't *take* control from you, you have to surrender it. There's a world of difference between the two.'

She kidded herself that it was the alcohol in her drink rather than the commanding way he spoke about sexual submission and profound pleasure that had a heavy warmth blossoming in her belly and chest. 'Not from where I'm

117

standing. Control is control. I'm never going to let anybody take it from me, let alone give it away. Not for *pleasure*, not for any reason.'

'Why not?'

'Are you serious?' She boggled at him. 'Because control is power, and power gets abused.'

'Often, yes.' He conceded with a slight nod. 'But not always.'

'Almost always. Believe me, I've seen it enough to know.'

He didn't speak for a moment, just regarded her with sharp-focused eyes. 'I can understand that you'd be wary, that you want to protect yourself from a life like your mother's.'

God, he was an astute bastard. She'd known him only a few days and already he seemed able to read her better than anyone ever had.

'Damned right. I've worked too hard to let you, or anyone for that matter, take my dignity or my independence away from me.'

'I'm glad to hear it. I respect that you respect yourself too much to let that happen.'

'Then why can't you respect that I don't want this –' she paused to wave a hand between them rather than try to find an appropriate label to give to their situation '– to happen?'

Aidan leant closer across the bar, his look drilling into her. 'Because as I've already said, I don't believe that's true. And deep down, neither do you.'

Deep down, something shivered and agreed with him. But that didn't mean acting on it would be the right thing to do. Sometimes the sweetest cravings left the bitterest of tastes. Struggling against the forceful quality of that scrutiny, she shook her head.

'Sorry. You're wrong.'

'*A mhuirnín.*' His voice dropped low but his tone broadcast his certainty loud and clear. 'I've never been so right in my life.'

Everything. He had to argue every last, teeny-tiny thing. And the fact that he somehow managed to pitch his pig-headedness with just the right amount of sexy self-assurance meant that fighting back was becoming downright exhausting.

As though to highlight just how exhausting, a wide yawn cracked her jaw.

'Didn't get much sleep last night?' Aidan gave an off-kilter smile as she rushed to cover her mouth with the back of her hand.

'Not much,' she muttered, blinking her watering eyes and trying not to blush at the memory of her stimulating nocturnal activities. She reached for the half empty glass and took another long pull on the straw, wondering when the effects of her Flynn Special were going to kick in.

'And why was that, then, Ms Frost?' Something about the pitch of the question set alarm bells ringing in her head. One look at his face told her he already knew the answer. But that was ridiculous. He couldn't possibly have any idea.

Could he?

She swallowed. 'I don't know.'

'Now I don't think that's true either. We both know what kept you awake last night. Why don't you admit it?'

Oh, God. He *did* know. *How?* She felt a flush of heat start deep inside and start to radiate outwards. 'I'll admit to not having a clue what you're on about.'

'Do you need me to be blunt? I want you to tell me about how you touched yourself last night. Tell me what you were thinking from the moment you pushed your hand between your thighs and slid your fingers through those cinnamon curls, to the moment you made yourself fly apart.'

The heat intensified, racing to the surface. 'I didn't—'

'You did. I can see it written all over your face.' He grinned

119

as she felt the furious telltale blush blossom across her cheeks. 'Were you thinking of me, of us together? I told you it would happen.'

God, his smugness was insufferable, making her want to slap that grin right off his face. 'Don't flatter yourself. It only happened because I was drunk!' she blurted out before realising he'd goaded her into making the very admission she'd been trying to avoid.

The grin got even wider, brighter – infinitely more slappable. 'No. It happened because for once your defences were down and you wanted it to. I saw how aroused you were when you ran out of Chino. What's so wrong with admitting it?'

What was wrong with it? It was humiliating! 'Why should I admit to anything when you didn't even react, just sat there and let me make a fool of myself?'

Unbelievably, she'd done it again. Said too much. But before she had time to give herself the mental kick she deserved, Aidan Flynn's expression hardened.

'You think I was unaffected by that nearly kiss?' he demanded, staring fixedly at her. 'Christ, Annabel, you must have been drunk if you couldn't see that I was just as turned on as you were. I couldn't breathe with the way you were looking at me, your eyes slightly unfocused, the hard lines around your mouth smoothed away by a surprisingly sweet arousal. Of course I wanted to kiss you – had been dying to long before I'd watched the sinful way you'd devoured Anton's desserts. What's more, I'd wanted to take that hand that was burning my thigh and shift it higher to press it over the hard ache in my groin so you could feel what you do to me. And I'd wanted to put my own hands on you. So badly I'd had to clench them into fists in a desperate attempt to keep them to myself.'

She'd felt desperate, too. That's why she'd bought the wine, to try to numb the unwanted feeling. But drinking more had only amplified the need. By the time she'd staggered to bed, she'd been able to think of nothing but Aidan Flynn. Trying to shame herself out of her thoughts by recalling how mortifying it had felt to be caught fantasising over the size of his fingers had only served to renew her fascination. It had been so long since anyone had touched her – since she'd thought of touching herself – that before she knew it her own hand had crept down to slip under the waistband of her pyjamas.

'Because believe me,' Aidan's voice continued in a growl. 'If I'd let myself touch you, I wouldn't have been able to stop.'

The truth of it was there in his eyes, piercing straight into her. Shocking, thrilling – leaving her in no doubt that he'd have crossed almost every line of decency right there in public and not given a damn.

'I've never denied that I want you. Or found any shame in admitting that I've fantasised about you. Why can't you bring yourself to do the same?'

He was relentless, ruthless. And it took all of Annabel's waning strength not to think of the powerful image of him pleasuring himself to thoughts of her. As keeping him at bay on a personal level seemed to be getting harder, she fought to keep a professional distance.

'What would be the point? I don't get involved with my staff members, remember? Especially not ones with secret ties to my boss.' She couldn't bear to contemplate the damage it would do to her career if anyone found out – not to mention the hold he'd have over her.

'And I don't take no for an answer, remember?'

'Well, you're going to have to. I value my job too much to risk it.'

'And I value the chance to have you too much not to take the risk.'

How very noble that sounded. 'Remind me what risk that is, exactly? You're *related* to the owner. I don't see that you have all that much to lose.'

'And yet of the two of us, I'm the one in receipt of a final official warning, about to be cast out into the street.'

And Annabel was even less sure how to proceed with that situation after Richard Landon's phone call. However things were going to play out, it was better right now if he didn't see her doubt.

'Why do you have to argue every single thing?' she deflected.

'I could ask the same of you.'

She ground her teeth to keep from screaming in exasperation. 'I'm not arguing, I'm saying no. Why not make life simple for yourself – try using your charms on someone who actually finds the Tarzan type appealing. Someone like Donna, perhaps?' she suggested, remembering the way she'd caught the waitress looking at him. 'She seems much more your type. I bet she'd be an easy catch.'

'I don't want easy. I want complicated and interesting. I want you.'

She gave a frustrated sigh. 'Only for the challenge of winning—' and as she said the words the light bulb finally went off in her head. Of course! Recalling Donna's mild-mannered, yet unrequited pining, it all suddenly became so simply, gloriously clear that Annabel wanted to face-palm herself for not having worked it out sooner.

The thrill of the challenge. The trophy hunt. That's what this whole thing was about for Aidan Flynn. He'd even told her as much early on – doormats didn't do it for him. That's why Donna all but serving herself up on a plate didn't stir the slightest reaction from him. That's why every effort Annabel made to resist just increased his resolve.

She stared at him across the bar as though seeing him

for the first time, noticing that while his lips continued to move, the sound of his voice was muffled by the electric buzz of that brain bulb glowing brighter with each passing second.

'Annabel?' He raised his voice loud enough to be heard over the buzz, but not enough to distract her from the truths now plainly illuminated. Like an idiot, she'd been going about this all wrong – right from the start when Aidan Flynn had swept into her life with the force of a whirlwind and she'd let him catch her off guard, blow her right off balance with his shock tactics—

'Annabel.'

—Well, it was past time for a change of plan. Surely the fastest way to make him lose interest in her would be to appear to give in. Stop putting up a fight. Metaphorically roll herself out at his feet with the word 'Welcome' stamped across her forehead.

Yes. She could see how that would work. Eager to find out how *he* liked being caught off guard for a change, she pulled out some shock tactics of her own. Arranging her features into a smile, she put all the sweetness and softness and docility into it that she could gather, trying to replicate the ingratiating, adoring expressions she'd seen women like her mother and Donna use.

She tried not to smirk as Aidan Flynn physically flinched away from her. 'Everything all right?' he asked roughly with a frown descending to shadow that sharp stare of his. 'Are you feeling ill again?'

'What?' Annabel felt the smile falter.

'Do you need me to get you a bucket? You're suddenly looking a bit peculiar.'

The smile dropped and she only just stopped herself from scowling. Maybe this wasn't going to be quite as easy as she'd thought.

Redoubling her efforts, she picked up the corners of her lips again. 'I'm OK, thanks,' she said, adding a little simper to her tone. 'But I'm really touched by your concern.'

Apart from the slight narrowing of his eyes, Aidan Flynn didn't move; he just gave her a long, suspicious look.

Oh, fine. If she was going to make this plan work, obviously she needed to learn to be more convincing. That would involve polishing up some techniques, maybe practising in front of a mirror first. She had to play for time.

She gave a dainty fake yawn. 'As much as I'd love to stay and talk, would you mind if we continued this another time?' She gave her eyelashes a few bats for good measure. Ugh, she might need that bucket after all if she had to keep up this sort of behaviour for any length of time. Hopefully, his interest would wane quickly. 'I really am tired.'

Aidan covered an odd-sounding little cough with his hand. 'Hmm. I can see that,' he said, still looking at her as though she were like nothing he'd ever seen before. 'How about after work tomorrow night?'

Annabel nearly fell off her stool. She'd assumed things would continue along as they had been, with Aidan Flynn undertaking his random perverted ambushes during work hours, enabling her to perform her new act within the relatively safe environment of Cluny's. She hadn't been expecting the action to suddenly shift to anything as risky as a private late night 'date'.

'Seeing as the last one was so – *enjoyable*,' he emphasised the word with a teasing glint in his eye, 'we could go for another coffee.'

Oh, shit. Coffee . . . *kissing*. Tomorrow night! That sounded too intimate, too soon. It would only give her twenty-four hours to prepare. 'Tomorrow's my day off.' She remembered with a spurt of relief. 'And I already have plans for the evening.'

She quickly tacked on the lie, only just remembering to pair it with a look of regret.

'No problem. How about breakfast, then, before my shift starts?'

Breakfast! God, no. That was worse. It would leave her with even less time.

'Do you know Height at The Hyde?' The question cut through her rising panic, stopping it dead.

'Height?' she repeated sharply. Sure she knew about it. Who didn't? The Hyde was the newest über hip addition to the Harcourt Group's stable of designer hotels and the roof terrace restaurant was reportedly the best in London. He couldn't mean . . . 'Isn't it impossible to get a table there at short notice?'

'I have it on good authority that if we're early enough to avoid the cool crowd, we're in with a chance.'

Good authority. Did he mean his uncle, or maybe he knew someone who worked there? Whichever, she doubted it could be as easy as he made it out to be.

'Half eight all right?' he asked with a raised brow.

Her instinct was, of course, to say no – to keep well away from Aidan Flynn. And what little was left of her dwindling good sense agreed, even if it meant passing up an opportunity like Height. Meeting so soon wouldn't give her nearly enough time to get to grips with her new act, let alone perfect it. But then, didn't the very basis of the act rely on her breaking her habit of resisting? If this invitation was Aidan Flynn's way of trying to call her bluff, catch her out, could she afford to fail at the very first test and compromise the best plan she had of escape?

Lord. How much more complicated could this get?

Even as she wrestled with indecision, Annabel realised that if she was committed to freeing herself, there was really only one way to go.

So – she'd only have precious few hours to cobble together a plan of action? She'd better get busy, then. It was just breakfast, after all. In a highly public place. How dangerous could that be?

'Eight thirty is perfect. I'll meet you there.'

TWELVE

Perhaps it was England's reputation for famously bad weather that made the odd sunny day in London seem so perfect. Whatever the time of year. Stripped of its habitual grey shroud, the sombre British dignity of the city and its inhabitants was transformed. Under a clear blue sky and a low-riding winter sun, timeworn stone glowed and some rush-hour commuters were even moved to smile. In public. At strangers.

On the wide, straight avenue of Piccadilly, where Aidan waited in the shadow of the restored Palladian mansion that housed The Hyde, it was still early enough for the morning air to carry a frosty bite. Having arrived some while ago, he could have chosen to pass the time at his reserved table up in the warmth of the glass-covered, sun-drenched roof terrace, but that would have robbed him of the pleasure of watching his breakfast companion arrive. And that would have been a shame indeed, he acknowledged as, despite looking as he'd never seen her before, he spied Annabel Frost through the crowds the instant she came into view.

Rooted to the spot by the sight of her ruby hair

billowing long and loose about the shoulders of a floaty swing coat which danced enticingly around the tops of a pair of tall, calf-hugging suede boots, he found himself forgetting to breathe. As much as the red-blooded male animal in him appreciated watching the way she moved – her long-legged stride, the sway of her hips – it was the underlying significance, the symbolism, of such a seemingly simple act that he was more interested in witnessing today. From their first meeting, he had been the one driving the fast and furious momentum, bulldozing Ms Frost with relentless intent. Now, for the first time, *she* was coming to *him*. Walking into whatever was about to unfold between them, freely, willingly. He wouldn't have missed the sight of that if he'd had to stand all night in a freezing blizzard.

As she drew closer, he could see that she looked much better than she had yesterday. With her eyes clear and bright, and her cheeks rosy from the brisk morning air, she looked beyond beautiful. It didn't take him long to pick up that, despite the unexpected change in image her clothes and hair style lent, there was something else there – an added straightness to her spine, a glint of steel in her gaze that suggested the outer packaging of soft femininity was just an act.

Well of course it was.

He'd known from her sudden turn of bizarre behaviour late last night that Ms Frost was up to something. Whatever that something turned out to be, one look at the badly concealed sassiness behind the smile she sent him now left little doubt that it was going to test him. Good. Inside the collar of his coat, the hairs on the back of his neck rose in anticipation as he watched her close the last of the distance between them. He couldn't wait to find out what she had in mind.

When she finally stepped up to him, he had to make a conscious effort not to embrace her as his instincts shouted at him to do.

'Good morning, Ms Frost.' He settled for a simple greeting.

'Aidan,' she returned, looking up at him with what he guessed was intended as some sort of simpering coquetry, but which more closely resembled a deranged kitten.

Mindful of this particular kitten's needle-sharp teeth and claws, he kept his own features straight and motioned her to precede him through the hotel doors. Following her through the entryway, he stepped up as close behind her as he could without risking an accidental touch and inhaled the fragrance of exotic flowers she trailed. 'You look breath-taking,' he murmured into her ear.

She gave a quiet gasp and half-turned in surprise. This time the semi-shy smile and the look she gave him through her lashes were genuine – and hit him with such force they very nearly laid him out for the count right there.

They both blinked and the moment passed as Annabel's attention was drawn to the stunning monochrome décor of the hotel lobby. A polished expanse of white marble flooring extended to walls lined with sheer panels of snowy voile, backlit by colour-change lighting and hung with great, gilt-framed original oil paintings – dark, solemn portraits of grand personages adorned in period finery. Oversized chairs and settees, upholstered in studded black velvet, were set in casual groups here and there. The silver-gilt reception desk stretched across the far wall, and glowed under the light of the countless candles burning in the four-foot-high Venetian glass candelabra that stood along its surface at regular intervals. The centrepiece of the space, cascading from the forty-foot-high ceiling like a waterfall, was an enormous cylindrical chandelier, its thousands of strands of crystals hanging all the way to the floor and spilling like rivulets across the marble. The hotel's seasonal decorations were understated, stunning in their simplicity – a series of identical 'Christmas trees' standing sentry around the perimeter of the space, each constructed entirely from blown-glass baubles of varying sizes, some silvered, some intricately etched, some patterned with glitter.

'This is beautiful,' she breathed in awe, eyes darting to take in everything as he led her towards the bank of elevators.

'Very,' he agreed, his own eyes focused on nothing but Annabel Frost, captivated by the way her fair skin appeared even milkier framed by the luxuriant length of loose hair that reached past her shoulder blades in thick waves.

They joined a group of people riding the express elevator up to the roof terrace and stepped out into a floating formal winter garden. Over the wonderland of clipped evergreen topiary, sculpted steel water features and dozens more of the delicate bauble 'Christmas trees', a vast retractable glass roof was fully extended, its state-of-the-art frameless design allowing diners the opportunity to bask in all the beauty of the cloudless day while enjoying protection from the attendant chill.

Annabel eyed the long line of people queuing for tables. 'We'll never get in,' she said, not bothering to hide her disappointment.

'Ah, Annabel, when will you learn to trust me?' he asked, leading her straight to the head of the milling crowds. He uttered a quiet word to the host, who in turn signalled a waiter to show them to one of the better tables set close to the building's edge, offering uninterrupted views of the London skyline. But again, Aidan found he only had eyes for Annabel as she removed her coat to reveal a round-necked dress of softest forest-green cashmere that seemed to cling to every curve.

Taking her seat and the proffered menu, Annabel waited only until the waiter turned away. 'How did you manage that?' she demanded with a snap of her old self.

'Friends in the right places.' He grinned. In the sunlight her hair ignited with highlights of flame and spun gold, hinting at the fiery natural colouring that not even a layer of dye could subdue. He couldn't help wondering how long her armour had been in place, what had prompted her to want to hide her true beauty from the world. He'd find out one day.

By the time the waiter came back to take their order, Annabel had apparently recovered enough to resume her act. Instead of ordering for herself, she sent Aidan the same faux coy smile and eyelash bat combo she'd tried out last night and breathily asked him to choose for her. Oh, yes. Miss Frost definitely had a game afoot.

Thinking back to the dessert episode during the tasting at Cluny's, he took full advantage of the situation, choosing her the sweetest thing he could find. When their food arrived, he was far from disappointed by the sensuous, and entirely genuine, display he was treated to as Annabel was helplessly transported to syrupy waffle heaven.

Intrigued to see how far she was willing to take things, he set about testing the boundaries, finding that, no matter what topic of conversation he brought up, she agreed with him. Even when he offered the most unfavourable views he could think of, she held character and did no more than simper. She deferred to him in every choice to be made – from whether she wanted more coffee to whether they required the nearby terrace heater turned up for extra warmth.

While he had to admit that it was all a hugely enjoyable show, Annabel really did make a terrible actress. Nearly as bad as she was a liar. He waited until their plates had been cleared to call her on it.

'You've a very interesting mood about you this morning, Ms Frost. And as diverting as I find it, why don't you tell me what it is that you're hoping to achieve?'

'Achieve? I don't know what you mean.' She gave an exaggerated beat of her lashes. 'I'm simply making an effort to be friendlier. I thought that's what you wanted?'

He snorted with incredulity. 'Despite the very entertaining performance, I'm not sold.'

She blinked at him with huge eyes. 'You don't believe me?'

'I'm not entirely sure what it is I'm supposed to be believing.'

'Simply that I've taken on board the things you've said about me, and that, on reflection, I've realised you're right – I need to be more –,' she paused, pursing her lips as she obviously cast around for the right word '– obliging.'

He felt one side of his mouth lift up. 'No. I don't believe that for a minute.'

She feigned a hurt look. 'That's a shame. So I suppose you also wouldn't believe that I've come dressed especially for you?'

His gut tightened at the cheeky undertone her voice had taken on. 'How so?'

She leant forward and lowered her voice. 'With no knickers.' Immediately her cheeks flamed bright red, all the evidence he needed to know she was telling the truth.

Sweet fucking saints save him.

He was beyond impressed when he managed to get his next sentence out in a steady sounding voice. 'If that's the case – and I sincerely hope it is – then you're playing with fire, Ms Frost. You realise that, don't you?'

She gave him a mischievous smile, her eyes skipping over his face. 'Don't worry, I think I'm big enough to take the heat.'

Oh, she was having the time of her life – thinking she was beyond safe, flirting and teasing him here in the middle of a crowd. She really didn't know him very well at all yet, did she?

Time to set her straight.

'Are you? Maybe we'll have to put that theory to the test.' He leaned across the table and lowered his voice. 'Open your legs. Show me.'

She gasped, looking around at the glamorous, wintry surrounds. 'Here?'

'Here,' he confirmed. 'Now.'

Her green eyes darted as though looking for an excuse to pluck out of the air. 'I'm not an exhibitionist, Mr Flynn. I dressed just for you, not for everyone else.' The words were still full of bravado but the nervous swallow that followed them rather ruined the effect.

He sat back and gave a shrug. 'Ah, not to worry, then,' he said, watching the breath she'd been holding rush out of her lungs. Her relief would be short-lived. 'I can have that fixed in a matter of minutes,' he said, calling her bluff. 'Have us tucked away in a nice private room. Shall I arrange that, Annabel, so we can see if you're still so sure of yourself, so ready to please me, then?'

The tension was back, tenfold. His gaze latched onto the fluttering pulse point at the base of her throat. Very soon, he'd be in a position to press his mouth over it, feel the rapid beat of her excitement against his tongue, let it set the pace of his own heartbeat.

'Sounds extravagant.' He watched her throat move

133

with the words. 'Are you sure it would be worth the cost?'

His gaze jumped back up to hers. 'Without a doubt.'

He caught the flicker of uncertainty in those green depths, noted that she couldn't quite keep from fidgeting, and was impressed that she made herself hold his gaze.

'All right,' she said, not nearly so certain of herself now but obviously deciding to risk a double bluff. Little did she know that as a seasoned player, he was already one step ahead of her.

'Then finish up your coffee.' Without ever taking his focus off her face, he produced the keycard to the hotel room he'd been keeping in his pocket and slid it into the middle of the table. 'Because I can't wait to get you all alone.'

Annabel stared with stunned horror at the keycard sitting on the table between them, hardly able to hear what Aidan was saying over the sudden roaring of her blood in her ears. The heated excitement that had been building as a result of their teasing had morphed into outright panic. This wasn't supposed to happen.

'You got a room? Here?' she asked dumbly. How? He was a barman. How could he have managed to secure, let alone afford the cost of a room in one of the most exclusive, expensive hotels in London? 'Who *are* you?'

He grinned across the table at her then signalled their waiter for the bill. 'I'm the man pulling every string at his disposal in the hopes of impressing you. Is it working?'

Was it working? Well, she wasn't running for the exit, which left her with an awful suspicion that *something* was. Shame it wasn't her brain. As if it wasn't bad enough that she'd given in to a moment of madness and come without her underwear – all for the sake of the kick she'd get out of parading that secret right under Aidan Flynn's oblivious nose – she must have totally lost her mind to then go and admit it to him. What had she expected would come from waving herself in his face like a giant red rag to a bull?

She was saved from having to inspect the answer to that question too closely when Aidan said, 'We're done here,' after she'd failed to respond. Signing the bill to the room, he pushed to his feet and stood beside the table waiting for her to make her next move.

Shit, what should she do? What *could* she do? Yet again she found herself backed into a corner, where her choices left a lot to be desired. She could say no – *should* say it – because this was too much. It was supposed to be a game, that was all, one that had gone too far, too fast. But it wasn't as simple as saying no and walking away. Performing that sort of U-turn now would be as good as admitting that the whole thing had been a farce. And that would surely only serve to make her look immature and foolish.

Right. Because she'd been the very picture of maturity and wisdom so far.

'Annabel?'

Aidan's voice broke through her mental wranglings. She looked up at the resolute set of his handsome face, into those beautiful eyes that questioned with a steely glint and felt the bottom drop out of her stomach as she realised that, short of a sudden convenient natural disaster, there was no way out of this. Pride wouldn't let her back down. Trying to ignore the traitorous voice in her head that whispered maybe she didn't want to back down, she reached for the keycard that Aidan had left sitting on the table like a gauntlet, and pushed to her feet. When she met the look of heated admiration he gave her, the whispers in her head turned to shouts for help. Come on! Where was an earthquake or a big bloody bolt of lightning when she needed one?

Carrying her coat over one arm, she followed Aidan back to the elevator lobby where he passed the clutch of people waiting to take the express ride back to the ground floor and continued to the lifts which serviced all the hotel's floors. She watched him push the button, jumping at the almost instantaneous pinging sound that preceded the swish of the metal doors opening in front of her.

In the mirrored rear wall of the empty car, she saw the reflection of Aidan Flynn move up behind her. 'First and only chance to back out, Ms Frost,' he whispered, his stare meeting hers over her shoulder. 'Be sure before you step inside, because if you want to play games with me, you'd better know that I play to win. And I play dirty.'

Yeah, she thought shakily. She'd already figured that out. She took a breath to try and clear her mind. Was she sure? Hell no. She'd never been so unsure of anything in her life. The only thing she could think was that maybe the best way to regain order and control was to face up to the test that Aidan Flynn represented. Didn't psychologists promote the theory of embracing fears in order to conquer them?

Almost as though her feet had a mind of their own, they led her into the elevator. Aidan followed, pausing to hit the button for the second floor before homing in on her. Backing up, she found herself bumping against the wall, unable to take her gaze off him as he closed in on her space.

His greater height and the unblinking intensity of his scrutiny were overwhelming. Her mouth was so dry she couldn't speak. It didn't help that she was as aroused as she could remember being in . . . well, in pretty much forever. Her last *encounter* must have been over a year ago, and so casual and perfunctory an affair as to be rendered utterly forgettable.

She forgot it even more when the doors started sliding closed, making her start.

'You look a little nervous, Annabel,' Aidan observed with a quirk of a brow, stepping even closer so that Annabel found herself pressing further back against the side of the elevator. 'Are you?'

She couldn't answer, just produced some sort of strangled squeak that drew a chuckle from the tall, dark wall of danger looming over her.

'You should be, if you're really wearing nothing under the skirt of that dress.' He lowered his head towards the side of hers so that he could murmur directly into her ear. 'If it's true, imagine the things I could do to you right here, right now?' He stopped and drew in a deep breath which hummed in his throat. 'Delicious, deviant things that in an instant would have you squirming against my mouth – begging for my fingers.'

She tried to gasp but found that all the air seemed to have been sucked out of the elevator.

'I'd only use two at first, to test how tight you are,' that soft voice went on, pouring more scandalous words into her ear, his breath making the fine hairs around her hairline tickle against her cheek. 'I'd make you ready so I could ease them in deep to explore every inch, to hunt out all your weak spots.' If he was trying to shock her, he was succeeding. It was too much, she needed to distance herself, gain some control of the situation. Already pressed as tight as she'd go against the wall, she tried to edge sideways, but froze when Aidan brought his arms up to the wall on either side of her head, trapping her. 'Then, once I'd got to know you better than you know yourself, when I felt you finally start to melt around me, I'd stretch you with a third and finger-fuck you, Annabel. Slow and easy to start, and then fast and hard.'

He played dirty, he'd said? Oh, no. This wasn't dirty, it was downright filthy. If she couldn't work out how to get some oxygen into her lungs soon, she was going to pass out. Maybe that would be her saving grace?

'But I don't think I'd let you come. Not for a long time. Instead, I'd use all that newfound knowledge to drive you to the edge and keep you there until you cried and pleaded and struggled for release.' Vaguely Annabel noticed that their descent had slowed but Aidan didn't move, ignoring the doors as they opened behind him. 'And when you thought you couldn't take any more, thought that surely I must grant you mercy, I'd take you somewhere private, tie you down tight and take my own pleasure in every way imaginable. Until I was the only thing you could taste and smell and feel. I'd claim ownership of every part of you, Annabel, and you'd surrender willingly and love every minute of it.'

She closed her eyes needing to take a moment, but opened them again as she sensed him move. He caught the button to hold the doors open just as they'd begun to close, turned back to her. 'Shall we?'

As though in a dream, she followed him down the hall, no longer able to remember whether she should be working to a plan of escape beyond the rather flimsy one of relying on the intervention of major disasters or acts of God. Before long she found herself entering the room, her heart beating so furiously she was surprised Aidan couldn't hear the thud. She couldn't even spare a thought to take in her surroundings as the door closed, all her attention on keeping an eye on Aidan, waiting for him to pounce.

He did no such thing. Simply walking past where she'd glued herself to the entrance wall, he crossed the room to push the heavy silk curtains back from their half-opened position so that the diffused sunlight shining through the panel of white muslin fell across the bed.

He turned back to face her. 'Come here to me, Annabel.' That voice, soft, almost sensuous with that lyrical lilt, coaxed her to listen, to comply. And lord help her she did, under the weight of that penetrating grey gaze she went to him.

'Sit on the end of the bed,' he said when she reached him.

Was she really going to do this? Apparently so. She sat, finding herself spotlighted by the sunlight while he turned to the desk behind him and pulled out the high-backed chair tucked under it. Positioning it back to front a foot from where she sat, he straddled it, leaning on his folded arms and stretching his long legs out to bracket hers.

He looked at her for long time, letting his eyes drift leisurely over her body. Eventually they met hers and held her gaze until she felt like she wanted to squirm.

'Put your things down beside you,' he said, and she noticed that she was hugging her coat and bag in her lap. She placed them on the mattress and looked back at him.

'Good. Now lift your skirt,' he said in same soft voice, a little husky around the edges, that silvery gaze drawing her in, sucking at her will.

She cast around frantically for a distraction but there was still no way out. Not a crack in the ceiling to indicate it would imminently cave in, nor a hole in the floor through which she could conveniently fall. There was just her and Aidan Flynn, filling the stylish greige-hued room with the palpable force of sexual tension.

Holding the hem, she swallowed, and edged the soft wool up over her knees. He didn't break eye contact until she rested her hands again on her thighs. Then his gaze flicked down to her bare legs and back up again.

'Higher.'

Sunlight continued to stream through the muslin, throwing every bit of her into high relief, the distinct lack of any portentous darkening telling her there was no sudden hurricane due to strike. She really was on her own. And she couldn't seem to stop herself. She took the hem an inch or so further up her thighs, determined to play for every second of time she could.

Adain raised an eyebrow. Waited. The fact that she was purposely keeping him waiting, denying him his desire, sent a thrill of power through her. Power, and a rush of her own desire that had her slowly dragging the hem to mid-thigh.

'Keep going, *a mhuirnín*,' he said, but his gaze stayed locked on hers, her legs seemingly forgotten. She tested the theory, daring to expose a good five inches in one swoop.

Sure enough, his eyes stayed on hers. 'Higher, Annabel.' His lips quirked. 'All the way up to your waist.'

It was impossible not to respond to the challenge in his eyes, that smile that said he didn't think she'd be able to do it.

And there was no point in pretending any longer that she didn't want to rise to that challenge. That she wasn't well and truly caught in this trap of her own making.

Barely able to breathe she took it up to her waist. He held eye contact for a long moment then finally dropped his gaze. She clenched her thighs tighter together.

When he spoke, his voice was even huskier. 'I had a dream very similar to this the other night. Do you want to know what happened next, Annabel?' His gaze met hers again and the weight of it slammed into her chest. No one had ever looked at her that way before, with such naked . . . *hunger*. 'You spread your lovely legs for me.' Despite that calm control of his, she could see that he was beginning to breathe a little harder himself. 'Do it for me now, *a mhuirnín.*'

Should she? Could she? It had become too hard to think.

'Annabel?'

'Please . . .'

'Please what?'

She shook her head, unable to catch her thoughts and form them into sentences.

'Please stop?'

Yes! The word was a shout in her head, but she couldn't get a sound to pass her dry lips.

'Please more?'

No! This shout was equally loud, but remained equally silent. She had to close her eyes in case he read the truth in them.

'Is that what you're asking for – for me to touch you? Is that what you want?'

More than anything and not at all. She'd shatter into a million pieces and lose herself if he did and would surely self-combust if he didn't. And she could no longer tell with certainty which one of those outcomes would be worse. Could no longer tell where the game ended and reality began.

'I want that too,' he went on as though she'd answered in the affirmative, his voice sounding tight, rough. She heard the slight rustle of movement, nearly moaned in relief when she opened her eyes again to see him reach one hand towards her. He plucked a red curl a little away from where it lay against the bodice of her dress and rubbed it between his forefinger and thumb. Annabel was mesmerised by the slow, sensual caress taking place mere inches from the curve of her breast. Her nipples tightened as she imagined the same careful touch there.

She closed her eyes and swallowed. She was going to fall, to give in, hand him the control he wanted . . .

'But I can't,' he said.

What? Her gaze sprang up to his and she stared at him. He was tense, from the muscle twitching at the side of his clenched jaw, to the stiff set of his shoulders. He didn't look any happier about his pronouncement than she did.

'I won't break a promise,' he said simply, dropping the curl. 'I can't touch you yet, *a mhuirnín*. Not until you're ready. But you can touch yourself. Why don't you do it?'

Her head spun with shock. 'No.'

'Why not?'

'B—because I won't,' she blustered.

'That's not a reason.'

The thought of doing something so intimate in front of him was outrageous. 'I can't.'

'Of course you can. Your hand is right there on your thigh. So close. Just slide it a little to the left and down.' His words were soft and slow, that melodic brogue mesmerising.

She shook her head. It was too much. Wasn't it? Were they really *her* fingers she could feel twitching with the need to move?

'Do it, Annabel. You're wound so tight, you know how sweet the release will feel.' That lovely lilting voice dropped into a soft rasp. 'Show me. I want to look and learn so that when it's my turn to touch you, I'll know how to do it right.'

She had to stifle a moan. 'I can't,' she gasped again, knowing she was a hair's breadth away from throwing caution to the wind and doing it.

'Touch yourself the way you'd like me to touch you. Imagine that it's my fingers on you, in you – thicker, longer, the skin rougher. Imagine how they'll feel.'

That pale gaze turned penetrating. The gentle coaxing was

gone. In its place was that demanding tone – the one that reached inside and spoke directly to that carefully hidden spot that wanted nothing more than to listen and obey. Surrender. The one that terrified her because it had the power to make her do just that. With a jolt she realised she was doing it again, letting herself fall under his thrall. She'd let herself forget that this wasn't about sharing pleasure. Aidan Flynn wanted to take things she wasn't prepared to give. This was a game of power to him. The reminder doused the heat of her passion as effectively as a bucket of cold water over the head.

'I said, I can't,' she reiterated with much more resolve, pulling her skirt back down and covering herself.

'You can. I can see how much you want to.'

Because she'd just made it more than obvious to him. Fool that she was.

'That doesn't mean I can, or will,' she snapped, gathering her belongings and pushing to her feet so she could make a long overdue dash for the door. 'Forget it. Forget these games. This was a mistake.'

She hadn't even made it two steps before Aidan was also on his feet, apparently reading her intent and blocking her way to the entrance passage.

'Get out of my way,' she demanded.

'No. No more running, Annabel. And I agree with you, no more games either. Stand and face this.'

She was about to tell him where to go when he said, 'Tell me what it will take.'

'Take?'

'Yes. I want you, and I'm not going to stop until I have you. So tell me, what will it take to get us to that place before we both go mad from frustrated desire?'

She looked at him, noticing that he had that coolly implacable look that meant he wasn't going to budge until they'd slogged this out. It was his absolute delight to toy with her like this, she was sure.

'How about you leaving me alone? That'd work perfectly for me.'

He gave her a one-sided smile. 'Now it's my turn to say I can't. Or won't.'

Unfortunately, he'd given her every reason to believe him. She could see this torment stretching on forever. The thought exhausted her. 'Please, just let me go.'

'No. Stop evading and answer the question.'

Why could he never leave enough alone – just accept a no instead of this relentless digging, this pitiless pursuit?

'And Annabel.' He stepped close and gave her such a stark look that her breath caught. 'Do us both a favour and be honest. Please?'

With him looming large, she noticed that it wasn't just his eyes that gave away his feelings. There was so much tension in the way he held himself, she knew that under the deceptively calm surface he was fighting hard against whatever strong currents were swirling inside. Self-controlled as always. She looked back in his eyes and found she had no defence against the naked need in that gaze. She swallowed, allowed the truth to come out, albeit in a tiny voice.

'Honestly? I need you to back off. You're too much, too intense. I can't think straight around you.'

He was quiet for a long time, studying every inch of her expression, standing solidly between her and escape. There was no way through him, or around him so she waited, braced for the inevitable refusal. But he surprised her.

'I can step back, slow down, if that's what you want,' he said, although the words sounded strained, missing their usual mellifluous ring. 'On the condition that we have no more charades, no more pretence.'

It was a compromise that cost him a lot of effort.

144

'But that's all I can offer you, Annabel,' he said, the edge of his voice rough with restrained passion. 'I won't stop until I have you. I can't.'

Those last words should have sent her heart plummeting, but Annabel was aware that she felt weirdly reassured by them instead. She nodded and tried to walk around him.

'No.' He stopped her. 'For once, I'll do the running. I have to get to work anyway. You stay and take the time to get yourself together.' With a lingering look and a pained smile that appeared even more crooked than usual, he turned and left.

Annabel continued to stare at the door long after it had closed behind him, knowing that she was in big trouble. God damn him. Every time Aidan Flynn crossed the line, he somehow managed to step right back over it and redeem himself in some surprising way. And the more of this reasonable side he showed, the more dangerous he became.

THIRTEEN

As weeks went, Aidan was convinced the one he was trapped in was the longest in history. He'd agreed to slow things down with Annabel, but having to apply prolonged pressure to the brakes was taking its toll. He was surprised no one had complained about the smell of his burning self-control. The memory of how Annabel Frost looked in that hotel room, turning his dream into a reality, was both a blessing and a curse. So precious yet so torturous as the days dragged past.

He did everything he could think of to distract himself lest he be tempted to give into the urge to bombard Annabel. His apartment was beyond spotless, his sock drawer ordered to within an inch of its life. His bike had been tuned until it purred like a kitten, and the gleam on the chrome work could only be safely viewed through a pair of dark glasses. All his bills were paid and his bank statements balanced. He'd completed his Christmas shopping and even remembered to buy a present for his sister's first baby – who wasn't due to be born for another month. He tried not to think about how long he'd have to keep this up; at this rate he'd have to start on next Christmas as well.

Oh how the mighty have fallen, he taunted himself, remembering back to his cocky assertion of how much fun it would be having Ms Frost naked and begging at his feet. He was the one currently on his knees. Fun sure felt like frustration to him.

If he had any sense, he'd drop the whole idea of this pursuit, save himself the pain, move on. But he'd already proved that he was lacking in the sense department by starting this in the first place. And he doubted he could stop now if he tried. Nothing seemed as important as winning over Annabel Frost's trust so he could finally get his hands on her, show her the depths of his passion for her. If he didn't know any better, he'd swear she was becoming his obsession.

Tim found him one afternoon when he had all the fridges empty and was vigorously washing down the insides.

'You all right, mate?' the Australian asked with a troubled look.

'Fine. Why?'

'You did those the other day.'

'Did I?' Aidan shrugged.

Tim's look deepened to one that made it obvious he thought Aidan had lost the plot. 'Donna tells me it's your birthday this weekend?' he said.

Aidan was taken aback for a moment, surprised that Donna seemed to know something he'd nearly forgotten about himself, before recalling that she'd asked for his birth date so she could read him his horoscope from one of her gossip magazines. 'On Saturday. Yes.'

'You got any plans?'

'Not for the day.'

'Good. I'll see who's up for a celebratory bevvy after work on Saturday then?'

'Great. Will we be heading for the Louche Lounge?'

'Why not? You know how hard it is to find a place with decent bar service in this town.' Tim gave him a wink and walked off.

Later during service he came up to the bar to give an order of drinks and to say that everyone was on for Saturday night.

'Everyone?' Aidan raised his brows and directed a look across the restaurant to where Annabel was conversing with a group of fresh arrivals at the desk.

Tim followed his gaze and turned back with a roll of his eyes. 'No way.'

'Are those your words or hers?'

'Mine, mate. I didn't even ask her.'

'Why not?'

'*Why not?*' Tim gave him a long look. 'I'm starting to worry about you. What are you? Some sort of masochist?'

'Hardly,' Aidan laughed, though he had to admit he felt like one this week. 'Why didn't you ask her?'

'No point.' Tim gave a shake of his head. 'She'd never come anyway.'

'How do you know?'

'Because she's made it clear she's not interested in socialising with us minions. We used to invite her to things all the time but gave up when she kept looking down her nose and refusing. Guess we're too far below her.'

'Ask her anyway,' Aidan said, starting to prepare the drinks.

'You going to tell me what's going on here?' Tim's question drew his attention to the speculative expression on the waiter's face.

Keeping his own expression neutral, he gave a casual shrug. 'Christmas spirit. Haven't you heard it's the season of goodwill?' He gave a nod towards where Annabel was now standing alone, head bent to the reservations book. 'She's free at the moment.'

'If you're so full of goodwill, ask her yourself. You've got the gift of the blarney.'

'Doesn't work on her.' He glanced Annabel's way again, careful to keep any hint of wistfulness firmly in check. 'She's immune to my Irish charm.' He turned his gaze back to Tim and gave a dazzling grin. 'But you're not.'

The Aussie drew a deep breath and shook his head again. 'Mate, you're one sick fella,' he grumbled and, giving a theatrical show of reluctance, headed off towards the front desk. Aidan watched the following exchange with interest. Although he was too far away to hear the conversation, the accompanying body language came across loud and clear. Annabel's spine turned immediately stiff, she threw a quick look at the bar and then shook her head before sending Tim scurrying off to a recently vacated table which needed clearing.

'That was a no, in case you couldn't guess,' he said as he arrived back at the bar several minutes later, depositing a selection of dirty glasses in front of Aidan. 'Count yourself lucky.' With that he picked up the tray holding his fresh order of drinks and huffed away.

Annabel herself proved so adept at avoiding him that it wasn't until half way through the Sunday lunch service that he found a quiet moment to catch her at the reception desk.

She gave him a wary glance as he approached, and he watched her fair skin colour as it had done without fail every time she'd looked at him since that morning at The Hyde.

He found the reaction charming, so sweetly sexy it was a wonder it didn't have him blushing himself. 'Everyone missed you last night,' he said.

'Last night?' she queried while keeping her attention on the weekly shift printout in front of her.

'Drinks after work,' he prompted.

The flash of recollection across her face was followed by an amused snort. 'No they didn't.'

'No, they didn't,' he agreed with a grin before leaning in and dropping his voice. 'But I did.'

Annabel stiffened and her gaze jumped up to his. 'Aidan, don't start—' she warned with a weary sigh.

'I'm not starting anything, apart from a conversation,' he assured her. 'Just interested to know why you didn't come along.'

'I was busy.'

'No you weren't. Tell me the real reason.'

She gave him a put upon look. 'Because no one seriously wanted me to be there. It was obvious my invitation was issued out of a sense of duty. I wasn't going to spoil the fun just because Tim felt obliged to ask me. I have nothing in common with anyone here. Nothing to talk about apart from work.'

Listening to her reasoning, Aidan realised that her dismissive reaction to Tim the other night had been an attempt to hide her discomfort at being asked. That she used her bluntness to contribute to her reputation as part of her effort to keep everyone at arm's length.

'Why not try? They're a pretty friendly bunch.'

'But I'm not their friend. I'm their boss. I have no interest in blurring the line between the two. I don't need them to personally like me, I need professional respect. It's easier to keep the roles clearly defined. Now if you don't mind,' she said, inclining her head towards the bar. 'Customers need drinks.'

He looked over to where Jon easily had everything under control, then turned a knowing smile back on her, holding her discomforted gaze for a moment before backing off.

Annabel answered a call and watched out of the corner of her eye as Aidan walked back to the bar. She'd barely been able to look him in the eye since their encounter in the hotel room – God, had barely been able to look *herself* in the eye after the way she'd exposed herself.

Willing away the flush of shameful heat radiating through her, she concentrated on taking down the booking details, ignoring the touchscreen monitor on the reception desk in favour of writing it in the big, leather-bound reservations book. It might be old-fashioned, but she loved the appeal of the traditional pen and paper way, even though she'd have to go to the bother of transferring the information into the system anyway. It was a sentimental link to the long-distant past when her father would sit her on his lap and together they'd run through the bookings, picking out names and making up fantastical characters to match, magically transforming their clientele from accountants and managers and housewives to explorers and spies and princesses from exotic lands.

Noticing the front door open in her peripheral vision as she repeated the details into the handset, she rang off and raised a smile to greet the new lunch arrivals.

That greeting stalled when she came unexpectedly face to face with her mother – and Tony Maplin, dapper in his ubiquitous blazer topped by a camel overcoat, his greying hair brushed back from his handsome face. She ignored the sharp-eyed look and set smile he gave her and looked back to her mother.

'Mum? What are you doing here?' she demanded, her tone urgent but quiet, mindful of the room full of diners behind her.

'This is a restaurant, isn't it?' Tony answered instead, his words slurring, telling Annabel he was drunk. Looking back to her mother, it was obvious that she'd been drinking heavily too. This wasn't going to be good. 'We've come for lunch.'

'You won't get any here,' Annabel said firmly.

'Now, you don't want to go causing a scene, do you? Not

in front of all your nice customers.' He looked around the room before turning back to her, his smile a slash of malicious intent. 'So be a good girl and get us a table.'

'I'm afraid the owner has a policy against serving nasty drunks, Tony,' Annabel said, showing him she wasn't going to put up with his threats. After the way he'd treated her mother, she couldn't resist adding on a dig. 'Besides, you couldn't afford it.'

Tony's face turned bright red. 'And whose fault is that?'

'Nobody's but your own. Now I'm going to have to ask you to leave.'

'You bitch! You can't tell me what to do.'

Before Annabel could answer her mother jumped in.

'Tony,' Ellen protested, giving him a shocked look. 'There's no need to be rude.'

'There's every fucking need.' Tony turned on her mother, his voice rising. 'I won't be judged any more by this meddling cow.'

Her mother gasped. She turned disbelieving eyes from Tony to Annabel. 'Bel, I'm sorry, I didn't—'

'It's all right, Mum,' Annabel said in a calm tone, trying to keep things from spiralling into an ugly drama in the middle of Cluny's. 'What is it that you want to prove here, Tony?' She looked him in the eye to let him know she wasn't afraid of his tantrum. Although his looks had become jaded through years of excessive living he was still a classically handsome man. Nearly six foot, his stocky build was only just starting to run more to fat than muscle. He was turned out as well as he'd always been, despite the fact that Annabel knew he currently didn't have a penny to his name. The uniform of the consummate con-man. Annabel had never been fooled by it. She'd always seen the rot lurking beneath the suave exterior.

'I've come to get what's mine.'

Whatever he thought that could possibly be. The only things Annabel had of his were a stack of creditors' demands. 'Fine. How about we go outside and discuss that?'

'Oh no, Miss High and Fuckin' Mighty. We'll discuss it here, right in front of your la-de-da friends so they can see what a fraud you are.'

Annabel hadn't taken her focus off Tony, watching for any sign that things were going to escalate. She could sense the unnatural quiet that had started to fall over the restaurant as the diners began to notice that something was wrong.

'No. Whatever we have to talk about doesn't involve these people. Let's take it outside.'

Tony's face turned redder. 'I've already said that you don't get to tell me what to do, you stuck up little bitch. Think you're so much better than everyone else, don't you? What'd these fine folk think to hear that you stole from me.' He ended, voice rising so it could carry to the diners.

What was he on about? The man was a thief, he had nothing of his own to steal. Annabel felt a presence move up close behind her. As soon as she felt the heat radiating against her spine, she knew it was Aidan. She didn't want him interfering, but couldn't spare a glance his way to tell him so. Tony was in a position to take a good look though; his scowl flicked over her shoulder.

'Who's the pretty boy? Can't fight your own battles, eh? Typical woman. So much for all your feminist clap-trap, your *independence*. You're just a pathetic little whore.'

Behind her she sensed Aidan stiffen and move in closer, but he remained silent, for which Annabel was eternally grateful. Jumping to her rescue would only give Tony's words the ring of truth they didn't deserve. Instead he did the best thing he possibly could, lending his quiet support. She drew strength from his presence.

'Tony, that's enough.' Ellen had no such subtlety, jumping

153

to her daughter's defence. She pulled at Tony's sleeve. 'I would never have brought you here if I'd known—'

'Get your hands off me, you stupid cow!' Tony screeched, shoving his elbow into Ellen's side as he tried to disengage. With a yelp, Ellen lost her balance, falling against the reception desk and sprawling over the floor.

'Mum!' Annabel lunged around the desk to help her mother, aware of Aidan moving a split second ahead of her. Except he was heading for a different target.

'Aidan, no!' Annabel gasped. Not wanting a brawl in the middle of restaurant. Already she could hear the scrapes of chairs against the floorboards as a number of customers pushed to their feet. But she needn't have worried. Tony had already seen what was coming for him and was half way out of the door in a heartbeat.

She bent and scooped her mother up by the shoulders and looked back in time to see Aidan about to disappear in pursuit.

'No, leave it!'

He stopped and swung around, glaring at her with wild eyes, his chest heaving. He was obviously spoiling for a fight and not happy about obeying her. She held his flinty gaze to make sure she was getting through the haze of anger she saw there.

'He's not worth it.'

His gaze flicked to the door again, his body still tensed.

'Please,' Annabel tried again. 'Help me here.' She was relieved when she saw his shoulders suddenly drop.

A few strides brought him back and he helped pull her mother to her feet.

'You should call the police,' he said quietly once they'd established that, apart from a swelling where Ellen had caught her jaw on the edge of the desk, there was no serious injury.

Annabel shook her head. 'No. I don't want to turn this into more of a circus than it's already been. He's long gone.'

Aidan looked as though he wanted to argue but instead gave her a nod and suggested she take her mother through to the office while he dealt with calming the ruffled atmosphere and getting the diners resettled to their interrupted meals.

'What the hell was that about, Mum?' Annabel demanded as soon as they were in the privacy of the office. 'What the hell were you doing with Tony?'

'I'm so sorry, Bel. I know you didn't want me seeing him. We met for a drink, that's all.'

Annabel wanted to shake her mother, but more from a sense of disappointment and frustration than anger. 'And what possessed you to bring him here?'

'We'd been having such a lovely chat about you. I'd been telling him how much I appreciated all your help, all your efforts to make me welcome and comfortable, how you were even helping me get to grips with the financial issues. He said he was so pleased to know someone cared, after all the bad luck that had befallen us – said he'd like the opportunity to thank you in person. He seemed so genuine. I never knew he'd turn like that. He must have had too much to drink.'

'You think, Mum?' Annabel couldn't hold back the sarcasm. 'Drink is only partly to blame, only shows what sort of man Tony Maplin really is. I can't believe you'd go behind my back like this.' She didn't think she'd like the answer to her next question, but she needed to ask it anyway. 'How many times have you seen him—'

A knock on the door interrupted her.

'What is it?' she called out impatiently.

The door opened a little way and Jon peered through the gap. 'Ah, sorry Ms Frost, Aidan sent me back to give you this ice for your mother's jaw.' He extended his arm through the opening, a linen towel filled with crushed ice clutched in his hand. 'He's keeping an eye on the door, in case there's any more trouble.'

Annabel went to him and took the folded towel. 'Thank you. But tell him he doesn't need to do that.'

'Aidan?' her mother's voice queried from behind as Annabel watched the door close behind Jon. 'Was that the man who was standing behind you out there?'

Annabel nodded as she crossed the room again and handed the icepack to her mother.

'Oh, my. You should have seen his face. He was so angry. I thought he was going to kill Tony. Is he the one?'

'The one?' Her heart jumped in her chest at the ridiculous thought.

'Yes. The one we were talking about the other day?'

Oh, right. She felt a little foolish. 'Um, yes. That's him.'

'The one you were pretending not to like. I think you're wrong about him. He likes you too, Bel. He likes you a lot.'

Like her mother was any reliable judge of character when it came to men. 'Perhaps you should get the ice on that jaw, give it a rest.'

FOURTEEN

Aidan tamped down on the burning urge to smash his fist through something hard and thick and satisfying and made himself knock softly on the office door and wait until he heard Annabel call out. Pushing the door open, his gaze went straight to her, running over every inch as though reassuring himself that she was unharmed, although he knew that bastard hadn't laid a finger on her. It was a shame the same couldn't be said of her mother, with a nasty bruising starting to darken her jawbone. He regretted having allowed that split second of violence to happen. But overriding his instincts to thump the lowlife in his obnoxious mouth had been a sense that Annabel needed to handle the situation herself. That'd teach him to try to hide his Neanderthal instincts beneath a civilised metrosexual veneer.

'How are you doing, Mrs Frost?' he asked, crouching down beside the frail-looking woman sitting at the desk. He couldn't help but notice her colouring, her hair the colour of autumn leaves, her green eyes, everything fading gently with age. He could only imagine the full glory of the natural beauty her daughter was trying to hide.

'Call me Ellen, please.' Despite being shaken she primped and preened under the attention, flirting. 'Has Tony gone?'

'Yes. And there's no sign of him. It doesn't look like he's coming back for now.'

'No. Like most bullies he's a coward,' Annabel spat. 'He won't be back because he knows he's got no way of winning.'

'What was that all about? I only caught part of it, but he sounded determined to get something back from you?'

Annabel gave a mirthless laugh. 'I don't know what he thinks that could be. He has nothing to take. If anything he should be giving my mother back everything he's taken from her.'

'Still.' He'd seen the look in the bastard's eye, and it hadn't been rational. 'Is he likely to try again? If not here then what about at home? Is it safe for you there?'

'I bought the place less than a year ago and he's never been there,' Annabel started to assure him, then looked questioningly at her mother. 'Has he? Please tell me that you haven't let Tony know where I live.'

Ellen shook her head. 'No. You were so adamant when you took me in that he shouldn't know that I was careful over the weeks to meet him away from there.'

Aidan almost couldn't bring himself to get the next words out, so white-hot was his rage at even having to think about voicing the question, let alone contemplate the answer. 'Has he a history of violence against you?'

'No,' Annabel said, and the rush of relief left his head spinning. 'Never against me . . .' She left the answer open-ended, casting a questioning look at her mother.

Ellen shook her head. 'No. I've never seen him like that before. It must have been the drink.'

Aidan felt some of the tension ease from his shoulders. He turned to Annabel.

158

'Why don't you take your mother home then, we can manage here?'

Annabel shook her head. 'I can't leave. Tim's not in today. I have to lock up.'

'If you leave your keys I can do it. I've seen it enough times to know the routine. And with the family connections, it's hardly likely I'll rob the place.'

The fact that she agreed almost immediately gave him a good indication of how shaken she was by the whole experience, even though she held herself as ramrod-straight as ever.

'I'll go grab you a cab.' Aidan made for the door. With that jerk out there somewhere he didn't want them standing on the street. 'Where are you needing to get to?'

'Highgate,' Annabel said.

It took no time to hail a black cab, and he made sure to scan the street thoroughly as he waited. He returned to the office to find the women ready to go.

'The cab's coming around to the back now.' The rear alley wasn't the most salubrious of locations, reserved almost exclusively for waste disposal, but he figured it was preferable to having to run the course of curious gazes through the kitchens and dining room.

'There are my keys.' Annabel, who was scribbling on a piece of paper, stopped to point her pen at the bunch of keys sitting on the desk. 'And here's the alarm code and my mobile number,' she continued, handing the paper to him once she'd scribbled some more. 'Ring me if there are *any* problems.'

He offered his arm to Ellen Frost who was still a little unsteady from a combination of shock and alcohol. Escorting her outside, he opened the rear door of the black cab and handed her in while, beside him, Annabel recited her address to the driver through the front window.

When she turned Aidan was close beside her, but instead of scurrying straight through the open door, she lingered, looking up at him in a way that had his heart racing with primal instinct all over again. But the only thing he felt like smashing now were his lips against hers.

'Thank you,' she said with soft sincerity.

'Don't mention it,' he told through a suddenly dry mouth. 'Take care, Annabel. Call the police if you have to.'

'I will. But I think he's done his worst.'

'Don't take any chances.'

He closed the door and stood watching until the cab slowed at the end of the alleyway and turned, disappearing from view. The surge of protectiveness that slammed through him caught him unawares, leaving him fighting the urge to pound down the alleyway after it, keep Annabel Frost in sight. Keep her safe.

As unpleasant as Tony Maplin's scene at Cluny's had been, Annabel had to acknowledge that at least some good had come of it. Her mother was now sworn off the man for life. Having tearfully admitted during a heated discussion that she'd been meeting him in secret and giving him money – Annabel's money – she'd finally seen him for what he was. Tony's goal today might have been to humiliate Annabel in public as retribution for some imagined slight, but he'd ended up disgracing himself into the bargain.

Exhausted after such an emotionally trying day, Annabel was already tucked up on the sofa for the night when her phone buzzed at around eleven indicating a message had come in. It was from Aidan to tell her that everything was all right. Cluny's was locked up tight for the night with no problems, and as he didn't have access to the safe, he'd stashed what cash there was down in the cellar and taken the spare key home. He'd finished the text with, 'Hope all is OK at your end.'

It was nice of him to have taken the time to put her mind

at ease. Considerate. Like the consideration he'd shown in backing her up today, respecting her authority rather than charging in all macho as though she was incapable of looking after herself. The same consideration he'd shown in the hotel room at The Hyde when she'd let things go too far. He'd respected her need to call a halt, had let her stay and sort herself out. And boy, at the time she hadn't realised what a favour he'd done her until she'd looked in the mirror after he'd gone and seen the state of herself – all flush-skinned and wild-eyed. She'd never had a man leave her so untouched yet looking so wanton before.

She felt herself start to blush at the thought of the things she'd let him drive her to do. While she'd never considered herself a prude, her sexual encounters had always been pretty swift and safe – efficient, functional ways to scratch a physical itch. She'd never experienced anything like the slow erotic build Aidan Flynn was subjecting her to. Between that and the considerate gestures, it was getting harder and harder to remember why she should stay away from him. Surely today's events were a timely reminder of what happened when you fell for the surface charm and ignored the dangerous man beneath.

But hadn't those events shown that, despite the charm, Aidan was nothing like the Tony Maplins of this world? Demonstrated that he was as protective as he was possessive, as respectful as he was relentless? In the time she'd known him, in the extreme situations he'd put her in, she'd never felt afraid. Even when she'd been at her most exposed and vulnerable.

Could she do as he wanted and give him her trust? Risk getting close enough to take some of that pleasure he offered? She felt her chest tighten, found it harder to catch her breath. But strangely the feeling wasn't caused by fear, it felt more like . . . excitement.

She should text him back, show him the same courtesy. But she couldn't. Not just now. As a gesture it would feel too familiar, too much like an invitation to more. And she needed to work out whether she could handle that. She'd deal with it in the morning when she felt more settled, more like her old self.

If her feelings hadn't gone back to normal by then, she'd know she was in trouble.

Annabel was in trouble.

All Monday morning she tried to ignore the warm glow in her chest every time she thought of Aidan Flynn. Which was too frequently. She tried texting him too – also frequently – but couldn't seem to find the combination of words to strike just the tone she was looking for. Friendly yet professional. Appreciative yet authoritative. Approachable yet cool.

It was easier by far to let herself be distracted by her mother's insistence that they put up a Christmas tree – something Annabel never usually bothered with. From mid-December, Cluny's opened every day to meet customer demand, and although she worked the shift rota to allow staff either Christmas Day or New Year's Eve off, she always worked both herself. She'd never seen the point in putting in the effort for something she'd rarely be home to enjoy.

As it was, she had to leave it to her mother to finish hanging the new box of decorations on the small tree they'd bought from the nearby florist shop while she headed off to work.

When she arrived and came face to face with a quietly concerned Aidan, who'd arrived early to open up, she realised just how deep in trouble she was.

'How's Ellen doing?' he asked, sliding the set of keys she had given him yesterday across the bar to her.

'She's fine. A bit of a stiff neck from the fall.'

'And you? Everything all right? No sign of any further problems?'

'No. The only way Tony has of getting in touch is via Mum's mobile, and I took the SIM card out of that, just to be sure. But I don't think he'll try to bother her, or me again. He was being a drunken idiot yesterday, he'll know he went too far.'

The usual clear brilliance of Aidan's grey eyes seemed as clouded as the overcast skies outside as he regarded her with concern. 'I'd take extra care anyway. And you have my number now. Ring me any time you need to.'

That sent a disturbingly warm and fuzzy feeling through her. 'I can manage,' she muttered to cover her reaction.

A glint of exasperation flashed in his eyes but he gave a wry half-smile and kept his tone level. 'I'm not suggesting you can't, Superwoman. But everyone needs a bit of back-up from time to time. Just know I'm there if you want me.'

If she wanted him? Well now, wasn't that the million dollar question? From a physical standpoint her body screamed yes! It had been more than a year since she'd been with a man, and never with one quite like Aidan Flynn. He stood there looking at her steadily, the ever-present spark of provocation and powerful attraction crackling in the air between them. Did she have the strength to keep trying to fight the temptation of him? Or was she going to save her sanity and take a taste of what he was offering, get it out of her system? She knew what the answer was – could feel her resolve faltering, her resistance melting away. She was going to do it. Despite all her rules and her carefully constructed defences, she was going to go against common sense and her better judgement. But she was going to do it on her terms. Take the lead, call the shots, retain control. After all, it wasn't really surrendering as long as she stayed on top, was it?

'That's very generous,' she said, keeping her tone super

casual, lest she come across as too keen. 'Maybe I can buy you a drink some time to thank you for your help yesterday as well.'

She suspected from the way he looked at her that he knew exactly what had been running through her mind. The smile that spread across his handsome face a moment later confirmed it, set a swarm of butterflies fluttering around her belly.

'I think that deserves dinner at least, Ms Frost, don't you?'

Pushy as ever. Trying to take more than she wanted to give. And in a funny way, that familiar, infuriating arrogance made her feel more confident. She knew where she stood with that, found it much easier to deal with than all the unsettling emotional touchy-feely. She snorted under her breath. 'We'll see.'

The following day, after dinner service, Annabel stepped out onto the street, glad to find that the rain and sleet which had been falling incessantly since she'd woken up that morning had finally stopped. The cold night air held a fresh-washed scent, the festive lights of the street reflected in the slick black surface of wet tarmac. As she turned back to lock the door, her attention brushed past a motorcyclist waiting on the other side of the road. She stopped in surprise and did a double-take when she realised it was Aidan, dressed head to toe in black leathers and looking very slick himself as he leant back against a huge bike, which was also black, relieved by shiny bits of chrome. From this angle, the flashing pink neon sign above the entrance to the adult club opposite was pointing its arrow and the words 'HOT SEX' right at the top of his head.

Oh, yes. He was that all right. Was he aware that he'd positioned himself so perfectly as to advertise the fact? Following her line of vision, he turned and looked at the sign, then back to her with a quirked eyebrow and an arch smile that only added to the devastating effect.

Annabel couldn't stop staring, couldn't help but follow the line of those long, leather-clad legs all the way down to where he had one booted ankle crossed over the other. Seriously, that was what she'd been trying to resist? No wonder she'd been faltering so badly.

When she continued to stand there and stare, he pushed himself upright and, grabbing a canvas bag from one of the panniers, he crossed the road towards her.

'What are you doing here?' she demanded.

'I've come to steal you away.'

'Pardon?' she said, thoroughly distracted by all that leather and how well it moulded to his body.

'You owe me dinner. I've come to collect.'

'Now?' Annabel felt her eyes pop. 'It's nearly eleven!'

'Guess we'll have to settle for a late supper then.'

She should have known he'd jump right on her earlier invitation, charge in, give her no opportunity to over-think it or change her mind. But at the moment her mind seemed to be in total agreement with her body, eager to send her down the path of destruction. Was she really ready to let this go further?

'Fine. Where?' she said, trying to keep her voice steady as she started to rattle off a list of local, late night places they could try. Aidan stopped her.

'We're going to my place. Hence the transport.'

'Your place?' Oh, no, no, no, her brain warned: on his territory meant in his control. Meanwhile her body was nearly self-combusting with anticipation. She didn't know whether to be relieved or disappointed to discover a major problem with his plan. 'I don't think so. There's no way I can get on that –' she pointed to the big bike '– in this.' She indicated her tight pencil skirt under her mac.

'No problem.' Aidan gave one of his lopsided smiles, the ones she had little defence against, and held out the soft canvas bag. 'I brought leathers.'

Of course he had. She stared at the bag, her pulse banging in her ears.

'Annabel. It's not going to bite.'

'What?' she muttered, her gaze focusing on Aidan's face.

'You look as though I'm handing you a sack of snakes. What's the issue?'

He knew damn well what the issue was. The man was too clever not to know. He knew what reaching out for that bag, getting on that bike, and letting him take her home signified. He knew, and he was laying down the challenge. She could see it in the tiny kick up at the corner of his mouth, the glint of determination deep in those clear eyes.

And she knew right then that this was decision time. This was where she had to choose, once and for all.

And for once in her safe, boring, regimented existence, she was going to break her rules and live a little. She was tired of fighting her attraction to the man, the excitement he offered. She'd never been on a motorcycle, for God's sake. Didn't know if she was likely to ever get the opportunity to do so again. And even if she did, what were the chances that she'd get anything anywhere near as sexy as a leather-clad Aidan Flynn to go with it?

'No problem, then.' She said, aware of her skippy heartbeat and trippy pulse. Taking the bag, she turned to push through the door again. 'Give me five minutes.'

Rather than traipsing all the way back and unlocking her office, she nipped into the customer loos to change. She phoned her mother first, keeping the conversation brief and avoiding any unwanted shrieks of excitement by telling her she had a staff meeting with her head barman.

She glanced at her reflection in the mirror. 'You'd better

know what you're doing,' it cautioned her. Of course she knew what she was doing. It wasn't as if she was going in blind. She knew the risks, as long as she kept her eyes open and her guard up, she could stay in control of this.

Opening the bag, she found a black biker jacket, some sort of thermal jersey, and a pair of leather trousers. She wondered briefly if they were Aidan's but discovered the moment she pulled them out that, apart from the jersey, the leathers were not only much too small, but also decidedly feminine in style. Although they were clean, the leather bore traces of wear that told her they weren't new. Whose were they?

She removed her mac and suit jacket first, pulling the jersey and leather jacket on over her shirt. Zipping it up to her neck she discovered it wasn't a bad fit. She pulled off her footwear, shimmied out of her skirt and pulled the leather trousers on over her tights. Stepping back into her ankle boots she checked out her reflection in the full-length mirror and nearly stumbled. Wow! Who was that black-clad biker babe looking back at her? She turned this way and that, astounded at the way the leather flattered her figure even though it was a little loose fitting. She especially liked the sexy edge the high, narrow-heeled boots gave the outfit, making her legs endless. But there was something not quite right, something a little off. Taking out the clip holding her hair in its usual tight twist, she shook out the long locks, fluffing it around her shoulders. That was better. Now she definitely looked more biker chick than kinky librarian.

She couldn't help but feel a thrill run through her when Aidan caught sight of her. He stilled, those amazing eyes narrowing in on her with the intensity of a big cat sizing up its prey through the tall grass. Dressed as she was, she found it impossible not to swagger a little as she crossed the road.

'Not bad,' he said, running what she now saw was a critical

stare over her from head to toe. 'A little flabby in places.' Annabel's swagger stumbled a bit as she gasped in outrage. Was he judging her? 'The leathers, *a mhuirnín*,' he qualified with a grin, letting her know he'd baited her on purpose. 'They're a little on the large side. The better the fit, the better the protection.'

'Oh. Whose are they?'

'They're not anybody's.' He took the canvas bag that she'd stashed her folded clothes and handbag in. 'I keep spares handy.'

Spares. Of course he did. For all the women who undoubtedly threw themselves in his path.

'For dates?' The question slipped out before she could stop it, sounding much needier than she'd have liked.

He looked up from where he was rearranging the contents of the panniers and crooked a brow at her tone. 'Yes, for dates. And for friends.' He gave her a slow smile that reached places she didn't know she had. 'And especially for lovers.'

Lovers.

'Are you jealous, Ms Frost?'

Yes. Surprisingly. 'I've got nothing to be jealous about, Mr Flynn.'

'Not yet,' he said. 'Now, let's try these for size.' He indicated a pair of sturdy flat boots and folded gracefully into a crouch at her feet, wrapping one hand around the heel of her boot.

'Oh, that's OK,' she said uncertainly, looking down at the top of his bowed head, resisting the pressure she felt at her heel. 'Won't mine do?'

'At a push, but I'd feel better if you were properly kitted out. Let's try them. If they're too big you'll be better off in these sexy little things.'

So he *had* noticed the heels. She tried to pretend that that didn't send quite such a thrill through her.

She yelped as he took advantage of her distraction to pull her foot off the ground and rest it on his thigh. She flailed her arms as she cast around for something to grab on to. That mop of glossy hair was the obvious choice, right there in front of her as it was. The same with those wide shoulders – with black leather stretched across them, they looked like a sturdy option. But she couldn't trust her fingers to behave and she didn't want to embarrass herself by fondling him in the street. In the end she went with resting one hand on the saddle of the bike and watched as Aidan pulled on the zip feature at the front of the boot. It could have been her imagination, but it seemed to take an age while she stood there having a pair of slightly too big biker boots scrutinised for fit. She was certain it never normally took *her* that long to undertake a simple change of shoes.

'They'll do for now,' Aidan pronounced. With a creak of leather he straightened to what, from her newly flat-footed perspective, appeared to be a very impressive height and looked down into her face. 'But you're definitely getting to put these back on at my place,' he said, and tucked her ankle boots into the pannier with her other belongings and buckled it closed.

He put the helmet on her head, making a noise of approval when he wobbled it to test the fit. It was certainly snug enough that Annabel felt it compressing the sides of her face, making it feel as though she had hamster cheeks. Tightening the strap under her chin, he then produced a pair of gloves which he pushed onto her outstretched hands. He pointed out her footrests and threw a leg over the bike with his usual easy grace before turning over the engine. The thunderous rumble made her jump.

At his signal, she climbed on behind him, her breath catching at the sensation of the purring vibrations of the idling engine coming up from the saddle, not to mention the feel of Aidan Flynn, solid and male, wedged snugly between her spread legs – so intimate despite the layers of heavy-duty clothing separating them.

'Put your arms around my waist,' he said as he unhooked his helmet from the handlebars. She did so, tentatively, barely putting any pressure on the leather.

Twisting his torso, he turned to look over his shoulder at her. 'Annabel, I'm not going to lie and say I'm not going to enjoy your touch, very much. But this is about your safety more than anything else. You need to get a good grip.'

She nodded. She was sitting on a giant vibrating machine clinging to Aidan Flynn and feeling like a giddy girl – of course she needed to get a good grip.

Tightening her arms around his trim waist, she felt the hardness of the man beneath the layer of soft leather. For once she couldn't feel the heat of him, not even where their bodies were pressed together, and it made her want to snuggle further against him in search of it.

'That's better.' He cast a look up to the night sky, still heavy with cloud and the threat of more sleet. 'With any luck we'll get a dry run.' After he'd donned his helmet, he turned to her again. 'Ready?'

When she gave a nod, he reached back and lowered the visor over her face; giving her a smile, he flicked down his own. She had a split second to notice that he didn't seem to have any issue with hamster cheeks before he shifted his body over the handlebars. Clinging to his waist as she was, she had no choice but to move with him, let him take complete control. She hoped he didn't hear the yelp she gave inside her helmet as he released the brake and the big machine sprang forward. Heart in her throat, she forgot her inhibitions and clung to him even harder. She hadn't been on so much as a bicycle for twenty-odd years.

For the first minute she forgot to breathe. For the first five, she kept her eyes closed, hyper aware of the flex and stretch of Aidan's movements as he manoeuvred the big bike through the streets. Less than ten minutes into the ride, she was watching the lights of the city streak past as though through a new set of eyes. Familiar sights that she hardly bothered to register on a daily basis suddenly took on a clarity they lacked when viewed through the filter of a grime-streaked bus window. The abundance of Christmas decorations and colourful store front displays appeared more vibrant, even the miles and miles of fairy lights which seemed to be draped, swagged and wrapped around every available surface twinkled with extra brightness. She felt a fierce grin push her hamster cheeks so hard into the padding of the helmet that they ached. She wouldn't say she reached the point of relaxation, it was too exhilarating an experience for that, but thanks to the way Aidan handled the powerful machine with his usual manner of deftness and confidence, she felt no fear. She let herself lean into his back which felt solid and strong and a mile wide.

She was buzzing with speed-induced adrenaline by the time they pulled into an underground garage beneath a converted warehouse somewhere in a trendy area of East London.

Up on the fourth floor, Aidan motioned her through his front door ahead of him. She stepped into a large, open-plan space with high ceilings and huge windows – like the arty New York lofts she'd seen in movies. Rather than try to hide the working history of the building, the décor embraced it, with lots of exposed brick and pipe work, the industrial feel barely softened by large pieces of dark masculine furniture. She wasn't sure what she'd been expecting, but nothing quite as impressive as this place, which she guessed was about three times the size of her little apartment. Modern, slick, expensive. How could Aidan Flynn afford this?

Family money, possibly? Richard Landon was wealthy after all. But if that was the case, why would Aidan need to work as a barman? Before she could decide if it would be too rude of her to ask, he indicated a door set off to the side.

'You can change in there,' he said, removing his jacket and pulling off a thick-knit sweater to reveal some sort of snug-fit base-layer top clinging to a torso of classically sculptured proportions that suddenly rendered everything else unimportant. Before she could get caught staring open-mouthed, she gratefully ducked inside so she could check out her own image, fearing the damage that the ride through the streets of London had wrought. While all it had taken for Aidan to look like his usual sexy ruffled self upon removing his helmet was a quick run of his hand through his black hair, she was sure she looked a right mess. The worst possible combination of hat hair and wind frizz.

She did a double take when she looked in the mirror, but not out of fright. The wind had tossed her locks so that they looked wild rather than woolly. If she'd barely been able to recognise herself earlier, she had no clue who this transformed creature was.

'Are you sure you know what you're doing?' she asked the stranger in the mirror. But there was no chance of a sensible answer to be had from the bright-eyed, pink-cheeked, giddily breathless girl in the mirror. 'Don't let yourself get lost in this. Remember to stay in control.'

As she pulled off the borrowed trousers, the zip caught on her tights and laddered them below the knee. Her hosiery didn't seem to do too well around Aidan Flynn. Even without the sudden flush of heat that assailed her at the memory of the scene that had taken place in Cluny's cellar, she realised the temperature in Aidan's apartment was warm enough for her to go without.

Which was probably just as well, she decided, quickly removing the ruined tights and shoving them in her bag. If she wanted to be the one controlling what would happen tonight, it would be best not to give him any reminders of that particular encounter.

FIFTEEN

'Come on through,' Aidan called out from the kitchen when he heard the cloakroom door close. Turning on the oven, he slid a flat square of rosemary focaccia bread into it to warm.

While Annabel had been changing, he'd taken the opportunity to swap his own leathers for a pair of jeans and had flicked the switch to ignite the modern gas-fuelled fire set into the wall.

She appeared through the doorway as he uncovered the serving plate of antipasto he'd had the little Italian deli down the road put together for him earlier.

'Nice place,' she said, wandering slowly through the living space towards the open-plan kitchen, eyes darting all over as she took everything in. From his position on the opposite side of the long central island separating the two areas, Aidan watched her. She was back in her skirt and little boots now, but he didn't think he'd ever forget the way she'd looked earlier, striding out of Cluny's in those leathers and heels with her red hair rippling behind her as she strode towards him. She'd been the living incarnation of every wet dream he'd ever had. And would no doubt be the inspiration for many more.

'Glad you think so.' Picking up his smartphone from the worktop, he set it into the speaker dock set at the far end of the island. 'What music would you like?'

'Anything which doesn't feature a combination of the words "merry", "white" and "Christmas", or involves the jingling of bells, mommy kissing Santa, or rocking around any trees.'

Her sardonic tone made him grin. 'Not a festive person?' Scrolling through the menu on the touchscreen, he chose a nicely unobtrusive and chilled compilation to play in the background.

She did a visual sweep of the apartment. 'No decorations, no tree. Seems you're a bit bah-humbug yourself.'

'Ah, but I've only been back in London for a matter of weeks after an extended time away,' he explained. 'I haven't had time to get around to decorations, much to the consternation of my cleaning lady, who insists on putting the cards on display at the very least.' He tilted his head in the direction of the window ledges and caught such an unguarded look of surprise as Annabel saw the forest of cards covering the deep surfaces, that he was left wondering how many well wishes she received at this time of year.

'Do you live here alone?'

'Yes.'

'The rent must be extortionate,' she muttered, almost to herself as she looked the place over again with a calculating eye.

'I don't rent. I own it,' he told her, watching her react with surprise again. 'A perk left over from my years working in the City.'

'Oh,' she said, giving a little grimace at his admission. It was a reaction he was more than used to. As a breed, bankers had hardly done much to inspire feelings of love and respect in recent years. 'So, is Cluny's part of some permanent change or just be a bit of a stop gap for you?' she asked.

'Still so eager to see me gone, Ms Frost?' he teased. 'To be honest, my plans are a bit loose at the moment, so you needn't give up hope. Now, why don't you sit down and tell me what I can get you to drink.' He indicated she should take a seat at the closest end of the long dining table – although after having her thighs cradling his arse and hips all the way home what he really wanted was to lay her across the solid oak surface instead so he could see how good they felt wrapped naked around his waist or clenched tight around his ears.

'Something soft,' she said as she pulled out a chair and sat. 'Water's fine.'

Seeing as he was going to be taking her home again a little later, he decided to join her.

'So, what about you?' he asked over his shoulder, taking a couple of glasses from a cupboard and turning to use the ice and water dispenser set into the door of the big American-style fridge. 'I gather you've been at Cluny's for a while?'

'Since it opened. I started as assistant manager.'

He turned to glance at her. That was roughly five years ago. She must have been young. 'What were you then, about twenty?'

She nodded, although she wasn't looking at him; her attention had been caught by the gentle flicker of the flames that danced up from a decorative bed of dark smooth pebbles in the fireplace. 'Twenty-one.'

Impressive, but not really surprising given her formidable drive and single-mindedness. 'And where does Cluny's feature on the Frost career plan?'

'What do you mean?' Her suddenly sharper tone had him turning to look at her again. Her air of general distraction was gone. In its place was focused suspicion.

176

Aidan hid a sigh. Well it hadn't taken long at all for the liberating effects of the bike ride to wear off. He'd hoped a spin on the big Triumph would serve as a bit of an ice breaker, and although he hadn't been able to actually see her reaction at the time, he'd felt her whoops and shrieks of laughter reverberate against his spine and knew she'd been having fun. It was the first time he'd known her to truly let go – and knowing he'd been instrumental in bringing that release of elemental joy to the surface had felt almost as good as having her plastered against him. Almost. For all that she might now be looking to scurry back behind the protection of her hard outer edges and spikes, he had undeniable proof that Annabel Frost was made of soft curves.

'I mean, do you still see yourself working there in ten years from now? You seem to be a very driven person.'

'Oh, well, I'm very committed . . .' She let her words dry up, obviously not wanting to be drawn on that particular topic of conversation. Hell, *any* topic of conversation. She really was the most guarded person he'd ever met. That only increased his determination to crack her open.

'I know you are, Annabel. That wasn't the question.' He carried the glasses of iced water to the table and set them down, looking at her across the expanse of wood. 'I'm not spying for my uncle.'

'Then why do you want to know all this?' she bristled, confirming that even this seemingly innocuous exchange of information was pushing against her boundaries, sending her into retreat.

'I want to get to know you,' he said, keeping it simple and straight to the point. 'Is that a problem?' If she wanted to keep trying to run and hide, keep trying to push him away, she needed to know that he refused to make it easy for her. 'If it is, why did you agree to come here tonight? What did you think was going to happen?'

She hit him with a green gaze suddenly ripe with provocative intent. 'I think you know the answer to that.'

'Do I?' He felt a tingle at the back of his neck. With supreme effort, he kept his tone level. 'Why don't you tell me, just so we're clear.'

She raised her eyebrows as though surprised he had to ask, then she was on her feet, rounding the table towards him with deliberate steps. He turned to face her as she came to stand right up close, his whole being lighting up in response to her unmistakably seductive attitude.

'I thought you wanted to fuck me,' she said in a low, throaty tone he'd never heard from her before – one that went to work on his straining libido straight away. 'Isn't that what this whole thing has been about?'

Well, he'd asked for it, and it certainly didn't get much clearer than that. Apparently Ms Frost had been making some decisions. Taking his cue from her bluntness, he returned it in style. 'I do want to fuck you.' God, how he wanted it. Right there, right then, with such a force that the effort it took to hold himself in check made even his teeth hurt. 'When you're ready for me, remember?'

'I am ready,' she proclaimed, boldly holding his gaze. 'I'm here, and I'm ready.'

Ready to take control of the situation, yes – ready to let things happen on her terms. Which told him one thing.

'You're not ready, Annabel,' he said. 'Nowhere near, if you've come here prepared to get naked and sweaty, but unprepared to carry out a simple conversation.'

She looked at him as though he was crazy. And maybe she was right. 'Most men like that I want to keep things simple, uncomplicated.'

'I can imagine.' And something about the thought of those faceless, emotionless men casually taking what she offered, taking the gift of her body without giving any thought to

178

the nourishment of her heart and soul made him seethe. Was that how she'd conducted all her intimate relationships? Had she ever been romanced? There was no point in asking her, of course, not when she was balking at discussing something so innocuous as her career path. And why should he even care? His body screamed at him. Why not just take what she was so obviously eager to give?

Because it wasn't enough. He didn't want to be just a convenient tool she could use to satisfy her physical needs and then easily discard. She could use a damned vibrator for that. He shoved the urges aside. 'But, that's not going to happen here,' he said, breaking eye contact and letting his gaze roam slowly, suggestively over her curves – curves that were so tantalisingly close. Most importantly he let her see the desire she aroused in him when he raised his eyes to hers again, to ease the sting of his necessary rejection. 'You're so beautiful,' he told her. 'I doubt you have any idea how badly I ache to touch you right now. How much I do want to fuck you. But I want to be the man who gives you more than that, who takes more than that. I want to make love to you, and for that we need to be more than convenient strangers.'

He caught a glimpse of unease slither across the back of her eyes, and she nearly jumped out of her skin as the timer on the oven sounded. As he'd suspected, even the thought of extending intimacy beyond the bounds of the purely physical was still enough to scare her.

'I don't want to fight,' he said, gently, ignoring the digital beeps, keeping his attention and his will focused on her. 'And I don't want you to run. Let's have something to eat and try taking this from the top again.'

He could see her indecision – took it as a good sign that on a deeper level the need generated by frustrated desire was warring with her life-long habit of protecting herself. He used it to press the point. 'It's the only way we're both going to end up with what we want.'

She took a breath in. 'OK.'

He let his out. 'OK.'

Together they carried the makings of supper to the table – Annabel taking the platter of cold meats, cheeses and olives while he grabbed the warm bread, a couple of side plates and napkins. He'd purposely kept the meal super light, super casual – finger food to nibble on, to dip, to tear and share. Not only was it late, but the food wasn't much more than another prop, a premise to get them sitting together, to get Annabel Frost talking. And despite her continued reticence, he would persevere. He would get her to open up to him. He would win this challenge and claim his prize.

'So, where were we?' he asked, careful to keep the thread of steely determination hidden and his tone light and easy. Instead of taking the chair directly opposite her, he went for the next one along, in the hope that the added space created by the diagonal offset would help her relax, make it appear less like they were facing off across an interrogation table. For much the same reason, he'd kept the lighting low and subtle – although he couldn't say the idea of shining a spotlight in her eyes to force her secrets out of her didn't hold a certain attraction. His patience wasn't infinite. 'Ah, yes. The working life and times of Ms Annabel Frost.' He tore off a corner of the bread and helped himself to a paper-thin strip of prosciutto. 'How did you manage to make assistant manager in an establishment like Cluny's by the time you were twenty-one? I know how exacting Richard can be. Be honest now. Did you fudge your CV?'

The little goad was all it took to get her off the back foot of defence and onto the attack. She bit instantly, like she always did.

'Of course not,' she said with affront. 'I'd had a good six

years' experience by then. I started working as a part-time kitchen hand at fifteen.'

'That must have played havoc with your teenage social life?'

She shrugged and picked up a crumbled piece of the tangy parmigiano. 'It was only my mother and me at that point. We didn't have enough that I could've afforded a social life without the job. And I didn't have any spare time for one with.'

Aidan nodded. He wondered if that answered the question of where all of Annabel Frost's friends were. It appeared Tim's observation had been right: there seemed to be no sign of anyone in her life apart from her mother. And that bastard Tony Maplin. If she'd had to sacrifice her youth for the sake of gaining some financial security, that would explain a lot.

He wanted to ask her. About that and so much else, but he knew he had to take things slowly, pick and choose very carefully what to push her on. So he went in the opposite direction from the one he wanted. 'Well, that would explain why you've no head at all for drink. Missing out on all those formative drunken years meant you never built up your tolerance.'

It worked. She gave him a little smile. 'And as you're such an expert with hangover cures I take it you're speaking from experience. Is that how you spent your formative years, then?'

'Face down in the gutter? Of course. It's practically the law in Ireland to start building a tolerance from birth, so it is,' he told her, exaggerating his accent for effect. 'And then to keep trying to increase it all through your adult years.'

That earned him a slightly bigger smile. He watched as she reached for the bread and tore off a pinch, dipping into the shallow dish of oil and balsamic before rushing the dripping mass to her mouth.

'So washing dishes at fifteen led you to assistant manager

at Cluny's at twenty-one, and now manager by twenty-seven. You don't need me to tell you that's as far as you can go there. Somehow, given your age and your, ah – *character*, I don't think you'll be content sticking with that. All the hard work, all that determination and drive, has got to lead you on to something bigger. Surely you've thought of where you go from here?'

She looked at him for a moment. Looked as though she had something she wanted to say, something that was simply bursting to come out.

'Ideally?' she said in a rush, obviously having no choice but to release the pressure he'd seen building. 'I'd like to run my own place.' She looked as though she could barely contain her excitement, then looked quite horrified that she'd actually revealed it. 'You, know. Eventually,' she qualified.

He didn't react to any of it, didn't fuss. Just popped an olive into his mouth and spoke around it. 'You'd be good at it. There's always a demand for quality places in London.'

'Oh, no. Not London. I'd like a place in the country.'

Now that did surprise him. Her carefully cultivated appearance was pure city girl – sleek and urbane. 'I didn't have you down as a bumpkin, Annabel.'

She went for another pinch of bread. 'It was where I grew up,' she said as she dipped in the oil. 'My parents owned a country inn.'

And then she'd lost her father, lost whatever that childhood had been. It made sense that she'd be drawn to something similar, maybe try to recreate something of what she'd lost. He studiously avoided asking about any of the things he really wanted to know about her past. 'Sounds fun. And you got to help out?'

She finished chewing and nodded. Another small smile played on her lips, but he knew this one wasn't for him. This faint trace of a curve was for the play of memories only she could see. 'I got to get in the way a lot. My father was a chef, Mum covered front of house and the accommodation. I was always running around. It was fun – busy, warm, always full of life . . .'

Her words trailed off and he saw a hint of sadness creep into those green eyes. Then she blinked and the shutters slammed down as she came back to herself. Sent him a wary look.

'You're doing fine, Annabel,' was all he said, even though he wanted to tell her that it sounded like she'd lost a lot, even though he wanted to gather her in his arms and make her forget about everything but him. Now.

'I don't . . .' she started and stalled. Reaching for her glass, she took a swallow of water. 'I don't like talking about myself.'

'I already know that, *a mhuirnín*. What I don't understand is why not?'

He could see her jaw beginning to set, knew she was preparing to retreat. 'I just prefer to keep my personal things private. I don't see why that's such an issue.'

Now that was the sort of non-answer he *was* prepared to push on. 'Listen to me.' He leant forward and rested his arms on the table. 'It is an issue, and whether you get past it now or try to hold out is up to you. Just be aware that when I do finally get my hands on you, you're going to be stripped bare, body and soul.' He kept his tone calm but let her see the resolve in his eyes. 'When I take you for the first time you're going to find I'm buried so deep in every part of you that there'll be nothing personal or private left.'

He saw her breath catch at the explicit image his words drew, but she wasn't happy with the attached conditions. 'Listen to you? Why should I, when you won't listen to me?'

'I am listening, Annabel,' he said patiently. 'The trouble is that you're hardly saying anything at all.'

She gasped in outrage. 'That just proves my point. I've been saying plenty. Right from the start. You just choose to ignore it and carry on demanding that everything happens your way.'

His gaze rested on the pulse point at the base of her throat, showing him how agitated she was getting. While he wanted her a little hot under the collar, and more likely to let slip her guard, he didn't want this to escalate into a full-out argument. Not with what he was planning next. He calmed his voice and leant back in his chair. 'So tell me now. What it is that scares you so much about letting me get close? Why are you so afraid to trust yourself in this?'

'Me?' Her eyes went wide with disbelief and she snorted. 'You're joking. You're the one who keeps insisting that I hand over complete control. It's not myself I don't trust.'

'Oh, but I'm afraid it is. You can't begin to trust me, or anyone else for that matter, until you learn to trust yourself. It's your own self-doubt that's keeping you locked up. Why is that? What do you fear will happen if you let me get past those defences?'

He'd obviously struck too close for Annabel's comfort.

'That I'll be trapped for eternity having to listen to you drone on and on.' The sarcasm dripping from her answer left no doubt that she was trying to deflect him.

'Do you actually do anything but talk?'

Aidan looked at her for a long moment, those pale eyes piercing into her and the merest hint of amusement kicking up one corner of his mouth. She sat, breathless, waiting to see if she'd pushed him into action. Seriously, couldn't the man just shut up and kiss her?

'Keep speaking to me like that, Ms Frost, and you'll find out exactly what I can do.' His voice had taken on a growling quality that brushed against her nerve endings. 'But not before time. Now, stop trying to push me away and tell me, what are you so afraid of?'

She didn't bother to try to hide her sigh. So, no action then. Just more talking.

'Who says I'm afraid of anything?'

'I do. Everyone's afraid of something.'

'Even you?' He'd left himself wide open with that. Let him see how he liked to be challenged.

He frowned as though he thought the question strange. 'Of course me,' he admitted easily.

Oh. Did he mean that? 'So if we're sharing it's only fair that you tell me what you're afraid of.'

He didn't miss a beat. 'I thought that was obvious? That we won't ever reach that place of trust we need to be in for me to touch you like you need to be touched. I'm afraid that you won't ever let me get close enough to know you.'

She was taken aback by the sincerity, his earnestness. He sat there looking at her. Looking at her and waiting.

He'd given her an answer and now he wanted one in return. And Annabel suspected he'd wait all night to get it if he had to. She might as well save them both the interminable bother. If he could be honest, so could she. It wasn't like she didn't have a considerable list of Aidan-Flynn-inspired fears to choose from.

'I'm afraid of giving you any more control. I don't like the idea of you making me do things I don't want to do.' Well, any *more* things, allowing for what he'd already made her do.

'But I can't. You wouldn't do anything you didn't want to do.' He frowned for a moment then his expression cleared. 'Maybe that's what's really scaring you.'

She shifted uncomfortably in her chair as that possibility sank in. Maybe.

Sitting forward again, Aidan pushed his plate to one

side and folded his arms on the table, the snug-fitting top making it obvious that not only did he have the sexiest forearms she'd ever seen, but that the leanly defined strength carried on all the way up to some pretty stunning biceps, too.

'Annabel, we said no more games, so here it is. Neither of us is trying to deny the obvious attraction we have for each other. And I don't think there's any doubt that we both want this thing between us to end in a sweaty heap of satisfaction. The only problem we have is agreeing on how to get there, and how to make the most of the journey. And that comes back to trust.

'You are afraid. And that's OK, as long as you don't let the fear rule you. And the only way to get past fear is to face it. Take a risk. With that in mind, will you let me try something, here, now?'

'Try what?' She eyed him with caution.

He pushed to his feet and walked to open one of the drawers set into the base of the kitchen island. He held up another of the white linen napkins, letting the pressed folds fall open.

'Will you let me blindfold you?'

Annabel grabbed the edge of the table with both hands as the room seemed to tilt around her. 'No way.'

'And now that you've got that entirely predictable knee-jerk reaction out of your system,' Aidan said, coming back to the table but choosing the chair directly opposite her this time, instead of taking the one he'd originally occupied, 'will you tell me why not?'

'Because I'm not stupid?'

'No. Far from it.' He laid the napkin out on the table in front of him and folded it in half lengthways. 'So why not?'

She cast around for a more solid reason. 'I hardly even

know you!' She couldn't drag her gaze away from where his hands, those deft fingers, folded the thickly woven, restaurant-quality napkin a second time.

'You know enough, Annabel,' he said quietly, his hands stilling. 'Do you think I'm going to hurt you?'

She looked up into his face. Into the translucent depths of those silvery eyes that threatened to steal so much from her. She'd be the worst kind of fool not to acknowledge that he was a danger to her wellbeing, capable of causing her considerable hurt if she wasn't careful, but not in the physical sense he meant.

'No. But it's still asking too much.'

'Is it?' He tilted his head a little to the side as he watched her. 'Even though you just jumped on the back of my bike and entrusted your life to me? Because the way I see it, nearly a third of a tonne of high-powered metal speeding down rain-slicked roads presented way more of a threat to you than a square of soft linen.'

She hadn't thought about it like that. 'That was different.'

'Yes and no.' He put a final fold into the napkin, smoothing the long, narrow length before sliding it to one side and looking at her again. 'It's still about trust. And as you've now proved that you can put your trust in me – because you've already, although apparently unwittingly, done so – then all that's left to prove is whether you trust yourself.'

Annabel felt her eyes narrow as she tried to keep up with his reasoning but the bottom line was, it didn't matter how he'd reached his conclusion. He'd challenged her to prove herself and her pride wouldn't allow her to leave that unanswered.

Her heart rate exploded into a frantic rhythm as she reached across the table and snagged the end of the makeshift blindfold to pull it towards her.

Picking it up by both ends, she looked pointedly at Aidan Flynn. 'This is me trusting myself,' she told him, raising the folded strip of linen and placing it over her eyes. She tied a knot at the back of her head and then brought her hands down to rest against the edge of the table. Forced herself to sit still, to appear calm.

SIXTEEN

The echo of her own breathing resonated in her head, making her realise that the blindfold had covered her ears as well as her eyes. She strained to pick up any hint of noise from beyond her dark, muffled world, but as the moments ticked by there was nothing but the rush of breath growing louder, faster.

She actually jumped when Aidan spoke at last. 'You can remove it any time you need to,' he said with gravity, and Annabel's sense of hearing instantly locked on the sound. 'And if at any point you find that you don't like what's happening, you can tell me to stop and I will. You have my word on that.'

She heard the rustle of his clothing as he moved, sat frozen and tried to calm her breathing so she could keep track of his whereabouts. Calming anything became impossible as she heard him approach and come to stand directly behind her.

'You have all the power in this.' His voice suddenly beside her linen-covered ear made her flinch. 'You always have had, whether you realise it or not, and that won't change.'

She didn't feel like she had the power. She felt like she'd

lost all control, felt small and vulnerable. There was a scrape as the chair beside her was repositioned, the grating sound making her fingertips dig into the table top.

Then she felt the pressure of his grip closing on the back of the chair she sat in. 'I'd like you to let go of the table, *a mhuirnín*. I'm going to swing you part way around so I can see you better.'

It wasn't an easy thing to do, give up the touch anchoring her to her surroundings. But then nothing Aidan Flynn wanted was easy. As soon as she loosened her grip, the chair beneath her began to move, and she grabbed onto the sides of the seat instead to keep her balance.

She felt even more vulnerable when she followed the sound of his movements around to the front of her. There was no barrier between them now. She felt exposed. Especially when he made no noise of any sort for over a minute.

She strained to try to pick up any sound that would give her a clue as to what he was doing, but there was nothing. The utter silence was unnerving. Was she sure he was even still there?

'Aidan?' she asked when she couldn't stand it a second longer.

'Yes, Annabel?' he answered from not far away.

'What are you doing?'

'I'm looking at you. Taking my time to study every inch of you in detail.'

She shifted self-consciously, pressing her legs together.

'How does that make you feel? Knowing I'm looking at you, when you can't see me?'

It made her feel prickly all over as she tried to imagine which part of her his gaze was on. She shifted on the chair again but couldn't bring herself to answer.

'It's amazing how losing your sight heightens all the other senses, don't you think?' he said, his voice starting to move

190

away to one side. 'Everything becomes so much more acute. Touch, taste – sound.'

She started as a soft mechanical whirring filled the air around her.

'Don't worry, it's just the automated blinds going down on the windows. I thought you might like a bit of privacy from my neighbours. I know I don't want to share you.'

His words sent a thrill through her. What were they going to be doing that required privacy? God, please let him get around to touching her at last. Surely this must be sufficient demonstration of her readiness?

'Something similar happens with trust and surrender. Giving up something of yourself to your partner intensifies the emotional and physical bond and amplifies the pleasure. Let's see how far we can stretch this new trust between us, right now.' His voice came close again, closer than before, drew down level with her face. 'I want to look at more of you, Annabel. Will you let me undo your shirt so I can do that?'

She swallowed. Gripped the sides of the chair. Nodded.

She heard him move, felt his touch alight on her shirt, fingers undoing one button at a time with such a lightness of touch that all she could feel was her shirt brushing against her skin like butterfly wings. She shivered at the sensation, at the feel of the fabric parting bit by bit and the slide of her shirt tails being pulled gently from her waistband. Tried not to pant as Aidan reached the end, undoing the last button and pushing the shirt open to her shoulders.

'You do have the prettiest underwear, Annabel,' he said in a voice that sounded like it scraped against a dry throat.

She did, she knew. It was probably her greatest indulgence. Today she'd chosen delicate mint-green satin sprayed with the tiniest red rosebuds. He rustled and moved, and she tracked the sound as he circled around behind her, then the shirt was lifted back off her shoulders, slid down her arms and off. Nothing done quickly, everything maddeningly, sensuously slow.

Annabel let out a long, shaky breath.

'So pretty that I'd like to take your skirt off, too.' Aidan's voice was close to her ear again. The heat of him radiated against the newly exposed skin of her shoulders. 'Check whether you're wearing a matching set. Or even better, nothing at all.'

A breath of nervous laughter escaped her at the teasing quality of his tone. She was so tense with anticipation, every muscle drawn so tight that she was almost levitating above the chair.

'Annabel?' She felt pressure at the waistband of her skirt as his fingers rested against the fabric there, waiting for her okay. 'Would you like that? Or would you like me to stop?'

She shook her head. 'Don't stop,' she whispered.

The button released and she felt the give in the material around her stomach as the zip lowered. Aidan moved back around to the front and when he asked her to lift up, she didn't even hesitate, so swept away on sensation that all she could do was react. She pushed up on her hands and felt him tug the skirt down by the hem, exerting a steady pressure that dragged it in a slow glide over her hips and buttocks.

'Oh, yes. Matching and very pretty indeed,' he said with rich appreciation as her skirt reached her thighs and revealed her knickers. 'So pretty I can't even feign disappointment at discovering you're properly dressed today.' The skirt continued its steady path down past her knees and shins and when she settled her weight back on the chair so she could lift her feet free, the wood felt shocking against her bare flesh.

Then there was nothing but silence again. As the seconds dragged by it increased the feeling of vulnerability. She felt the tremble in her muscles as she pushed her thighs tight together. Senses on high alert, the entire surface of her skin tingled as though a brush of static electricity was making every tiny hair rise. After what seemed like an eternity she was driven to break the tension again. 'Aidan?' she whispered.

'I'm here,' he replied, stopping to clear his throat. 'Momentarily struck dumb by the picture you make. I don't remember anything at my table ever looking quite so appetising.'

Another little breath of laughter, another release of tension.

'God. Do you know how beautiful you are when you do that?'

'Do what?'

'Smile, laugh. It lights you up.'

As compliments went, she didn't think she'd ever received such a lovely one. She felt the warmth of her reaction to it blush across her cheeks, across her upper chest. Her mouth had turned so dry it took her a couple of attempts to re-moisten her parched lips with her tongue.

'I was concerned that maybe it wasn't warm enough in here, but you look as though you're starting to feel the heat, Ms Frost,' Aidan said. There was a rustle of movement and she heard the clink of ice against glass. 'Here, let me help.'

Annabel gasped at the freezing sensation of a wet ice cube meeting her mouth and Aidan took advantage to rub it over her parted lips, leaving her to lap up the moisture before it could run down her chin.

'Is that better?'

Annabel nodded. It was better. It was contact at last. Not quite skin to skin, but close enough for a start. 'Would you like me stop there, Annabel?' he asked, removing the ice.

'No,' she snapped with more force than she'd intended.

'You'd like me to cool you a little lower down?'

She nodded, ignoring the slight hitch of amusement in Aidan's tone.

The ice touched unexpectedly on her collarbone, tracing the line of it inwards to the little dip at the base of her throat, where she could feel her pulse pound against it. Goose flesh sprang up in its path.

'Tell me if you get too cold,' Aidan murmured, but Annabel was too busy concentrating on the feel of the ice cube painting watery paths across her skin as it glided downward to the swell of her breasts. 'But I have to say, right now you look like fire. The flames are casting a glow over your skin here, *a mhuirnín*, turning it to gold.' The ice dipped into the top of her cleavage, held there until a droplet broke free and started trickling its way southward, making her shudder at the tickly feel. In no particular rush, the cube traced along the upper edge of one bra cup, followed by the other, leaving tingling trails in its path and making her nipples push hard against the constraining fabric.

And then it was gone. Annabel heard a humming sound of pleasure before Aidan spoke. 'You are delicious, Ms Frost.'

He'd tasted it? Licked it, sucked it into his mouth after it had been on her skin?

'Would you like me to stop there?'

Would she hell. How could he even ask it? She gave her head a vehement little shake.

'You'd like me keep going lower?'

She nodded.

'Tell me, Annabel.'

'Yes.'

'How far down? Just to here?' The ice touched her solar plexus, traced slow figures of eight across her ribs, the warming effect of her flesh causing little rivulets to begin trickling down her stomach.

'Or here?' It followed the vertical line that bisected her

abdominal muscles down to spiral leisurely around the dip of her navel.

'Or even further – all the way down here?' It inched its way down to the waistband of her knickers.

Lips pressed together to keep from moaning like a wanton, Annabel nodded again.

'Which one? You'll have to tell me.'

'All the way down,' she said, hyper aware that all that stood between his fingertips and her flesh was one little block of ice that was melting fast.

He followed the upper edge of silk all the way out to one hipbone and then all the way to the other before coming back to the centre and stopping. Annabel waited as the tension grew thick again.

'Open your legs a little.' Her body obeyed before her mind could object. She couldn't breathe as she did it – parted her thighs, just a little. Just enough that Aidan took it as an invitation to run the ice cube down over the silk of her underwear, the thin barrier offering no protection from the freezing sensation against her sensitive flesh. Up and down he ran it in sensuous strokes, applying just the right amount of pressure for her to feel it to delve into the valley of her sex, making the secret flesh there ache and leaving her shivering with want and need as much as cold. She began to squirm, to arch her back, push against the chilly caress, seeking more. Seeking the warmth of his fingers instead. When she let out a shuddery sigh at the thought of how good they would feel, Aidan broke the silence for the first time in ages.

'Are you imagining how it will feel when I make you come for me? I've been wondering how it will be. If you're the type to cry out loud, or gasp and bite your lip in an attempt to hold it all in,' he told her. 'If you tremble and shake all the way down to your toes, or bow your body in a graceful arch. Whether you'll come hard and fast against me, or unravel soft and slow in my arms.'

She made a little noise in her throat.

'Take the blindfold off,' he commanded in a rasping voice.

Considering her earlier resistance to putting the thing on, Annabel was surprised by the rush of reluctance she felt at the idea of now removing it. Somehow it was easier to hide from her doubts and fears in the dark.

She removed it and blinked a few times in the subdued lighting. Aidan was on his knees between her legs, his eyes dark with desire. Lowering his gaze, he let it run slowly down the front of her to where he withdrew the ice cube from between her legs.

'I've made your underwear all damp.'

God. Not just her underwear.

He slowly lifted the melting cube up to his mouth. 'Do you think this tastes of you, Ms Frost?' he asked, then opened his lips and sucked on the dripping ice.

She felt an answering flutter between her legs. Nearly moaned out loud when his tongue swept out to lick at the drops clinging to the full curve of his lower lip and said, 'Now it tastes of both of us.'

He brought it her mouth and slipped it in past her lips, careful not to let even a fingertip come into contact with her. Technically, he still hadn't touched her. Despite the state she was in, he hadn't let his skin touch hers.

She sucked on the ice cube, which of course tasted just like ice. Not that that made the sharing of it any less sexy.

'Annabel, I'd like to ask you something.'

As long as it was permission to remove her underwear and see to the ache he'd created between her thighs, she had no objection. She'd demonstrated her trust, hadn't she? She was ready. In fact, she'd rarely been so ready in her life. She closed her eyes and felt a delicious shudder of anticipation run through her. 'What?'

'As you know, I've booked a day off the Saturday directly after New Year.'

Wait . . . *What?* Her eyes sprang back open. More talking? About *work*?

'A friend of mine has taken a table at a charity ball and I have two tickets. I'd like you to come as my guest.'

She was utterly taken aback. Stunned into silence. Aidan Flynn wanted to take her to a ball? Who was she, Cinderella?

'It's going to be quite a big event by all accounts, very lavish.' He dropped his gaze to allow it to roam over her still semi-naked form, drawing in a deep breath of appreciation. 'And as much as I'd love to take you looking just as you do now, I think the dress code calls for a little more formality. Do you have a suitable gown?' he asked.

She had something long and black that she'd bought years ago hanging somewhere in the back of her wardrobe. 'Yes, but—'

'Good. What about a current passport?'

That shocked her out of her stupor. 'Passport?'

He nodded. 'Yes, the ball's in Vienna.'

'*Vienna!* I can't go to Vienna.'

'Why not?'

All sorts of reasons. Starting with the fact that she kept a passport as a useful form of ID, but she'd never had cause to put it to its proper use. Had never been out of England.

'I don't have any time off scheduled for a start,' she went with offering the least complicated excuse.

'No. But the trip's only for two days. Flying out on Friday – New Year's Day, when we're closed anyway, and back in time for Sunday lunch service. It would mean taking one day off. Tim can cover for you easily.'

'Of course he can't. No one at Cluny's can know anything

197

about this . . . us.' She gave him a sharp look and crossed her arms as a horrible thought flitted across her mind. 'You haven't mentioned it to him, have you?'

'No. And there's no need for you to mention it either. You're the only member of staff who'll have been working without a break over the Christmas period. It's perfectly reasonable to swap a shift and take a day off without arousing suspicion.'

'But not a Saturday,' she insisted a little desperately, worried that the conversation was running away from her.

'The quietest Saturday of the year,' Aidan countered with that composed implacability she recognised only too well. He was settling in to argue his point until he won.

'Why do we have to talk about this now?' Annabel complained, uncrossing her arms again and arching her torso forward in invitation. 'Don't we have something more important to finish?'

She was pleased to note Aidan's gaze drop to her chest and felt a thrill run through her at the potent intensity of it when it came back up to lock onto hers. 'We do. That's why I want you to come away with me. I want you all to myself, and I don't want to have to rush things.'

'Why do we have to be away for that? You're hardly rushing things now,' she said with an accusatory edge to her tone that only made him smile.

'I'd like the chance to spend some time getting to know you better, far from everything here – all the distractions, the excuses,' he said. 'Say you'll think about it at least.'

He was trying to bribe her with sex. No two ways about it. And while it was impossible for her to make a decision until she could think straight, she couldn't see the harm in agreeing to give it some thought, especially if it would make him stop talking and get back to action. 'I'll think about it.'

'Good.' He flashed her such a beautiful smile that she felt an answering one curve her own lips. His gaze immediately dropped to her mouth, darkened in a way that made her hold her breath even as she felt herself drawn slowly forward.

'And now I'd better get you home.' Aidan pulled back and rose to his feet.

Annabel's spine snapped upright. '*What?*' she demanded, watching in disbelief as he reached for where he'd draped her clothes over the back of a nearby chair.

'It's nearly one. Already Christmas Eve. We've got a busy day ahead,' he reasoned, holding her shirt for her put on. 'Time to go.'

'Oh no.' Instead of hooking her arm in the waiting sleeve, Annabel snatched the garment from Aidan's hand. 'You are *not* doing this to me again.'

'Doing what?' he asked, looking down at her with infuriating calm.

'Leaving me in this state!' she nearly screamed. He was not going to turn this into another exercise in frustration and shame like The Hyde. She couldn't stand it.

A slow, wicked smile curved his lips, telling her she was going to have to stand it. 'But I like you in this state, Annabel,' he admitted. 'And if it's any consolation, I'm as frustrated as you are.'

She glanced down and saw that he wasn't lying. The hard evidence of it was plain in the bulge of his jeans.

She looked determinedly back up into his face. 'Hey, simple solution here.'

Aidan just laughed at that and retrieved her skirt. 'As I've already told you, *a mhuirnín*, I don't want simple.' He passed the garment to her. 'Now wrap up warm, it'll be cold on the bike.'

By rights, the look she gave him should have incinerated

him on the spot, or turned him to stone at the very least. But instead it only encouraged him to give her one of his lop-sided smiles. 'Trust me, the pay off will be worth the wait, Annabel. I promise.'

SEVENTEEN

'Hi, Aidan.'

Glancing over his shoulder from the open locker in front of him, Aidan smiled as Donna came into Cluny's small staff room set across the hall from Annabel's office.

'Donna, hello. How are you today?'

'I, um, have something for you.'

'For me?' He closed the locker door and turned to face her, noticing the small pink polka-dot cake box in her hand.

'What's this?' he asked, taking the box and opening it to reveal a cupcake decorated with tiny white and pink and red heart sprinkles. Oh, no. 'Ah. You made this?'

Donna nodded shyly. 'You said how much you like cake the night of your birthday.'

Had he? He remembered chatting to Donna in the Louche Lounge but in all honesty couldn't recall much of what had been said. It had been a Saturday night after all and the volume of the music had been pumped right up to satisfy the weekend party crowd.

'Well, thank you,' he said, watching her head to the lockers and hoping his suspicions about the motivation behind the offering were wrong even though those bright edible hearts declared otherwise. 'That's very kind. It looks delicious.'

She fiddled with the lock in front of her for a moment before looking at him out of the corner of her eye. 'Taste it now if you like.'

What could he do? Taking the cupcake from the box he took a hefty bite and swiped little hearts off his lips with his thumb. 'Mmm. Tastes as good as it looks. You're a great cook.'

'I don't know about that,' she demurred at the same time as looking delighted by the compliment. 'I just love to bake. Perhaps you'd like to come over some time and I could show you? I make brilliant croissants.'

Oh, dear. If she was offering breakfast food it was definitely a come-on. The bashful Donna had found the courage to flirt, but the last thing he wanted to do was lead her on. As uncomfortable as a rejection was going to be, especially to that budding newfound spirit, it was better to end this now, and to do it as kindly as possible.

'Thank you for the invitation but I don't think that's such a good idea.'

'Oh?' She looked suddenly crestfallen.

'Forgive me if I'm wrong, but I think our expectations might be a little different.' He watched her expression drop further. 'You're very lovely, Donna. And I'm immensely honoured, but believe me, I'm not the man for you.'

She looked momentarily pole-axed but rushed to pull on a brave face. 'Oh, I didn't mean . . .' she started to lie then nodded as her face crumpled. 'Oh God, I'm sorry,' she cried, turning her attention to getting her locker open and depositing her handbag inside.

'Hey, now.' He gave her an understanding smile. 'There's nothing to be sorry about. As I said, I'm honoured. I just know we're not right for one another.'

202

At that, a tear escaped and ran down her cheek, making him feel like a total heel. Reaching across the distance between them, he gave her shoulder a fortifying squeeze. 'Please don't be upset.'

'I – I'm just so embarrassed,' she said, staring hard into the locker and not at him.

He gave her arm a bolstering rub. 'You want to hear embarrassing?' he confided. 'I once crushed so hard on a colleague that I did everything to try and put myself in her path, up to and including arranging to "coincidentally" run into her one day at this yoga session I'd discovered she attended. There I was, posing in my gym kit thinking I was everything cool as I smooth-talked her into thinking I was an expert at this particular form of yoga when she called me out by asking how many weeks gone I was. Turns out it was a specialist class for strengthening the birth muscles in pregnant women.'

It worked: her own distress had been momentarily forgotten, wiped from Donna's face by the look of fascinated horror that had replaced it as she turned to face him.

He nodded. 'True story.'

'Oh, no!' she said, her hand covering her mouth in shock. 'What happened after that?'

'Not the happy ending I'd been hoping for, that was for sure. And to this day I can't see anything to do with yoga without cringing.' He popped the rest of the cake into his mouth.

That earned a giggle from behind her hand.

'When you're quite finished there, Donna,' Annabel's voice came from the doorway behind them, icy and clipped. 'Perhaps you'd like to get on with what you're paid to do?'

Donna jumped before he released her and turned.

Annabel looked right at him. 'And if you've nothing better

to do with your time then I'm sure the kitchen staff could use some help putting out the rubbish.'

She spun and stormed through the door into her office.

Donna rushed to close her locker and scurry off to the dining room while he gave the door opposite a thoughtful look before approaching it.

Before he'd made it across the hallway, the door opened again, revealing a glinting-eyed Annabel. 'What are you still doing here?' she demanded, cuttingly cold.

He made sure to meet that daggered look. 'I want to know what that was all about.'

'How dare you! You don't get to question me here. I was doing my job, which is more than could be said for you. This isn't a social club – if you want to fraternise with your colleagues, do it in your free time, not on the company's. Just get out there and do what you're paid to do. I have nothing more to say to you.'

She looked about to charge past him so he stepped forward, filling the doorway.

'Sorry, Annabel, but I think you've still got plenty to say. And I think you need to say it.'

'And who cares what you think?' Instead of trying to battle her way past, she let go of the door and turned and walked back inside the office.

Aidan followed her before it could swing closed. 'I think *you* care about something here to be getting so worked up.'

She swung on him. 'Oh, I care. I care that I get value for money out of my employees. I care that they respect that they're here to work, not flirt with each other.'

'Flirt? That's what you think was going on with Donna? She was upset, Annabel. I was offering her some comfort.'

Annabel actually advanced a few steps towards him, seething. 'You were *laughing*! Both of you. I heard it. I saw it. Laughing and touching. So I guess the joke's on me, eh?

204

I deserve it for being such a fool, for letting you try and fuck with my head with your twisted games when it's obvious you're capable of being entirely normal with women.'

'This is about me touching Donna? It was a sympathetic hug nothing more. It didn't mean anything beyond a casual act of kindness. I'm flattered by your jealousy but Donna is nothing to me but a colleague.'

'I'm not jealous,' she raged.

'Oh, yes you are.' And the idea delighted him to the extent that he couldn't help the smile that stretched across his mouth even though it was likely to get him killed. 'Those lovely eyes are flashing as green as emeralds.'

'You can forget about this,' she sneered before turning and walking towards her desk. 'I'm finished with you. This is over.'

No, it wasn't. He felt his fists clench at his sides. 'It hasn't even begun, Annabel.'

'Exactly!' She pirouetted to glare at him. 'And I'm starting to doubt it ever will. You keep saying you'll touch me but you never do. If you really wanted me then you'd show me. You'd stop this silly power game and touch me!'

Annabel's angry taunt ignited the smouldering fuse of his own frustration. In a few strides he was across the room, bulldozing her back against the bank of filing cabinets.

He slammed his hands onto the metal cabinet either side of her, bent his face close. 'Do you have any idea how hard it is to keep my hands *off* you?' he all but shouted back. 'Every fucking day I have to fight myself, Annabel. And every day it gets harder.'

She breathed hard as she looked up at him, grabbed his shirt front in an attempt to pull him closer. 'Then don't fight it, do it.'

For a split second all he was aware of was the feel of her touch. He wasn't sure how, but he found the strength to resist. He hadn't come this far to risk it all in a moment of weakness. 'The moment you're ready, so help me, I will.'

Her hands stopped pulling and shoved sharply against his chest instead. 'That's such bullshit. I've done everything you've asked.' She was shaking with anger, but more importantly, with emotion. Whatever she might say otherwise, that was proof enough for him that Annabel Frost did care.

'And this is your definition of ready?' He ruthlessly pushed his advantage. 'You think this little hissy fit is a demonstration of your trust?' Her eyes widened at his insult but he didn't give her time to get sidetracked by it. 'Do you?' he demanded, right in her face.

'I don't know,' she yelled back in his.

'Keep your voice down,' he warned. 'Someone will hear.'

'I don't care!' she raged, her ire over-riding her common sense. 'I don't know what more you want from me.'

'For fuck's sake, Annabel.' He slammed both his palms against the filing cabinet in frustration, making her flinch. 'You do know. I just want you to say yes. Say yes and mean it.'

'I've said yes.'

'You've said the word, but you're the one still fighting. Stop! Stop fighting and show me that you mean it right here, right now. Say yes to Vienna. Say yes to giving me everything. Say yes to it all.'

Her eyes were flashing, chest heaving, her lips parted so she could suck in air. Sexual tension was thick in the room. Their heated exchange had ignited more than her temper, it had fired her blood. His too. He felt every bit as aroused as she looked. Christ, he could only imagine the mess they'd make of each other, their clothes, the office if he let his control snap, if he wedged her roughly against the filing cabinet and claimed her mouth, her body, like he wanted to do.

He let his chin drop to his chest, closing his eyes, breathing

206

deep. The exotic scent of her filled him, left its taste on the back of his tongue.

'Annabel.' His voice was a reedy scrape of sound but he didn't try to hide it, or cover the depth of his yearning. She needed to know how much this meant. He opened his eyes and opened himself, letting her see just what it meant to him right there in his gaze. 'Say yes.'

Her own eyes widened as they searched his and caught a glimpse of what he'd laid bare. Then she seemed to shrink in height as all the tension drained out of her body. She let out a sigh and when she answered him, her own voice wasn't much better than a thready scratch either. 'Yes.'

When Annabel tried to casually mention the news over Christmas breakfast the following morning, her mother's reaction was everything she'd dreaded it being. Beside herself with excitement, Ellen all but started compiling lists of names for her future grandchildren.

As they sat there wearing paper crowns from the crackers her mother had insisted they pull as part of the only celebratory meal they'd share for the day, it was impossible for Annabel not to feel a stab of guilt over leaving her. 'But are you sure you'll be all right on your own?'

'I'll be fine.' She brushed Annabel's concern away in favour of apparently more important matters. 'What are you wearing?'

'Really? That?' she asked critically once she'd harried Annabel into the bedroom and assessed the dress that was pulled from its protective dust cover.

'Yes. Why not?' It smelled slightly musty from neglect but, having only been worn once before, was as long, black and classically practical as the day she'd bought it. She couldn't see anything wrong with it that a trip to the dry cleaners wouldn't sort out.

'You're going to a Viennese ball to waltz in a skirt that tight?'

Waltz? Was she serious? Did anyone under retirement age waltz any more? Annabel eyed the slim column of silk. 'Well I don't have anything else.' And as she'd already insisted on paying her share of the trip – including having a room of her own – she wasn't wasting any money on getting something new. 'It's this or nothing.'

Although Ellen didn't say anything further, the look she tried to hide by turning away said she considered 'nothing' to be the better option.

And that look haunted Annabel for days until a fit of doubt had her asking questions of Google that swiftly led to her seeking answers from one of Cluny's regular customers, Ivy Lord, a local businesswoman who ran an exclusive dress hire company.

'Oh, yes. Viennese balls are all about the dancing,' the vibrantly dressed Ivy said, sizing Annabel up where she stood in the centre of an equally vibrant private Soho showroom lined with rails of clothing. 'And they're taken very seriously. There are over two hundred major balls crammed into their winter carnival season alone . . .' she continued talking as she walked to the rear wall of the showroom and started skimming her fingers over the tops of the hangers '. . . most of which preserve and observe strict traditions that represent the height of civilised society.' Fingers stopping suddenly, she grasped a hanger and unhooked it. 'Now this Westwood would be perfect.'

Ivy spun to face her, holding a strapless but full-skirted gown in shades Annabel would describe as olive and khaki.

'Not many people can carry the colour,' Ivy said, her thoughts running in the same vein as Annabel's. 'But with your ethereal complexion . . .' She pursed her lips in contemplation. 'Try it on.'

Twenty minutes later, still doubtful about the entire adventure, let alone the dress, but having succumbed to Ivy's firm assurances, as well as the special discounted deal she offered, Annabel stepped out onto the street with the roped silk handles of a large dress bag looped over her shoulder.

Annabel knew she'd been too rash in agreeing to this. Of the multitude of reasons she could list in support of this being the worst idea of her life, she was currently preoccupied with just one. She'd never been on a plane before. And as the engines roared to life and the force of the acceleration down the runway left the craft shuddering around her, she doubted she'd live to find herself on one ever again. Gripping the armrests of the window seat she was plastered to, she tried not to throw up as, with a sickening lurch, the plane left the earth – and her stomach – behind.

However, that sensation was nothing compared to the bottomless horror she felt when she glanced out of the small window a moment later and saw the ground drop away beneath her at an alarming rate. Nor did it come close to the sheer terror that gripped her when the frightening view was suddenly obscured by a dense grey blanket and the plane started bumping around in mid-air.

Certain that something catastrophic was going on, that the aircraft was about to plummet back to earth, she cast frantic looks at her fellow passengers, only to find them in various states of relaxation – some reading, some chatting, some even snoozing. No one, it seemed, was paying the slightest bit of attention to the rough ride, or her panic-stricken fidgeting.

No one apart from Aidan, that was, who she found looking at her out of the corner of his eye with interest as she turned back around to resettle in her seat.

'All right?' he asked, the twitch at the side of his mouth telling her that, plainly, he didn't think she was.

For once she didn't care if he was making fun of her. She was too damned scared. 'I don't know. Am I?'

His expression changed to a frown at the starkness of her tone, all traces of amusement disappearing. 'What do you mean?'

'I mean, I've got no idea if any of this is right. I've never flown before.'

He blinked at her in astonishment. 'Why didn't you say something? I thought you seemed unduly fascinated by the crew safety demo.'

'And that's not helping,' she yelped as the plane gave another jump. 'Where did they all go? Why have they disappeared?'

'Everything's fine,' he assured her. 'The crew have to be seated for takeoff the same as everybody else. We're going through the cloud layer at the moment and the slight change in air density can make it a bit bumpy. We'll be out the top end in no time and things will smooth out then.'

Even as he said it, the plane emerged from the impenetrable grey mist into a sky of endless blue and sunshine.

'See? Look how beautiful it is,' Aidan coaxed, leaning forward to look out of the window beside her. 'So much nicer than the drizzle we left down below.'

But after only a quick glance, she turned away, preferring to keep her eyes trained on the solid bulk of the fuselage around her. No matter how beautiful the scenery, there was too much – *nothingness* out there for her liking.

'Once the seatbelt sign goes off we can swap seats if you like,' Aidan offered as he continued to regard her carefully.

She liked. The second the illuminated sign above their heads pinged off, she scrambled as far away from that window as possible, but didn't manage to relax at all.

210

She was only glad that none of Aidan's friends were travelling with them to witness her make a fool out of herself. By the time they were due to meet at a pre-arranged dinner tonight she was sure she'd be back in control.

When a member of the cabin crew appeared beside them pushing a trolley, Aidan tried to convince her to have a drink, a 'small one, just to take the edge off', but all she could manage was a glass of water. Ordering a Bloody Mary for himself, he waited until the trolley moved away down the aisle, then decided to pry: 'So where do you usually go on your holidays, Ms Frost, if you don't fly?'

'Nowhere.' Noticing that she was squeezing her plastic tumbler to the point where it might snap, she released it, resting her clenched fist on the little pull-out tray instead.

'Sorry, I don't follow you.'

'I mean I don't go on holiday.'

'Never?' Aidan sounded disbelieving.

She shook her head. 'Not for a long time.'

'Where was your last?'

'A weekend on the south coast. Brighton.'

'Great party town. Were you there for the clubs?'

'Hardly. I was nine.'

'Ah. That would have been a little young,' he laughed. 'So, that was with your family, then?'

She gave him an aggravated look and shifted in her seat, growing uncomfortable with the personal line of questioning.

As usual, he was quick to read her body language, and as usual he seemed determined to use it to his advantage, to push for maximum discomfort. 'We don't have to keep chatting if you don't want, Annabel. All things considered, I thought you might appreciate the distraction but –' he shrugged and let his head drop back against the seat, closing his eyes '– you can simply sit there and enjoy the flight if you prefer.'

She felt her own eyes narrow. He really was ruthless, but she had to grudgingly accept that he did have a point. 'Our family summer holiday,' she said. 'My parents' business meant they never had time for much more than a few days away.'

'Running your own place takes huge commitment and dedication,' he said, head up again and eyes regarding her intently. 'Obviously their work ethic rubbed off on you.'

She thought. 'The inn never seemed like work. Not to me, and I don't really think to them. It was – just our way of life.' Her bedroom had been in the eaves of the antiquated coaching inn, above the public rooms. She remembered lying in bed at night with the sound of laughter and conversation floating up through the old floorboards, her father's deep tones – sounds of happiness and security. Sounds that had wrapped around her like a blanket offering comfort and safety, offering the promise that everything in her world was all right. How wrong she'd been, how cold and uncertain a place her world had so quickly become.

How determined she was to create a safe place for herself again, one that no one could take away.

'Why don't you have holidays now?'

'I don't need them. To be honest, I don't even really think about them. I'm working towards something more important.'

'Your plans for your own place?'

She didn't answer. But yes, everything she did was towards that. The saving, the crippling mortgage to give her a credit rating, the perfect employment record, anything and every-thing she could do to present a loan-worthy prospect to the banks when she went looking for her start-up investment.

'You do realise that once that happens you'll likely be

back to the no holiday option. Don't you want to see the wonders of the world?'

'Of course. But I want security more. And, frankly, if flying is the best way of getting around then, I'm happy to stick with virtual travels through the internet and TV holiday shows.'

A little later into the flight, Aidan tried to sway her views by encouraging her to take advantage of the clear conditions and look out onto what the captain announced as the 'dramatic scene' of the snow-covered Alps. Intrigued despite herself, she took a peek out of the window, but quickly looked away again when her stomach somersaulted at the sight of how small and insignificant the majestic mountain range looked from this height.

Their descent into Vienna, which for Annabel couldn't come soon enough, brought a whole new set of challenges for her to panic about including the changing pitch in the engine noises, and the weird pressure in her ears, but at least there was no cloud layer for them to bump through, as the blue sky and sunshine stayed with them all the way down to the snow covered ground.

Bright though the afternoon was, there was nothing warm about the minus zero temperature that greeted them when they stepped outside the terminal.

Relieved to find herself back on solid ground but left shaken by the flight and feeling totally out of her depth, Annabel was more than grateful to hand over the reins and let someone else organise her for once. And Aidan Flynn was very adept at it. Before long they were ensconced in the heated comfort of a dark limousine heading right to the historic heart of Austria's capital.

Drinking in the sights as they swept along wide boulevards lined with grand mansions and museums it was easy to see why Vienna was classed among Europe's great cities. Seat of the powerful Habsburg Empire for centuries and a renowned centre for culture and music, it still retained much of the glory and grandeur of its imperial past. And dressed for the festive season as it currently was, it also offered the most perfect storybook representation of a traditional winter that she'd ever seen – with its scenes of pristine snow-covered parks and squares dominated by Christmas trees swathed in multi-coloured lights. In front of the magnificent gothic style town hall, an outdoor skating rink held more magical appeal than any equivalent set up in rain-drenched London could hope to. And everywhere she looked, there were decorations – even the trams trundling along the roads had their rooflines bedecked with ribbons and bows and baubles. As if she needed it, the whole experience gave her even more of a sense of being on a fairytale adventure.

As the car slowed to take a turn, Aidan pointed out the opera house, a beautiful Renaissance-style building fronted by two tiers of classical arches, where the ball was due to be held the following evening. Rounding the building, the driver pulled to a stop at the entrance to a pedestrianised shopping street which was flanked on each side by imposing Neoclassical-designed buildings housing five-star hotels. One, she noticed from the monogrammed burgundy canopies over its windows, was the Hotel Sacher, home of the famous Sacher-Torte, arguably the best chocolate cake in the world. The other – an equally grand-looking place – sported canopies of duck-egg blue with gold-printed lettering identifying it as Haus, their hotel for the next two nights. With its five-storey ivory-rendered façade embellished with snow-dusted pediments and each of the balustraded balconies decorated with a large tied bow of the same delicate blue to match the canopies, the place looked like a very large, very luxurious Christmas present.

Leaving the driver to deal with their luggage, Aidan guided

Annabel toward the entrance beside which two seven-foot high white Christmas trees stood sentry, adorned with silver bells and smaller velvet versions of the large blue bows.

Stepping into a hushed haven of refinement which continued the external colour theme of ivory and duck-egg blue, Annabel registered the sort of tastefully-understated, yet highly-finished décor that was the reserve of only the very finest of establishments and had to admit she was getting worried about the cost of this trip. Although the figure Aidan had quoted her for her share amounted to a large chunk of her Christmas bonus, she'd been adamant about paying for herself, keeping a level of autonomy, safeguarding her independence. But with the premium seats at the front of the plane, the chauffeur-driven car, the rarified opulence of the hotel, she was wondering how his calculations could possibly be right.

She was almost relieved to discover upon check-in that they'd been booked into a two-bedroom suite, which she supposed might help keep the costs down.

Or not.

The top-floor suite, when they were shown up to it, was enormous – taking up an entire corner of the building and offering views over the snow-blanketed rooftops and gothic spires of the old imperial centre. When Aidan offered her first choice of the bedrooms, she figured she may as well go for the whole fairytale and picked the one dominated by a spectacular carved four-poster bed.

With swift efficiency, the porter deposited their luggage and departed, pulling the door closed with a soft click behind him. And suddenly, finally, they were alone, and issues such as flying and finances no longer mattered. With no more distractions, the sexual tension that had been lying muted during their journey surged to the fore, charging the atmosphere as she looked across the room and met Aidan's eyes.

There was possession in the gaze he ran over her. Voracious, triumphant possession. Annabel's pulse set up a pounding in her ears as she watched his lips part to start forming the words she could hardly wait to hear.

But rather than suggest anything remotely along the lines of 'let's get naked', what he actually said was, 'Before you start getting any ideas, the answer is no – not yet.'

Before her mouth even had time to drop open, he continued. 'For one thing, you must be starving, you didn't eat anything on the flight.' Well no, she hadn't. She'd felt too sick to even try the light lunch that had been served, but . . . 'For another,' Aidan went on, crossing the space with a fluid prowl and stopping close to look down at her. 'There's no way I'm going to start something I won't have time to properly finish before we're due at the Reiser's in a couple of hours.'

Ah, yes, dinner, she vaguely recalled, helplessly caught by the intensity of that penetrating silvery gaze. 'Remind me who they are again?'

'Friends of the friend who invited us. I've met Karl before but not his wife Astrid. It's she who's on the fundraising committee for the charity that the ball's in aid of.'

'And remind me why we have to go to their dinner party tonight instead of staying here?' The piercing clarity of those eyes turned a little smoky as his stare dropped to her mouth, locking onto the hint of a pout she felt pulling at her lower lip.

'Because we said we would,' he said, with a definite note of regret in the words. 'And it'll give you the opportunity to meet some of the people we'll be attending the ball with tomorrow night.'

It was obvious to Annabel that they had a wildly differing set of priorities. While she was intrigued to find out what sort of people Aidan Flynn called friends, she wasn't so interested that she couldn't wait until tomorrow night. As thoughtful as it was that he was thinking of setting her at ease, years of dealing with customers from all walks in the restaurant trade meant she was more than capable of easing her way through most social situations.

'Having waited this long for you, Annabel, I don't intend to rush,' he said next, in a tone of absolute certainty and with a firm set to his jaw that blew out any idea she had of trying to make him do just that. 'For now, order something from room service, have a hot bath to soak away the stress of the journey, relax.'

Knowing it wouldn't get her anywhere, she didn't see the point in trying to argue with him. Especially when, if she was honest, the alternative he was offering didn't sound too bad at all. With the possible exception of improving on one point. 'Actually, instead of room service I'd love to go across the road for a slice of Sacher-Torte. It's my favourite cake.'

His gaze sharpened, dropping to her mouth again. 'Remembering how much I enjoyed watching your reaction to Anton's desserts, that sounds like the perfect foreplay, Ms Frost. Get your coat.'

Back in her room a while later, with her sweet tooth satiated and her queasy stomach calmed by coffee and, yes, very possibly the best chocolate cake in the world – which she may have consumed with a barely concealed rapture that had left Aidan shifting in his chair – Annabel flipped open the leather-bound guest folder as she waited for the bath to run, hoping to find some clue as to how much this little exercise in madness was going to set her back. She almost wished she hadn't looked when she spotted the small print at the bottom of the information sheet which proclaimed Haus as 'Part of the Harcourt Group of Hotels' – which was code for pricey. Too pricey for a bartender that was for sure.

Even one who lived in a very swish apartment and used to work in the world of finance.

When he'd mentioned his past connection to the City she'd assumed that, like many of his peers, Aidan had been a casualty of the global financial crisis. A lot of reputations had been ruined, jobs lost, and a lot of banking refugees had found themselves suddenly beggars instead of choosers, having to turn their hands to different forms of employment. It was that type of situation she'd figured Aidan must be in, because why else would a man so obviously used to a certain level of wealth and power be working the bar in his uncle's restaurant?

But if that was the case, she couldn't understand how the hell could he still afford things such as this hotel?

Wandering back into the en suite, she recalled the oblique comment he'd made about 'having contacts' when he'd wangled them into The Hyde. Maybe those 'contacts' were the same 'friends' they were meeting here in Vienna? She certainly hoped so, because if it turned out that Aidan had been less than honest with her about the cost and there were no mates' rates on offer, her weekend of playing Cinderella really was likely to end with her dressed in rags.

Stripping out of the fluffy robe she'd donned, she slipped into the warm, scented water of the bath, sighing in bliss as she reclined into the bubbles and closed her eyes. There were things about Aidan that just didn't add up and she was determined to confront him about it. But not until after they'd finally made it into bed together. She wasn't willing to risk a disagreement causing any more delays to that long-awaited event.

It was dark by the time they set off once again in the limo, Annabel wearing her trusty black cocktail dress that relied on the quality of its cut rather than any bling to see it through almost any occasion, while Aidan was possibly the sexiest she'd ever seen him – beyond stylish in open-necked shirt and midnight-blue lounge suit. Leaving the thriving commercial centre behind, they headed towards the western edge of the city, to a quiet, expensive residential area where the snow lay thicker and whiter on the ground, and the streets were lined with elegant mansions.

Turning into the drive of one such mansion – a pale stone affair, invitingly aglow with golden light spilling from its multitude of French windows which cast illuminated reflections across the pristine blanket of snow covering the front garden – the car swept them through open gates and pulled to a stop outside the front entrance.

Annabel shot Aidan a look of disbelief as they climbed the shallow steps of the portico, but before she could say anything, the glossy black, double-width door still decorated with a large Christmas wreath of evergreen, pine cones and red silk ribbons was swung open by a young man dressed in a black waistcoat who motioned them through a second set of doors.

They stepped into a vast double-height reception hall dominated by a curving staircase that swept up along one wall to a galleried mezzanine level that appeared to extend to the rear of the building. Through the ornate wrought iron balustrade, garlanded with more evergreen foliage and ribbons, groups of guests could be seen milling, and the sounds of chatter and laughter as well as the soft tinkling of piano keys drifted enticingly back down to the entrance.

In the centre of the expanse of polished parquet floor over which Annabel's heels clicked, a pedestal table held an enormous display of red calla lilies, roses and red holly berries, and against the wall opposite the staircase a wood fire crackled in a carved marble fireplace, offering a blast of welcome warmth to counter the freezing temperature outside. Annabel had no problem handing her coat over when requested.

'Flynn, you bastard!' A voice crashed through the refined air from above, snapping her attention up to where a large man with striking angular features and a bald head was leaning precariously over the balustrade. 'About time. Get up here and have a drink, boy.'

Annabel was too busy staring to properly hear Aidan's reply. That man looked remarkably like . . . *no*. It couldn't be.

'Annabel?' She realised Aidan was standing at the foot of the sweeping staircase waiting for her.

He motioned for her to precede him up the stairs but she wasn't having that. She followed him up instead, using a stage whisper to get his attention for the question she was dying to ask. 'Was that—'

'Aidan.' A cultured British male voice interrupted from above. 'Good to see you.'

'Damien,' Aidan replied, reaching the top step and embracing the man standing there. 'Good to see you too.'

They exchanged a few manly back thumps before breaking apart and stepping back to make room for Annabel – who nearly fell back down the stairs in shock to find herself face to face with infamous playboy and scion of the Harcourt family, Damien Harcourt. Even without his trademark sunglasses in place, there was no mistaking the thick golden brown hair and chiselled features of Europe's most photo-graphed billionaire bachelor.

He swept a warm, amber-coloured gaze over her. 'And you must be Annabel?' he asked with that crystal-cut accent. She hadn't thought it possible for anyone to radiate more charisma than Aidan Flynn, but she felt it blaze out of this man, who with his tawny colouring shone like the sun to Aidan's dark, silvery moonlight.

'Annabel Frost,' Aidan said. 'Damien Harcourt.'

Damien held out his hand. 'How—'

'Move over, now.' The big man who had yelled at them over the balustrade barged in between Aidan and Damien Harcourt and gave her his own hand to shake. 'It's just like you two runts to try and hog all the real beauty for yourselves. I'm Bal, my darling one,' he said in an accent every bit as polished as Damien Harcourt's and which was a direct contradiction to his hard-man leather and studs look. 'I've come to rescue you while these two peacocks preen each other's feathers.' He threw an arm around both men's necks and gave a playful squeeze. 'You look like you need the attentions of a real man.'

'And that's you I suppose?' Aidan laughed, loosening the headlock and clapping the man on the shoulder. 'Annabel Frost. Balthazar Hunt.'

Annabel stared at the six-foot-five Viking of a man, who was not actually bald at all but sported a crop of fair, close-shaved hair. So she hadn't been seeing things. And she no longer needed the stairs to fall down. She could easily collapse in a heap right there as the exotically-slanted blue eyes of the lead singer of heavy metal band Absence and bona fide rock god Bastard Bal crinkled with a smile as he took her hand again.

'Annabel, you don't need these losers. Come with me, darling.' He tugged her after him as he began to back away, adding, 'I've got something special I want to show you. ' Too stunned to do anything else, Annabel went with him.

'Steady, Hunt,' Aidan warned. 'Be nice. That's my boss you're talking to.'

Annabel blinked at that and turned to see Aidan's easy smile, surprised by how readily he'd made an admission a lot of men might have preferred not to draw attention to. Especially in such glaringly alpha company.

'Is it now?' Bal said, sounding impressed and giving his eyebrows a wiggle as he tugged her again towards the main group of people milling about. 'Lucky me. I do so love a woman on top. Have you met our hosts, Annabel? No? Then let me introduce you.'

More than a little star-struck she allowed Bal to lead her further into the open space. Obviously designed and used for entertaining on a grand scale, it was furnished with various grouped arrangements of casual seating and low tables, as well as featuring a full mahogany bar and – set against a rear wall of frameless glass beside a beautifully decorated Christmas tree – a grand piano. Wide double doorways along each of the side walls were swagged in more festive greenery and ribbons and showed glimpses of large, well appointed rooms beyond. And finding herself led through it all by a world famous star who introduced her to a stream of glamorous and important strangers had to be the most surreal experience of Annabel's life.

Karl and Astrid Reiser turned out to be generous and welcoming hosts, and all of their twenty-odd dinner guests were equally charming and polite – apart from Damien Harcourt's girlfriend du jour, Georgiana Savill-Jones, a blonde so faultlessly polished, so immaculately manicured that Annabel, who was certainly no slacker when it came to presentation herself, reckoned it had to be full-time job just to maintain such groomed perfection. Georgiana wasted no time in showing her claws, casting a critical eye over Annabel as they were introduced.

'What a lovely dress,' she said in a tone that implied she thought exactly the opposite. 'And how socially-minded of you to adopt "austerity dressing" – so relevant these days. I have to say, you're a much braver sort than I am.' She tinkled with a delicate shudder. 'I can't quite bring myself to tackle the High Street jungle.'

Annabel didn't react with anything beyond a chilly approximation of a smile as Georgiana turned and glided off. She knew a prize bitch when she saw one.

Unfortunately, she also knew enough about fashion to recognise that, while her classically cut prêt-a-porter dress wasn't quite the cheap rag Georgiana had insinuated, every other woman in the place did appear to be draped in top end designer. And that put her at a distinct disadvantage. Cinderella indeed.

She made a conscious effort not to narrow her eyes as she scanned the room for Aidan Flynn. That man really had some explaining to do.

EIGHTEEN

Champagne flute in hand, Aidan circulated, greeting old friends and new acquaintances, all the while keeping half an eye on Bal leading Annabel around the group, introducing her, breaking the ice in his own inimitable fashion. He knew she couldn't be in better hands. Underneath that show of outlandish rocker attitude, the big man was a gentle soul, his natural disposition about as tough as a pair of old corduroy slippers, his humour infectious and irresistible. And despite what surely must be a sizeable sense of shock, Annabel seemed to be coping like the impeccable social hostess she was. But from the odd occasion that their gazes clashed, he knew that he was going to have strips torn off him at some point. That was fair – he had pulled a hell of a surprise on her.

He was on his way back from visiting the cloakroom when she caught him, slipping away from her self-appointed six-and-a-half-foot guard dog and stepping into his path.

'This?' She flung out a hand gesture that he took to indicate both the lavish surroundings and the eminent guestlist. 'You couldn't have told me about this before throwing me in at the deep end?' she demanded in a furious whisper.

He did so love the spark her temper lit in her eyes. When he'd told her he wanted to get her away from the distractions and excuses in London, what he'd really meant was that he wanted to get her out of her comfort zone, shake her up a bit. She was too guarded, too well protected behind the walls of her carefully constructed existence she'd built for herself there. Here she was adrift, exposed. Real.

'I considered it, but honestly, Annabel, would you have agreed to come if I had?' And, more importantly, if she had agreed to come, would it have been because of the lure of celebrity, or because of him? He would have had no way of knowing.

'Probably not,' she said. 'I'm not sure any of this is even real.'

'You're doing fine.'

She shot him an annoyed look, telling him how much she didn't care for his opinion. 'Apart from being hideously under-dressed compared to every other woman here.'

He glanced around the mezzanine, noting the gathering of beautiful, glamorous women in cocktail dresses. To be honest, the only difference he could see was that Annabel lacked some of the glitz that sparkled on shoes and bags and dresses, and to his eyes, she looked so much better without the fuss. Maybe his genetics left him predisposed to the archetypal ideal of Celtic beauty, or maybe it was her green eyes that reminded him of the lush landscapes of home? But to him she looked perfect, with the lustre of her fair skin like a pearl against the black of her dress and her red hair piled up – not in its usual precise twist, but in a softer, looser style tonight – to expose the delicate curve of her shoulder, the graceful length of her neck.

Still, whatever he saw, she obviously didn't see it herself, and that little glimpse of insecurity was a reminder that as capable as Ms Frost seemed on the surface, she wasn't solid ice to the core. For all her front, the more he uncovered of her softer centre, the more he realised how vulnerable she actually felt, how tight she had her true self locked up. And that stirred his protective instincts like nothing before. The fact that she'd felt able to let her guard down enough to share her doubts, to let him see what no one else here would suspect from her outward show of cool confidence, signified something very important. The thing he'd been waiting so long for. An almost subconscious display of trust that would at last allow him to take things to the next level.

With the weight of anticipation squeezing his chest, he raised his hand and let his palm settle around the nape of her neck. He felt her stiffen beneath it instantly, felt the jolt ricochet between them at the shock of the first touch, skin to skin. The feel of her was divine – warm, velvety, so smooth. Better than he could have imagined. And he'd imagined a lot.

He could tell that Annabel was feeling the impact of it too. Looking at her parted lips, her shocked thousand-yard stare across the room, he moved his thumb, ever so lightly, ever so slowly, stroking it over the incredible downy softness beneath her ear. He felt and saw her shiver as he leaned in close.

'You're the most exquisite thing here,' he whispered into her ear. 'Relax.'

For a second it seemed as though she'd done exactly that. She exhaled slowly and leant into his hand as though her very bones had melted. Another sign of trust. Of surrender. A fierce surge of something primitive and possessive had his hand tightening instinctively around her neck, the movement causing her to gasp and turn her eyes up to his.

The instant their gazes locked, he became trapped by what he saw in her eyes. The tension, the need, the desire, all laid bare. He was sure she could see the same things reflected in his stare because she didn't seem able to look away any more than he could. Not until Bal came up with Georgiana on one arm and the sleek Russian heiress Yuliya Nubova on the other and broke the spell by thumping him hard on the shoulder.

'Afraid you're going to have to keep it in your pants for the time being, boy. Didn't you hear the call for dinner?'

'No,' Aidan cleared his throat and shook his head, noticing that all the guests were making their way down the stairs.

'Didn't think so.' Bal barked a laugh. 'Anyway, I insist on having all the brains and beauty sit beside me, so I've come to claim your lovely boss.' With that he scooped Annabel into his bevy and herded her away down the stairs. Aidan watched her go, his stomach tight with hunger, but not for food. That one touch had awakened a ferocious appetite that demanded instant appeasement, made him want to ravish her on the spot. Giving himself a moment to get a grip on his control, he waited until the rest of the party had filed down the stairs before surreptitiously adjusting himself inside his trousers so he didn't trip himself up. It was going to be a long night.

After dinner, which had been served at a long, candle-lit table in a grandly formal panelled dining room, the party drifted back upstairs to the mezzanine. Roughly half the number of guests broke into smaller groups, seating themselves at the bar or sinking into the available sofas and chaises to sip coffee and digestifs while they chatted or listened to the pianist. The other half made for one of the rooms off to the side.

Pausing on his way through the doorway, Damien Harcourt turned to raise an expectant eyebrow at Aidan.

Obviously catching the gesture herself, Annabel spoke beside him. 'What's going on?'

Motioning for Damien to give him a minute, Aidan turned to her. 'Nothing serious, just a game of poker. We can join them, or not. Your call.'

'I don't know how to play poker,' she blurted with a slightly horrified look.

'You're not expected to play,' he reassured her with a smile. 'There's only a handful that will, a pretty regular group.'

She gave him a shrewd look. 'And you're part of that group? You're expected to play – and you're expecting to?'

'Well, I wasn't expecting to, no. I had no idea it had been arranged until Damien mentioned it over dinner. Karl set up the game in support of Astrid's fundraising and they've insisted on counting me in as I haven't played in a while.' He moved in closer, dropped his voice. 'But I'd had a much more exciting game planned just for the two of this evening, *a mhuirnín.*' He let his gaze trace her face, come to rest on her lips, let her see how much the thought of kissing them aroused him. 'If you prefer, I can make my excuses and we can leave now.'

For a moment she looked like she was going to agree, swaying towards him slightly, caught by the irresistible pull of the attraction between them. Then as though breaking free of a spell, she blinked and looked away, her gaze taking in the other guests. 'And have everyone here know what we're up to by you dropping out and leaving early? No thanks, not when I have to look them all in the eye again tomorrow night. You should play if your friends have included you, it would be rude not to.'

She was right, but that didn't stop the rush of disappointment he felt to hear her say it. Since that earlier moment when he'd finally let himself touch her, all he'd been able to think about was doing it again. And again. All night. All over. Until he'd mapped every inch of Annabel Frost with the feel of his fingertips, his palms. As if it hadn't been bad enough having had to sit through the meal, being driven to distraction by the sight of Bal flirting and putting his big hands on her. Now he was going to have to drag his blue balls to the poker table and try to keep his mind on the cards? He didn't fancy his chances.

OK, how many other surprises could possibly come her way tonight? Annabel was still trying to process everything that had been thrown at her over the past few hours: the famous people, the fabulous wealth, that heart-stopping first touch from Aidan. And now gambling – one of the things in life she really couldn't abide? She felt a near-hysterical laugh bubble up as she recalled her earlier concerns at the hotel about certain things relating to Aidan Flynn not quite adding up. She'd had *no idea*.

It was apparent now that there was no way to put off a confrontation once they were alone, but where the hell was she supposed to start? Recognising the need to try to get everything straight in her own head first, she made herself swallow down her deep aversion to any form of gambling and encouraged Aidan to stay and play his game of poker, figuring the best way to buy some thinking time was to have him preoccupied for a while.

She accompanied him into the room, which turned out to be a library with walls lined with neatly stacked bookshelves and display cabinets. At the far end of the room, in front of a flickering open fire, a number of her dining companions had made themselves comfortable on a selection of high-backed armchairs and cushion-laden sofas. Set a little way apart was a table at which Karl Reiser, Damien Harcourt, Bal, Yuliya and two other guests were already settling into position behind stacks of coloured chips and baiting each other with good-natured competitiveness.

When one of the serving staff walked by Annabel on his

way towards the fire-side group, trailing a heavenly aroma from the tall silver pot he carried, she didn't need Aidan's suggestion that she go relax and enjoy a coffee. She was already on her way, leaving him to join the other players at the table.

Of the two available places left to sit, Annabel took the one slightly further away from Georgiana, though in a funny way she felt quite comfortable with the aloof, untouchable blonde – perhaps recognising a bit of herself in the prickly act. Besides, there was no point in trying to avoid the woman after discovering over dinner that she, Damien and Bal had been forced to come straight to the Reiser's from the airport having flown in late by private jet from Switzerland, but would be checking into Haus later tonight.

No sooner had they exchanged equally brittle smiles, and Annabel had been handed a steaming cup of coffee, than their hostess arrived with a plate of petit fours and took the last remaining seat in between them.

'Well, ladies, I see our partners have abandoned us,' she said in crisply accented yet impeccable English as she offered the plate to Georgiana. 'I have to say, Damien is looking very bullish tonight. I hope he remembers that Karl and I have three growing boys to feed and doesn't push the betting up too much. Even if it is all for a good cause.' She turned to Annabel, extending the plate. 'And I hear Aidan is a force to be reckoned with at the table. Do you play, Annabel?'

'No. Never.' Annabel took one of the tiny biscuits and popped it whole into her mouth, surprised by the kick of spiced gingerbread on her tongue.

'Is that a hint of disapproval I hear?' Georgiana asked.

'Partly.' Annabel took a sip from her cup.

'Even when all the winnings are being donated to charity, as they are tonight?'

230

Annabel gave a little shrug. 'I don't agree with leaving things to blind luck.'

'Neither do I,' Astrid said, leaning forward to slide the plate of biscuits onto the coffee table so that others could reach them. 'But there's more to poker than luck, there are many complex skill factors involved, from calculating the odds to psychological strategy.'

'Well, I really don't know that much about it.' Annabel said, hoping to move the subject onto something else.

'If you like, I can try to give you a real time explanation of what's happening while they play,' Astrid offered, turning her attention to across the room.

Unable to think of a way to refuse that wouldn't sound impolite, Annabel turned as well, noticing that over at the table, the banter had subsided and the game started. With a new air of focus, cards were being dealt, bets called, chips tossed.

As the play moved around the table, Astrid began briefly outlining each player's actions, explaining whether they were meeting a bet, raising the stakes or dropping out of the hand.

Annabel nodded, making an effort to seem interested for her hostess. When she heard Bal say, 'Raise five' she turned to Astrid for verification.

'So Bal's just increased the stake by five euros and the next player will need to match that to stay in the game?'

She thought she'd got it wrong when Astrid just blinked at her. But before she could say anything, Georgiana gave a delighted shriek of laughter.

'Oh, that's too funny! Did you all hear Annabel's brilliant joke?' she declared immediately turning to the others sitting nearby. She relayed the remark, looking back at Annabel with a malevolent gleam in her eye. When everybody else started laughing, Annabel joined in, though she really didn't get the joke at all.

Astrid, who'd been watching her closely throughout Georgiana's performance, must have picked up on her doubt, because she leant forward and said, 'Let's go take a closer look at the game, shall we?'

When they rose from their seats, several other people followed suit, wandering closer to the table. Standing as part of the loose group of spectators gathered around, Annabel watched the action as Yuliya turned up the corner of the cards lying face down in front of her before casually 'raising' by tossing two rectangular chips into the centre of the table. Watching them come to settle amongst the messy pile of plastic tokens already there, it took Annabel a moment to register the fact that the number value printed on each of them represented five thousand. Not five as she'd thought.

Five *thousand*.

These people weren't playing in multiples of ones, tens, or even hundreds. Now she knew why everyone had been laughing at her 'joke'. She looked at all the chips on the table and her mind spun at the idea of how much money those stacks of plastic represented, how much some players had already lost in that central pile. Then she looked at the stacks neatly lined up in front of Aidan and knew that if she didn't want to embarrass herself by starting to hyperventilate on the spot, she needed to get out of there.

She ignored the quick smile he spared her before snapping his attention back to the game. Taking advantage of everyone's attention being riveted on the table, too, as the next player raised again, she slipped out of the library and made for the cloakroom where she hid for as long as reasonably possible.

Studying her reflection in the mirror, she noted that against the dyed red she'd rushed to redo in anticipation of the ball, the skin of her face looked bone white. Staring, she wondered who this woman was that had let herself be led to a strange house, in a strange country, by a man she obviously knew so little about. A man with secrets. A big-time, regular gambler. It actually made her feel slightly sick to think that she could have been so blind, so stupid, as to ignore all the warning signs and let herself be taken in by a charmer, a player, a Tony Maplin.

She emerged from her hiding place wondering what to do with herself. Her natural instinct was to leave, to escape, but simply walking out would not only seem a rude way to treat the Reisers who had welcomed her into their home, but would leave her stranded in sub-zero temperatures in the middle of who knew where with no way of knowing if she could even find a taxi to take her back to the hotel.

In no rush to end up back in the library, Annabel wandered slowly across the mezzanine, noting that there were only a few people gathered near the bar who, for the most part, were sitting quietly and listening to the pianist. With the music providing the perfect excuse not to have to engage in conversation, it seemed like a good place to park herself and try to work out her next move.

She'd barely got her backside onto a seat before she was approached by one of the ever attentive serving staff and asked if she'd like a drink. She thought for a moment before ordering a martini.

Why the hell not? As she seemed to have stumbled out of the pages of a fairytale and straight onto the set of a James Bond movie, it would no doubt help her fit right in.

NINETEEN

Aidan stepped out of the library, his searching gaze pulled like a magnet to the vibrant flash of Annabel's hair. She sat at the end of the Reisers' bar slightly apart from the few other people nearby, seemingly absorbed by the pianist who, over the course of the evening, had been doing his best to pay homage to every famous composer ever known to have set so much as a fleeting foot in Vienna.

Coming up behind her, he noted the half-empty martini glass resting on the bar by her elbow.

'Ah. Must be trouble,' he teased, quietly enough not to draw anyone else's attention from the lively first movement flourish of Beethoven's Emperor Concerto, but loud enough to make Annabel stiffen and whip her head around to glare at him. Oh, yes, trouble indeed, if the set of her jaw was anything to go by. He nodded towards the drink. 'Is it helping?'

She followed his gaze and made a little moue of distaste. 'No. It's disgusting.'

Picking up the glass, Aidan tilted the clear liquor to his lips to taste it. 'Mmm. Vodka martini. A good one.'

'You're welcome to it.' Annabel said dismissively and

turned her attention back towards the piano. Setting the glass down again, he studied her profile, trying to accurately gauge her mood. Tense didn't begin to cover it.

'I didn't realise you'd left the room. I'm sorry if the game bored you.'

She turned to him again, letting out a laugh that had no trace of humour in it. 'Bored me? No. I found it –' she paused as though trying to find the right words '– terrifying and obscene, but certainly not boring. In fact, it made me realise what a mistake this all is. I should never have agreed to come.'

'Ann—' he started, only to be cut off when she threw up her hand.

'Don't bother trying to argue,' she interrupted. 'Just take my word that this isn't going to work.'

'Just take your word for it? No, you know I can't do that. And I don't argue – I discuss. Tell me, what's not going to work?'

She gave her head a violent shake. 'I'm not doing this here.' She reached for her small clutch bag and swivelled on her stool. 'I'm tired and I want to leave. I need to get a number for a taxi.'

'If you want to leave, that's fine, the car's still here. We'll get our coats—'

'No,' she interrupted him again. 'I'll be fine taking a taxi on my own. Please just get me a number and go back to your game.'

'I'm not letting you leave alone, Annabel,' he stated flatly.

That earned him an angry look. 'What I do isn't down to you!' Slipping from her stool, she began striding towards the staircase.

He followed, hot on her heels and overtook her on the small landing half way down, swinging around to stand in

235

front of her with his arm stretched out to grasp the hand rail to cut off her escape.

Annabel stopped dead. 'Get out of my way.'

'No. I'm not going to let you run away without at least offering some sort of explanation as to what the problem is.'

'What the problem is?' She puffed out a breath. 'Jesus, there's so much wrong here that I don't even know where to start!' she muttered almost to herself, rubbing fretfully at her forehead before almost immediately finding a starting place. 'Because I had no idea about any of this,' she accused, whipping her hand away and pinning him with a wild look. 'How does any of this fit in any way with you parading as a barman? These people . . . the amount of money you had stacked on that poker table . . . It's ludicrous. And you've got the nerve to keep going on about trust! Like you're some sort of honourable, dependable saint of a man, worthy of it. But you're not, you're plainly a liar. I haven't the first idea who you really are.'

The breathless rant finished as quickly as it had begun. 'Yes, you do, Annabel,' he said calmly. 'I'm still me.'

She closed her eyes and drew in a breath. 'But that's exactly the point, I don't have a clue who "me" is. I thought I did, but now I realise that I don't know anything about you.'

He waited until she opened her eyes again so he could look directly into them as he asked, 'And why do you think that is, Annabel?'

'How the hell should I know?' she blustered. 'Because it gives you some twisted kick to be all secretive and manipulative and deceive people?'

He let the insult pass and held onto her gaze. 'Or perhaps it's simply because you've never bothered to ask me about myself.'

236

She paused as that stunningly clear piece of reasoning sunk in, but rather than accept the possibility that her own actions – or more specifically, the lack of them – were responsible for her current state of discomfort, she came right back on the defensive.

'That's ridiculous. You could have offered the information. At any time. It's not as though you don't like to talk my ears off!'

He wanted to throw his head back and laugh at the tartness of her tone, but with the rapid rise and fall of her chest telling him how high her emotions were running, he suspected she'd likely push him down the stairs if he dared. 'In the same way that you offer so much about yourself, you mean? Annabel, the only reason I've been learning what little I have about you, is from dragging it out of you word by stubborn word.'

Again, she paused, recognising the undeniable ring of truth in his words. But she was still rattled and not ready to admit it. 'Well at least I've never misled you,' she threw at him. 'Never pretended to be someone I'm obviously not.'

Skirting around him, she continued down the stairs. He allowed himself a small, secret smile before he turned in pursuit. Helping educate Ms Frost on the requirements needed to conduct any sort of personal relationship was proving to be hugely rewarding.

He caught up with her again at the bottom of the stairs, putting himself right in her way. She gave an exasperated sigh. 'I don't like being taken for a fool, Aidan.'

'And I don't take you for one, Annabel. Not for a minute. I've never pretended to be anything. I am who I am, nothing's changed.'

'Oh, how can you say that? Everything's changed.'

'No. Only your perception has. I'm essentially the same

man I've been since you met me. You're just seeing another side from the one you're used to.'

Although her chin remained at a stubborn set, it appeared Annabel had nothing else to add at present.

He took advantage of her silence. 'Let me call for the car so we can finish this in private.' It may have been phrased as a question, but he delivered it in a tone that made it a statement.

'Fine,' Annabel snapped, accepting defeat, but not very graciously. 'I'm too bloody tired to keep fighting you.'

In less than ten minutes they were in the back of the car, gliding through quiet, snowy streets towards the lights of the city centre.

Turning his back on the window, Aidan angled his body to look across the darkened interior to where Annabel sat staring out at the passing scenery and asked what it was that she'd discovered about him tonight that she found so objectionable.

He wasn't overly surprised to learn that it had something to do with the poker game. Given her current family situation, she had good reason to be wary of something that had so much potential to wreak havoc. But he felt she was placing the blame in the wrong corner.

'I understand that you've had a difficult time with what happened to your mother with Tony Maplin, but don't you think it's a little unfair to judge all gambling based on his actions? Surely you can see the difference between his behaviour and what we were doing tonight to raise money for charity?'

Annabel sent him a look across the car's interior. 'You could have easily just given the money to the charity. Gambling is all about unnecessary risk taking.'

'And what's so bad about taking risks, *a mhuirnín?* Lots of things in life are a gamble, involve some element of risk. There's not much reward to be had by playing things too safe.'

'Yes, but if you risk too much you stand to lose everything.'

He tried to read her expression in the occasional flash of a passing street light. She was obviously much more relaxed and open here in the enclosed, semi-dark intimacy of the car than she had been back at the Reisers', where she'd felt exposed and vulnerable.

'And is that what you're saying, Annabel? That this, us, is too much for you?'

He heard the long intake of breath she took, watched her head sink back into the seat. 'I'm concerned that the price that's going to have to be paid in the end is too high.'

That was a remarkably candid admission from her. Perhaps his plan to shake her out of herself was working after all. 'And you think you're the only one who's afraid of that?' He repaid her openness in kind. 'You, me, every person on the planet has to take that sort of gamble at some point. All any of us can do is decide for ourselves whether the reward is worth the risk.'

His heart nearly stopped as he saw her shake her head. But instead of telling him he wasn't worth it, she said, 'It's not always about deciding for yourself, though, is it? Somebody else made the wrong decision for my mother.'

'What happened to Ellen was devastating, unforgivable – but you need to stop using that one bad relationship as a marker for all.'

Annabel's gaze went back to the window. 'It wasn't just one,' she said quietly. 'There were a few – not necessarily playing her for her money like Tony did, but who definitely played her emotions, her trusting nature.'

He let that sink in. 'Is that why you find it so difficult to trust anyone? To trust me?'

Her head turned to him sharply. 'That's not fair. I've already trusted you more than I should.'

He held her gaze. 'Why more than you should? I've done nothing to betray anything you've given.'

'Haven't you?' One of her brows quirked. 'You've not exactly been honest about yourself.'

'Because I didn't immediately spill my life story in minute detail all over you uninvited? The words pot and kettle, spring to mind, Annabel.' He shifted again in the seat, turning to face her head on. 'But I'm an open book. Ask me whatever you want.'

And she did. Starting with how someone working as a barman could possibly afford his lifestyle, how he came to have friends and acquaintances who were some of the richest and most powerful people in Europe.

'Ah, now that's something you already know. That very successful City career I told you about? I landed Damien as a client, and over the years we became friends.'

'But . . . I assumed when you mentioned it that some disaster must have befallen you. That you'd ended up at Cluny's because you'd lost your job in the banking crash.'

'Ultimately, I did lose the job as a result of the crash, but only after I'd managed to get myself and those of my clients who would listen, out without the huge losses that a lot suffered.'

Annabel frowned. 'So why haven't you gone back? I mean, serving drinks in your uncle's restaurant can hardly be fulfilling after that.'

'I can't ever go back into that world, Annabel, even if I wanted to.'

Her look of confusion deepened. 'Why not? I'd have thought someone who'd managed to save a few fortunes would be considered a big asset. And you obviously did come through it quite well if you can still afford a lifestyle like the one you appear to have.'

'It's not that I wouldn't be welcomed back,' he told her. Indeed, there'd been more than a few keen offers made based on what he'd managed to achieve. 'But the effort involved in trying to shore up the solid foundations I'd built against the force of that catastrophic financial avalanche cost me my health. One day I was storming through a solid sixteen hours of work, the next I was laid out helpless in intensive care having suffered a stroke.'

'Oh.' Annabel's eyes went wide. 'I had no idea. You – you look so healthy.' Her gaze dropped to run over him in a way that made his abs tighten. 'Are you fully recovered now?'

Since he'd met her and had her bring back his dreams and ignite every one of his senses to blazing life, he had to admit that he felt better than he had in a long time.

'It's taken a while but I'm almost there.' He smiled at her. 'But now that the damage has been done, it wouldn't be wise to go back into such a stressful profession. I've been forced to re-evaluate, to find a new direction. And I'm fortunate that I'm able to do that from a position of comfort and security. From a strictly financial point of view, I don't need to be at Cluny's, but I'm not really the type to just sit around waiting. I'm a social creature and I hate to be useless. When I learnt Richard needed an emergency staff replacement, I'd been recuperating back home in Ireland for some time and had reached that point of recovery where I'd begun to drive my family, my friends, and myself crazy. I'd worked bar as a student and was desperate to get back to independence so it seemed like the perfect solution all round.'

Absorbing the information, Annabel gave a slow nod and faced forward, her gaze wandering to the windscreen.

'It's started to snow,' she said with sudden and apparent delight.

Looking out of the window himself at the fat, lacy flakes that had begun tumbling from the sky, he also noticed that they were now back in the centre of the city. He felt a hot tingle of anticipation wash through him at the thought that they were very nearly at the hotel.

He turned back to Annabel. 'Anything else you want to ask?'

Picking up on the slight crack in his voice, Annabel's attention snapped back to him. When their eyes met, he saw her chest rise on a quick, deep intake of breath. Their gazes stayed locked for a moment before she managed a soft, 'no'.

Aware of the car slowing to take the final corner, Aidan reached a hand across the space between them and caught one of the wisps of hair that hung down from where she'd pinned the red tresses up.

'Then there's only one question that remains, Annabel,' he said, smoothing his fingers slowly down the silky tendril. 'Are you ready for me?'

Annabel watched as Aidan closed the door to their suite behind them, hyper aware of the force of the intensity radiating from him. He'd not spoken since she'd offered a ragged 'yes' in answer to that one last question.

She held her breath as he stepped towards her and set about silently removing her coat. Tossing it onto the nearby console table, he kept his eyes on hers as his own coat followed suit, then he stepped close again, the fingers of one hand, warm and strong but gentle, wrapping around hers and raising it his lips to press a kiss against her knuckles. Still without a word, he led her towards the bedroom he'd taken as his.

Drawing to a halt in the doorway, he broke his silence at last.

'Go and stand in front of the mirror,' he instructed, indicating the full-length mirror hung on the wall at the end of the bed. Compelled by the tone in his voice, Annabel did, watching in the reflection as he moved to close the door before turning back to meet her look in the mirror. Even from across the room he looked commanding yet elegantly at ease in that well-tailored midnight-blue suit, the searing look in those pale eyes hiding nothing of his intent. She shivered and realised that his prediction had turned out to be true. All he had to do was look at her across the room to make her know she was his. How quickly that had happened . . . within weeks. How long it had seemed, an eternity.

She couldn't take her eyes off his reflection as she watched him shed his jacket and throw it on the bed before beginning to roll up one shirt sleeve as he slowly came up behind her. When he was within reach, she turned to meet him and put her arms around his neck. He stopped her.

'No. Face the mirror. From now until I make you come for me, you don't do anything I haven't told you to do. Understand?'

There was something electrifying in his tone that short-circuited her need to argue. She could feel the hairs on her arms rising in response to the thread of power that was as irresistible as it was intoxicating. She did as she was told, her eyes glued to his reflection that stared back at her from over her shoulder.

'I'm going to start with the bit that's been intriguing me all evening,' he said as he finished rolling up his other sleeve. 'The first bit of you I touched.' One hand came up, the back of one finger stroking down the side of her neck, causing her to arch into the touch. Lowering his head, he put his lips to

243

the curve of shoulder and neck. The lightest brush, like the one he'd pressed on her knuckles. He planted another a little further up. And then another and another. Turning his cheek in to rub against her hair, he tucked his nose behind her ear and breathed her in.

'You smell so good,' he murmured before swapping to the other side, this time running the kisses down from her ear to her collarbone. 'And you taste even better.' Pulling back, he took the pins out of her hair. Let it cascade down, smoothed the curls over her shoulders.

He circled around to the front of her. Placing himself between her and the mirror. 'I've been wanting to kiss you since that first night we met, when you put me in my place,' he said, cupping her cheeks with his hands, his fingertips spearing into her hair as his gaze locked onto her lips. He tilted her face up to his. 'Every time you've opened your mouth I've wanted to smother your sass.' One thumb moved to rest on her lower lip, to gently stroke back and forth. 'I've wanted to share every gasp and sigh I've watched pass through your parted lips.' He leaned in close. 'I've wanted to run my tongue along that tight seam every time they've been pursed with disapproval.' He stopped with mere milli-metres to spare between them, their breaths mingling, raised his eyes to look into hers. 'Have you thought about me kissing you, Annabel?'

'Yes,' she admitted in the merest whisper, her bottom lip catching on the pad of his thumb.

That pale gaze dived back to her mouth. His thumb slid up to the centre of her lips, pushed in and pulled down, dragging her bottom lip with it, teasing her open.

'How have you imagined it? I've thought about it soft, like this.' He closed the scant distance between them and grazed the very edge of her mouth with his lips. 'And this.' He swept the tip of his tongue lightly along the sensitive inner edge of the bottom lip he still held. 'And harder, too.' He moved his thumb and sucked her lip between his, barely nipped it with his teeth. 'Like that. But most of all –' his hands shifted further into her hair, taking a firmer hold, his eyes met hers again '– I've thought about it being like this.' He pulled her to him and covered her lips with his, pressing them against her teeth, his tongue sweeping into her instantly.

God, he tasted good. So warm and rich and elemental that a little whimper of pleasure rose up from her throat as she opened under the hot, silken caress. The sound drew an answering rumble from Aidan as he accepted her invitation to take the kiss deeper. Eyes looking deep into hers he invaded her mouth, demanding, conquering.

Annabel grasped at his forearms as sensation swept her away. She'd never been kissed like it. Had never felt so completely and passionately *claimed*. She wanted to close her eyes, hide away, but the intensity of his gaze held her captive.

Taking his time, Aidan delved into every part of her mouth, his dominating exploration sending warm tendrils of desire through her entire body – weakening her knees, fizzing through her belly, pulsing between her thighs. When he finally broke the seal of their mouths, he didn't move back but kept their parted lips just touching as they shared panting breaths, gazes still locked.

'But I have to say, Ms Frost,' he murmured huskily after a moment. 'That nothing compares to the real thing. I could kiss you all night.'

And she'd take that happily, along with discovering what-ever other amazing talents he had hidden.

'Then do,' Annabel said, kissing him this time with all the urgency she felt. Her hands released their grip on his arms, found his waist instead. The heat of him, the hardness through the cotton was too much of a tease to resist. She ran her palms up over his abdomen and chest, feeling the tight contours of the man beneath the clothing. Her fingers went for his shirt buttons, needing the contact of skin on skin.

Aidan broke the kiss again, his hands closed over hers to still them before she'd got more than two undone.

'Slow down, *a mhuirnín*. We're not going to rush this.'

She gave him a murderous look, which just made him laugh.

'Trust me on this. The more we let the anticipation build, the better the pay off.'

Like there hadn't been enough anticipation already? She was *desperate*. 'No more waiting.'

'You don't like it slow?'

Annabel shrugged, trying to get her hands free from his and back to losing his shirt. 'I've never tried it slow.'

One of his hands let go of her then, came up to tilt her chin back so he could look into her eyes. 'Good. I'm glad I'll be a first for you.'

'Really, there's no need. We're both ready and willing.' Taking advantage of her freedom she wasted no time in getting a couple more buttons undone. 'Let's just get to what we both want.'

He gave a shake of his head and recaptured her busy hand. Tightening his grip on both, he forced them away from his chest and behind her back with surprisingly easy strength. He held her there, fingers ringing her wrists gently but inescapably.

He was waiting for the glare she cast up at him when she failed to wriggle herself free.

'You can struggle all you want, but let's get one thing clear. You're not in charge here, Annabel,' he said quietly. 'I am.'

The beautiful silvery hue of his irises seemed to have

suddenly hardened to a solid steel. The calm authority of his voice sent a thrill through her, slowed her struggles.

'I say what happens, when it happens and how it happens. Can you cope with that?'

If the alternative was missing out on what promised to be mind-blowing satisfaction, she hoped to hell she could.

'Let's try it and see,' she sighed.

TWENTY

Aidan smiled at her persecuted tone, knowing how difficult it must be for her to go against everything she'd spent years conditioning herself to be. But he wasn't about to stop pushing her now. The fact that she was even here had him more convinced than ever that he was right about her true nature. A little dose of surrender was exactly what Annabel Frost needed.

And it would have to be a *little* dose this first time, he reminded himself as a jagged bolt of lust ripped through him at the thought. As much as he wanted her completely at his mercy, unleashing the full force of his dominating desire on her too soon would likely send her packing.

He leant forward and kissed her again, leisurely, thoroughly – taking his time to savour her. And good lord, she was addictive. His head spun with the taste, the scent, the feel of her trapped against him, leaving him already wrestling with the primal urge to rush to take more, take all of her. Make her his. Despite all his assured talk, he knew the strength of the need she inflamed in him meant that keeping a hold on his control tonight would be a grim challenge indeed.

Closing his eyes, he lost himself in the pleasure of kissing her for so long that when he pulled back, Annabel swayed towards him, soft and pliant. Her eyelids fluttered open when he released the hold he had on her wrists. Her unfocused gaze followed him as he circled back around behind her.

He gathered her loose hair, draped it over the front of one shoulder, dropped a kiss to the back of her neck. 'Time to unwrap my prize.'

Forcing himself not to hurry, he pulled at the zipper on the back of her dress, lowering it all the way down to the base of her spine. Slipping his fingertips under the gaping neckline, he guided the garment over the curve of her shoulders and down her arms.

He watched in the mirror as the bodice of the dress lowered to expose her bra. Made of some sheer black gauzy material it veiled but certainly didn't hide the creamy swell of her breasts or the pale pink nipples contained in the push-up cups. If the panties matched he was in even more trouble than he'd thought. He swallowed. Unable to speak, he peeled the dress lower, his gaze eating up every bit of her that he uncovered inch by tantalising inch.

When the bunched fabric reached her hips, he dropped into a crouch and pressed a kiss into the dip of her lower spine before continuing to ease the dress all the way down her legs, his cock twitching at the sight of the sheer, lacy-topped hold-ups she wore. Once she'd stepped out of the dress, he tossed the still warm sheath onto a nearby chair and wrapped his palms around her ankles – just above the straps of her sexy high shoes – and started the slow glide back up over her silk-clad shins, her knees, the front of her thighs as though dressing her again. From behind, his eyes matched the ascent, sliding up over her calves, up, up, over the strip of bare thigh . . .

God help him. The pants did match. Scant inches in front of his face, he could see the shadowy cleft of her buttocks bisecting that triangle of black gauze. Hands grasping her hips, he let his forehead drop forward to rest against the small of her back, closing his eyes and taking a couple of deep breaths to steady himself. It hardly helped as the scent of warm, aroused Annabel Frost filled his lungs.

Pushing to his feet, he ran his hands up the long curve of her back as he went. When he was fully upright and looked in the mirror over her shoulder, the sight that greeted him knocked every bit of that sex-infused air out of him.

Her eyes were wide in her face, pupils huge, the dark depths of desire drowning out the green. Her lips parted as she drew in rapid breaths. Her hands, hanging by her sides, were gripped into fists. And that black underwear against her pale skin – stark, sexy, sophisticated. So different from the pretty pastels he'd seen her in previously. His gaze dropped to the juncture of her thighs, where the shroud of dark gauze barely dimmed the vivid flash of the fiery curls beneath.

'That underwear is the work of the devil,' he rasped through a sandpaper throat. 'I think we need to keep it on for a while.' He stepped in close, feeling her shoulder blades against his pectorals through the cotton of his shirt, and the curve of her arse against his erection through the crotch of his trousers. He ran his fingers down the lines of the bra straps from her shoulders to her chest.

'I like the tease of being able to see through it.' He traced the upper line of the cups inward across the swell of her breasts. 'The suggestion of being able to glimpse almost every-thing, but not quite.' When his fingers met at her cleavage, he let his hands cover her, scooping the weight of her up with his palms, testing the soft flesh with splayed fingers. She was a perfect fit.

A moment later he felt her shudder under his touch as he moulded the shape of her and his thumbs brushed over the puckered peaks of her nipples, that one caress drawing them even tighter.

250

It was all the sign he needed to repeat the caress, making Annabel gasp and shudder again.

'Always so responsive. So sensitive.' He concentrated on circling the ever tightening buds. 'I believe some women can orgasm just from having their nipples stimulated.' He caught the hard tips between fingers and thumbs and squeezed, making her jolt. 'Are you one of them, Annabel? If I used my mouth on you as well as my fingers could I make you come for me that way, do you think?'

She didn't answer, seemed lost to herself as she arched forward, pushing further into his touch as her head dropped back onto his shoulder and gave a restless toss.

He raised a hand to grasp her chin, turned her to take another deep kiss while the fingers of his other rolled her nipple until she cried out into his mouth.

The sound shot right to the heart of him. He pulled back.

'Jesus, you test me,' he muttered, moving both hands to her shoulders and pushing her off his chest and upright again. He waited until their eyes met in the mirror before smoothing his palms outward and down her arms. When he reached her wrists, he did a U-turn and ran his knuckles up her inner arms until his palms found her hips, curved around her sides as they ran up to her waist and around to glide over her abdomen. He was transfixed by the sight of how large his hands looked on her slim figure, how much darker his own skin looked against her milky complexion. His gaze tracked the motion as his hands glided lower, passing over the front of her briefs and down onto the front of her thighs, splaying his fingers to exert gentle pressure.

'Open for me,' he murmured in her ear. When he felt her give, he swept his hands back up over her hips and belly, pressing her tight against his groin with one while the other plunged straight down over her pubic mound and into the space between her newly parted thighs to cup her.

251

They both gasped at the sensation.

'Fuck, you feel hot,' Aidan ground out, dragging his hand firmly back up over the fabric of her knickers only to dive it back down again. 'Hot and damp.'

He added pressure to his fingers, circled them over the thin barrier separating their flesh.

Annabel shuddered, arching, riding his fingers, pushing her backside against his erection, trapping it tight between their bodies.

'Yes,' she breathed.

'You want more?' He raised his eyes to hers in the mirror. Her look alone gave him his answer. There was nothing cold or reserved about Ms Frost now.

Pulling his hand from the heavenly heat between her legs, he ran his fingertips along the waistband of her briefs, letting one slip its way beneath the elastic.

'You want me down in here?'

Annabel grasped his wrist as though she was afraid he'd move his hand away. 'Yes,' she repeated more assertively.

He pressed his lips to her ear, watched her face in the mirror. 'Then put your hand over mine and guide me,' he whispered, seeing the shock of the request widen her eyes.

She stared at him for a moment, then settled her small hand over the top of his and slid them both down into the front of her knickers. Aidan felt the incredible softness of her skin, the silky tickle of her pubic hair, the plump ripeness of the flesh below as Annabel steered their joined hands deeper.

'Oh, *a mhuirnín*, you feel divine. Guide me all the way. Show me where you want me.'

Her hand took his further between her legs, to where she was slick and smooth to the touch. She stopped when his fingertips were aligned with her entrance.

He had to force himself to wait. Rubbing his cheek against

252

hers, he spoke against her jaw. 'You're so very wet. Are you ready to take me here?'

She didn't answer, didn't even nod, just applied pressure to her middle finger, pushing his in turn into the hot, moist heat, just breaching her entrance.

'That's it,' Aidan groaned. 'Show me what you want while I tell you how I'm going to fuck you. The first time will be hard – no,' he stopped when her eyelids fluttered closed, 'keep your eyes open and look at me while I'm talking to you.' He waited until she'd refocused on him, felt her fingers press him deeper. 'The first time will be hot and hard and heavy, because that's the way you'll want it, the way we'll both need it. Then once the edge is taken off, I'll take you again, slow and long, up and down and sideways until you can't think, can't walk. Do you like the sound of that?'

She moaned.

'I like the sound of it too. The only thing that could possibly be better is if I had you tied up, unable to move, unable to disobey me. Don't panic,' he said at the look of horror that flashed across her face. 'I'm not going to do it. Not yet. Not until you're ready to appreciate the added – *dimension* it brings.' He pressed his lips briefly against the fluttering artery in her neck. 'The games I want to play with you will push your boundaries. It's human nature to want to fight against things that make you feel uncomfortable so I expect to be hearing a lot of the word "no" from you.' He gave her a wry smile. 'But I'll be looking to push you past that place of denial so we need a word we can use to signify your limits – the place where you'll go no further. That word will simply be "stop". And when I hear it, that's what I'll do. I'll stop whatever we're doing. Promise me you'll use it if you need to. I can only get to know how to please you properly if you're honest with yourself and with me. Do you understand, Annabel?'

She looked wary but nodded.

'Good. Now put your palms flat on the mirror and let's see how long you can leave them there.'

Again, she hesitated – no doubt fighting an internal battle over whether to accept his authoritative tone – before reaching forward and resting her hands on the mirror.

Sliding his hand up from her stomach to span her throat and frame her jaw, he told her to spread her legs wider. Even as she adjusted her stance, he took charge of himself, rocking his finger gently to push his way into her. God, she was wet. So ready.

'I can't wait to find out what those limits will be, Ms Frost. Just how far will you let me go, I wonder?' Tilting her head back against his shoulder he turned her so he could look directly into her eyes. 'Where will you make me stop?' He kissed her, slipping his tongue into her mouth at the same moment he pushed a second finger into her down below, using both to tease her with slow, searching caresses that had helpless noises bubbling up from her throat again.

Running his hand over the arch of her neck and down her chest, he found her bra and hooked his fingers into the top of one cup, drawing it down to expose the full curve of her breast. Then he reached across and pulled the other cup down. He brushed his fingers lightly over the exposed peaks, felt them tighten as he plucked and teased until he had to break the kiss to look at her.

And what a sight she was, half naked. Her breasts with their hard pink tips thrust forward towards the mirror, her fair skin flushed.

'You're so beautiful, Annabel.' He raised his hand to trail over the blushing heat of her upper chest. 'I love that I can see the effect I have on you. That you light up like a neon sign for me, react with such abandon.' Between her legs, he pushed the heel of his thumb against her, watched her hips undulate in response.

'I'm going to make sure I'm buried deep inside you the first time I make you come for me, so I can feel every pulse of that unrestrained pleasure constricting around me, squeezing me tight.'

'Yes,' she panted, obviously liking the sound of that too. 'Yes, do it.' She took her hands off the mirror and reached back to grab him by the hip pockets, pulled him closer to urge him to hurry.

Her urgency was nearly his undoing. He clung onto his control by a thread. 'Hands back on the mirror, Annabel.'

Caught up in her need, she didn't seem to listen. 'But I want—'

He stilled his movements. 'Put your hands back on the mirror,' he repeated more clearly, using the sound of his implacable tone to regain his own focus. 'Don't you remember what I said to you at The Hyde?'

That got him her attention in the form of a furious frown. '*What?*'

'After breakfast, in the hotel lift. Do you remember what I told you about taking my time to learn all your weak spots? About using them to drive you to the edge and keep you there for a long, long time?'

Her green eyes narrowed. 'You wouldn't dare.'

'You know I would. So put your hands back on the mirror while we remind ourselves of what else I said.'

She struggled for a moment with her need to argue, but put her hands back in place. Every small capitulation was a gift. As a show of gratitude, he renewed his caresses between her legs, pressing here and rubbing there until she was panting and gyrating helplessly again.

'That's it. Are you remembering now that I promised to use two fingers to start with, like this?' he asked, twisting and stroking deep inside her, gaze fixed on her face in the mirror, reading her every reaction. 'And how I said that when

255

I felt you start to melt around me, I'd add another?' He withdrew his fingers to her entrance, circling as he added a third before pressing his way steadily back inside. 'Jesus, you're tight,' he uttered as Annabel keened at the stretch to accommodate him. A sharp twinge seared through his groin as he imagined the mind-blowing sensation of pushing his swollen cock deep into that snug velvet vice. Crushing his pelvis against the curve of her backside in an attempt to appease the ache, he took a moment to re-gather his thoughts.

'Do you recall me saying how I'd finger-fuck you slow and easy?' He followed the words with matching actions, unable to move at any other pace while her body adjusted around him. He kept up a gentle rhythm that had her knees trembling, had her leaning back against him for support.

When he was sure she was ready for more, he wrapped an arm tight around her middle, bracing her as he said, 'And then fast and hard.'

'Oh, God,' she cried out, head snapping back up from his shoulder and her hands curling into claws on the mirror as she trembled and shook under the pressure of his increased pace.

The sight of her on the verge of falling apart was too much. Pulling his fingers from her, he walked around and dragged her hands from the mirror. 'About having you squirming against my mouth?'

Encircling her with his arms, he scooped her up against him, arching her backwards over his hold and latching onto her upturned breast. He hummed in pleasure at the taste, the feel of her hard nipple against his tongue; he swapped to the other side eager to get the flavour of that one too.

Then his mouth and hands were making their way swiftly down her body, he could feel her skin twitch and her stomach muscles tighten in their path. When he was on one knee before her, his face level with her groin, he looked up the long line of her torso and smiled at her dazed expression.

'Hands on the mirror,' he said, waiting until she obeyed before hooking his fingers in the sides of her briefs and tugging them down to her knees.

Dropping his gaze back down, he reached one arm between her legs to splay his hand against her buttocks and jerk that glorious blaze of colour forward to meet his open mouth. Annabel's startled cry snapped his attention back up to her face, drowned out his growl as her lush wet heat hit him hard. She was like cinnamon and spice. He used his free hand to tug her underwear the rest of the way down and off over each shoe, then raised it to join the other, using his arms to push her thighs wider. Another rumble sounded deep in his throat as she opened to him. Tightening his grip, kneading the firm roundness of her arse, he held her fast against his mouth as he delved into every part of her as though he'd devour the rich taste of her desire for him down to the very last drop.

He lost himself in the pleasure of it all, in the sight of her swaying and trembling above him, beautiful in her abandon, features transformed into an expression of sweet agony as she watched the scene in the mirror, her nipples hard little exclamation points of her arousal. He wasn't sure how long it was before she started chanting *God, yes. God, yes.* Then, when his ravenous pace showed no signs of slowing, the plea changed to *God, no. God, no.*

He wanted to listen, to back off and savour her, to re-tighten the leash on his control that seemed to be slipping so badly, but he couldn't get enough of her. Sliding one hand from her arse, he pushed two fingers inside her, curling them forward as he pumped to stimulate the ultra-sensitive bundle of nerves with every pass.

Eventually, her words started running together in an incoherent stream. Aidan felt her start to shake, adjusted his grip to hold her up. Her hands landed on his shoulders, pressing hard.

'Aidan,' she panted, eyelids heavy as she looked down at him. 'God, I'm going to come.' One knee buckled. 'I'm going to fall.'

He managed to tear his face away from her before she tipped over the edge. 'No you're not.' He surged upright again, hands grasping his half unbuttoned shirt and ripping it off over his head. 'You're going to stay on your feet for me, Annabel.' He speared his hands into her hair, forcing her pleasure-dazed eyes to look up at him. 'I'm going to fuck you right now. Right here in front of the mirror.' He toed off his shoes as he spoke. 'So I can see everything. So you can watch as well as feel me take you for the first time.'

Annabel had never been in such a state. Could barely keep her balance with the force of desire swirling though her. With the force of Aidan's passion battering her senses.

She was so unsteady that she was grateful when he told her to put her hands back on the mirror as he walked around behind her again. She'd known from the start that the man had a dangerously wicked mouth – she just hadn't appreciated how wicked. She watched his reflection as he made short work of stripping off the rest of his clothes.

Naked, he was breathtaking. A picture of masculine power tempered by lean elegance – his musculature defined and strong without being bunched and heavy, his tall frame well proportioned with those broad shoulders and chest tapering to lean hips and long legs.

The rip of a condom packet brought her eyes back up to mid-height. To where a fine line of dark hair trailed down from his navel and his hands were busy smoothing the latex sheath over the length of an equally powerful and well proportioned erection. It seemed there were no half-measures where Aidan Flynn was concerned.

His head came up, those eyes caught her looking, and with

258

a wolfish grin he was moving towards her again. Coming close behind, he pressed all that bare skin to hers, his hard contours a solid wall for her softer curves to yield against, the heat of his flesh warming her so that she couldn't help but melt back into him, leaving only her very fingertips touching the mirror, feeling the hottest, hardest part of him nestle between her buttock cheeks.

He unhooked her bra, snagging the straps and sliding them down her outstretched arms, letting the garment drop to the floor when he pulled her hands from the mirror. Grasping her by the wrists, he guided them up and back behind his neck.

'I want you to link your fingers together, Annabel, and keep them there,' he ordered, as he caressed his way back along the underside of her upraised arms and to her breasts, so prominently offered by her new position which left her arched taut as a bow into his touch.

'Stunning,' he said into her ear as he cupped and squeezed, thumbs circling the outline of her areolae, brushing with the lightness of a feather but the zap of electricity across the puckered tips of her nipples. 'Are you squirming from pleasure, Ms Frost, or from discomfort at being on display for me? So exposed, so accessible?' His fingers plucked, thumbs and forefingers tightening on her nipples, just enough pressure to make them tingle when he released them and the blood came rushing back.

'Both,' she said, shakily.

'Good.' Flashing one of his gorgeous smiles in recognition of her honesty, he pressed a kiss to the hollow beneath her ear and swept his hands down to spread her legs wider. Bending at the knees, he let his erection slip into the space he'd created. Rocking his pelvis slowly back and forward so that he rubbed along the length of her cleft, he slid a hand between her thighs to guide the blunt tip of him into her entrance.

'Watch,' he commanded.

He entered her slowly with a strained string of curses while they both watched, wide-eyed and slack-mouthed, his fingers holding her parted to provide an unimpeded view of their joining.

He slid in deep to the sound of their combined groans, reaching places even his insistent fingers hadn't, filling her. Once he was seated as far as he could go, he pulled out again, every bit as slowly, dragging himself over every nerve ending his explorations had brought to life. He paused at her entrance and pushed back in again, his teeth scraping her earlobe.

'Jesus. It looks like I'm fucking fire,' he breathed in awe, the fingertips of one hand moving to brush over the bright patch of her pubic hair and down into her slick folds. 'Feels like it too. You're so hot, Annabel, so hot and tight around me I can barely stand it.'

He found her clitoris, scissored his fingers either side and squeezed. His other hand captured her breast, his fingers creating a corresponding sensation as they pinched and rolled her nipple. She undulated under the double assault, unable to keep still.

'Have you ever watched yourself being fucked before?'

She shook her head. She never had. And she didn't know if she could take the sight of it now. It felt almost unbearably exposing, overpoweringly intense.

It seemed that Aidan was similarly affected. For a moment his eyes closed, his jaw clenched as he continued to slide smoothly in and out. It was too much and too little at the same time. She needed it faster, this slow torture was going to kill her. She thrust her hips back onto him.

His eyelids flew open, the pale grey of his irises almost completely flooded by the black of his pupils. 'Don't move,' he croaked.

'I have to. I want to,' Annabel insisted, rocking her hips again.

'Not tonight.' His fingers dug into her hips to still her. 'I'm too close.'

That was all she needed to hear. Knowing he was already at the edge of his impressive control made her want to push to see him lose it. For her. Because of her. Taking her hands from around his neck, she reached down to grasp him by the hips to pull him deeper inside.

'Then let go.' She dug her nails into the hard muscles of his backside and rolled her hips, dared to tempt him, shock him with a dose of the dirty talk he so liked to give out. 'I want to watch you come inside me now.'

Aidan swore then, as though helpless against her words, his arms wrapped around her and he exploded into a flurry of action. Hot gaze locked on hers, he pumped into her hard and fast.

Clamped to him with nowhere to go, she watched his restraint shatter, took everything he had to give. 'God, yes! Like that,' she demanded, urging him on, surging towards the peak of her own pleasure.

With a growling sound, Aidan raised a hand and buried it in her hair, pulling none too gently to force her head back onto his shoulder. 'Jesus, Annabel,' he said, hot breath thundering in her ear. 'You're going to ruin me. Going to make me lose . . . oh, fuck, I can't . . . YES.'

He pressed his face hard into the side of hers as his hips gave two fast, powerful jerks that all but lifted her right off her toes and threatened to send them sprawling. Flinging an arm out to the mirror to steady them, Aidan jerked once more, held deep inside her as far as he could go for a long moment before he shuddered and groaned and his whole body slumped.

Panting, he raised his head and looked at her in the mirror, pulling his lips into a self-deprecating smile. 'Well, that was over much faster than I'd expected it to be.' Using the hand still buried in her hair, he turned her face so he could kiss her. 'You do test my control, Ms Frost. Round one goes to you.' The hand tightened just enough to cause her scalp to sting, his teeth nipped at her lower lip. 'But don't think you're going to get away without paying for it,' he promised darkly.

Annabel had been so close to her own release that she was still shaking like a leaf as he pulled out. She stumbled on a low moan of frustration, reaching out to the mirror for support.

'Steady,' Aidan said and guided her towards the bed, sitting her on the edge of it and lifting her chin as he leant down for another kiss. 'Don't move. I haven't finished with you yet – not by a long shot. I'll be right back,' he said, and made for the en suite to no doubt deal with the used condom.

Feeling suddenly drained of energy, Annabel let herself keel gently over to one side and sprawl on the mattress. She felt boneless, utterly spent, the place between her legs tingled with warmth while somewhere deeper, something spread that felt very much like the heavy weight of post-coital satisfaction. But how could that be when she hadn't even had an orgasm? It seemed too hard to think about the answer right then, too hard to fight the soporific trance that deepened her breathing, closed her eyelids, slowed her thoughts . . .

TWENTY-ONE

Satisfaction? Had that seriously been her last waking thought the previous evening? Annabel lay motionless on her back, keeping her eyes closed and her breathing even. Judging by the way her nerve endings hummed like she'd been jump-wired to a high voltage battery this morning, it hadn't been satisfaction that caused her to pass out last night, it had been utter exhaustion.

And to prove just how dissatisfied her body felt, it had woken her with an insistent throb of frustration. Even the brush of the bed covers against her skin was almost more than she could stand. If she didn't get some relief soon, she'd scream.

She could sense Aidan beside her in the bed. Although their bodies weren't touching she'd been aware of the heat of his presence since she'd first surfaced from sleep. And that aware-ness, combined with the memories of what he'd done to her last night was only making her predicament worse.

At least her preoccupied state meant she didn't have to obsess too much over the significance of having shared his bed all night. She'd never fallen asleep with a lover before, let alone woken up beside one. It felt strange. Nice. Strangely nice.

Given her current situation, she'd have thought that having a big, sexy, and no doubt naked man next to her in bed would be the perfect answer to her needs. But as the man in question was Aidan Flynn, she doubted it would be so simple. After pushing him to the point of losing control last night she couldn't help but worry that he'd make good on his promise to make her pay.

She suppressed a shiver at the thought of what price he'd exact, knowing it would more than likely involve more torturous frustration for her. For the sake of her own sanity, then, she knew she had to take some alone time before she could even contemplate surviving another round with him. Maybe she should take advantage and sneak out now, tend to urgent matters before he even woke?

The prospect of imminent of relief caused the most inflamed parts of her anatomy to twinge with enthusiasm. Cautiously, so as not to risk disturbing him, she turned only her head, cracking one eye open to check Aidan's sleeping form.

She found him lying on his side facing her, black bed-hair ruffled around his face and his pale eyes, bright and wide open, waiting. Disappointment barely had time to register against the warm wave of desire that washed over her when he smiled, teeth very white against a shadow of morning stubble which lent him even more of a roguish look than usual.

'Good morning, Annabel. I wondered how long you were going to lie there pretending to be asleep.'

She couldn't even be irritated by the dig, not when the covers were down around his waist, showing those wonderful broad shoulders and chest, the ridges of his abdomen. That maddening throb of frustration intensified. God, what wouldn't she do to get him to provide the relief she needed.

'I'm sorry I fell asleep on you last night.'

'It's all right, I didn't take it personally. You'd had quite a stressful day all in. You were out cold in a matter of minutes – still in your shoes, too.'

His voice husky with sleep, he sprawled lazily, the very picture of sexy, mellow contentment. Her pulse picked up. Maybe she'd get what she needed after all. Maybe he was more amenable now that he'd had his own satisfaction?

She turned on her side to face him, slid one hand slowly across the sheet toward his chest. 'We could pick up where we left off.'

He caught her hand before it reached him. 'We will. All in good time,' he said, and looking closer she saw that the core of steely determination was still there, lying beneath the relaxed exterior.

Damn it.

She jumped as the door chime sounded. Honestly, being around Aidan Flynn was playing havoc with her nerves.

'That'll be breakfast,' he said, kicking off the covers and rolling to his feet. Annabel got her first good view of the back of him as he walked naked to the bathroom and she had to admit it was nearly as good as the front view. He reappeared tying on a towelling robe a moment later and let himself out of the bedroom door.

There was no way she was going to sit through breakfast in the state she was in. Rising from the bed, she gathered her scattered clothing and slipped through the interconnecting door to retreat into her own bedroom.

She used the toilet and rinsed her hands, checking her reflection to gauge the damage a night in make-up had done to her face. Not too bad. Her lipstick hadn't survived long enough to make it to the bed anyway, and her mascara had smudged only a little. As she checked the state of her hair, her eye caught on the shower cubicle reflected over her shoulder.

'Oh, thank you,' she murmured when she spied the hand-held spray attachment fixed to the wall beneath the shower head, already imagining the delightful tickle of those fine jets against her highly sensitised flesh. Oh, yes, a quick wash was definitely in order.

She turned on the water and pulled on one of the robes that hung behind the door. Grabbing a hair clip from her wash bag, she twisted her hair up as she went to tell Aidan that she'd be out in a minute.

Opening her bedroom door, she saw him crossing the spacious sitting room, heading back towards his bedroom door with two glasses of orange juice. He detoured when he saw her.

'I was going to see if you wanted breakfast in bed,' he said as he came up and held one of the glasses out to her.

'Oh. That would be nice.' She took the glass and watched him take a long drink from his own, gaze locked on that strong throat working to swallow. 'But I'm a bit, you know, sticky after last night.' She indicated the sound of running water coming from behind. 'I'm going to jump into a quick shower first.' She took a hasty sip of her own juice to cover any inadvertent clues she might give away as he studied her face.

'Good idea.' He smiled, and she nearly sighed with relief at having got away with it.

'Great,' she said, trying to close the bedroom door but finding him in the way. She gave him a look. 'I won't be long.'

Instead of retreating he advanced a step.

'Er, I meant I'm taking that shower right now?'

'Yes, I know what you meant,' he said, reaching out to take her glass from her.

'But – I can manage from here.' She watched as he strolled past her into the room to place the glasses on the dresser.

'Oh, I'm sure you can, Annabel.' He turned back to her.

'Which is why we'll be showering together. Don't think I don't know what you're up to.'

He knew. Of course he did. At this rate she was going to have to start wearing a balaclava to avoid him reading her face. Her plans for self-pleasure foiled, she scowled.

Laughing, he came up in front of her and used the belt of her robe to pull her to him. 'And don't think I've forgotten about last night or am inclined to let you off payment.' Wrapping one arm around her, he clamped her flush against him, reminding her of all the hard strength hidden beneath his robe. His other hand clasped lightly around her jaw, tilted her face up to his. 'I know you must be nearly climbing the walls by now.' He gave a satisfied smile, his eyes glinting as they searched hers. 'But you won't be coming until I'm buried deep inside you again,' he said. 'And that might not be for some time yet.'

Before she could complain, he lowered his face and claimed her mouth with a kiss. A kiss that went on and on until her anger and his humour had melted into liquid desire. A kiss so lovely that it had her raising her hands to his head to hold him there forever, her fingers burying themselves with delight into the silky black waves of his hair.

Behind one ear, she found an unexpected ridge that ran in a long thin vertical line. Long enough to have her breaking away in surprise to see what she'd discovered.

'What's this?' she asked, brushing his hair aside and gasping at the sight of the six-inch scar that ran all the way down to the top of his neck.

'A souvenir from the stroke.' Aidan turned so that she could see better. 'Where they operated.'

'I had no idea,' she said quietly, laying a gentle touch at the base of the raised silvered line. 'It must have been bad.' What was she saying? Of *course* it must have been bad, when was a stroke ever good?

'I had a bleed in my brain that needed to be stopped. For the rest I've been lucky; the only other souvenir I have is this.' He turned back to face her and pointed to his lopsided smile. 'For some reason a few of my facial muscles haven't returned to normal after the paralysis.'

Paralysis? Annabel could barely believe it. He seemed so dynamic, so strong. She brought her fingertips around to touch that spot too, thinking how strange it was that something that seemed such a charming part of him should have come from something so devastating.

He grabbed her fingers and kissed them before using them to tug her after him towards her bathroom. The room was already warm and humid from the running water but even so, she shivered when he undid the sash of her robe with a single pull, swept it back off her shoulders and ran that intent silvery gaze over her. His robe followed a moment later, joining hers in a pile on the floor as he wordlessly used his big, naked and very vital body to herd her into the large shower cubicle.

He followed her in, filling the enclosure not only with his physical size but with the palpable force of energy that radiated from him. He overwhelmed the space with his very presence – she could feel the weight of it pressing in around her, stealing the air.

That didn't seem to matter a moment later as she forgot how to breathe anyway, watching him step under the spray, tip his head back into the water and stretch that torso as he reached his hands up to slick his sodden hair off his face.

He smiled knowingly at her as he stepped out from under the stream and reached for the shower gel. After squeezing an amount into his palm, he passed it to her.

Annabel took the bottle, but couldn't seem to do anything beyond clutch it as Aidan began to wash himself in front of her. Couldn't look away from the sight of his hands slipping

268

over the contours and ridges of his torso, sliding over long, lean muscle.

She stared as his ministrations worked lower, until he grasped the shaft of his erection in his fist, soaping the thick length of it, lifting to allow his other hand to cup the taut testicles beneath.

'Something on your mind, Ms Frost?' his husky voice snapped her attention up to his face. But she couldn't answer, she was speechless, had never shared a moment of such intimacy with anyone.

'If you keep looking at me like that, I'll be obliged to jack myself off for you.'

The thought of him pleasuring himself, putting on such an unashamedly carnal show for her was enough to make her breath stutter, which of course he saw. With a growling sound he stepped closer, crowding her back against the tiled wall. He pinned her with those eyes, which looked paler and more penetrating than ever fringed by black lashes clustered together into wet spikes.

'Would you like that?'

'Yes,' she breathed, unable to deny the truth when she could feel the rhythmic brush of his knuckles against her stomach, could see the flex of his biceps in the periphery of her vision as he continued to stroke himself.

'Even if it meant that you'd have to wait longer for your own relief?'

Did she want to put that off in order to watch him bring himself to the peak of pleasure, to see all that control, that masculine strength disintegrate, to see him tremble and lose himself for her viewing pleasure?

'Yes.'

He bent his head and pressed his wet lips softly to hers, brushed his tongue against them until he coaxed them apart, then dipped inside. Even as she was aware that he continued

269

to work himself, she felt the touch of his other hand on her neck, felt his fingers slide down over her chest and the curve of her breast, felt him circle her nipple once, twice, his touch a slick, feather-light tease that had her dropping the bottle of shower gel and raising her hands to his shoulders as she arched forward for more.

He cupped her in his palm for a moment, then ran his hand lower, his soap-slippery skin gliding effortlessly over waist and hip and belly. He deepened his kiss as his hand delved between her legs, fingertips only tracing her cleft. She was so sensitive with need down there that she whimpered into his mouth.

Taking her bottom lip between his teeth Aidan pulled it with him for a moment as he drew back to look at her.

'How long do you think you can wait?' he asked, eyes on hers as he added just enough pressure to slip his fingers deeper, to run a light caress back and forth through her hidden folds.

She didn't bother answering his question. He was smart enough to see the state she was in, to know just how devastating she found his taunting gentleness.

Her only concern was encouraging him to get a move on. Sliding her hands down over his chest she scored her nails lightly over the rises and ridges of his pectorals and abs, heading for his groin. 'Would you like some help?'

'No. I'd like you to put your hands on the tiles beside you.' There was no give in his tone or his look. 'You wanted to watch, so watch.'

Disobeying now would only lead to more delays, and that she couldn't face. So she did as he asked. Drinking in the sight of him touching himself as all the while he continued to touch her too, his fingers between her legs driving her mad.

He held nothing of himself back, letting her see his

excitement grow. And she'd never seen anything so erotic as when his control started to fracture, had never heard anything as sexy as when he said, 'I'm going to come for you, Annabel,' before rocking back on his heels to gasp in a breath. The movement put him under the spray of water, which cascaded down over his shoulders, and ran down his tightly tensed torso in rivulets. She couldn't resist, leaning forward she licked at one such rivulet. It was enough to push him over. With a ragged grunt he froze in place. Annabel pulled back in time to see a creamy ribbon of release pulse out of him, then in the next instant he unclasped himself, his hand reaching around the back of her thigh to lift her leg to his hip as he ground his pelvis against her, crushing her back against the wall. The position opened her enough that his previously teasing fingers slipped right inside at the same instant she felt a second release erupt from him in a splash of liquid heat against her stomach. His mouth came down hard on hers to swallow her desperate sounds of pleasure. He crowded even closer against her, his erection trapped between them, big and solid and no damned use to anyone at all where it was. Annabel insinuated a hand between their bodies, wrapped her fist around him, the soapy residue letting her glide up and down his length with ease. Aidan's hips gave a little jolt as he groaned into her mouth, pulsing in her hand he continued to come squeezed between their bodies.

He shifted, grabbed her other thigh and hauled it up so that she wrapped both legs around his hips. His hands came under her buttocks to support her. His hips began thrusting, driving into the grip she kept on him. Spread so wide, pressed so tight against him, she felt the delicious friction, the pressure of every movement they made. Pushing back against him, she was sure she could ride herself to completion with just a few thrusts.

She tore her mouth away from his. His wet hair smoothed

into ribbons clung to his neck, exposing the end of his scar. She pressed her lips gently against it, moved further down to the tendons in his shoulder and bit into them, her groan hitching against his hot, wet flesh as his soapy fingers dipped into the valley of her buttocks and swept shockingly over every part of her.

'Oh, God,' she gasped, rearing back when he repeated the caress, her head resting against the tiles. He was watching her intently as he passed over that sensitive spot a third time, his touch slower, more deliberate. The sensation, so new and exciting, made her eyes lose focus, her eyelids flickering closed as the pleasure mounted and she strained for the summit. 'Oh, yes.'

'No,' he ordered gruffly. 'Not yet. Not until I'm inside you.'

'Then hurry.' He was still hard where she gripped him. She tried to guide him to where she wanted him, felt him jerk when she pushed him against her entrance.

'Wait. Condom.' Pulling her away from the wall, he ducked their clasped bodies under the spray for a rinse. 'Turn off the water.' He barely waited for her to do so before taking a firmer grip and carrying her out of the bathroom and all the way back to his bed.

Sopping wet as they were, Aidan crawled right onto the mattress and deposited her on her back before rearing back onto his knees. Grasping her inner thighs he spread her legs, wide. The gaze he raked over her most private parts left her struggling, trying to close against the acute rush of self-consciousness, but his grip tightened, holding her just where he wanted her.

'Don't. I want to look at you, Annabel. I want to taste you again.' She shivered, not sure whether from the intensity of those silvery eyes or from the air against her wet skin. Still holding her wide, he lowered himself between her legs. Turning his head, he trailed open-mouthed kisses up the inside of one thigh, his wet hair dripping and his morning

272

stubble scratching deliciously against the soft skin until he reached the crease between leg and groin. There he licked instead – a slow, light, brush of his tongue that made her shudder and rotate her hips, looking for more. Ignoring the movement, he turned and took his time to repeat the process on her other thigh until she pleaded, 'Aidan.'

She grabbed handfuls of the sheet when she felt his thumbs slide in to part her, closed her eyes as she felt nothing but his breath for an endless moment, heard him rasp the word, 'Beautiful,' and then his mouth was there at last, hot and wet and hungry. She rocketed skyward where she floated on a cloud of bliss, aware of nothing but the intense pleasure Aidan generated using his tongue and teeth and lips, not to mention that prickly stubble, to bring her to such devastating heights, only to ease her back down again without release. Again and again, until she was a moaning, groaning, writhing wreck of need.

Aidan eventually raised his head to interrupt her stream of babbling. 'Are you asking for more, Annabel?'

'Yes.' Her voice sounded raw as she answered him fervently. 'Yes.'

She nearly cried out when he pulled away from her, but as she lay there spread, her body pulsing with need, she realised he was going for a condom at last. It was impossible not to ogle him as he moved about naked and graceful and assured in the tightly defined contours of his own skin. When he bent his head to the task at hand, her gaze strayed to the mirror on the wall behind him, the surface smudged with hand prints – lots of her smaller ones and only one large. Recalling how he'd looked when he'd lost himself for her last night, her hand crept down to touch the place where she throbbed most as she closed her eyes. Just the lightest touch had her arching, ready . . .

Then she felt the bed dip. Opened her eyes to see him move over her again.

'You look captivating touching yourself,' he murmured, his warm palm covering the hand she had between her legs. 'One day soon I'll get you to make yourself come like that for me while I watch you. But not today.'

He captured her other hand and moved both, pinning her wrists to the mattress either side of her head as he settled his weight onto her. His mouth came down, took hers in a kiss that tasted intimately of her. His tongue delved deep as further down his hips started to rock his readiness against her spread sex. He rubbed back and forth, grinding the solid length against her, teasing her entrance with the broad tip, but never breaching it. Never giving her what she craved. She broke the kiss for need of air, her moans growing more vocal the more her frustration rose.

'So sweet, and so loud. No doubt the other hotel guests are getting to enjoy this as much as we are.'

He thought torturing her was funny? 'Aidan!'

'Annabel?'

'*Please.*'

'Please, what?'

'God,' she shouted, infuriated. 'You *know* what!'

'No. I'm not a mind reader,' he said calmly but with a flex of his hips that suggested the statement was a lie and that he did, indeed, wield impressive psychic powers and know exactly what she wanted. 'You need to learn how to tell me what you want from me.'

She half sobbed with frustration and anger and need. She lifted her head to glare her intent right into his eye as she threatened, 'Fuck me now or die.'

He laughed. 'Well, seeing as you asked so nicely.' And with a small adjustment he surged inside.

Aidan clenched his jaw as he entered Annabel in a smooth, seemingly endless glide that had her sucking in a lungful of air. She was so wet for him, the position allowing much greater access than he'd had last night, that her tight heat welcomed him all the way home. She obviously noticed the difference too, her spine arching off the mattress at the invasion, offering her lovely breasts up in an invitation he couldn't refuse. Ducking his head, he sucked one pink nipple into his mouth as he held her pinned beneath him and slid the last inch home, filling her up.

'God, you're perfect,' he said, trailing kisses back up to her neck as he started to move, keeping it slow and steady and controlled. 'How does it feel?'

'Good,' Annabel croaked. 'So good.'

As he pushed all the way into her again, he had to agree. Being buried to the balls in Annabel Frost felt like heaven on earth. 'You've got all of me, *a mhuirnín*,' he said, feeling the solid pressure of her pelvic bone tight against his own. 'I couldn't get any deeper into you if I tried.' He rotated his hips instead, drawing out long groans from both of them.

With the edge of his own need already blunted, he could take the time that her forthright antics had stolen from him last night. The slower he kept things, the easier it would be for him to read her reactions, learn what she liked. And it wasn't long before she was giving him all sorts of clues – most notably the impatient twist and pull of her wrists in his hold. He couldn't blame her. After the teasing build-up of sexual tension he'd subjected her to he could only imagine how agonising the slow pace must be. He was ready to give her anything she needed, but he wanted to hear her beg for it first. The independent Ms Frost liked taking what she wanted. Time she learnt how to ask for it.

With the next slide home she bucked beneath him, gave a ragged little cry. Lowering his head, he followed the taut line of the tendon up the side of her neck with his tongue.

'Tell me,' he whispered when he reached her ear.

'Faster. God, go faster.'

He increased his rhythm a little, enough to draw another cry from her, but judging by the way she continued to writhe in his hold, not enough to bring her the satisfaction she sought. For every push of his hips, she thrust back against him, quicker, harder, the noises she made full of frustration.

'Ask me for what you want, Annabel.'

'More. Faster!'

She looked surprised when he suddenly flipped their positions, laying himself out flat on his back with her straddling him.

'Show me how fast.'

She stalled for only as long as it took her to get over the shock of being handed control, and then she didn't hesitate at all. Placing her hands on his chest, she rode him, her pace growing faster, her need increasing. His own hands filled with her breasts, he watched her move above him, watched her fight for a release that hovered on the periphery but that she couldn't seem to reach.

Running one hand down her stomach, he pushed his thumb between her legs, searching out the place she needed him.

'God, yes,' she gasped a moment later. And then everything was shifting, lifting, tightening around him. He knew she was close, mere moments away. When she closed her eyes and flung her head back he was ready.

'No,' he growled, transferring his hand from her breast to the back of her neck, forcing her head forward again. 'Open your eyes. Look at me.'

Her eyelids flew open again, her green irises bright with desire as she focused on him. He exerted more force on her neck, bringing her down closer, until her torso was angled over him and she had to push her hands into the mattress to support herself.

'You keep your eyes on mine as the pleasure takes you,'

he said, increasing the pressure of his thumb as he dug his heels into the mattress to punctuate his thrusts. 'I want to see you come.'

And he did see it, right then. He saw the rosy flush wash over her skin, saw her eyes widen and her mouth open on a silent moan. More than that, as he held their gazes locked, he saw what he'd been hoping to see – the masking layers of protection, of years of social conditioning dropping away to reveal a glimpse of her true self. And in that unguarded moment what he saw of her was delicate, passionate, so beautiful it made his chest hurt.

'Annabel,' he breathed, and her whole body clenched before it began to shudder. He picked up the pace, driving himself deep as her internal muscles started to flutter around him, massaging his own release from where he held it boiling inside him. As Annabel reached the peak of her ascent and hovered just before the freefall back down, he pulled her mouth down onto his and let himself go with a shout.

Ten minutes later he was pleased he'd ordered everything sweet and sugary he could find on the breakfast menu as he watched her devour two enormous almond croissants. If things continued like this between them they were both going to need all the energy they could get.

TWENTY-TWO

Aidan's reaction when she appeared from her room that evening dressed for the ball went a long way to reassuring Annabel about the green gown. She'd spent ages in front of the full-length mirrors, checking out her reflection, worried that the draped and ruched asymmetric layering of the shot silk skirts was too much. She'd left her hair down, pinned to one side with a crystal-studded clip to let the long loose curls cascade over her shoulder. A matching crystal choker sparkled around her neck, leaving her décolleté bare above the pleated neckline of the boned bodice.

Turning from where he'd been looking out through a window over the night-time city lights twinkling beyond, he tracked her entrance into the room. Rustling her way to the dining table where their coats were slung over the back of a chair, she placed her clutch on the polished surface and, hands smoothing over the voluminous skirts, she turned to face him. He remained silent for a moment as his gaze swept over her.

'You look breathtaking,' he said with a sort of rasp that suggested he was indeed struggling to find air.

'You don't look so bad yourself,' she returned, in what was a gross understatement. He looked like he'd stepped right out of the glossy pages of *GQ* – tall, dark and incredibly handsome in a classic black tie ensemble that fitted his body like it had been tailored personally for him. Which was very probably the case, she realised, given the circles he moved in.

He crossed the room towards her with his usual fluid grace, those keen eyes taking in every detail of her appearance. He stopped in front of her, gaze mapping her face. 'I want to kiss you,' he said, attention dropping to focus on her mouth. 'But I wouldn't be able to stop myself messing up that perfect lipstick if I did.'

With the way he was looking at her, she was about to say she could easily reapply it, but he spoke again first. 'I'll just have to get creative.'

Hands reaching for her hips, he pushed her back a few steps until she felt the press of the table against her skirts. Dropping to his knees, he began gathering up the fabric of the dress, giving her a wicked smile before he disappeared underneath it. Annabel leaned back against the table, hands gripping the edge as she felt her underwear being pulled aside, felt Aidan's fingers opening her a second before she felt the light press of his lips, the warm, wet flutter of his tongue over her clitoris which sent a shudder through her. Then he nudged her thighs apart and deepened the intimate kiss, his mouth closing over her, sucking at the tender flesh as his tongue stroked through her folds.

Her knees were jelly and fine tremors were chasing each other all over her body by the time he re-emerged.

'Jesus,' he muttered, rising to his feet to loom over her where she continued to lean against the table in an attempt to support her weight. 'I want to be inside you.' He licked at his moist bottom lip, the slashes of high colour across the ridge of his cheekbones evidence of his own arousal. 'Right now. All night. Feeling you come around me again. Listening to you scream my name.'

279

She was on the verge of screaming it right then from frustration – the hint of regret in his voice telling her that he was going to leave her in this state even as his words ratcheted up the tension. Luckily, she bit back the urge as the door chime sounded.

With a last, lingering look that promised all sorts of pleasures later, Aidan stepped back from her. Running a hand through his mussed hair, he reached for their coats.

'Time to go.'

They caught the lift down to the lobby with Bal, who, apart from the array of silver and jet-studded skull rings adorning both hands, some sort of black crystal encrusted cod-piece attached to the front of his trousers and the obvious lack of a bow tie, was conservatively dressed for the occasion given his reputation for outlandish costumes. Arriving on the ground floor, they found Yuliya, dramatic in blood-red satin and a queen's ransom worth of rubies, speaking to the staff at the reception desk.

'Perfect timing,' she said, leaving the desk and coming to greet them. 'I just arrived and was having them call you.'

Bal kissed her on both cheeks. 'We're here. Damien and Gee are on the way down. And you look absolutely ravishing,' he said, taking her hand and giving her a little twirl. 'I wish I'd been slower getting ready so that you'd have had to come up to find me.'

'I'm sure my fiancé would love to read about that in tomorrow's papers.' Yuliya all but rolled her eyes. 'Though, you obviously do need help dressing yourself.' She flicked a finger at his open shirt collar. 'Where's your tie?'

'Tie?' Bal said with theatrical horror. 'Watch your language, woman. I can't be seen in a tie! And it would serve that idiot Viktor right to worry about you. What sort of man leaves such a beauty to travel around unaccompanied?'

Yuliya patted Bal's cheek. 'A very busy, highly evolved one, my dear Neanderthal. This isn't the dark ages. He's not even locked me in a chastity belt.'

Bal was making a show of trying to get her to prove it when Damien and Georgiana stepped out of the elevator a minute later, their arrival drawing the attention of pretty much everyone in the lobby. Damien looked effortlessly dark and sexy in black tie, the perfect foil for Georgiana's pale gown with its bodice of silver ribbon lace and floating dove-grey chiffon skirt. Her blonde hair had been gathered into a perfect chignon with tiny pearl pins scattered throughout. Elegant diamond and pearl drops hung from her ears.

Watching Georgiana glide as though her feet didn't touch the ground, Annabel braced for the sneering judgement on her own dress that was surely to come. But although the blonde gave her a thorough going over, she followed it with no more than a shallow, fleeting smile before letting Damien lead her towards the doors.

As the hotel was situated directly behind the opera house, the party set off on foot. In their strappy evening shoes, the women all felt the bite of the freezing air on their toes while the light snowfall decorated heads and shoulders with a dusting of icy jewels.

The snow had been falling pretty much since the middle of the day, when Annabel and Aidan had finally left the hotel to rest tender muscles and take in the sights. The settling drifts and twirling flakes lent the city a magical winter wonderland feel, especially in the pretty squares and amongst the stalls of the Wintermarkt, where the sweet-spiced scents of fresh baked goods mingled with the more potent aroma of warm glühwein and only added to the charm.

To Annabel's mind, however, the best thing about Vienna, had been the abundance of beautiful cafés the cold weather had given them the regular excuse to stop in and warm up on truly excellent coffee. What wasn't to love about a city reportedly famed for having created the first coffee house in Europe?

Rounding the corner to the front of the Opera House, Annabel saw that the pavement directly outside the arched entrance had been covered by a red carpet around which crowds of onlookers and paparazzi had gathered.

An explosion of noise and flashbulbs erupted as their party crossed the red carpet – mostly frenzied shouts vying for the attention of Bal and Damien. When Bal 'raised the horn' – the ubiquitous rock'n'roll hand signal symbolising the devil's horns – the screams of delight became almost deafening. Damien, on the other hand, didn't react at all. The son of legendary musician Drake Harcourt, he had a rock'n'roll pedigree and a scandalous family history that made him a favourite obsession with the popular press. But watching as he breezed past as though he'd not noticed a thing, Annabel figured the feeling was far from mutual.

They made their way under the arched canopy of the loggia, up a shallow set of steps and through the doors. Inside the lobby, more photographers waited, crowding around the base of the magnificent ivory marble staircase as they encouraged celebrity guests to pose on the steps to great effect.

With a protective hand against her spine, Aidan guided Annabel up to the first floor where the cream of the international jet set and A-list stars rubbed shoulders with influential political leaders and corporate bigwigs. A select guest list of two hundred had been invited to the exclusive VIP dinner which was taking place prior to the ball opening its doors to the greater public at nine p.m.

One of the long intermission halls – a beautiful room with tapestry-lined walls and unique golden chandeliers – had been transformed into a dining room. Round tables had been covered with white linen and the places set with decorative gold-plated cutlery while tall, ornate gold candelabra rose from exquisite white floral centrepieces.

At Damien's table, which was set to one end of the room by a low stage, Annabel found herself in the company of some of the guests from the previous night's dinner party. And she was once again seated beside Bal, who made the first two courses of the meal pass quickly as he flirted and joked and shared salacious, not to mention utterly libellous, bits of gossip about many of the room's occupants.

At the next table were the Reisers. Astrid – resplendent in gold couture, to match the colour theme for the night – managed to look the epitome of gracious calm even as she kept an organisational eye on every detail of the evening she'd been responsible for creating.

Over dessert, she made her way onto the stage and introduced the president of the charity – the Future Bright Foundation – who in turn formally welcomed them all to the inaugural Bright Ball, an event which the charity intended to host annually as the major fundraiser for their cause. There followed a projected presentation which highlighted the charity's commitment to bringing education to every child across Europe, regardless of race, gender, religion, or social or economic standing, and showcasing how the generous donations from their benefactors were being put to good use.

'And now that we have filled your stomachs and emptied your wallets,' the president finished up to ripples of laughter, 'I would ask that you all join me in the auditorium as the doors have been opened and it's time to get the dancing underway.'

Damien led his group of guests to two private boxes, plushly decorated in red with velvet-cushioned seating and small linen-covered tables holding ice buckets chilling bottles of champagne and wine. Stepping into one of the boxes, Annabel took in the sight of the grand auditorium before

283

her. Opposite, across the expanse of the ground floor which had been cleared of seating and was full of milling crowds, an orchestra filled the stage providing a classical backing track to the noise of hundreds of chattering voices. Meeting each side of the stage, three tiers of private boxes and two upper galleries festooned with festive garlands and wreaths, ringed the enormous space in a horseshoe shape, the whole luxuriously decorated in golds, reds and creams.

A sudden fanfare from the stage cut through the noise and drew everyone's attention to the conductor, who bowed to the crowd before asking that the floor be cleared for the debutants. Obediently, the crowds parted, pushing back against the walls.

Yuliya took two glasses of champagne that Aidan had poured and handed one to Annabel. 'You've not been to a Viennese ball before?' she asked.

'No,' Annabel shook her head as the orchestra struck up with new vigour.

'Then you'll enjoy this spectacle – I always do. It's a tradition here to officially open balls with a processional Polonaise – a type of court dance which is performed by debutants.'

As she spoke a column of young women dressed in snow-white gowns and men in black tails filed into the auditorium. Four abreast, gloved hands linked, row upon row promenaded down the centre of the dance floor at a dignified pace, their gliding steps in keeping with the music's tempo, every third one accentuated by a slight bending of the knees.

And the rows kept coming, until the dancers numbered over a hundred. When the head of the column reached the opposite end of the dance floor, the couples parted, with pairs looping right and left to double back along either side of the advancing centre ranks. Once all of the couples had been divided into two separate trains, the dance became more complex as the group performed patterns – winding, criss-crossing, side-stepping, their precise formations and contrasting black and white costumes giving the illusion of a giant moving chequerboard.

The dance finished to great applause, leaving the debutants drawn into two circles on the dance floor. As the noise died down to be replaced by the sweet, slow strains of a violin, the couples turned to each other and performed a courtly bow, the young women placing their fingers lightly in those of their partners before folding into low, graceful curtsies and the men bowing at the waist to almost touch their foreheads to their grasped hands. When the women rose, each couple came together in the closed position before moving as one in the first turning steps of the waltz.

Applause erupted again at the sight. After the stately symmetry of the Polonaise, the fluid swirl of the waltz created a dizzying spectacle of black and billowing white. As, here and there, the guests started to step from the sidelines and join the circling mass, Annabel had to admit that her mother had been right about the dress. A waltz required big skirts.

Beside her, Yuliya put down her glass. 'I'm going to dance,' she announced, grabbing a surprised Bal by the arm and dragging him from where he stood chatting at the back of the box, laughing dirtily at something one of his companions was saying. 'Anybody joining us?'

Two other couples quickly followed, and Annabel returned her attention to the dancing below. After only a moment, she felt a hand descend onto her shoulder and turned to see that Aidan had stepped up beside her. 'How about you, Ms Frost. Would you like to dance?'

She cast another glance at the spinning sea of humanity and shook her head. 'I don't really know how.'

'Doesn't matter,' Aidan said. 'Nor do half the people on that floor. And wait until Bal gets out there. You'll actually be able to see him counting the steps aloud.'

Annabel laughed, diverted by the unlikely picture that

would make – one of the bad boys of rock counting steps like a child. 'That reminds me of—' When she realised she'd been about to share a silly memory of her counting the steps while she danced on her father's feet, she stopped herself. 'Never mind,' she dismissed, self-consciously turning away.

She felt Aidan shift closer. 'Reminds you of what?' he prodded gently, but with enough interest in his tone to tell her that he wouldn't let it drop.

So, taking a sip of champagne and keeping her eyes averted, she told him. For a moment he stayed silent by her side, then reached for her hand and raised it to his lips. Surprised by the gesture, she turned to be met by a gaze warmed by something that looked like pride. 'Finish your drink and then you can use my feet.'

'You don't waltz,' she challenged, flustered

'I do. I grew up with four sisters all of whom attended the local dance school and all of whom found it useful to have a practice partner at home. You should see my *pas de deux*.' He gave a formal little bow and held a palm out to her. 'Would you do me the honour, Ms Frost?'

Seriously, she was beginning to think the man wasn't even real.

Ten minutes later she could feel how real he was as they found themselves all but wrestling in the middle of the dance floor.

'Stop trying to lead,' Aidan muttered through clenched jaws as he tried to manhandle her into a spin.

'I can't help it,' Annabel snapped with frustration, nearly wrenching her knee as she mis-stepped in the wrong direction again. 'I told you I couldn't do it.' She made to pull away from him and retreat back up to the box but he firmed his grip, preventing her escape by holding her fast against him.

She felt the rush of his breath stir the hair at her temple

as he exhaled in frustration. Then he lowered his mouth to her ear. 'Close your eyes,' he said, the low command brushing over her skin like velvet.

'I don't think that's going to help.'

'Just try it. You're overthinking things. As usual.'

She bristled. 'And how is me bumbling about blindly going to simplify things?'

Aidan slowed their pace, pulled her even tighter against his body. 'Remember the night at my place when you were blindfolded? Remember how liberating it felt to let go? To give control up to me?'

Annabel licked her suddenly dry lips, remembering with a shiver the delicious helplessness she'd felt that night, waiting to feel the play of ice against her hot skin.

He pulled back a little to look down at her. 'Let go again,' he bid, eyes sharply focused with his will. 'Let me take care of you now.'

She held his gaze for a moment longer and then let her lids drift shut. She felt him pull her close again, felt the long fingers resting between her shoulder blades splay wider as he moulded her against his hard chest and swept them confidently into a series of smooth revolutions.

His mouth found her ear again. 'You thrill me, Annabel Frost,' he whispered. 'Your trust is like a gift.'

The words flowed through her, washing some of the tension out from her limbs. As she felt herself relax she was aware of Aidan's strength taking up the slack, aware of the graceful flex and stretch of his muscles as he took control and guided them both around the floor.

When the music stopped, Annabel opened her eyes to find him smiling at her. She couldn't help but smile back. 'Thank you, that was amazing.' She pulled back to break out of his hold, but again, he wouldn't let her go.

'I agree,' he said, gathering her close as the orchestra struck up a new piece. Let's try another. I like the feel of you in my arms.'

Almost as one, the countless couples on the dance floor began to move again, swirling around Annabel and Aidan in a fantastic, ever changing kaleidoscope of coloured gowns and glinting jewels and beaming faces. But she realised that it was the brilliant flash of Aidan's eyes, his smile of fierce satisfaction and pure enjoyment that really sent her senses into a dizzying spin.

She waited for her warning system to set off the alarm bells, waited for the defensive panic to hit, but in the midst of the mad whirl, all she felt was the solid presence of Aidan, wrapped around her like a strong tether that promised to keep her from being blown away in the maelstrom of new sensation. She shouldn't let herself fall for the illusion of security, but she found that the pull was irresistible.

Relaxing into him, she closed her eyes. The music swelled and the tempo quickened, spinning them faster and faster until it felt as though her feet barely touched the floor. Throwing her head back, she laughed with delight, and opened her eyes to see the lights of the auditorium swirl dizzily above her. When she lowered her gaze to Aidan's face, she was met with a look of such intensity and naked desire that it stole the laughter from her throat.

Caught up in the magic of the moment she had a sudden desperate urge to make the most of this fairytale before the spell got broken. Like Cinderella, her fantasy came with a time limit, and she wanted nothing more than to make the most of it before midnight struck and returned her to the hard practicalities of real life.

With an urgent squeeze to the hand that held hers aloft, she said, 'Take me back to the hotel. Now.'

TWENTY-THREE

Aidan had enough time to throw his jacket over the back of one of the armchairs before Annabel had herself pushed up against him, mouth stretching to meet his, hands groping with single-minded determination. As he'd noted previously, if there was one thing Ms Frost wasn't backward in being forward about, it was taking what she wanted. And that in itself wasn't a bad thing – as his spring-loaded erection could testify – except when it was obvious to him that such behaviour came less from conscious choice than from the fact that she knew no other way but to take pleasure on her terms. He'd bet no man had ever got close enough to *give* her anything.

He looked forward to being the first to teach her the gift of receiving.

Allowing himself to accept and enjoy her kisses, he held her away when he felt her hands start to undo the zipper of his trousers. It would be better if they both remained dressed for the moment.

'As flattered as I am by your enthusiasm, Annabel, I'm afraid to say you've already had all the rope you're going to get from me.'

She frowned at him. 'What do you mean?'

'I mean that I've given you all the slack I'm prepared to give, allowed you more than enough freedom. It's time to tighten the ties so I can do all the things I want to do to you.'

She looked at him in uncertainty for a moment.

'Do you mean tie me up – literally?'

He bent his head a little so she could see the intent in his gaze. 'Yes. I do mean tie you up. Literally.'

'No.' She tried to pull away but he locked his arms around her and caged her to him.

'Why not?'

'You know why not. I'm not into giving up control.'

'And yet, you've given up quite a bit to me, especially during the past twenty-four hours.'

She shook her head. 'Not easily. And not on the level you're asking for now. I can't do it.'

'You can't. You don't. You won't. You say things like that a lot. But how do you know you can't if you've never tried?'

'Because this is too much. I know better than to put myself in a position where I can't defend myself.' Although she wasn't struggling, he could feel the rigidity in her spine, feel the steady pressure of her palms against his chest as she sought to put some distance between them.

'What is it you think you'll need to defend yourself against?' he asked with quiet earnestness. 'For my part, I've already promised that I'll never hurt you. Whatever else you think you've learnt about me, you should know by now that I'm a man of my word.'

'It doesn't matter. You can't expect me to go against my better judgement and give you that much control.'

'But I do expect it. The issue is whether you can agree to it.'

She shook her head, pushed harder against the hold he refused to relax. 'It scares me.'

Oh, he was already acutely aware of that. 'Yes, I know it

does. I can see how you're reacting to just being held trapped against me like this. And I can't deny that fact is a big part of the attraction – can't say it doesn't excite me to see your eyes widen.' Keeping one arm clamped around her waist, he raised the other and brushed a strand of red hair from her cheek. 'To feel your pulse pounding.' He traced his fingertips over the fluttering vein in her neck. 'The rapid rise and fall of your chest against mine.' Settling his palm over her breastbone, he felt the racing patter of her heartbeat. 'Not because I want you to be frightened of me, but because I understand that a little bit of the fear of the unknown can be a good thing. All that adrenaline-spiked blood pumping extra fast to every part of your body, flooding your nerve endings, feeding your brain, putting every sense on high alert. You can see better, hear better, feel better.' Ducking his head, he pressed a kiss to the side of her jaw. 'Every touch is amplified, every taste and scent more distinct.' Because he couldn't resist, he put his nose to her neck and took a deep draw of her scent before raising his head to look at her again. 'It's about giving you pleasure like you've never known before, Annabel. It's the place I want you to be every time I put my hands on you, so that not a single touch is wasted, so that every sensation is maximised.'

Even though her green eyes showed a touch of heat smouldering around the edges of fear, she shook her head, said, 'What if I say no?' – but in a voice far softer than it had been a moment ago. It was enough of an advantage for him to press.

'Then I'll keep pushing. Because "no" is exactly what I'd expect you to say. I know what I'm asking of you, Annabel, know how far out of your comfort zone this falls. But I'm asking it anyway. If you can't do it then the word you need to use is "stop".' He raised his hand and clasped her chin so that he had her full attention. 'But if you say it, be sure that's really what you want.'

She closed her eyes, obviously torn.

'Let me show you something, before you decide.' Making himself release her, he went into his en suite and retrieved the towelling sash from the bath robe, hoping that – like the dinner napkin he'd used as a blindfold at his apartment – the mundane nature of the item would help make the prospect of its intended use seem less threatening. Coming back into the sitting room, he noticed she hadn't moved from where he'd left her. Going directly to the dining area, he pulled one of the ladder-backed chairs out from the table and looped the strip of towelling around the top strut. Explaining the workings of a slip knot, he tied one, demonstrating how she could free herself with one simple tug.

'Will you let me try it on you?' he coaxed easily – as though he wasn't holding his breath like her answer was the most important thing in the world. 'One hand only.'

She looked at him, at the sash, with trepidation. But then she moved, and it was the first step she took toward him that told him her true desires. That first step that had lust raking its claws so deep it was almost painful.

She stepped near, but not too close, and extended one arm. Calling on every ounce of will power he owned he managed to keep his movements slow and casual as he tied the sash around her slender wrist and let her see for herself how quick and easy it was to release it.

'Now the same thing with two.' Watching her carefully he gathered her hands and held them together in front of her, wrapping the sash around both. Tying the knot, he pressed the loose end into one of her palms and watched as she again freed herself with ease.

'How's that?'

'It would be just like this?' she asked.

He nodded, sliding the sash from her fingers. 'Just your hands this first time, yes. Tied together like this. Just for fun.' He kept an eye on her expression as he reached for one of her hands again and raised it to his mouth to press a kiss against her pulse point before he began to wind the sash around it again. This was the moment he found out if he'd done enough to earn her trust. 'Do you want me to stop?'

She did but she didn't; he could see it warring all over her face.

'No.' She hit him with that green gaze and offered her other hand this time, rather than wait for him to take it – a show of courage that slayed him where he stood.

He grasped it loosely, turning it to expose the inside of her wrist as he brought it to his mouth and this time traced his tongue along a delicate web of blue veins there, leaving Annabel shivering as he began lashing her wrists together.

Once the knot was complete, he cupped her face and stepped close to kiss her, deep and long, because the sight of her bound for him made it impossible not to claim her in some way. Those claws of lust were shredding his insides.

With her hands trapped between their bodies, it didn't take the industrious Ms Frost long to discover his iron-hard erection within her reach. This time when she groped him through his trousers, he let her. Not only because he was greedy for her touch, but because giving her a sense of control to start with would help ease her into her first bondage experience, would hopefully allow him to take her deeper without scaring her off.

He nipped her bottom lip as he broke the kiss. 'As you like to be so useful with your hands, *a mhuirnín*, why don't you see if you can undress me?'

Maybe this really wasn't so bad after all, Annabel thought as she reached her bound hands towards the studs of his dress shirt – she was tied up but somehow gained all the power while Aidan Flynn stood as passive as she'd ever seen him, moving only to assist her efforts, letting her do as she pleased.

And it pleased her to uncover that masculine strength as quickly as possible. Starting at the top, she found it easy to get his shirt off to expose the width of his shoulders, the contours of his chest. She knelt low to remove his footwear and then rose up on her knees and reached for the belt of his trousers. As she went to work on the buckle, the backs of her fingers brushed against the silky dark hairs that ran south from his navel in a fine line. She saw Aidan's abs clench sharply in reaction, felt his palm come to rest on the crown of her head. A moment later his breath hissed as her wrist grazed against the hard bulge of his erection through his trousers, his fingers twitched against her scalp.

She glanced up to see his fiercely focused expression. It was obvious he liked the picture she made on her knees before him, and it wasn't hard to figure what ideas were running through his mind.

As she undid his flies, uncovering more of that treasure trail of body hair leading down into the waistband of his boxer shorts as she went, her own mind became suddenly set on the same idea. Once loosened, his trousers fell easily away, leaving her only to pull his underwear down. He was fully erect when he sprang free, and Annabel left the boxers hanging around his thighs as she reached to cup the swollen weight of him between her palms.

A wordless noise, deep and appreciative, escaped Aidan's lips as she slid her bound hands up and down his length. She licked her lips in anticipation and felt him jerk in response – felt the fine tremble running through him as she opened and took him into her mouth, the tiny shudders speaking volumes about the effect she had on him. He was hot, of course, and hard. But as she began to move her mouth and hands in tandem along his length she discovered an incredible softness also, all that hard heat wrapped in a layer of silken skin. His scent enveloped her, musky and male, his taste slightly salty on her tongue when she began to suck.

The cadence of Aidan's breathing changed, and although his hand stayed light on her head, she was aware of the tension in his fingertips increasing. His hips started to rock, the movements tight and retrained, but the restraint came at a cost. She could feel the leashed power of him. Understood for the first time the effort he exerted to keep all that passion and strength so controlled. Wondered what it would take to make him lose it again, as thoroughly as he'd lost it for her last night.

Spurred on, she grasped him tighter, took him deeper, wrenched a groan from his throat.

Then he was pulling away from her.

Bending to haul her to her feet, he pressed his lips briefly to hers when she was upright. 'As amazing as that feels, you're not getting the better of me tonight, Annabel.' He released her to tug up his boxers at the same time as kicking out of his trousers. 'Let's take this to your room.'

Reaching down to his discarded trousers, he plucked his wallet from a pocket before leading the way into her bedroom.

Making his way straight to the bedside, he placed his wallet on the side table and turned to sit on the edge of the bed.

When Annabel made to close the short distance between them, he held up a hand. 'Stay where you are, *a mhuirnín*. I'd like to watch you undress for me now. Why don't you untie yourself so you can get that gown off?'

She stopped, the sight of all that finely moulded male beauty exposed and so tantalisingly close, made her waste no time in complying. Pulling on the short end of the sash, she felt the knot unravel, allowing her to slip her bonds in an instant. The reminder of how easily she could free herself was reassuring, and she had no doubt that was why Aidan had suggested she do it. Shrewd man.

He reached forward to take the sash from her, then sprawled back again to watch as she released the cleverly hidden fastenings of her gown and stepped out of it, leaving herself in a pair of appliquéd burgundy lace knickers.

'Shoes next,' he directed – and once released, her toes wriggled against the soft carpet with relief.

As she went to hook her fingers into the waistband of her underpants, he ordered her to stop. 'I'll do the rest.'

Rising to his feet, he came with loose-limbed grace toward her. Without the added inches lent by her heels, the difference in their height was overwhelming apparent. He towered over her, a wall of taut strength, close enough that she felt the heat from his bare skin beat against hers as he spent an unhurried minute retying the sash around her hands.

Then his free hands were on her, smoothing down over her waist and hips. His fingers dipped under the elastic of her briefs and slid them down her thighs, leaving Annabel to step out of them as they dropped to pool around her ankles.

Grasping control of her bound wrists in one hand, he delved the fingers of the other between her thighs. His face lit with a pulse-hitching smile. 'I do believe you're enjoying this more than you thought you would, Ms Frost,' he said as his fingers slipped through the unmistakable slickness they'd discovered there. 'How do you feel about your hands being bound to one of the bed posts?'

Her gut reaction was to refuse – she'd accepted a big enough compromise as it was. Being tied to something added an extra element of helplessness, would deny her the opportunity to steer the course of events, to touch him.

'You'll still be able to free yourself whenever you want,' Aidan said, obviously reading the doubt flitting across her features. Then he lowered his face to hers to steal another soft kiss before whispering against her lips, 'I'll make it worth your while. I'll make you come, and come, and come.'

The husky promise left her knees so weak that she swayed against him. He was fighting dirty again, bribing her with sex. And as she'd previously found out, what defence did she have against that?

'Let's try it and see,' she said somewhat shakily, in what she recognised was becoming an all too familiar catchphrase.

Without giving her the chance to change her mind, Aidan helped her onto the bed, coaxing her to lie diagonally across the mattress before climbing on himself and crawling his way up over her legs to straddle her hips. Taking hold of her bound hands, he raised them above her head, holding her arms stretched while he lowered his mouth to kiss her. He broke away only when she began squirming beneath him, reaching to tie the sash to one of the posts and making sure to tuck the release tab into her grasp.

For a moment then he sat above her, gaze sweeping hungrily over her bound and stretched form. 'What a picture you make, Annabel.' And then his hands swept over her too, running up her arms and back down her sides before curving up over her ribcage to frame the undersides of her breasts. Squeezing, he lowered his head and gave her a grin that went beyond pulse-hitching and into heart-stopping.

'Shall we see how close we can get you to coming just from nipple play?' he asked, giving one pink tip a slow lick, and then the other. He took her reaction as his answer, falling on her with an open mouth even as she arched and shuddered beneath him.

He feasted – there was no other way to describe it, savouring her with the decadent indulgence of a gourmand. And the sensations he conjured were exquisite. Whipcords of white-hot pleasure ran from her breasts to her groin, where she felt the answering echo of every tug, every graze of his teeth, every lick and suck.

He pushed her right to the edge of her pleasure before he stopped to take some of his own. Losing his boxers, he crawled up her torso until his thighs bracketed her shoulders, and pushed his thumb into her mouth.

'Open for me. I want to watch those lips slide up and down my shaft again.'

He was gentle yet demanding, setting the pace and pushing himself into her mouth over and over, his eyes ablaze, his breathing ragged, until the muscles in his thighs began to tremble.

Pulling himself free, he shuffled back down to renew his attentions to her already tender breasts, leaving her thrashing against the twin bonds of the sash and his weight.

When she couldn't stand it any longer, she managed to articulate a begging word in between pants. 'More.'

With a sucking pull on her nipple, Aidan lifted his head to look up at her. 'What was that?'

'More.' She moaned as she felt his fingers replace his mouth, teasing her over-sensitive flesh.

'You want more? Where?'

She thrust her trapped hips up against the hot, heavy bulge of his groin 'There.'

Still straddling her to keep her snugly confined beneath him, he began to slide down her body, kissing and nipping as he went. The tendrils of that black hair felt like cool silk trailing over her hot, feverish skin

Then he dropped a light kiss on her curls. 'Here?'

His hands ran up the sides of her thighs and hips and met in the centre of her belly. Palms pressing over her pelvis, his thumbs teased her labia apart a fraction.

'Yes,' she hissed in desperation.

'With pleasure, Ms Frost. I've been thinking all night about putting my mouth on you again, tasting you come against my tongue.'

He speared that tongue into the small opening he'd made, hitting right on the target of her clitoris and concentrating all his efforts there. Annabel cried out and arched at the intensity, making Aidan clamp down and hold her fast. Legs trapped shut between his and arms anchored by the sash, Annabel found the inability to move push her over the edge with surprising speed. With his name bursting from her lips she came fast, and hard.

Leaving a short trail of kisses up over her curls and stomach, Aidan climbed off the bed. She watched, panting and limp as he drew a condom from his wallet and sheathed himself.

Then he was on the bed again, spreading her legs apart and lifting her thighs over his so he could kneel between them. He murmured how lovely she looked spread out so helplessly, so shamelessly, before him as he let his fingers begin to explore her. Taking hold of his erection with one hand, he held the very tip of it against her entrance as he worked her sensitised flesh towards another climax. Waiting, watching, gauging, he pushed into her at the moment she began peaking again, forging his way in past the contracting muscles. The feel of his inexorable invasion driving right through the heart of her orgasm shot Annabel to another level of intensity like she'd never known. Before she could come down, he began to thrust his hips, his fingers never letting up, holding her trapped on a plateau of mindless sensation that wrung pleasure out of her until her teeth rattled.

Dazed, she heard the grunting oaths Aidan uttered, felt him withdraw and abruptly flip her over onto her stomach. Taking only the time to shove a stack of pillows under her hips he nudged her legs apart and re-entered her from behind, pushing into sensitive tissue in a relentless glide, going deeper than ever before until his pelvis was pressed flush up against her buttocks.

With a groan of satisfaction, he lowered himself onto his elbows, the hard contours of his chest and stomach blanketing her spine, pinning her torso to the mattress.

His mouth pressed to her ear. 'I love making you come for me, Annabel. I'm going to make you do it again. Just like this.'

She groaned herself at that idea, but she'd never orgasmed from penetration alone before. 'I don't think I can . . . I've never . . .'

'Let's try it and see,' he murmured, echoing her earlier words.

He stayed plastered to her as he pushed in and out, slowly, carefully, adjusting angle and pace according to her response. His blanketing heat had her skin prickling as he gradually moved faster, his body sliding against the sweat trapped between them.

She was aware that where he slid inside her felt just as slick. After a while Annabel felt a tingling pressure build until it was almost a burn, and cried out when he shifted slightly and caught a certain spot.

'There,' he breathed into her ear, triumphant. He concentrated on hitting that spot, again and again, pushing up onto his arms to improve the angle even more, each jolting thrust making her tender nipples rasp over the bed cover.

The orgasm hit her hard, her body clenching tight, fingers and toes curling, the air squeezed from her lungs. The sudden fierce clamping of her muscles brought a hoarse shout from Aidan. He dropped back onto her, one arm moving up to curl tight around her head, his hand spearing into her hair to hold her face against his.

'Jesus, I'm coming too,' he rasped as he lost his rhythm,

lost control of his muscles, twitched and panted and shook as he emptied himself into her.

Trapped under his weight, drained and delirious, Annabel felt the irresistible tug of exhaustion pulling at her. Although she no longer really doubted it, Aidan had proved he was a man of his word all right – he'd made her come, and come, and come. As the darkness of sleep encroached, she thought it was just as well that they were leaving for London first thing in the morning, because spending much more time at the mercy of Aidan Flynn would likely be the end of her.

TWENTY-FOUR

The cab pulled up outside Annabel's apartment block and before she could move to get out, Aidan slid closer to her across the back seat and nuzzled her neck. Their flight from Vienna had been so early that they hadn't had time to make love again that morning and he was apparently feeling the loss.

'Are you sure you wouldn't prefer to come and get changed at my place?' he murmured in her ear. 'Then we could travel into Cluny's together.'

She arched her neck and let him nibble for a moment, mainly because it was too damn hard not to. 'If I come back to yours then there's no way either of us would make it to work.'

'True,' he said, with a sigh of resignation. Releasing her with obvious reluctance, he moved to help her with her overnight case.

'No. I can manage. Stay where you are.'

'I can at least see you to the door.'

'No. I want to say goodbye here so I can do this.' She turned and launched herself at his chest, pushing into him with enough force to slam him back against the seat. Kissing

302

him fast and hard, she pulled away when his dominant instincts started to take over.

'See you in a couple of hours.' Slamming the door, she strode towards the communal entrance to her apartment block and swiped her security tag to open the doors. Aware that the taxi continued to idle at the kerb behind her, she turned to throw a very un-Ms-Frost-like look over her shoulder as she stepped into the lobby, laughing at Aidan's answering grin as she headed up the stairs.

As she stopped outside her apartment door to fit the key in the lock, she thought she heard the intercom buzz for a moment. She smiled. If that was Aidan thinking he was coming up here as a substitute for going to his place, he had another thing coming. What did he imagine they could get up to with her mother around?

'Mum, I'm back,' she called out as the door swung open, revealing a mess in the hallway. The drawers of her console table, along with their contents lay strewn on the floor. Immediate confusion gave way to a chill. 'Mum?' she called out again.

'In here, love.' Her mother's voice, sounding strained and strange came from the sitting room. Something wasn't right. Had they been burgled? Her case dropped from suddenly nerveless fingers as she rushed from front door to sitting room. The place was like a bomb site, overturned furniture, cupboards emptied, contents scattered all over the floor. The only thing that was upright was the sofa, from which her mother was staring at her with eyes wide with fear as she silently mouthed 'I'm so sorry'.

'Mum?' Annabel picked her way towards her as quickly as she could through the debris, noticing even the Christmas tree decorations had taken a beating. 'What the—'

'I didn't tell him how to find us, Bel, I swear,' her mother rushed on. 'He followed me.'

'Who did?' Annabel asked, having difficulty taking everything in.

'I did,' said a voice behind her.

Spinning on the spot, she saw Tony Maplin, glass in one hand, bottle of gin in the other, standing in the sitting room doorway.

'As you weren't here when I arrived, I thought I'd set up a nice welcome home surprise, Bel. We've been having a drink in your honour while we waited for you.' He raised the nearly empty bottle.

Annabel backed further away from him, headed nearer her mother. 'What the hell is going on here?'

'Oh, you mean all this?' He swept his arms out to indicate the mess. 'Retribution.' He sneered.

Retribution? Annabel frowned. 'You did this? Why?'

'I've come to get back a little of what you took from me.'

In the hallway the entrance buzzer sounded another short burst. Could it possibly be Aidan? If it was, it didn't make a blind bit of difference as she had no way of getting past Tony to let him in. She didn't like the look or the sound of him. He was drunk on gin and bitterness, a nasty cocktail simmering under the surface.

'What are you talking about, Tony? We've already had this discussion. I haven't taken anything of yours. You need to leave.'

'Liar! You always had a grudge against me – couldn't wait until my back was turned for a second to swoop in like a vulture and shut me down.'

'Shut you down?'

'Yes. Don't pretend you didn't enjoy letting the bailiffs take everything, watching me lose my house.'

'How is that any of my fault? I had no authority to stop the repossessions, and you can't keep a house you don't pay for, Tony.'

'And as if that wasn't enough for you, you resentful little cow, you've been busy since, closing all my lines of credit.'

'*Your* lines of credit? I assume you mean the accounts you got my mother to open for you? The ones that left her solely liable for any debts you ran up?'

His face flushed a vivid red. 'I'm talking about things between me and your mother that were none of your fucking business,' he shouted. 'Who the hell do you think you are interfering in somebody else's relationship? Especially as you don't have the first clue about what that involves – frigid bitch that you are.'

'Tony,' her mother spoke out loud for the first time. 'Please stop this. I told you, all Annabel has done is help me.'

'And I don't want to hear another fucking word from you.' He turned to Ellen. 'You were so quick to run when she turned you against me.'

Annabel shook her head. 'She didn't need me to do that. You managed to turn her against you all on your own. You ran off and left her with less than nothing. What sort of person does that?'

The red flush darkened to a mottled purple. 'Don't you dare look down your fucking nose at me. You think you're so smart trying to shaft me, but I've seen just what you're worth.' He waved the bottle in the direction of a mess of papers spread across the floor – most of them her bank statements. 'And I'm telling you you're going to pay me back for the fucking trouble you've caused me.'

The buzzer sounded again and she grabbed at the opportunity it presented. 'Talking of trouble, that's my boyfriend. If I don't answer he'll use his key to get in,' she bluffed. 'You'd better get out of here.'

Tony laughed nastily. 'Lover boy? No, I was watching you arrive out of the bedroom window. I saw him take off down the street in the taxi. It's just you and me, ladies.

And I'm not going anywhere until I've received some compensation.'

She couldn't tell whether it was booze or belligerence that fuelled Tony's refusal to accept a word she was saying, his determination to blame her for his own shortcomings. Either way, she wasn't taking any more of his threatening behaviour. Her heart thumping, she was determined to show no fear as she pulled her phone out of her bag.

'Sorry to disappoint you, Tony, but the only thing I'm going to do is make more trouble for you. With the police.'

Tony roared, his face puce with fury. He dropped the bottle and threw the glass against the wall, lunging as it shattered, coming for her. With a scream, her mother jumped to her feet and lunged into in his path.

'Bitch!' He threw her, literally through the air. Ellen hit the wall, hard, and crumpled to the floor.

Annabel shouted and raced to her mother's assistance, but Tony swung toward her and struck her on the side of the head with enough force that white lights exploded across her vision and she staggered, dropping the phone.

She'd never been hit before and the shock was absolute. Before she could properly process the enormity of what was happening, there was another blow, every bit as hard as the first that made the world lurch and brought her to her hands and knees. A forceful shove from the side had her sprawling on the floor, a kick in her side stole her breath and then Tony Maplin was on top of her straddling her. How had it happened so quickly?

Annabel fought with everything she had to get him off her, pummelling him with her arms, kneeing him in the back, twisting and bucking. She screamed at the top of her lungs, hoping the racket would draw the attention of any of her neighbours still at home.

'Shut the fuck up.' Tony's hand clamped over her mouth

and nose, cutting off her oxygen. In terror she bit into his palm, tasting the iron tang of blood.

With a shout, Tony whipped his hand away. 'You'll pay for that, you little bitch!' he yelled, backhanding her across the cheek, adding more searing pain to her face as it snapped to the side. As her vision righted, she saw the photo of her and her father lying close by. Without thinking she reached for it, grasping the frame and swinging it at Tony's face with all the strength she could muster.

Glass shattered and wood splintered at the contact, but it inflicted only enough hurt to make Tony angrier.

'You think it's fun to fuck with me?' He wrenched the broken frame from her hand and tossed it aside. 'See how you like this.' He raised his fist high to bring it down onto her face. Annabel put her arm up to deflect the blow, which landed on her forearm. She heard the crack of what surely must have been bone a split second before agony shot up her arm.

Tony must have heard the noise too, because even as she tried to bring it closer to her body to protect it, he got his hands around it and squeezed, the grating sensation making her scream again.

He laughed. 'Not so fucking high and mighty now, are you?' He squeezed tighter, the pain so sickening it left her choking on the bitter burn of vomit that seared the back of her throat. In a desperate bid she went for his balls with her free hand, her fist striking him in the groin. Not hard enough to dislodge him, but hard enough to incense him further.

One of his hands clamped around her throat. 'I'll fucking kill you,' he screamed, his spittle spraying her face. And then suddenly he was gone.

Gone where? For a weapon? A knife? God, she needed to move, get her mother and get out before he came back. She could hear him banging about, grunting, swearing; the fury in the sounds was the most frightening thing she'd ever heard.

She tried to pull herself up, but her body didn't seem to want to obey her commands. Fire shot through her arm and every movement was slow, heavy, like pushing through treacle. An insidious blackness pulled at the edge of her consciousness. No. *No.* She had to fight against it, knowing that if she passed out . . .

Too late. He was back – through the darkening spots in her vision and the blur of tears she saw the shape of him bend over her again but she couldn't focus enough to see what he was about to do to her.

'No!' she screamed, frantically trying to get her limbs to propel her away, to put up some resistance as she felt his hands take hold of her shoulders to turn her onto her back.

She knew she must be in a bad way when she realised that she could no longer feel the pain those hands were inflicting. She'd gone mercifully numb. She heard shouting as if from far away. Her name? She couldn't be sure over the ringing in her ears, the blackness pulling insistently at her.

The hulking shape loomed close and she sobbed, trying to shrink back from what was to come, knowing she had nothing left. Like a coward she embraced the darkness that rushed up to meet her.

TWENTY-FIVE

Aidan hadn't thought twice about lying through his teeth to the duty sister to make sure he could be by his fiancée's hospital bed when she woke.

Annabel's green eyes blinked a little blearily to start with and then looked around the six-bed ward with wild eyes as she got her bearings. Her gaze landed on him as he pushed to his feet from the visitor's chair he'd set by her side.

'Mum?' she asked anxiously.

He laid his hand gently over her good wrist. 'She's going to be OK, Annabel. They've put her on another ward.' The specialist spinal ward to be exact. She'd suffered a fracture in her neck and would need to be put in traction for a while, but he didn't think Annabel needed those details right at this moment.

'I want to see her,' she insisted and tried to get up. Almost immediately she subsided again, even the small movement she'd managed making her cry out in pain.

'I'm sure you can. But not on your own.' He reached for the call bell looped around the head of her bed and pushed the button. 'Let a nurse help.'

'I feel strange, woozy.'

'Probably groggy from the meds they gave you. Try to take it easy.'

The sister he'd conned his way past earlier came into the room to be greeted by Annabel's curt demands to see her mother. With professional equanimity, she promised to check, unhooking the clipboard from the end of the bed and retreating.

Annabel sank back into the mound of pillows, the tension leaching from her body as her eyes closed and she seemed to drift for a bit. When she reopened them she seemed calmer but still somewhat disorientated.

She looked down at herself noting her arm, heavily bandaged and strapped with cool packs as though in surprise. 'I've got a broken arm,' she said. 'I've never had a broken bone before.'

Aidan stroked his thumb over her other slender forearm, aware how much more delicate her bone structure was than his. Than Tony fucking Maplin's. 'And here's hoping you never have another one.'

Suddenly her eyes snapped wide with a terror that tore at him. 'Tony?' she said on a gasp.

'It's all right, Annabel,' he assured her firmly, wanting to wipe the fear from her eyes. He grasped her hand as panic threatened to take hold. 'He can't hurt you now. Just breathe.'

It took her a minute to overcome the threatening hysteria. 'Where is he?'

'In police custody and waiting to be taken down to the station as soon as he's been patched up.'

'Patched up?'

'Yes. I believe he was in need of some immediate medical attention himself.' Out of sight, he flexed his right hand, relishing the sharp protest from his stiff knuckles. With any luck the bastard would find himself eating his meals through a straw for a while yet.

Annabel sank back into the pillows at that news, her eyes drifting shut only to jerk open again. 'Work!'

'All in hand. Tim's got everything covered for today and Tuesday. I've spoken to Richard. You don't need to worry about anything but yourself, *a mhuirnín*.'

The sister came back into the room with her chart, wheeling a blood pressure monitor. 'You'll be able to see your mother briefly in an hour or so, Annabel,' she said, closing the curtains around the bay. 'I'll book a porter and chair to take you. In the meantime we need to carry out a few checks.'

Aidan moved aside to allow the woman access to Annabel's uninjured arm.

'When can I go home?' Annabel asked.

'Bored of us already? You've only just got here.' The sister smiled, manoeuvring the monitor close to the bed. 'You'll be here overnight at least so we can keep an eye on you. As well as the arm, it looks like you took some nasty blows to the face and head.' Annabel's hand rose to feel her face, but the sister caught it and wrapped the wide cuff around her biceps. 'Doctor has also requested more X-rays once we've got the swelling around the bone to go down a bit. If everything looks all right you'll probably be OK to go tomorrow.' She pushed some buttons on the monitor before turning to Aidan. 'Providing there's some full-time care at home for a couple of days?'

Obviously catching the look, Annabel blurted, 'Oh, no,' as the cuff began to inflate. 'We don't live together. We're work colleagues.'

The sister raised an eyebrow and gave him a pointed stare, to which he just smiled and shrugged. Let her try and turf him out now.

'Well.' Deciding to let his deception pass, she turned back to Annabel. 'As long as someone can be there to care for you.'

'I'm used to being on my own, I'll be fine.'

'You might think so but it'll be a condition of your discharge nonetheless. Hospital policy.'

Aidan watched Annabel's face fall, her energy deflate. She closed her eyes and rested her head back on the pillow. It didn't surprise him that she'd hate the idea of lying around in hospital being reliant on others – he'd hated it himself. What did surprise him was what he seemed to be thinking of doing to help her with a solution.

She slipped back into a doze before the observations were complete and he took the opportunity to stretch his legs, get a cup of coffee and clear his thoughts. But twenty minutes later he was back by her bedside, still in the same frame of mind.

When she woke again she was a little more together.

'How is it that you're here?' she questioned with a small frown. 'I mean, you dropped me off and then left. How did you find out what happened?'

Although she'd come around during the ambulance ride, she'd been so disorientated that he wasn't surprised she couldn't remember much.

'I saw Tony at the window as the cab was pulling away,' he explained. He'd still been grinning at that look she'd given him as he'd signalled the driver to move off. What had made him glance up at the building, he'd never know, but that's all it had taken for him to catch a glimpse of a face – one that had seemed familiar and which had punched a fist of fear into his gut when he'd managed to place it.

'I got the driver to stop and call the police and I came back to do what I could until they got there.' It had taken precious moments and too many yards before the driver had pulled over again and the automatic lock released to let him fling the door open. Then he'd hit the pavement at a dead run. He hated to think what would have happened if chance hadn't played its part. 'It was pure luck that I looked up when I did.'

'You were there?' Annabel said, surprised. 'I remember the intercom buzzing and hoping it was you. But how did you get in?'

He remembered sliding to a stop at the entrance and frantically trying to work out how he was going to get past the security doors. 'The only thing I could think of doing was pushing as many buttons to as many flats as I could in the hope that someone would let me in. Luckily someone did. I heard your screams, followed them. Somehow the handle of your case had become wedged in the door, stopping it from locking shut by an inch.'

'I dropped it, I think. In shock at seeing all the mess.' Annabel said slowly as she pieced the fragments of her memory back together.

'Thank God you did. I burst in and found . . .'

His voice stalled, his throat too tight to speak as the image of Annabel sprawled on the ground, trying to fight off the much larger bulk of her half-crazed attacker came back with sickening clarity. Tony had been threatening to kill her, one meaty hand clamped around her throat, the other raising a gin bottle, ready to smash it down onto her face.

'I dragged the bastard off you and fought to subdue him.' And what a fight that had been. Tony Maplin was not only solidly built, he was also being powered by a wild, alcohol-fuelled rage. By the time Aidan had knocked him out and had rushed to check on Annabel, she'd been too far gone in fear and pain to recognise him or respond to him calling her name. Horrified, he'd frozen when she'd shrunk back from him, sobbing, realising that she thought he was Tony, back to finish what he'd started, back to make good on his threat.

'You passed out shortly before the police arrived. You don't remember the paramedics treating you? The ambulance ride?'

The frown deepened on her brow. 'Snatches only.'

313

In the circumstances, he thought 'snatches' were probably the best thing for her.

She reached her good hand out and touched his arm. 'Thank you,' she said, her chin wobbling and her eyes filling up.

Carefully he leaned over and placed a light kiss on her forehead. 'I only wish I could have got there sooner.'

He remained silent for a while as Annabel pressed her lips together, making an obvious effort to get her emotions under control.

'You don't need to stay,' she said eventually. 'You've done more than enough already.'

He suggested that he wait with her at least until the porter arrived to wheel her to see her mother. When she didn't argue, he also broached the subject of her going home.

'Even if they release you on your own tomorrow, you know you're in no condition to face the state your place is in, don't you?' He could see by her expression that she hadn't even thought of it.

'Oh, God. My flat. All my things.'

'I know. Is there someone I can call? Family you can stay with while it gets sorted out?'

'No.'

'*None?*'

'No.' She sighed and looked up at the ceiling. 'I'm an only child. So is Mum – to quite elderly parents who are so long gone I can barely remember them. My father's parents and sister emigrated to Canada years ago, before he died.'

It was hard for him to imagine being so alone when he'd had such a full, often maddening, family life, surrounded from childhood by a comforting circle of people to call on, lean on – people to help and care for.

'Friends?'

'Not an awful lot of those either. None in London that I

could ask something like this.' Even though she said it matter-of-factly he found the statement incredibly saddening, and the desire to help her grew even stronger.

'You have me,' he said, unsure which of them would be more astonished by the next words to come out of his mouth. 'You can come and stay at my place.'

Aidan carried the grocery bags up to his flat and let himself in quietly so as not to disturb his sleeping patient. Considering the way she'd reacted to his invitation at the hospital yesterday it was a miracle she was even here. Needless to say, her astonishment had been the far greater initially, but he'd been left somewhat surprised by the force of his subsequent determination to turn her flat refusal into reluctant acceptance.

She'd caved eventually, but only because she didn't have the strength to keep resisting him, he reckoned. Had he felt bad about taking advantage of her weakened state? Perhaps – until he'd swung by her place this morning to pick up a few items before collecting her from the hospital to bring her home. Having seen the mess, such a brutal reminder of the violence that had happened there, he'd felt no question that he'd done the right thing.

After getting her settled in, he'd realised that the only thing he hadn't had time to do was pick up something for them to eat. She'd been out cold when he'd gone in to check on her prior to nipping out. Wearing one of his white T-shirts – the easiest thing to get on over her temporary splint – she'd looked small and pale and bruised, lost against the white sheets of his big bed. Whatever the pain medication was that the hospital had sent her home with was good and strong.

Expecting to see her in exactly the same place that he'd left her, he detoured past the bedroom and opened the door a crack. The first thing he registered was that his bed was empty. The second was the sound of sobbing coming from the other side of the room. Swinging the door wide, he spotted Annabel in a heap on the floor just inside the en suite.

'What's happened?' Dumping the bags, he strode towards her and dropped into a crouch. Arms reaching for her, he hesitated, not knowing where was safe to touch. 'Did you fall? Have you hurt yourself?'

She looked up at him through the tangle of her long hair. 'I'm all right. I didn't fall. Just felt dizzy and ran out of steam.'

'I'm sorry I wasn't here to help you.' He reached to brush her hair from her eyes, but she flinched away. 'Why are you even up?' he asked softly, letting his hand drop. 'Did you need to use the bathroom?'

'No. Yes,' Annabel wailed, raising her good hand and brushing her hair aside with much more force than he would have used. Her face was blotchy from where she'd been having a good cry, her eyes and nose streaming. 'And I wanted to get clean. Wash my hair. The last shower I had was in Vienna. I feel a mess.' She snivelled piteously.

God. If the sight didn't turn something over in his chest. He gave her a gentle smile. '*A mhuirnín*, you *are* a mess. And only making it worse by trying to do too much, too soon. I know you want to do things yourself, but I wish you'd waited for me to help you.'

'I'm not a child,' she groused, wiping her nose with the back of her hand.

'No,' he said soothingly, aware that it was pain and frustration that was making her act like one. 'You're not.'

His calm reply took the heat out of her temper. 'I hate being helpless,' she said, which he took as an apology.

'Believe me, I know the feeling. I hated it too. Come on. Let's get you off the floor.' He put his hands under her arms and pulled her to her feet. She was shaking and wobbly on her bare legs as he walked her back to the bed. 'I remember

316

how frustrating the road to recovery can be, but rushing things isn't the answer. Take it from someone who learned the hard way – you'll only set yourself back.'

He sat her on the mattress and moved the box of tissues from the bedside table to beside her. 'Having said that, nothing feels as good as being clean. I think if we're careful we can manage a bath, but no hair washing today. Will that do?'

Plucking a tissue out, she nodded.

Aidan went to the en suite and set about running a bath. He had various potions and salts that would work well for relaxing Annabel's muscles, but he was concerned that they'd aggravate her cuts and grazes. That bastard Maplin had been wearing rings when he'd laid into her – chunky rings that had not only gouged the skin on her cheekbones, but on her hands where she'd tried to protect herself.

However, he did have something that might be good. Annabel had a clump of tissues held to her face as he passed through the bedroom and made for the storage cupboard in his hall. There he found the enormous cellophane wrapped basket of organic baby products that some bouncy sales assistant had convinced him was the perfect gift for his pregnant sister. Raiding it, he discovered a bottle of hypo-allergenic, 100-percent natural, pure plant-extract, gently foaming baby bath. Perfect.

He took the bottle back into the en suite and squeezed an amount under the running water. Leaving the tub to fill, he returned to the bedroom where Annabel sat dry-eyed now but looking completely drained.

'All right if I put your hair up?' he asked. When she nodded he retrieved her toiletries bag from the overnight case he'd packed and handed it to her. 'Pass me your hair brush.'

Climbing onto the mattress behind her, he ran the brush through her hair in long, soft strokes, easing just enough of the tangles out to allow him to braid it.

'How did you learn to plait hair?'

'Sisters, remember?' he answered, folding the long rope up to the crown of her head. 'Clip?'

With her hair up out of the way it was a matter of making her cast waterproof, which he easily managed with the use of surgical tape from his first aid kit and a plastic bag. He led her back into the bathroom where she eyed the bubbly water with longing as he stripped himself first, then helped ease his T-shirt and her underpants off her. They stepped into the bath and he settled himself with his back against the end of the tub, pulling her down on top of him, supporting the bits that needed to stay dry.

Helping her settle into position lying on her side with her injured arm resting above the waterline on his shoulder, he held her loosely against him, careful not to press against the bruises blossoming darkly on the side of her ribcage. None of her ribs were cracked, thankfully, but he could tell by the way she held herself, by the way she sometimes caught her breath, that they were painful. He'd been by her bedside when she'd given her statement to the police, had heard how she'd sustained her various injuries – had wished he'd been a little more thorough with Tony Maplin.

Annabel sighed, her head sinking onto his other shoulder as he picked up a wash cloth and slowly ran it over her waist and hip. She felt heavenly fitted against him, relaxing into him, trusting his support. When he raised the cloth to wash her upper arm with gentle strokes, her good hand came up to lightly brush the bubbles from his split knuckles.

'You got these because of me. I don't know what would have happened if you hadn't got to us.'

'I'm only sorry I didn't get there sooner. I thought I'd have to kick right through those damned security doors before someone let me in.'

'You did more than enough. Thank you.'

He wanted to tilt her face up to his and kiss her. Kiss her long and slow and deep, but he didn't know whether he could trust himself to stop once he'd started. Getting physical should be the last thing on his mind but he recognised that what he felt for Annabel went beyond the desire for sexual gratification and into the realms of some primal life-affirming need. His cock agreed. He felt her tense as he stiffened inexorably against her hip.

'Ignore it,' he said, pressing his lips to her hairline and trying to take his own advice. 'I'm just happy you're here.'

There was a moment of undeniable tension before she sniffed and broke it by saying, 'Do we smell like—*babies*?'

He chuffed out a laugh. 'I'm afraid to say we do,' he admitted, and explained about the gift for his expectant sister.

'You said you have four?'

'Yes. The eldest is Deirdre, then Una – the one who's expecting. I come next in the pecking order, and then the twins, Caitlin and Ciara.'

'Five children. Sounds like chaos.'

'With so many girls it was certainly noisy. Especially with the twins. We grew up in a rural Irish backwater, living in the gatehouse of a decaying old mansion so we had lots of freedom to run around the estate – mostly wild. I think that saved my parents' sanity. I only remember us ever coming indoors to eat and sleep, before heading back out to explore.'

'Wasn't that a bit dangerous, not to mention creepy, playing in an old, empty house?'

'We liked to scare ourselves witless with ghost stories and such, sure. But the house itself was off limits, boarded up tight and covered in no trespassing signs.' He paused for a moment, looking back to see the place through the eyes of the skinny, dirty-kneed bundle of curiosity he'd been. 'Not that it stopped us finding a way in. Deirdre and I braved it a few times but the others were always too scared even

319

though there was nothing but dust and darkness to be found inside.'

'Do you know what happened to let it get that way?'

'Nothing nearly so fanciful as some of the horror stories our fertile young imaginations had dreamt up. Teach na Tulaí had belonged to a family called Tully for generations – that's what the Gaelic name translates to, Tully House – whose fortune came from the whisky business. According to local legend, a sibling feud sprang up over a technical glitch in a will which resulted in the business closing and some of the estate land and tenant buildings being sold off to pay duties and legal expenses. The house itself and the distillery seemed to be the bones of contention and were left to rot out of spite. My parents bought the gatehouse when the estate was divided up. They sometimes used to talk about buying the big house with a view to renovating, but it never came up for sale.'

'It's probably just as well,' she said with a small yawn. 'Sometimes places keep hold of that sort of history. It might never have made a happy home.'

The heat of the water must be relaxing her more than he'd thought. He'd have never put her down as the superstitious type.

'It's funny, but it never came across to me as an unhappy place.' Just the opposite: for as far back as he could remember, the classical proportions of the colonnaded stone façade and the grand size of the empty rooms had filled him with nothing but dreams and aspirations . . .

'Are you still close to them, your sisters?'

Annabel's question pulled him out of his reverie. 'Yes. In fact you'll meet Ciara tomorrow – she's going to come and sit with you while I take my shift.'

In a heartbeat, the relaxed stupor had left her and she tensed against him. 'That won't be necessary. I'll be fine.'

'Doctor's orders, Annabel.'

'But—' she started to argue.

'Non-negotiable,' he interrupted to save her wasting her breath. He wasn't budging.

'So what happened to "rules were made to be broken"? You're suddenly a stickler for them now?' she huffed.

'I'm always a stickler for the rules that matter.'

'Meaning mine don't?'

He sighed but kept his spike of frustration out of his tone. He knew this wasn't about her rules. 'Why do you do this? Push people away when they want to help?'

She was silent, stiff as a board against him now.

'Annabel, relax,' he murmured, pressing his lips into her hair. 'Let me in. You can't keep living your life this way.'

'And one weekend together doesn't give you the right to tell me that. You have no idea about my life,' she said in a flat voice, closing herself off.

He was damned if he was going to let her, not when they were lying there pressed naked against each other from top to toe. 'Then talk to me.' He dropped the cloth into the water so he could grasp her chin and tilt her face up to his. 'Tell me how a beautiful, intelligent woman ends up with no friends in the world.' He looked into her eyes, caught her before she could slam that cold green curtain down over the swirl of conflict and confusion in their depths. 'Tell me.' He lowered his lips to press them softly against hers. 'Because I can't understand it at all.'

'You *don't* understand. That's exactly my point,' Annabel said, twisting her head to escape his grip. She lowered it back to his shoulder, tucking her forehead into his neck. 'How could you? You grew up surrounded by a big family. You're handsome and charming, you've got everything. I was an only child, a red-headed one at that. Do you know the sort of shit that gets piled on a "ginger", how you're judged on and defined by your looks over everything else? How you're made to feel ashamed of your own appearance, like it's something you have any control over?'

No, he didn't know, but he could imagine. Kids were cruel. He picked up the wash cloth again, started slowly stroking over her hip, gentling her.

'It's bad enough if you're confident, outgoing, but for a shy kid . . .' She stopped and he felt the careful breath she sucked in. 'The only place I ever felt really safe, really accepted was with my parents. My dad loved redheads, after all.'

Aidan felt her cheeks shift, as though she was smiling at the memory and rubbed his jaw over her hair. 'He was a man of very good taste, then.' He wasn't sure whether it was because of the meds, the trauma or the fact that she was beginning to trust him – hell, it could even be the comforting smell of the baby bath, whatever – but he couldn't quite believe that Annabel was opening herself up when a minute ago she'd been on the verge of shutting him out.

'Everything was all right when he was around. I didn't need anything else. I loved him and Mum, loved the inn, had my life planned out where I'd work alongside them, learn the business, eventually take it over.'

He could picture her as a little flame-haired girl, full of dreams and determination.

'Then the day after my ninth birthday everything changed. My father left to meet with a new supplier and died in a car crash. It didn't seem real – that one day he could be there, and the next gone forever. I think the only thing that got me through it was clinging to those plans – like the inn was a way of staying connected to him. I lost everything when Mum sold it. She had to, I know that now. She felt the opposite, couldn't bear the memories, found it too heart-breaking to stay. But at the time I couldn't see past my own grief. I swore I'd find a way to get the inn back – it was all

I could think about. When we moved I was so stuck in the past that I had no chance of starting afresh. Not only was I shy and ginger, but I was angry and difficult too. Hardly friend material.'

His heart ached for the matter-of-fact way she said it, as though it meant as little to her as she pretended it did. He didn't dare say anything, though. He'd never been in her shoes, could only imagine what it must have been like. Any attempt at comforting her would be taken as pity or sympathy and savaged accordingly.

'By the time I hit my teens, well I told you, I was so focused on getting back my life plan – working, saving – that I didn't have the time or inclination for anything else. And by that time I was so used to getting along on my own that I actually preferred not to have anyone getting in the way. It's paid off too, because I'm nearly there. Another year or so and I'll be in a position to buy my own place.' She stopped as a yawn overtook her. 'So now you know.'

Yeah. Now he knew all right. Knew she deserved better than she allowed herself.

'Thank you. Come on, the water's getting cold. Let's get you dry and fed. You must be starving after a day of hospital food.'

TWENTY-SIX

Annabel woke in a dimly lit room and for a moment couldn't place where she was. Then it came back to her. Aidan's place, Aidan's bed. But no Aidan beside her where he had been last night.

The diffused glow of daylight surrounding the drawn blinds told her she'd slept the night through. Hardly surprising on the drugs the hospital had given her. They packed a punch worthy of a horse tranquilliser. They also left her mouth feeling beyond foul. From the nest of pillows Aidan had built to stop her inadvertently rolling onto her broken arm in her sleep, she stretched over to the bedside table and grasped the glass of water sitting there, bringing it shakily to her lips and taking a couple of blissful swallows, letting the cool liquid wash the rank fuzz from her mouth.

Putting the glass back, she misjudged and knocked the plastic bottle of pills off the table, which clattered loudly onto the floor.

'Hello?' a female voice called out a moment later. 'Are you all right in there?'

Annabel had time to register a soft Irish lilt to the words, similar to Aidan's, before a black-haired head popped around the semi-opened bedroom door.

'Hi, Annabel. I'm Ciara, Aidan's sister. He asked me to come and sit with you while he went to work today. Can I help you with something?'

'No, I'm fine.' Annabel made to swing her legs over the side of the bed to pick up what she'd dropped, but getting her limbs to move seemed to be really slow going and Ciara was there in a flash.

'Here.' She handed the bottle to Annabel. 'I'll get you some fresh water so you can take one.'

'No. I don't want one.' Annabel eased limply back into the pillows. Her arm and head were throbbing, her face aching, but not enough to make her want to knock herself out again.

'Oh, OK.' Ciara smiled. 'How about a cup of tea or coffee then? I've just boiled the kettle.'

Coffee. Yes, maybe caffeine would help clear this thick cloud in her head. 'Coffee would be great. Thank you.' She scratched at an itch behind her ear. 'What time is it?'

'Just after one,' Ciara said, turning to leave the room. 'I'll be back in a minute.'

It took what seemed like an age for Annabel to work out she'd slept for a solid ten hours, like her brain was grinding slowly through rusty gears. How come she felt thick-headed and exhausted instead of refreshed?

Ciara came back with a tray which she set down across Annabel's thighs. 'I don't know if you're hungry but Aidan said you like these.' She pointed to an almond croissant sitting on a plate. 'He picked up a bag of them this morning.'

How did he know she liked them? Of course – breakfast in Vienna. Seriously, was there anything that Mr Observant didn't notice? She wasn't feeling particularly hungry as the medication left her feeling queasy, but if she had to force something down, she could think of worse things.

'He also said you'd probably feel like shit and not to talk your ears off. I'll be just out here. Give me a shout if you need anything.'

It sounded to her like Aidan was just too high-handed for words, she snarked internally and then immediately felt ungrateful for everything he was doing. If it wasn't for him, she'd still be stuck in the hospital – or worse. She hated to think what Tony Maplin would have done to her. Aidan had thrown himself into the midst of a dangerous situation for her, looked after her. She'd tried to show him how much that meant last night in the bath, tried to repay him by giving him the trust he seemed to value so highly. Lying there with his heart beating steady and strong beneath her ear, the feel of his body providing gentle yet solid support, she'd felt secure enough to open up to him, let him see parts of her that she'd never showed anyone else.

She drank the coffee, which was made just as she liked it, and picked at half the croissant. The first did clear her head a bit and the second settled her stomach. After a while she started to feel restless but attempting to move the tray with one arm ended with her nearly tipping the lot over the bed.

Obviously hearing the clank of the crockery, Ciara reappeared. 'Oh, good. You managed to eat.' She came up to the bed. 'Aidan won't kill me.'

'He's set you to report on me?' Annabel asked as Ciara righted the fallen mug and lifted the tray away, allowing her to move her stiff legs.

'Of course. Don't worry, it's not as control freakish as it sounds. He just gets a little overprotective sometimes.'

Personally, Annabel thought it had control freak written all over it. 'I told him I didn't need you to come today,' she said, scratching at another tickle on her scalp. 'I appreciate it but you don't have to stay, really.'

Ciara looked at her with grey eyes a few shades darker than Aidan's and not nearly as penetrating. 'You haven't known my brother very long, have you?' she asked with a laugh. 'We're stuck with each other until he gets back tonight. Can I get you something else – help with anything?'

'Actually, I'm going to get up,' Annabel said, sliding her legs to the side of the mattress. She sat for a moment while her head pounded from just that minimal movement. Then scratched some more. 'What I really want to do is wash my hair.'

Ciara shook her head. 'That's going to be virtually impossible for you to manage on your own with that splint. Unless you want to bend over the sink and I could do it for you?'

The thought of bending over made Annabel's head pound even more. 'No,' she sighed, resigned to an itchy scalp.

'Hang on a tick,' Ciara said. 'I think I might have an alternative.'

She disappeared with the tray and came back a minute later with an aerosol can. 'Dry shampoo,' she announced triumphantly. 'It's not the same as the real thing I know, but it should help.'

'Yes!' Annabel reached for it.

Ciara handed the can over and watched her struggle to untangle the remnants of the braid Aidan had done for her.

'I'm happy to help,' she said.

'No.' Annabel was horrified. 'It's dirty and knotty and disgusting.'

'It doesn't look anywhere near as bad as Aidan's when he was taken ill, believe me. We couldn't wash it for ages after the surgery – the half that hadn't been shaved off, in any case.' She picked up Annabel's brush from the bedside table.

'Honestly, it's not a problem. Do you want to come and sit at the table and I can do it for you?'

Annabel gave up her struggles. Yes, she really did want that. Incapacitated as she was, she knew she'd only make a mess of doing it herself.

'This was when he had the stroke you're talking about? He had half his hair shaved off?' That beautiful hair!

She pushed herself to her feet as Ciara nodded. 'He had a haemorrhagic stroke, where the blood vessels burst rather than get blocked by a clot. He needed emergency surgery to repair the damage and stop the bleeding. His hair had to be shaved so the surgeon could cut away a section of his skull.'

Annabel wobbled over to where her suitcase sat on an upholstered stool. Aidan had been back to her flat to pick up some essentials and she noticed that he'd done quite well as she pulled on her robe and a pair of woolly socks. 'I've seen the scar. It must have been a terrible time.'

Ciara nodded and fell into step beside her as they made their way out to the main living room. 'To tell you the truth, I don't think I've ever been so scared. We knew he'd been under a lot of stress with his job, but his neurologist said that it took dangerously high blood pressure to cause that sort of damage. To start with we didn't even know if he'd pull through, or what state he'd be left in if he did. I could hardly bear to look at him after the operation when he'd been put on a ventilator. Seeing him lying there unconscious, hooked up to machines that were basically keeping him alive . . .' Ciara shuddered as though trying to shake off the memory. Aidan radiated such force of energy that Annabel couldn't even begin to imagine what it would be like to see all that vitality drained from him. 'But he's Aidan. He pulled himself through, though he was no picture, I can tell you. As soon as we were able, we shaved off the other half of his hair.'

'I bet he wasn't happy about that,' Annabel said as they reached the table and she lowered herself into a chair. 'I know I wouldn't have been if I had such fabulous hair.'

'It's not fair is it? I'm jealous.' Ciara came up behind her, hands gentle as they began to untangle the braid. 'He's only started wearing it long since it grew back. He didn't like that his scar was all people could talk about when they saw it. At the time, though, he didn't mind being shorn; it was easier all round while he was bed-ridden.'

Thinking of her mother currently stuck in bed in traction, Annabel was thankful that her own injuries had at least left her mobile. She'd go mad being confined to bed for any length of time.

'Was he in hospital for long?'

'The family wanted him home so we could care for him. We got him back to Ireland as soon as we could. And I have to say he was a pretty easy patient until he started to improve. Then he was a bit like you, raring to go, wanting to do things for himself, frustrated not to find himself bouncing straight back onto his feet.'

Annabel felt the first soft stroke of the brush as Ciara continued to chat away, making sense of the reference Aidan had made regarding his 'especially' noisy twin sisters yesterday.

'In his case it took nearly a year of sheer determination for him to overcome the paralysis and regain a degree of mobility. And another year after that until he was fully self-sufficient again. That was the time frustration made him truly horrible – as fractious and impatient as a toddler, as sullen and stroppy as a teenager.'

'Two years. So long?'

'Yeah. And every day was a battle for him.' Ciara started dividing her hair into sections. 'To start with we all feared the paralysis would be permanent, that he'd have to stay at home for constant care. But he was insistent that he'd recover, that he'd get back to independence. He wouldn't let us sell this place, even though it sat empty for all that time. He wanted to keep his options open.'

Annabel closed her eyes. To meet Aidan, you'd never guess what he'd been through. With his mind so sharp, and his body – not an ounce of flab or hint of weakness to signify how wasted his muscles must have become during that time he'd been incapacitated. It wasn't until you got to know him that you discovered how much more lay behind that gorgeous crooked smile, that sexy tousle of hair.

Behind her, Ciara sprayed on the powdery substance, section by section, then brushed the whole lot through before gathering it up to begin plaiting it again.

'Oh, is this your natural colour?' she asked as Annabel felt the brush pass over the wisps of hair at the nape of her neck. Ever mindful of her budget, she home-coloured and so didn't always get perfect coverage at the back.

Ciara didn't wait for her reply. 'It's beautiful. No wonder my brother is smitten. Redheads have always been his weakness.'

Annabel blushed, thinking that he did seem to be particularly fond of the colour of a certain other set of curls. But *smitten*?

'That's his usual type then, is it?' She hated herself for asking, for feeling the need to fish for information. 'Redheads?'

'Usual? No, not at all. More like his ideal. His ultimate.' Ciara's hands were busy weaving and then slowed as though her attention turned elsewhere. 'In fact, I don't think he has a usual. He's always been choosy.'

'Oh?'

'Yes. He's never had a shortage of female attention – well, no surprise, you know yourself what he looks like. Those eyes alone had pretty much the entire female population of County Cork swooning in his wake, not to mention the most popular girls vying for his attention. Caitlin and I always had a sneaking suspicion that we were only so popular with the other girls at school so they could get close enough to throw themselves at his feet.'

Annabel gave a soft snort. 'That would explain his –' she only just stopped herself saying *arrogance* '– confidence.'

'You'd think so, wouldn't you? But it never really went to his head. Unlike most hormonally charged teenage boys he refused to take advantage of everything offered to him, and he was very protective of all of us too – policed any boy that came near the house. Maybe growing up surrounded by females gave him a sense of respect that most boys lacked. As far as I know he's never been involved with anyone unless he's serious about them. He's always had a calm intensity about him that makes him kind of an all or nothing guy.'

An all or nothing guy. Annabel couldn't think of a more perfect description for Aidan Flynn.

Ciara smoothed the braid down her back. 'There, all done. Would you like another coffee?'

'As long as I can make it,' Annabel insisted. 'I'm sick of being useless.'

By the time she'd finished drinking her second mug, she'd learned quite a bit more about Aidan. After phoning the hospital to check on her mother, she visited the bathroom, and began to feel taxed and sore enough that another horse pill didn't seem like such a bad idea after all. Climbing back into bed while she waited for it to take the edge off, she drifted into sleep.

TWENTY-SEVEN

The following morning Annabel was back at the hospital to have her permanent cast fitted and visit with her mother. Although she'd insisted that she was fine to go alone, Aidan was just as insistent on accompanying her. Apart from offering a few grumbles to satisfy her sense of independence, she didn't really fight that hard to dissuade him – in all honesty she was still feeling a bit shaken and it was nice to have him around.

Very nice, she discovered later when, instead of being ferried straight back to Aidan's, she found herself detoured to a hairdressing salon where she got the shampoo she'd been hankering after, although her still tender head meant she had to pass up the rigours of a sleek blow dry in favour of a rough dry. The resulting fluffy curls seemed to fascinate Aidan, who teased them with his fingers for the entire cab ride back to his apartment.

'I hear you have a particular thing for redheads,' Annabel said.

Aidan looked at her, his black brows raising. 'Ciara?'

She smirked and nodded. 'Ciara.'

He hooked an arm around the back of her shoulders and

pressed himself closer to her whilst sliding the palm of his other hand up her thigh, stopping just short of her groin.

'You didn't need her to tell you that, surely? I thought I'd made it quite obvious.' He pushed his mouth to her ear and lowered his voice to murmur throatily. 'Especially the prefer- ence I have for *natural* redheads.'

Annabel tried not to squirm at the feel of his lightly circling fingertips.

He pulled back to look at her hair. 'Tell me, after what you said the other night about the way you were taunted for it, I've been curious – why hide red with red?'

'I'm not. I'm hiding bright orange with red. There's a difference.'

He leaned into her again, resumed his circling. 'Mmm. I've seen the difference – bright and fiery and beautiful.'

She couldn't help but melt against him with a sigh. Stroking her hair, he held her against him for the rest of the journey.

Not long after their return a bouquet of flowers arrived for her from Richard Landon.

'He's knows I'm staying here?' she asked with something akin to panic, but once Aidan had assured her that Richard, and only Richard, knew for the sake of necessity, she soon found her concern outweighed by the novelty. She'd never received flowers before.

A whole raft of emotions assailed her. It was shocking to discover how easily she could let herself fall into all the warmth and togetherness, the caring and sharing. But she needed to remember that this wasn't her life. It was a temporary situation born of extreme circumstances, a situ- ation that wouldn't exist in the normal scheme of things. It was because she was shaken, susceptible, that it seemed so seductive – all the more reason not to prolong it. She should get back to reality, let Aidan get his life back too. As patient and empathetic as he was, it couldn't be much fun for him to have to play nursemaid to a woman he barely knew. She was on the mend, no longer needing care. There was no reason for her to stay and get comfortable with things she couldn't have, shouldn't need to rely on.

As Aidan made to leave for the evening shift at Cluny's, she announced that she'd be going home tomorrow, although she didn't fancy the thought of the mess that awaited her there.

'I need to get back to work, too,' she said. 'I'll hide out the back in the office,' she added, not missing the look he gave the cuts and bruises to her face.

All he said was, 'Let's see how you get on tonight.'

And as it turned out, the night was horrid. Her new cast felt tight, the skin beneath it prickling with discomfort, leaving her tossing and turning alone in Aidan's bed. She'd insisted on coming off the heavy painkillers in favour of a standard over-the-counter option but found that the lighter meds meant more pain and less sleep. And lighter sleep meant dreams – nightmares of violence and panic and choking fear.

She awoke gasping and sweating in the dark to find Aidan back from work, a warm, solid presence beside her in the bed.

'I've got you,' he murmured. 'You're safe. I've got you.' His voice soothing and velvety in the darkness, relaxing her back into slumber.

But it was only the start of a long night of broken sleep. Not even his assurances or the comforting heat of his strong body curled lightly around her were enough to keep the dream demons at bay. It wasn't until dawn that they both succumbed to exhaustion.

Annabel didn't surface until late in the afternoon, finding herself alone again, with a note from Aidan telling her that he'd gone to work. She huffed at being left behind. He'd known she wanted to get back to Cluny's today. Grabbing her phone, she messaged him.

I don't appreciate you making my decisions for me. You were supposed to wake me for work.

She thought about trying to rush to make it in for the evening service at least, only to realise that she had no suitable work clothes with her anyway. She huffed some more.

A reply came in a short time later. *Hello to you too. Feeling better I assume?*

Well enough not to have to put up with his sarcasm. *Changing the subject won't change the fact that you have absolutely no right to make choices on my behalf!*

I'm going to take that as a yes. You were certainly starting to sound more like your old self when I tried to wake you and you told me to fuck off. Twice.

She paused for a moment to take that in. *Ah. That was real? I thought it was a dream.* She hit send, then as an afterthought followed up with a *Sorry?*

He replied, *I took it to mean you needed more sleep. And after last night, maybe you'll consider staying at my place a little longer, just in case.*

The offer surprised her, given how snappy she'd been, and for once she didn't even think of putting up any resistance. The thought of coping with those nightmares while surrounded by the devastation Tony had wrought held no appeal whatsoever.

After she sent a further message accepting his offer of another night's board, she phoned the hospital to check on her mother and began making a list of things she'd need to start sorting with regard to insurance, repairs, replacements.

A while later Aidan responded. *Good. Another night with you in my bed is no hardship, Annabel, trust me.*

After what he'd had to put up with last night, she knew that couldn't be entirely true.

In case you're asleep when I get back, the police have been in touch to say they need to interview you again. Tomorrow morning if possible. Nothing to worry about, clarification on a few points. I've arranged for them to come to my place for 10am.

She wondered why the police were bothering Aidan instead of coming to her direct, then remembered that he'd given them his own number as part of her contact details at the hospital. Now that her phone had been retrieved from the mess of her flat, she'd have to remedy the situation with them in the morning. One of many steps she needed to start taking to get control of her life back.

When Aidan came home late from a busy shift, dog-tired but still too wound up to crash, he discovered that Annabel wasn't asleep. Far from it. Wearing one of his shirts, unbuttoned to show an inviting amount of cleavage, she sat pert and alert in his bed, looking like the perfect ending to his day.

Which was why he needed to get away from her as quickly as possible.

'You do look better. How are you feeling?' he asked, stooping over the mattress to brush a quick kiss of greeting against her lips. He got the answer when he felt her open beneath him – nearly lost his resolve to walk away when she brought that sweet, warm tongue into play. Forcing himself to pull back, he wished her goodnight and got out of there while he could.

Pouring himself a healthy shot of single malt, he flopped onto the end of the sofa, one hand clutching the glass to his chest, the other hanging loose from the end of the upholstered arm. Legs sprawled, he closed his eyes and let his head fall heavily back against the oversized cushions.

Friday tomorrow – and a busy weekend to get through before he got a day off. Not only had he found himself sleeping lightly with Annabel here, his body keenly aware of hers, his senses alert to her unguarded noises of discomfort and distress in the night, but his waking hours had been somewhat taxing too – spent trying to do whatever he could to help her without actually looking like he was doing too much. Being a sneak was surprisingly hard work.

Given the upheaval to his life, he should be looking forward to her going home, but when she'd mentioned doing just that yesterday, relief had been the last thing he'd felt. As unplanned and disruptive as the situation was, he found he liked having Ms Frost in his home, in his space and in his bed. Places that no woman had occupied seriously for a long time, places whose sudden and total invasion he should have resented.

Yet he didn't resent any of it. He welcomed it on all sorts of levels. Despite his efforts to keep to his own side of the mattress to avoid knocking her injuries, he found that every time he woke, he'd be wrapped around Annabel again, as though even in sleep he craved the touch of her. And the touch made him crave more, too.

God, the things he wanted to do to her – would be doing to her if she weren't injured. Her reactions to the testing teases he'd tried out in Vienna had left him little doubt that there was a well of latent desires embedded deep in her psyche that maybe even she didn't know about. If he tapped that reservoir right, he reckoned that eventually Ms Frost would let him dive a long way down into the tenebrous depths before calling 'stop'.

A soft noise had his eyes springing open. Speak of the devil. Annabel stood before him, barefoot and beautiful in the lamplight, and with another damn button of his shirt undone – the very epitome of temptation on earth.

'I want to apologise for earlier,' she said, looking contrite and cautious and adorably uncomfortable with it. 'For being a bitch. I'm – I'm not very good at this . . .' She stalled, a frown of frustration creasing her brow as though she couldn't find the right words to express herself. With a huff, she settled for, 'I'm used to having to think only for myself.'

Of course she was. But that little acknowledgement of self-awareness gave him hope that things could change.

'I know. Tetchiness is part of the recovery process too.' He took a swig of whisky to try to wash the telltale sensual rasp from his voice. 'It's not a problem. Go back to bed, I'll be in soon.'

'I'm not tired,' Annabel said, stepping right into the space between his legs. 'I hope you don't mind that I borrowed this.' She pulled at the hem of his shirt in a move designed to get him noticing her legs. Like he hadn't already thought of them wrapped around his ears. 'I managed a bath and wanted something fresh to put on.'

His throat was desert-dry again already. 'And none of your own clothes would fit?' he asked, calling her out. No point in being coy when she was making it obvious what she was after. Her forthright manner again reminded him that she was used to taking control. The fact that she could be so open sexually yet so closed off emotionally told him that she didn't connect the two. Yet.

'I thought none of them looked quite as good,' she returned with a knowing smile, stepping even closer. He was glad to see her cocky assurance coming back.

'You're right about that.' And because he was a sucker who obviously didn't have the good sense to know any better, he lifted the hand that dangled off the end of the sofa arm, and ran a finger up and down the side of her thigh. Soft and silky. 'But I'd still like you to go back to bed, Annabel.' It was a lie. What he'd *like* would be to run his finger high enough to lift the edge of his shirt and see what he'd discover. 'There's only so much I can resist.'

'I don't want you to resist.'

He'd expected a battle of wills over this from the moment

338

he'd picked up the vibe in the bedroom. What he didn't expect was for her to climb straight onto his lap, but a second later, that's where she was, her knees bracketing his hips as she settled over his spread thighs.

'I can tell. But I don't think it's a good idea.'

The gleam in her eye and the stubborn set of her chin said that she couldn't care less what he thought as she said, 'Well I do', and moved in for the kiss.

With his next intake of breath, the scent of her arousal hit him, shooting directly from his nostrils to his cock, which went from semi-hard to rock-solid in an instant. He very nearly didn't get his glass to his lips in time to stop her.

Annabel rocked back, eyes narrowed as she watched him take a mouthful. Fine. Let her give him the evil eye if that was the worst she could do.

But then she did something much worse. She undid another button. Then she let one side of the shirt fall open to show the alluring inner curve of her breast. He clutched the glass tighter, realising it was a poor weapon as his gaze was helplessly drawn to her chest, to where he could see the smooth white cotton of his shirt pushed into peaks by her nipples.

Jesus. She was ready for him under there. And he was beyond ready for her. How he wanted to get his mouth on those delectable little buds again, wanted to feel the way she responded to the caress of his tongue. Wanted to have her writhing in his arms.

He was losing ground, fast. 'I'm not convinced that you're up to what you're offering.'

Staring at his mouth in a way that made his abs clench, Annabel started to lean forward again. She stopped when she saw him move the glass back into a defensive position.

'Don't you think I'm the best judge of that?' she asked with a snap of annoyance.

'All right. Then I'm not convinced I can give you the pleasure you're after without accidentally hurting you.'

'Again,' she said, raising her good hand to his glass so she could stick a finger in the amber liquid. 'Isn't that for me to decide?' And she painted a line down into her cleavage with it. His gaze followed her movements and he knew he was going straight to hell.

Placing the glass on the side table next to the sofa, he snaked a hand around to the back of her head and pulled her gently towards him.

'Stubborn woman. You don't know what you do to me.' He brushed a kiss over her lips while his other hand pushed the gaping shirt off over one shoulder, the cotton falling away to expose her breast. 'You shatter my control like I've never known,' he confessed, tightening the hand in her hair and pulling to hold her where he wanted her so he could lower his face and lap up that daub of whisky. It tasted so good off her warm skin that he raised his head so he could kiss her, properly this time, his tongue sweeping into her mouth to share the flavour with hers. When he drew back he kept his hand in her hair so that their gazes locked. 'And while I'm far from averse to inflicting a measure of erotic pain to inflame the throes of passion, causing you genuine hurt is something I never want to do.'

A flash of wariness cooled the heat in her green eyes. 'What are you talking about? There's nothing pleasurable about pain, believe me.'

He touched her cast with his free hand, ran his palm up her arm so that his fingers could peel the shirt back over her other shoulder, letting it drop to catch at her elbows, leaving her naked to the waist.

'Not always, no.' With the violence she'd recently suffered, now wasn't the time for a discussion on varying degrees and applications. He'd simply show her the possibilities instead. 'But the by-products of it . . .' He cupped one breast with the lightest of touches, kept his eyes on hers as he lowered his face again and this time licked at the peak of her nipple.

Annabel nearly left his lap.

'Oh, God,' she said on a low groan.

'Feel good?' he asked.

'It feels incredible. Do it again.'

He swapped to the other breast and obliged her. Smiling when he got the same reaction.

'Your pain receptors have fired up your nerves – putting your body on high alert. That sort of stress leaves you feeling achy and tense, makes your skin feel stretched tight, so sensitive to even the gentlest stimulation.' He licked again, tracing a slow circle, using his thumb to mirror the caress on her other nipple. When she arched into him with a deep sigh of pleasure, he opened his mouth on her, laving and sucking. He set the edge of his teeth around one puckered nub, pinched his thumb and forefinger around the other and pulled both lightly as he drew back, leaving them pert and pink.

Annabel's eyes were already dazed.

'Imagine what it would be like if I changed the tempo, sucked those pretty nipples hard. Sucked and bit until they were swollen and rosy and raw and then put a dash of whisky on them? Do you think that would burn?' A shudder ran through her. 'You're nice and warm so I'd leave it there for a little while, watching you squirm while your tender flesh heated up the flavours. Then I'd lick it off, soothing you.' He ducked forward to brush the very tip of his tongue over each peak, seeing goose flesh spring up over her chest. 'Savouring the sweet taste of your body under the sharp hit of booze again.

'And what if I decided to repeat that on certain *sensitive* areas down here?' He ran his palm up one bare thigh but he'd put money on his words being responsible for the gasp

341

that escaped her. 'Oh, yes. I think I'd have to sit on you for the way you'd thrash and buck against that.'

His fingers edged beneath the edge of his shirt, met with nothing but warm skin, soft curls and slick satiny folds and it was his turn to let out a deep groan.

'Why, Ms Frost,' he croaked once he'd regained the power of speech. 'You seem to have forgotten your underwear.'

'How careless of me,' she returned breathily, squirming against his light exploration, a cheeky little kick-up of her lips filling his chest with a bubble of warmth. Her genuine smiles were still rare, precious things that he realised he'd go to great lengths to encourage.

'Just so long as you intend making a bad habit of it,' he said. And using the hand at her nape he guided her forward for another kiss as, further down, he slid a finger slowly into her waiting heat.

Aidan insisted on being beyond careful, bringing her to the softest release she'd ever experienced. With the double magic of his fingers between her legs and his mouth at her breast, currents of pleasure washed back and forth between the two until the ebb and flow coalesced and flooded through her in a gentle wave.

Spent, Annabel flopped boneless against him. He held her loosely for a while before pulling the shirt up over her shoulders and trying to encourage her back to bed.

She resisted. 'I want you.' Apart from tonight, he hadn't touched her properly since the attack, and she knew it was because he was giving her time to heal. She also knew that he wanted her – could hear it in the strained tone of his voice, had been able to feel the evidence of his arousal each night when he spooned around her in bed. 'I want you inside me.'

She heard him curse under his breath. His eyelids drifted shut as he drew in a breath. When he opened his eyes again, the silvery hue smouldered from within. Bringing his hands up, he framed her face, kissed her tenderly. 'I want that too. Very much. But it's too soon, Annabel.'

'It's not,' she insisted, realising that if she wanted to see any action she was going to have to push for it. She nearly laughed. That must be a first – having to talk a guy into having sex.

'Trust me, it is. Because as gentle as I want to be, there comes a point where I lose myself with you. You like to push me beyond control and I won't risk that, not until you're healed.'

She liked hearing him admit that she messed him up, liked the feeling of power such knowledge gave her. 'Then let me return the favour at least,' she persevered, palming him through his trousers. She wasn't surprised to hear him hiss. He must be in some considerable discomfort trapped behind his flies – he'd been unflaggingly hard since she'd crawled onto his lap.

Which was a state of affairs that turned out to be to her benefit. There wasn't a millimetre of give in the taut fabric, making it quick and easy for her to lower the zip. By the time Aidan even thought about stopping her, she was already pushing her good hand through the opening to grasp him through his boxers. His words of protest melted into mindless noises as she traced the shape of him from root to tip.

She used his distraction to swiftly pull him free of his underwear, wrapping her palm around the thick shaft. He was so swollen that beneath the hot, velvet feel of his skin there was no give at all to his flesh. She toyed lightly to start with, teasing that hardness with feather-light fingers, tracing the shape of him, imagining how good it would be to feel him inside her.

She closed her fist around him, tightening her grip as she began to administer slow pulls that had him fighting to keep his hips still. His impatience fired her own. She wanted more. Now.

Hindered somewhat by her arm, she shuffled none too elegantly backwards off his lap, making a frustrated noise when she couldn't move fast enough.

Instantly he was full of concern. 'Are you all right?'

'Need to get off,' she grunted.

His hands were there in a flash, helping her find her feet. 'I told you it was too soon . . . what are you doing?'

Folding onto her knees between his legs, she glanced up at him with a smile. 'Just getting into a better position.' She took hold of him again, started lowering her face.

'No, Annabel,' Aidan pleaded, sounding suddenly desperate. 'Not your mouth. I won't be able to – sweet Jesus!'

He went rigid as she ran her tongue along the length of him. She looked up to watch his expression as she parted her lips and took him in. His piercing grey eyes were glued to the sight, his body taut as he held his breath. When she reversed the action, dragging her lips back up over the broad tip, the air rushed out of him, his eyes rolled up and his lids fluttered down.

The cuts on her face had begun to pull tight as they healed, leaving her unable to take him as deep as she'd like, but he didn't seem to mind when she employed the use of her fist to compensate for any shortfall. His muscles were held under such tight control that he trembled all over with his effort to keep still, his hands digging into the seat cushion so that his knuckles turned white. Glancing up to his face again, she saw that his head had fallen back against the sofa, the tendons in his neck standing out. It was heady to see Aidan Flynn reduced to this by her touch.

Humming with satisfaction, she took him slightly deeper. He jerked against her tongue, made a strangulated sound.

'Enough. *Enoughenoughenough*,' he panted, sitting forward

344

and sliding his hands under her arms to gently force her up. As soon as her mouth released him, he moved one hand down, wrapping it tightly around hers where she still gripped him and dragging it up and down his shaft. With his other hand coming around to the back of her neck, he brought their faces together, lightly resting his forehead against hers, panting, chanting her name.

'Oh, God.' He released his grip around her fist and together they watched her hand continue to work him in the rhythm he'd set. 'Yes, like that, *a mhuirnín*. Just like that.' Bringing both his hands to cup her jaw, he tipped her head back so he could press his lips to hers between hot breaths. 'Make me come for you.'

Another little kick of power – his choice of words making her realise she held his pleasure, quite literally, in her hand. And she'd seldom wanted to make anything happen more. She looked into his eyes. 'Do it then,' she said. 'Come for me.'

All it took was a few more strokes before with a shudder and a groan Aidan Flynn began to fall apart, his striking crystalline gaze locked on hers as he gave himself up to her, his release erupting against his shirt front, a few warm streamers landing across her hand.

Annabel had never seen a more beautiful mess in her life.

TWENTY-EIGHT

Aidan entered his apartment and called out a greeting. After the welcome home he'd been treated to the previous evening, he'd offered Jon a hefty bribe to cover his evening shift today so he could get home early to attend to his lovely patient.

He got no reply even though he could hear definite sounds of movement coming from his bedroom. He smiled, hoping she was choosing herself another of his shirts to wear. He liked the look of her in his clothes almost as much as he liked her in her own – or nothing at all.

'Hey,' he said, turning into the doorway and stopping at the sight of Annabel's overnight bag open on the bed. His gaze flew to where she bent over the bedside table, trying to gather too many of her possessions into her one good hand, and failing. When she turned back to the bed he saw her face was a cold, expressionless mask, her pallor parchment-white.

His guts gripped with unease. 'Annabel. What's wrong?'

She didn't look at him. 'Nothing,' she said, shoving the items she'd managed to grab into the top of the holdall and then turning back for the others.

What the hell? 'Are you going somewhere?'

'Home.'

'Right now?' When he wasn't even supposed to be here? She hadn't said anything about it earlier. If he wasn't mistaken, he'd caught her in the act of sneaking out.

She picked up her things and made for the bag again. 'Yes. I should have gone the other day. I've got things to do.'

He walked towards the bed, watching her snag her wash bag and spin in the direction of the bathroom.

'Annabel, what is this?' He changed course to match her, reaching out to take hold of her good arm to slow her down. 'What's happening?'

'Don't touch me,' she spat, wrenching herself away with enough force that she winced in pain.

Immediately, he put both his hands up in a calming gesture. He didn't want her hurting herself. As much as she was playing it cool, that reaction spoke volumes. 'Then talk to me. Look at me at the very least. I haven't the first clue what this is but I can see it's not "nothing".'

She glanced at him then, her eyes icy green, her features set, every fibre of her being held stiff. Fuck, he felt a trickle of something cold down his back. Ms Frost was back with a vengeance.

'There's nothing to talk about. It's just time I left, that's all. I don't see what the problem is.'

The problem was that something had made her fling her defences back up and he had no idea what. 'Neither do I. But there obviously is one if you're running away.'

'Running away?' she scoffed. 'Isn't that a bit dramatic?'

Damn. She was giving him nothing. 'You tell me,' he said as he watched her walk past him and into the en suite. But as she turned to close the door behind her, he swore he caught her blinking rapidly as though fighting back tears.

'Annabel.' He rushed forward but was too late; the door closed in his face and the lock clicked into place. 'Oh, no. Don't you shut me out. Not now.'

347

There was a moment's silence and then her voice came through the door. 'Aidan. I don't see why you're trying to make an issue out of this. I appreciate your hospitality but it's past time I was gone.'

He knew it was. But not this way. 'I'm not going to try to stop you leaving. I just don't understand why it has to be like this. As though suddenly there's nothing between us.'

Another moment of silence, then, 'There *is* nothing between us. A few days of casual sex, that's all.'

She was lying. She had to be. 'You know that's not true. We've shared a lot more than that. Enough for me to feel entitled to know what's going on.'

This time the slight pause made him hold his breath. Perhaps he was getting through to her.

'What's going on is that I have a life to get back to.' Annabel's words soon dashed that glimmer of hope. 'As do you. Which reminds me, there's a message for you on your answer phone. It sounds important.'

Not more important that this. Unless . . . Unless it had something to do with whatever the hell was happening. Why would she have mentioned it otherwise?

He strode out of the bedroom and through the living space towards the small room set off the kitchen area that he used as his study.

He entered, noting the property details and extensive documentation for Teach na Tulaí covering the surface of his desk where he'd left them. He pushed the play button and listened to the automated voice telling him the call had come in about half an hour ago. Next came the voice of his property agent in Ireland, Niall O'Roarke, excitedly relaying the news that Aidan's bid on the house had been accepted and then, in typical O'Roarke jokey fashion, he crowed that, subject to contract, Aidan could be installed as lord of the manor and be warming his toes at the great hearth in a week. Aidan

348

understood by the gale of laughter following this statement that Niall thought he was the funniest man alive. They both knew the sprawling Tulaí currently had no roof.

If Annabel had been drawn in here by the sound of the phone, heard Niall's update and seen the paperwork and architect's plans, she wouldn't get the joke. Taking the evidence on face value she'd probably think he was about to up sticks and leave London. Was that what had triggered this? She was particularly vulnerable at the moment, had just started to open up and trust him. Could the idea of him leaving have hurt her somehow?

Only if she cared – the seductive thought slid through his mind. Only if she'd started caring enough to see it as some sort of betrayal.

'Shit.'

Picking up the photo of the old house, he made his way back to the bedroom, wondering how best to play this, pondering how much he should tell her of his plans when he wasn't entirely sure himself about the recent shift in direction his thoughts about the future had been taking.

When he reached the room however, it was empty. The door to the en suite was open, showing that too was empty. The bed was devoid of the overnight bag. Annabel had gone.

He strode to the windows to look down onto the street just in time to see the flash of her ruby-red hair disappear into the back of a cab.

Oh, she was running all right.

He checked his instinct to give chase. He'd been telling the truth when he'd said that he wasn't trying to stop her from leaving. After the intensity of the past few days he realised it would probably be a good idea for both of them to get some distance, take a breath. He was much less concerned with her physical departure than her total emotional withdrawal. Her ability to just shut down and walk away.

As the cab pulled out from the kerb, he knew he wasn't ready for this to be over – not yet, not when it had barely begun. But seeing how swiftly, how absolutely Annabel had reverted to type had him thinking that maybe what he wanted wasn't going to be anywhere near enough.

'Fuck it,' he barked, slapping a palm against the glass as he watched the cab carry her away.

Leaving had been the right thing to do. The only thing to do. Annabel stared out of the cab's window but hardly noticed the passing blur of London streetlights. She hadn't counted on Aidan's unexpected return interrupting her clean getaway, but the force of the feelings the sight and sound of him had stirred up made her even more convinced that she was doing the right thing. She'd known it had been foolish to ignore the voice of reason telling her to go home the other day, known it had been dangerous to stay, to give her mixed-up emotional state the opportunity to get the better of her. Yet she'd continued to drag her feet long after she'd had any reason to. Thank goodness that phone call had come in to help put things back into perspective.

She hadn't meant to snoop. Hadn't meant to go into his study at all. But when she'd heard the landline ring and the answer phone kick in, followed by the sound of a deep, lilting Irish accent, she'd thought that maybe it was Aidan calling. By the time she'd reached the doorway she'd realised it wasn't. She'd been about to turn away again when her attention had been caught by the papers scattered all over the large desk that took up most of the small room – her interest piqued in particular by the image of a beautiful old mansion house.

And then the meaning of the disembodied words filling the room had sunk in. Aidan had bought it. And from what she'd been able to tell, the house was the one he'd told her about, the one from his childhood in Ireland.

350

He was leaving. Going home.

'You all right, love?'

When the cab driver's question snapped her out of her musings, she realised she'd been absently rubbing her chest where an unpleasant tightness ached.

'Fine,' she muttered back, wondering if she really was. She'd been shocked by how much the thought of him leaving had hurt. The strength of her immediate reaction – a visceral stab of pain to the very place in her chest that still ached – had been so frightening that she'd known she had to leave. What had happened to her in just a few short days? She wasn't supposed to care. Had promised herself never to care, never to leave herself open to hurt or betrayal.

Except the rational part of her brain knew that there was no betrayal. Aidan owed her nothing. Take away the extraordinary circumstances following Tony's attack and what they had between them was physical, casual – only, that didn't seem to stop the pain. Nothing about Aidan felt particularly casual.

The irony wasn't lost on her that not much more than a week ago she'd have been celebrating the news of his departure rather than succumbing to inappropriate feelings. More proof that she was not herself. Thank goodness that wake-up call had shown her how relaxed and reliant she was becoming.

Aidan must be breathing a sigh of relief to have his life back.

Annabel paid the taxi driver and made her way down the path to the entrance doors of her apartment block. Her progress up the stairs was slow, not so much hampered by her injuries as a reluctance to face the destruction she remembered from that fateful morning. At least she knew she had nothing more to fear from Tony here. She'd learnt from her visit from the police yesterday that his arrest had uncovered a long list of outstanding charges that had ensured he'd been kept in custody.

351

Inserting her key into the lock, she tried to brace herself with the reassurance that it was easier to be home, facing having to put possessions back together, than to still be at Aidan's, getting sucked deeper and eventually be left trying to put herself back together.

Pushing the door open and turning on the light, she gasped. The hallway she stepped into was tidy and clean. As was the sitting room, which she walked into in a daze, for a fleeting moment wondering if any of the events of the past few days had actually happened. However, the empty space on the bookshelf where the photo of her father should have sat signalled that it was more than a bad dream. If it weren't for that, plus a very few other missing items, things that she assumed had also been broken, there would have been no way of telling what violence had gone on here.

She started to shake as everything that had happened recently finally caught up with her. There was no way she didn't know who was responsible for this. There was only one person it could be. Aidan.

She swiped her hand across her cheeks, cross to feel the moisture of a few errant tears. *Get yourself together, Annabel.* She didn't have time for this. Not when there were still plenty of things she needed to do.

She walked into the kitchen, looking forward to finding some tasks with which to distract herself from the increasing roil of emotions threatening to break out and overwhelm her. But she found that room to be beyond spotless too. On the worktop beside the sink she found a business card from a cleaning company propped against a cardboard box containing a selection of broken items. She rummaged inside, looking for the only thing that mattered, the only thing that was irreplaceable. But neither the photo of her father nor the frame were there. Had the police taken it as evidence? She'd used it as a weapon after all.

She checked the rest of the flat, a sense of desperation growing as she realised there was nothing left for her to do. In the bedroom even her bed had been stripped, the pillows and duvet left stacked neatly at the foot of the mattress.

Her desperation threatened to tip over into panic. There must be *something* she could do? Going back into the kitchen, she was suddenly struck with inspiration. Ha! The fridge. That would need clearing out. She bet Mr I'm-So-Bloody-Wonderful wouldn't have thought of that. She opened the door and looked at the sparsely stacked shelves, the empty vegetable crisper. No curdled milk, no browning lettuce, no mouldy tomatoes.

'Oh, for God's sake!' She slammed the door shut and burst out crying. Bloody Aidan Flynn! Why did he have to be such a considerate bastard? She didn't want it to feel so nice to have things done for her, didn't want it to feel so warm and comforting to be cared for.

In fact, she'd feel a whole lot better if she could just hate him at the moment. But she couldn't. All she felt was an overwhelming sense of loss and sadness.

Making her way back into her bedroom, she crawled onto the bare mattress and gave herself up to a good bawl.

It was mid-evening by the time she clawed her way back out of her pity pit, feeling bruised by emotional and physical exhaustion but with her conscience scoured to a raw clarity. It had been a long time since she'd taken a good look inside herself. And what she'd seen there left her knowing what she had to do.

She called Aidan's mobile. He didn't pick up. He probably didn't want to talk to her. He was probably angry, and why wouldn't he be when she'd flung all his care and kindness back in his face? She hung up, not knowing where to start with leaving a message. She'd try again later.

She tried later, before she went to bed, but again got no reply. She cut the call, still not willing to leave a message.

The following morning she called her insurance company, Richard Landon, the hospital, and her hairdresser to arrange for a twice weekly wash and blow dry until her cast was removed. She got through to each and every one of them. She called Aidan's number twice and got no answer. When her landline rang she jumped out of her skin, but it was someone checking in from the victim support team the police had passed her details to.

It was well into the afternoon before she finally got hold of him.

'Annabel,' he answered the call, his tone cutting the word short in a way she didn't like at all.

'I've been trying to call you.'

'I've been busy,' he countered, words still clipped, his accent devoid of its usual soft edges.

Yeah. He was angry. And rightly so.

'Well. I wanted to thank you for sorting out my flat. And for everything you've done. You've been really kind. You must tell me what I owe you for the cleaning company.'

That was greeted by silence, although she was aware of a fair bit of background noise. Was he at work?

'And I also wanted to apologise for walking out the way I did. After everything you've done for me it was incredibly rude.'

She heard him sigh. 'But not entirely unexpected.'

He expected her to be rude? Well of course he did, because she was. But the thought of him thinking ill of her bothered her.

'I was hoping maybe I could take you for a coffee or something, say thanks.'

'You've said it.' He paused and she could hear muffled voices in the background. 'Nothing else is needed, Annabel.'

Boy, he wasn't making this easy. 'I'd like to see you anyway.'

There was a short silence and then another sigh. 'I don't think that would be a good idea.'

'Oh.' That place in her chest ached again. 'Well, I'm back at work tomorrow,' she said, hoping the little twinge of excitement at the prospect of seeing him didn't make her sound too desperate.

'That's good.' His voice faded a bit as though he'd turned his attention away from the phone. 'I'm glad you're feeling better.'

God, this distant politeness from him was horrible.

Before she could think of what to say that might reach across that distance, he said, 'Listen, Annabel. I have to go.'

'Oh, OK. I'll see you—'

'Take care,' he muttered as though he wasn't listening and then the phone went dead.

He'd shut her off, quite literally. And just because she knew it was no more than she deserved, didn't make it hurt any less.

She stared at the phone in dismay, realising that she'd been relying on him to forgive her with his usual equanimity, been counting on him to have read and understood her fears in the way he seemed to be able to do. But although he'd been civil and calm, there'd been none of his usual warmth – just a coldness she hadn't experienced from him before. Even when he'd been annoyed and frustrated he'd always remained engaged.

Trying to look at things objectively, she should take his withdrawal as a good sign. He obviously just saw what they'd had as a fling. At least one of them had kept their head. This distance would make things easier between them at work until such time as he left.

So why didn't the idea feel as good as it should?

On Tuesday, just over a week after the attack, Annabel applied a covering of make-up to the rapidly healing injuries on her face and went to the hairdresser. She arrived at work in her cast but otherwise looking like Ms Frost. Inside she felt like someone else entirely. Who, she hadn't a clue. She pushed through the doors, her eyes already sweeping behind the bar to spot Aidan's mop of black hair.

Instead, she saw a head of cropped brown hair. 'Who the hell are you?' she demanded.

From across the room Tim answered. 'Ms Frost! This is Stu Price. Cluny's new head barman.'

Her head spun, but she fought to keep her thoughts and her voice straight. 'Where's Aidan?'

Tim looked at her worriedly. 'Uh, Aidan's gone. Back home to Ireland. I thought you knew? Richard Landon's been about for the past couple of days to deal with it all.' He stepped in closer, hands rising as though to reach out and catch her. 'Are you all right? You look a bit crook. Are you sure you should be back yet?'

'Yes.' Annabel pulled herself together, put on her brave face. Aidan hadn't wasted any time in getting away from her. 'Yes, I'm fine.' She smiled at Tim to show him she meant it. From the way he hastily backed up a step, she knew she hadn't managed to get the expression quite right. If it reflected anything close to what she was feeling – a crushing vice-like grip squeezing her chest – it probably looked like she was having a heart attack.

TWENTY-NINE

Annabel folded another of her mother's freshly washed night-gowns ready to take along on her regular Monday afternoon visit to the hospital. For the past several weeks, Ellen had been insisting on having her own sleepwear rather than wear the unsightly surgical gowns – mostly for the sake of presenting an attractive package to the doctors and male physiotherapist. Her recovery from the emotional – if not yet the physical – trauma of her relationship with Tony Maplin had been remarkably quick, and she'd wasted no time in using her flirty tricks and playing the helpless female in the hopes of catching the attention of any man who wandered too near her bed.

The same rapid recovery certainly couldn't be said of Annabel's emotions where Aidan Flynn was concerned. The month and a half since he'd left had been long and bleak. With the bright lights and colourful cheer of the festive season packed away for another year, all that was left were the dark days of deep winter – the gloom of which reflected her mood perfectly. Unlike her mother, who had a seemingly limitless capacity for affairs of the heart, Annabel's one and only foray into that world had been more than enough to last her a lifetime.

And it *had* been an affair of the heart, she'd been forced to acknowledge against all her efforts to pretend otherwise, because that was the precise location where a dull, constant ache had set up permanent residence since – an unremitting, unpleasant reminder that she'd been right all along in her decision not to let anyone get too close. Well, once was all it took to learn her lesson. She wouldn't be making the same mistake again.

As she packed the nightgown into the holdall sitting open beside her on the dining table, the buzz of the intercom sounded, announcing the arrival of her grocery delivery. With only one good arm, the usually simple weekly routine of a trip to the supermarket had become something of an ordeal of heavy bags and unwieldy trolleys. Discovering the convenience of online shopping and home delivery had made one aspect of her life that much easier.

Now if she could only get things like her sleep sorted out, she thought, giving her tired eyes a rub as she moved into the hallway. She pressed the answer button on the intercom panel. 'Hello?'

There was a moment's pause. 'Hello, Annabel.'

Her heart leapt into her mouth. Even though Aidan had never been far from her thoughts over the past weeks, his rich Irish brogue was the last thing she'd expected to hear. Ever again. Had she imagined it?

'Can I come up?' That unmistakable voice sounded again, filling the stunned silence and rasping over her senses like a physical touch. Not her imagination, then. Real. What was he doing here?

A tiny spark of something that felt like hope flared, escaping with worrying ease from the shadowy corner in the back of her mind into which she'd been determinedly trying to cram every feeling and memory associated with Aidan Flynn. 'Why?'

'We need to talk.' His tone was enough to extinguish that futile glimmer. Although he didn't sound as cold and remote as he had during that last, stilted conversation on the phone, his voice didn't carry its usual warm notes either.

'About what?' she asked guardedly.

She heard an impatient exhalation. 'What do you think? About the way you finished things between us.'

His accusatory tone put her straight on the defensive. 'I already tried explaining that to you. You didn't want to know.'

'I told you I was busy, I had a lot of things to organise.'

'That was six weeks ago,' she tried to keep control of her voice but she could feel the sound level rising. 'And you've only just found time to get around to it now? Sorry, but I don't know why you're bothering if it's that unimportant to you.'

There was a slight pause during which she heard another exhalation. 'Do you really want to do this over the intercom?' he asked. 'Or are you going to let me in? Your choice, but I'm not leaving until we've got this squared.'

Did she want to do 'this' over the intercom? No, she didn't. Did she want to let him in and do it face to face? Hell no, she wanted that even less – seeing him would risk having a light shined in that dusty corner and exposing all the things she wanted to keep hidden from herself. Really, she didn't want to be doing 'this' at all. And a few short months ago she wouldn't have hesitated to say no, to tell him to go away and leave her alone. But since then something had changed – *she'd* changed. After the way she'd thrown his kindness and generosity back in his face, he deserved better than more of the same sort of treatment from her. He deserved another attempt at an explanation at least. She'd give him that much, if that's what he wanted. No matter how angry he tried to make her.

Without a word she pushed the button to let him into the building, then went straight to the door and braced her good hand against it as she closed her eyes and breathed deeply to compose herself. Even though she was expecting it, the knock on the other side a minute later made her jump.

She put her eye to the spy hole and there he was – tall, dark and devastating, those pale eyes staring directly at the little bubble of glass as though they could see right through it. Could see right through her – to pierce that dull, empty ache into a pain so sharp it made her breath catch. His handsome features were set hard. He looked all business, and all of it serious.

She made herself open the door right then, before the seductive voice of cowardice could talk her out of it, noticing he was dressed in his black bike leathers before she forced herself look him in the eye.

Only, his gaze wasn't directed at her face. Instead it was locked on the top of her head. It took her a moment to realise that he was looking at her hair. Of course he was – he hadn't seen her since she'd given up her home dying because of her cast. For the first time in years her hair was almost back to its natural shade.

Self-consciously, she raised a hand and smoothed a bright strand behind her ear, holding her breath as she waited for him to comment. But after another moment, his gaze dropped to meet hers without a word. The rush of disappointment she felt left her to realise just how much value she'd placed on his opinion when she'd made the decision to go natural rather than pay salon prices instead.

'I was told you'd gone back to Ireland,' she covered the unexpected hurt with a cold, flat tone.

'Not permanently. Not yet. I'm back and forth between

here and there.' Aidan's voice was just as flat, and hard. As were his eyes. Used to seeing their striking beauty lit by a heated glint or gleam, she nearly flinched away from the flinty coolness with which he regarded her.

But there was no escaping now. May as well get it over with as quickly as possible. Stepping aside, she let him in, trying to ignore the way her body responded to his presence as he passed, his height and the width of his leather-encased shoulders filling her narrow hallway.

When she motioned him towards the sitting room, his attention caught on her cast. 'How's the arm?' he asked with the polite indifference of a stranger as he moved ahead of her.

So, they were going to start off by observing the niceties.

'Better.' She followed him into the room. 'The cast comes off this afternoon.'

She watched him cross to the table, trying not to notice how the soft leathers clung to his backside and long legs like a second skin. He placed his upturned helmet and gloves beside the open holdall and turned to face her as he unzipped his jacket. 'And your mother?'

'She's all right. Coming out of traction and should hopefully be home next week.' Annabel kept her eyes on his face rather than let them drop to admire the unveiling of what appeared to be a well-fitting cream jersey. She had no right to ogle him – she had given up any claim she may have had on that strong, lean body and every intimate pleasure it offered.

'Would you like something to drink?' she offered, less in accordance with the niceties and more because she could use one to moisten her suddenly dry throat.

'No. I'm not going to stay long. The only thing I've come for is the truth.' He took a couple of steps back in her direction, pinned her with those piercing eyes. 'About what happened the day you left. I want to know why you acted the way you did. Why you ran out without a word, without a reason.'

Try as she might, she couldn't help but take exception to his tone. She latched onto the hot spurt of indignation like it was a lifeline. Better to feel anger than hope. Or hurt.

'As I said, I tried to. You were the one who wouldn't give me a chance to explain.'

There was a pause before he said, 'Like you gave me any such chance, Annabel? You made your choice that day without paying a moment's consideration to me. And you think I owed you any more than the same in return? Your double standards astound me.'

She opened her mouth and then shut it when she realised there was nothing she could say to deny it. He was right of course, she knew he was. In her panicked state she'd jumped to conclusions and made decisions without letting him explain. By shutting her off the way he had, he'd only given her back a taste of what she'd dished out to him first.

She looked up at him, looming nearby. Although he was making a good show of outward control, the tension in his shoulders made it obvious that he was angry. And why wouldn't he be after the appalling way she'd treated him?

All right. She could do this. Explain, apologise, file it under major life fails, move on. God, though, where to start? She swallowed and tried to get her thoughts straight. 'Because I—' she began only to be interrupted by the buzz of the intercom. She didn't know if she was pleased or pissed off to find herself temporarily saved by the bell. 'That'll be my shopping,' she said, turning back into the hallway to let the delivery driver in.

Rather than face Aidan again immediately, she went and opened the front door instead, using the wait to think what

362

it was she needed to say. When the uniformed driver appeared, she directed him to place the bags in the kitchen before signing his delivery sheet and seeing him out again.

'I'd better get the cold stuff into the fridge,' she told Aidan, who sauntered after her and stood leaning against the kitchen doorway watching silently, expectantly.

Which made it all but impossible to concentrate, to order the turmoil of her mind. All too soon she found she'd run out of things to put in the fridge, so started piling things into the cupboard in front of her instead, buying every second she could. She heard the creak of leather as Aidan moved, felt the heat of him as he came up close behind her in the small space.

'Why?'

She froze with a jar of coffee in her hands, closed her eyes. 'Because I panicked.'

'That much was obvious.' His voice was a deep rumble behind her ear. 'I want to know the reason behind it.'

Annabel cleared her throat. 'I heard a call come in, about the house – the one in Ireland. I hadn't meant to listen but . . .' She shrugged. 'And when I realised you were going back . . .'

'Yes?' he prompted when she left the sentence hanging.

The last thing she wanted to do was expose herself, open up and leave herself vulnerable, but there was no point in trying to lie, not to a man who could read her so easily, who would relentlessly pursue the truth.

'I was scared.'

'Scared of what?'

Of how the thought of him leaving had turned her inside out, left every sensitive place exposed and raw. Of the strength of that reaction after so short a time.

'Of myself mostly. Of what I felt.'

'Turn around, Annabel.'

She shook her head. 'No. I won't be able to do this if I look at you.'

Thankfully, he didn't force it.

'Then tell me,' he said in a low voice. 'What did you feel?'

'Things I had no business feeling.' She clutched at the coffee jar and forced out the admission. 'I – I didn't want you to leave.'

Her words hung in the air for long seconds before he returned with a fair dose of irony. 'So *you* left instead?'

'I know. It doesn't make sense. It *didn't* make sense. I was confused.'

'You were confused. Confused and distressed. You think I didn't know that? After everything you'd been through you were in no fit state to think rationally about anything. But what about now? Are you still confused?'

Terribly. But she wasn't going to admit it, she needed to be strong to get through this. 'No.'

'Good. Because I want to know clearly why the prospect of my leaving would have bothered you so?'

And if he thought she was going to give that much of herself away when it obviously didn't matter any more, he was mistaken. 'I don't know.' She shook her head stubbornly.

She heard him move, saw the black of his leathers out of the corner of her eye as he came to stand beside her. She kept her attention firmly on the coffee jar.

'You do know, Annabel.' His tone was insistent. 'Was it because you wanted more?'

She swallowed but didn't move. Didn't speak.

'What if I'd wanted more, too?' He leaned in to utter in a hard voice. 'Did you think of that?'

Her pulse pounded in her head. No. At the time she hadn't thought of it, because she'd never been used to thinking about anyone but herself.

'I figured if you were leaving, that you'd be glad to get your life back,' she said. 'You didn't come after me, wouldn't answer my calls, didn't want to listen to what I had to say . . . and then you just left.'

'I very nearly did come after you as it happens. I was so incensed, all I could think about was dragging you back, forcing you to open up to me. At least I had enough sense left to realise what a disaster that would have been. You didn't need that then, you had enough on your plate.' He let out a breath. 'And once I'd calmed down, I couldn't see the point in trying to pursue someone who considered me so easily disposable, someone who was willing to treat me with so little regard.'

Disposable? That he could even think something like that of himself made her feel terrible. For all that he'd left her feeling turned inside out and upside down, he'd also given her joy and safety and friendship when she'd needed it most – had been there for her when she'd had nobody else in the world. No matter how torn up she felt, she owed him for that at least.

She turned to face him at last.

'I am sorry, Aidan. I really am. It was a childish and selfish way for me to behave after everything you'd done for me. I knew how wrong I'd been almost straight away – especially when I got back here and discovered you'd done even more than I could've imagined.'

He looked at her intently, eyes scanning her features and for once she hoped he could read the truth, the sincerity, there.

'That reminds me,' he said. 'I have something for you in the other room.'

'Something for me?' She followed him back into the sitting room where he pulled a flat rectangular package wrapped in brown paper from inside his motorcycle helmet.

Ripping the paper off, he drew out a photo frame and held it towards her.

In a daze she raised her hand to take the familiar photo of her and her father standing outside the White Harte.

'I thought this had gone,' she murmured as she stared at it, her voice cracking.

'It's actually a copy. The original was damaged beyond repair when the frame smashed. I found somewhere that was able to patch it up enough to make a decent reproduction.' A brief silence fell as they both regarded the golden-hued picture. 'I'm guessing the White Harte was the inn your parents owned?'

Annabel nodded. As hard as she tried to fight back the overwhelming rush of emotion, she felt the hot prickle of tears.

'Thank you.' Turning away from him, she made her way towards the bookcase, blinking rapidly to clear her blurring vision. 'I don't know what else to say.' She stood the photo in its rightful place. 'I don't deserve this.'

Almost immediately, she sensed Aidan come up beside her, felt the touch of his fingers against her chin, the pressure increasing as he forced her to face him. She didn't have the strength to fight him. Not without losing it completely. Instead, she kept her eyes lowered, trained on the strip of cream jersey visible beneath his open leather jacket, where she could see the steady rise and fall of his chest.

'Annabel,' he said in a voice much softer than it had been. 'Look at me.'

God, he was going to leave her a jibbering wreck at this rate. She firmed her jaw. Raised her eyes. Fell into his gaze.

'Tell me one thing.' The fathomless silver held her riveted as he asked, 'If you had the chance to do that day differently, would you?'

Now that she understood the hurt she'd caused to both of them? In a heartbeat. She swallowed and nodded.

'Why?' He dug deeper. 'What's changed?'

She blinked harder and gave a shrug. 'Me, I think.'

His hand moved up from her chin to catch a tear that had formed on her lower lashes.

'*A mhuirnín*, don't cry now,' he whispered, the steel in his gaze turning to molten silver. 'That's all I wanted to know.'

He lowered his head towards hers looking for all the world like he was going to kiss her. Annabel's head spun. What was going on?

She put a hand against his chest to hold him away, instantly feeling the warmth of him seep through the wool and into her palm. Even though his breathing was steady, she discovered that his heartbeat wasn't. It beat against the cage of his ribs like a wild thing caught in a trap. 'What are you doing?'

His other hand came up to cover hers, pressing it tight against the firm contours of his pectoral muscle. For the first time since he'd arrived one of his lopsided smiles appeared. 'I'm going to do what I've been dying to do for weeks – kiss you.'

Had she missed something? Her own heart thumped so fast it was a pounding echo inside her skull. Added to the spinning it wasn't helping her to get a handle on matters at all. He wanted to kiss her? Goodbye? She didn't think she could handle that.

She shook her head. 'What's the point?' Surely only more upset could come from such a reminder of what they'd shared? To her horror she felt a tear break free of her lashes, but before she had a chance to swipe it away herself, Aidan's thumb moved to stop it in its tracks.

'The point?' he smiled, stroking her cheek. 'I can offer a few but they'll have to wait. I have to kiss you first. I doubt you have any idea how difficult it's been to stay away from you these past weeks. To give you the space you needed to think about what you really feel. I've thought of nothing but you—'

She tried to process the words but it was difficult to focus when he was looking at her like that, lowering his head. She should stop him. Letting those parted lips touch hers would only make an impossible situation even worse. But trapped by the captivating beauty of those eyes she was helpless to resist. Suddenly greedy for one last farewell kiss, whatever the cost, she stood there and let his warm, firm lips make contact, lightly at first, taking small tastes until her own parted and with a groan he came at her like a starving man, using tongue and teeth and lips to devour her.

The heat and scent of him washed over her as she melted against the wall of soft, warm leather and wool he made, giving back with everything she had, savouring every second to store in her memories. More tears escaped from between the closed mesh of her lashes to run down her cheeks, but she couldn't do a thing to stop them. It was only when she thought her knees might give way that he started pulling back, finishing as he'd started, with small, light nibbles and tastes that gave them both time to catch their breath.

'That was worth the wait.' Still holding her face between his palms, Aidan's gaze followed the tracks of her tears as his thumbs swiped them away. 'But if you're thinking that was in any way goodbye, Annabel,' he stated, eyes locking onto hers, 'you're wrong. Come and sit down, let me tell you about the house in Ireland – my plans.'

She let herself be led to the sofa where she sat and listened to him explain about his childhood fascination with Tully House, his dream of restoring it to its former glory which had been rekindled while he was convalescing from the stroke.

'I decided to look into the situation with the owners, to see whether a new generation had finally been able to settle their differences and would be prepared to sell it. When I didn't get an outright no in reply, what had started as an interest to keep me from going mad during the long months of painfully slow rehabilitation soon became an obsession. I opened tentative negotiations via their solicitors but even right up to the moment Niall called I'd had no idea whether my offer would be accepted.'

She looked at the photos he'd taken on his phone only a week ago. Apart from the façade, which looked largely intact bar a bit of romantic crumbling around the edges, the place was pretty much a wreck. Aidan was so animated showing her shots of roofless rooms, collapsed walls, gaping holes where floors should be, that his passion for the project was obvious.

He finally stopped long enough to draw a breath. 'What do you think?'

What did *she* think? His ideas for the place were breathtaking and she thought she hated it. Hated it all with as much passion as he loved it, because it meant he was leaving.

'It's brilliant,' she said with a forced smile, refusing to admit just how far she'd fallen by acknowledging that she was jealous of a building. 'But I don't understand why you're telling me all this.'

'I'm intending to make it more than a just a home – I'm putting together a planning application for a hotel. Nothing too grand, a dozen or so luxury suites and a top end restaurant. I aim to reinstate the old distillery too, start producing fine Tulaí whisky again. Between the consents and the licences and the restoration work it means that it will take years to get anywhere near completion.' He turned to her a little more, reached out to curl his fingers around hers. 'It will be years before I'll be in a position to move there.'

Annabel watched a slow smile spread on his face, the curve of his lips as genuine as Annabel's had been forced.

'Years that we can use to see how crazy we can drive each other.'

Aidan watched Annabel's face closely as she took in everything he was saying. Not surprisingly, she looked a touch shell-shocked. She also looked incredibly young and more than a little fragile. He'd caught her fresh-faced, with the faintest sprinkling of freckles visible across the bridge of her nose, and her long lashes fair above the dark smudges he noticed she was carrying under her eyes.

And that hair! He'd planned on playing things so cool the first time they came face to face, to remain detached until he'd had a chance to assess her feelings. But he hadn't counted on that bright fall of rust and copper and spun gold framing her face like a fiery nimbus. He'd had a tough time trying not to let her see that he'd been a goner from the second she'd opened the door.

No, Flynn. You were a goner way before that. From the moment she'd run out and taken a piece of him with her, he'd known he needed to get her back. He'd told her the truth about being angry. He had been furious enough to do something stupid if he'd chased after her the way he'd wanted to. At least he'd had enough sense to recognise that another desperate man trying to impose his will on her by brute force would be the last thing likely to help his cause.

Even knowing that she'd behaved the way she had through fear of her own emotions, he couldn't deny that it had hurt after the enforced closeness they'd shared. But he'd realised that it would take more than a few days of intimacy to undo the defensive, insular habits she'd been cultivating for a lifetime.

So he'd tamped down the urge to follow her and forced himself to get on with his plans instead. But every day of the six weeks he'd managed to stay away, he found that everything he worked towards featured Annabel Frost some-where in the picture. The waiting had been hard but he'd known he needed to be patient, give her the time she needed to recover from the shock of the trauma she'd suffered, and get her head on straight before she'd be able to see what it was that she wanted.

Because what he wanted wasn't anything temporary or casual. What he wanted involved words like lifelong, serious, and commitment. Words he daren't say out loud just yet. He realised he was way ahead of her in what he saw for their future, and hoped he'd have the opportunity to keep her close while he did everything in his power to help her to eventually reach the same conclusions.

'You want us to see each other again?' She blinked in confusion. 'I don't know if I can.'

He held his breath. 'Because you don't want to?'

She shook her head. 'No. Because whether it's sooner or later you will leave and it will have to end.'

'It scares me too, Annabel.' He addressed the unspoken crux of the matter. 'The stakes are just as high for me. There are no guarantees in anything in life except that nothing lasts forever – we both know that only too well. Suffering that stroke taught me not to waste a minute, that life's too precious not to grab at what matters with both hands. You've tried to keep yourself safe from hurt, but that's not the same thing as being happy. I'd rather take the risk and live a little than settle for nothing at all.'

'Spoken like a gambler.'

He shook his head. 'Perhaps. But to tell you the truth, I can't read the play on this one. This is an entirely new game for me.'

'And for me.'

'Then we can learn it together, *a mhuirnín* – make up the rules as we go along,' he urged, trying to keep the hint of desperation out of his voice. He'd already decided that he wasn't too proud to beg – but only if he absolutely had to.

He watched Annabel close her eyes and let out a big sigh. When she opened them again, he saw both fear and determination warring in the lovely green depths, held his breath to see which one would win.

With a slight raise of her chin she took total command of his heart. 'Let's try it and see.'

His wish
was her
command.

THE
Silver
Chain

PRIMULA BOND

Book One of The *Unbreakable* Trilogy

Bound by passion,
she was powerless to resist . . .

The first in the sexy,
passionate and addictive

Unbreakable Trilogy

Passions will be awakened at...

the **naughty girls'** book club

'Deliciously addictive'
Justine Elyot

sophie hart

A quaint suburb.
A quiet little reading group.

A very
naughty
reading list . . .

Follow Avon on
Twitter@AvonBooksUK
and
Facebook@AvonBooksUK
For news, giveaways and
exclusive author extras

AVON